Gloria Cook ⋯⋯⋯⋯⋯⋯⋯⋯⋯⋯⋯⋯er
village upbringing ⋯⋯⋯⋯⋯⋯⋯⋯⋯⋯l-
ing countryside and coastline which permeates her
writing. She is married with two daughters and a
granddaughter and lives in Truro.

Roscarrock is her eighth novel. Her first three
novels were the highly successful Pengarron trilogy,
Pengarron Land, *Pengarron Pride* and *Pengarron's
Children*, and these were followed by *Trevennor's
Will*, *Trevallion*, *Kilgarthen* and *Rosemerryn* (all
available from Headline).

Roscarrock

Gloria Cook

HEADLINE

First published in 1996
by HEADLINE BOOK PUBLISHING

First published in paperback in 1996
by HEADLINE BOOK PUBLISHING

10 9 8 7 6 5 4 3 2 1

ISBN 0 7472 5396 X

Printed and bound in Great Britain by
Cox & Wyman Ltd, Reading, Berks

HEADLINE BOOK PUBLISHING
A division of Hodder Headline PLC
338 Euston Road
London NW1 3BH

To the joy and delight of my life,
my little granddaughter, Kerenza

Prologue

'Why don't we go take a peep at Roscarrock?' Hannah Spargo suggested to the six other children sitting on the curved stone quay of Porthellis. They had just come out of Sunday School and were debating what to do for the rest of the afternoon. 'We haven't been up there for ages.'

All except one boy looked up across the fishing village where behind the tips of a small wood on the cliff top the long slate roof and tall chimneys of a large house could be seen. The house was set well back from the cliff face but seemed to overshadow Porthellis. It had been there for centuries, the original occupants once owning the village and surrounding land and beaches. A gull was wheeling above the house and the children watched fascinated to see if the bird would rest on the roof. They weren't surprised when it flew away; Roscarrock was rumoured to be greatly haunted and only the bravest children had ever dared take a step on its land.

Six pairs of eyes then zoomed in on the uninterested boy. Daniel Kittow, the oldest of the group at fourteen years, and four years Hannah's senior, was rough and ready and almost fearless, qualities which were reflected in his bold features and striking red hair. He had led them on many an adventure, often receiving the belt

1

across his broad back for his troubles; they wouldn't be afraid if Daniel went with them.

Daniel was throwing pebbles to skim expertly over the grey-green waters slapping against the high wall on a full tide. He watched the passage of a smooth grey pebble as it leaped between the boats riding on their moorings until it sank and disappeared, then he scowled. He was in a dark mood. Sunday afternoons were always boringly quiet owing to the village's staunch Methodism and the adults' desire to nap in peace, but today his grandfather had made him attend Sunday School, a mortifying experience not least because he'd had to sit with boys two years younger than he was. It had not been because the old man cared for Daniel's soul but as a punishment for catching him swigging from his whisky bottle. Daniel took the next pebble from the supply Hannah was feeding him. Because of her pretty fair face and sunny nature she was the only girl he would tolerate near him.

'We could've played on the beach if the tide wasn't in,' Eileen Gunn said from her perch on a granite mooring stone. Although it was winter, the air was fresh and warm, the sky clear and pale blue, the waters of Veryan Bay inviting.

Daniel had no time for anyone who stated the obvious and he threw the pebble at the mooring stone and Eileen shrieked and gathered in her silk petticoat.

Hannah turned her lively blue eyes sternly on Daniel and it stopped him hurling verbal abuse at Eileen to add to her fright and indignation. Daniel swore often and if a grown-up heard him swearing on the Sabbath they would all be ordered home in disgrace. 'What do you want to do then, Danny?'

'I'm thinking of taking my grandfather's tosher round

Slate Rock and on to Hidden Beach.'

There was a hushed silence, then Mitch Spargo, Hannah's brawny, twelve-year-old brother, said in awe, 'But we'll be skinned alive for taking out a boat without permission, specially on a Sunday.' Added to that, the tosher was prized by Rufus Kittow who had won it off a rival fisherman from Mevagissey in a poker game.

'You scared, Mitch?' Fred Jose, who was leaning his scrawny back against Mitch's, asked a trifle scornfully. Fred was scared at the very thought of such blatant mischief. He was a coward by nature, it showed in every inch of his pale startled-looking face, and he was even more scared of this idea than going up to 'peep' at Roscarrock. But Fred was confident that Daniel was only trying to impress them and this gave him a rare opportunity to sound braver than Mitch, his closest friend.

'Course I aren't scared,' Mitch said, embarrassed. 'But it'll take even more courage to go up to Roscarrock at the moment. My gran said old Jago was heard wailing up on the cliff the other night.' He added ominously, mimicking his grandmother's solemn voice, 'And we all know what that means, don't we? Someone is going to die.'

'There really have been some strange goings-on at Roscarrock, you know,' Jowan Rouse chipped in. He was Hannah's cousin, a quiet, studious boy who took a deeper interest than most in what went on around him.

'We all know the rumours,' yawned another of Hannah's cousins, little sprightly Lizzie Spargo. She went on hastily, for Jowan was given to lengthy explanations, 'Jeremiah Jago was gardener to the Bodinnicks who had Roscarrock before the Opies, and one of the Bodinnicks was s'posed to have murdered old Jago and at certain times of the year he can be heard wailing in torment because he won't rest in peace until justice is done, but no one knows what justice it is he's looking for.'

'And don't forget that when old Jago wails, terrible screams are heard coming from Roscarrock,' Jowan grinned.

'Right then,' said Fred, clambering up on his gangly legs and rubbing at his numbed bottom. 'Let's go up and listen for the screams.'

The other five children looked at Daniel for confirmation. With an expression of grim determination he was looking at his grandfather's tosher, moored between the old man's lugger and the steps leading down to the beach. 'I'm going to take out the *Wynne*.'

The tide was still coming in and there would be plenty of time to row out of the cove, skirt round Slate Rock, the tall outcrop of rock that sheltered and formed part of the natural harbour opposite the quay, arrive at the long narrow strip of pale golden sand which Slate Rock hid from view, stay for a couple of hours and row back. No doubt his exploit would be discovered and his fractious grandfather would wield his belt again, but what was life for if not for taking a few risks? Daniel displayed the welt marks he'd already received on his back and legs like badges of honour, and he was getting smug in the knowledge that he was now bigger and stronger and could be fiercer than Rufus; one day he would stay the old man's whipping arm for good. Daniel got to his feet.

'So,' he said, somewhat arrogantly, ignoring the girls and looking into the avid faces of Mitch, Fred and Jowan. 'Who's coming with me?'

'I am,' Mitch said at once, eager now to go along with Daniel's decision.

'Me too,' echoed Eileen, springing to her feet and clapping her hands coquettishly.

'You'll get into trouble,' Hannah cautioned Daniel, staying put on the granite-paved quay. 'Someone's bound to see you.'

She was feeling uneasy. Among the row of pink and whitewashed cottages, fish cellars and workshops behind them was the pub; she thought she had glimpsed a face at an upstairs window. It had looked like her father but Jeff Spargo had said he was going to spend the afternoon in his shed busy at his hobby, making a ship in a bottle, and woe betide anyone who disturbed him. Hannah seemed to be her father's least favourite child, often receiving punishment when she had done nothing wrong and unfairly taking the blame for her brothers' and sisters' misdemeanours. She would take the full brunt of her father's fury if he knew any of his family had gone with Daniel.

'Do you really think you ought to go, Danny?'

Daniel looked warmly into Hannah's eyes for a second, then gave her his disarming smile. 'You girls can either walk along the cliff path and meet us on the beach or go home and help your mothers get the tea.'

'Oh, that's not fair,' Eileen grumbled, fussing with her dress. 'Why do we always have to be left behind?'

'You couldn't go anyway in that stupid frilly dress,' Daniel taunted her, stretching his long legs and flexing his thick arms.

Eileen bit her bottom lip and looked away, something she always did when her feelings were hurt.

'But I want to go with you,' Lizzie angrily interjected. 'I'm not afraid to get into trouble any more than you are, Daniel Kittow, and Eileen won't get her dress wet or dirty if we're careful.'

'Go on, Danny, let the girls come,' Fred pleaded. He would feel safer with the girls on the boat; Daniel was less likely to do anything foolhardy. His next statement was true. 'Hannah's always sensible, she'll keep Lizzie and Eileen in check.'

Jowan didn't have the aversion to girls that most boys of his age did and also spoke up on their behalf. Mitch said nothing, leaving the decision to Daniel, but hoping he would send the girls away as they were likely to spoil the fun.

Daniel eyed Hannah. 'Do you want to come?'

'Yes,' she answered. If she was to get into trouble because Mitch and their cousins were going on the adventure, she might as well be in on it too.

'Be quick getting into the boat then,' Daniel snapped and the group pattered towards the stone steps. Painted white, nineteen feet, eleven inches long, the tosher was usually taken out by one man and driven by a three and a half horsepower Kelvin engine which Rufus had stowed in his shed. Daniel took a pair of oars from another boat.

Afraid of being seen and ordered home, Daniel and Mitch quickly helped the others into the boat. Mitch was about to free the mooring rope when there came a breathless shout. 'Wait a minute, wait for us!' It was seven-year-old Leah Spargo, tearing along the granite slabs towards them, her long skirt flying, one hand on her straw hat, the other clutched by her toddler brother, Edwin.

'Tell your sister and brother they can't come, Hannah,' Daniel said impatiently. 'I've got enough in here already.'

Hannah made to leave the boat. 'Edwin will make a

din if he's left behind. I'll get out and run along the cliff path and meet you there.'

'Stay where you are,' Daniel ordered sternly. He didn't care for Edwin Spargo, the youngest child of the large family and a thoroughly obnoxious brat. 'They can walk.'

He motioned for Mitch to sit down beside Fred and dipped the oars in the water. Edwin began to wail, his handsome dark features distorting into the expression that preceded a violent tantrum.

'You can't leave us behind,' Leah muttered indignantly as she carried Edwin down the top steps. 'I'll go back and tell Dad what you're up to and he'll tell old Rufus.'

'She means it,' said Lizzie. 'Talk Danny round, Hannah. Leah's only little and won't make much difference and Edwin can sit on your lap.'

'Danny?' Hannah glanced nervously up at the pub window. There was no one to be seen but the longer they stayed and argued, the more likely their departure would be discovered. Her father was one of many in the village who saw Daniel as a 'bad lot' who would no doubt grow up to be like his rogue of a grandfather. Jeff Spargo had warned his children that if there was any more trouble involving Daniel, he would ban them from even talking to him. Hannah would hate that.

'Me come, me come,' Edwin was chanting as Leah carried him down another step.

'Oh, let them come, for goodness sake,' Lizzie said in a huff. If they didn't go soon they'd end up going nowhere at all, except perhaps to bed with no tea to look forward to.

'Get in then,' Daniel scowled, but he was uneasy at having so many children crowded in the boat.

Mitch helped Leah into the boat then lifted Edwin onto

Hannah's lap. Edwin shifted about as if in protest and glared up at his sister; he had two more older sisters who had stayed quietly at home, Sarah and Naomi, and a grown-up brother, Josh; he loved them as he did the other family members in the boat, lapping up the way they spoiled him, but Hannah could never do anything right for him and he seemed to despise her.

When Leah was settled beside Lizzie and Jowan, Mitch released the mooring rope and took his seat, and Daniel used an oar to push the boat away from the quay. The children kept their heads down until they had passed all the luggers and punts and were too far away to be called back. When Daniel eased the boat round to head upcoast, they broke into excited chatter and Hannah relaxed. Mitch was an unrelenting practical joker and he made Fred splutter and giggle at what he was whispering into his ear.

With powerful ease Daniel rowed round the towering outcrop of Slate Rock which vessels kept well clear of to avoid the underlying treacherous rocks. Playful breezes, reflecting the children's mood, cooled the sweat on Daniel's back and sifted through the girls' hair. Eileen squealed when Mitch and Fred tugged on her ringlets.

'Stop it,' Leah shouted at them. It greatly irritated her that her big brother and his soppy friend always tormented Eileen, often to the point of tears. It wasn't Eileen's fault if her mother thought she was a cut above the rest of the villagers and didn't let her beloved only child get grubby and have tangled hair and run about in bare feet like the rest of the girls.

Fred snickered and tapped Hannah on the shoulder. She shrugged his hand off. The movement annoyed Edwin and he elbowed her in the stomach, making her wince. To mask her hurt, and the same sinking feeling she experienced when her father was belligerent towards her, she looked out across the sea – miles and miles of Channel water. There wasn't a ship, big or small, to be seen, no sea birds bobbing on the water or hovering above it; it seemed everyone was enjoying a lazy Sabbath afternoon. The gentle waves, topped here and there with white foam, stretched up ahead to the Dodman Point and to Zone Point behind them.

Hannah loved the sea. She watched it a hundred times a day. She might be just a child but she understood the words grown-ups used to describe it – a vast force of nature, a magnificent living creature with colours and moods to match anything manmade. It excited her and awed her, and although it could be savage and threatening, it also gave promise, hope and a balm of peace like nothing else could. She felt she belonged beside it, had a right to live wherever it was. The smell of sharp tangy sea air, the feel of salt water spray on her skin, the sound of the waves were as important to her as the air she breathed.

She lowered her gaze and saw that Daniel was watching her. He gave her a wink and a smile. He had seen Edwin's spiteful act and as usual sought to comfort her.

As soon as they were round Slate Rock they could see Hidden Beach, for generations a favourite playing place of Porthellis children. It was known as Hidden Beach because of the mass of rock and gorse which hid its access from the cliff path. Only the locals knew how to reach it. The sea was running a little higher in this exposed part; the boat swayed and Daniel had to pull harder on the oars.

There was a loud splashing and Eileen squealed as

Mitch batted sea water over her back.

'Oh, stop it and grow up,' Lizzie muttered crossly at her cousin, much to everyone's surprise. She had a happy-go-lucky approach to life coupled with bags of energy; usually she found Mitch's pranks funny, but the anguish on Eileen's scrubbed face made her feel Mitch was going too far this time.

Mitch took his big hand out of the water and looked shamefaced, for a moment. He put his wide jaw on Fred's shoulder and soon they were giggling again.

As Daniel turned the boat to approach the beach, Hannah said, 'I think we'd better walk back, Danny.'

Edwin immediately bellowed his discontent but Daniel agreed that it was a good idea. He had already resolved it was too much trouble taking out small children and girls, except for Hannah.

Suddenly the tops of Eileen and Hannah's dresses were pulled down, and, feeling their backs on fire, they screamed in unison and shot to their feet, making the boat rock precariously. Edwin, who had pushed away Hannah's grasp on him a moment earlier, tumbled on to the deck.

'Sit down!' Daniel shouted urgently.

Hannah obediently fell down on the seat and despite a pain searing a red-hot path down her back tried to grab Edwin, but Eileen kept screaming and was doing a frenzied dance. Edwin was sent forward, banging his face on the seat between Daniel's legs and knocking an oar out of his hand. The boat rocked crazily. While Daniel and Jowan tried to retrieve the oar and Hannah attempted to pick up Edwin, Fred cowered in a tight ball, refusing to move so Mitch could grab Eileen and yank her down to stop her putting them all in peril.

In a rage over the pain he was in, Edwin kicked away Hannah's hands and clung to Daniel's leg, biting it viciously between his wails. Daniel left the retrieval of the oar to Jowan and the other girls and fought to get the child back on Hannah's lap. Mitch cuffed Fred round the head in exasperation then stood up to grab Eileen, but his weight made the boat lurch heavily to one side. The next moment there were frantic screams as the *Wynne*, hit by a large roller, spilled her contents into the sea.

Hannah closed her mouth as she hit the water. Her first instinct was to search for Edwin. All the children could swim except for him and she hoped the others would make the shore safely. She swam about but could not find the little dark-haired boy.

Then Mitch was beside her, shouting into her ear, 'Swim for the beach. I'll get Edwin.'

Hannah did as she was told. Next to Daniel, Mitch was the strongest swimmer and Edwin's best chance. She saw Lizzie clinging to the upturned boat. 'Come on, Lizzie. It's not far to the beach. We've nearly swum out this far before.'

Lizzie nodded and together they left the scene of the accident.

Fred had been thrown several yards from the *Wynne*. He was too afraid to strike out for the shore with the girls and instead trod water, desperately wiping salt water from his eyes and jerking back his head to avoid his face being swamped by the waves. He was waiting for Daniel or Mitch to come and haul him back to the boat so he could cling to it. 'Help!' he shouted at regular intervals.

Daniel was making for Fred when he heard a more urgent cry for help. Leah's dress had been snagged at the shoulder on the boat's gunwale and she was being dragged under. There was blood streaming from her cheek. Fred seemed safe for the moment so he swam for Leah. It took a few moments to reach her then holding her from behind he tore the dress from the boat. He turned her in his arms and looked at her face. There was a deep gash down her right cheek and she looked about to slip into unconsciousness. Daniel started for the shore with her.

'Help me!' Fred was screaming in sheer terror.

'I'll come back for you,' Daniel shouted at him. 'Hold on.'

Jowan was the first to make the beach and he stayed in the surf to help Hannah and Lizzie on to the sand. They were too weak to stand and fell in a huddle, praying that the others would soon join them. They could see Fred thrashing about making spumes of white foam all round him. Daniel was swimming towards them with Leah tucked in against his body, keeping her head above the water. When Hannah saw the blood on her little sister's face, she got shakily to her feet, ready to help Daniel.

An agonising pain on her shoulder made her shriek and she was spun round with a terrible force. Jeff Spargo was glaring at her with rage in his dark eyes. He gripped her arms and shook her violently. 'What the bloody hell's going on?'

'Uncle Jeff,' Jowan cried, tugging on his shirt. 'Fred's in trouble. Swim out and get him.'

Jeff pushed Hannah down heavily on to the sand. 'Take your cousins home with your sister when Kittow's brought her in. Tell Josh and your two uncles to come here and help.'

Jeff pulled off his boots and rushed down to the water's edge. He stopped long enough to scowl at Daniel as he carried Leah up the beach and to reassure himself that Leah was breathing, then he ran on and plunged into the sea.

Hannah stayed sprawled where her father had thrust her. Daniel put Leah down on the sand beside her and gently laid Leah's head on her lap. Leah's face was still trickling blood but she was conscious, blinking in disbelief at what had happened. Hannah stroked her sister's dripping black hair away from the wound and shuddered at how deep it was.

'Can you manage to carry Leah home between you?' Daniel gasped breathlessly as Lizzie and Jowan gathered round them. 'I'm going to get my breath back then see if I can pull in the boat before my grandfather turns up.'

'Will they be all right?' Lizzie asked anxiously, wringing out a handful of her skirt.

'Should be,' Daniel said. 'Your uncle's gone for Fred and Mitch is getting Edwin.'

'Eileen!' Hannah shrieked. 'Where's Eileen?' She eased Leah's head into Jowan's arms then ran down to the water.

Daniel caught hold of her before she plunged into the sea. 'I'll get Eileen, you do what your father said.'

Hannah stood numbly and watched Daniel take to the waves again. Lizzie tugged on her arm. 'We must go home at once, Hannah. Uncle Jeff will be even more furious if we hang about here.'

With a piece of cloth ripped from Hannah's petticoat and held against Leah's gashed cheek, the three unhurt children half walked, half carried her up the beach and squeezed through the gorse bushes that lined the steep incline of rock to reach the cliff path. No one said a word as they followed the narrow path, glancing anxiously at the sea where they could see small figures battling against the waves until Slate Rock hid them from sight.

As if some premonition of trouble had roused the village from its Sunday torpor, people were standing about on the quay, beside the pump and in their doorways.

Rufus Kittow was the only one who had noticed the *Wynne* was missing. While the men talked about the week of hard work ahead and the women what they would put on the table for tea, the children ruminated in whispers on what adventure they had missed with Daniel and the eight other children missing. Rufus was standing on the quay steps, legs planted wide apart, elbows sticking out of his ragged jacket, muttering under his whisky-laden breath what punishment he would dole out to his wilful grandson for stealing his precious boat. With his worn and seamed face, hooded eyes, his heavy unkempt whiskers and missing left earlobe, the result of a fishing accident, he looked hardly human as he mentally flayed the flesh off Daniel's back with his belt. Nonetheless, he was alert and he was the first to see the pathetic sight of Hannah's group struggling down off the cliff path.

'What's going on up there?' he shouted, waving his hand at the children.

Fretful stillness gave way to commotion and a rapid scurry along the narrow cobbled streets towards the cliff path. Rufus was nearing sixty, but despite his hard drinking and the fact that his legs were steadier at sea than on land, he was as sprightly as a man half his age. He scrambled up the steps and passed most of the villagers to reach the children with the fastest runners.

'What happened t'she?' he demanded in the thick voice that was virtually unintelligible to outsiders. ''As Danny anythin' to do with this? What about my boat?'

'It turned over,' Jowan whispered, his voice husky with shame and the soreness the sea-water had etched on his throat. 'Danny was swimming out for Eileen when we left.'

'Eileen?' a female voice shrieked. 'Did he mention my Eileen?'

Rufus Kittow thrust himself in front of Hetty Gunn and lifted the wilting Leah into his arms. He turned to face the crowd who were swarming behind Hetty, who was being held comfortingly on the arm by the pub land-lady, Maggie Curnow.

'You got nothing to worry about, woman,' Rufus said harshly. 'My boy will bring she in safely.'

Hetty Gunn went into hysterics anyway and pulled herself away from Maggie Curnow, whom she considered a common hussy.

Hannah's mother, Prim Spargo, came forward and gulping at the sight of Leah's wound, put her plump arms round her only fair-haired child. 'Come along, Hannah, dear. We'd better get you all home and into bed, questions can come later.' Her pale blue eyes were on Leah's stricken face. 'Will someone run and fetch the doctor for Leah?'

'I'll go,' offered Matt Penney, a young fisherman who fished with Rufus Kittow and who had been staring intently at Hannah, and he promptly ran off.

Roy and Janet Rouse, Jowan's parents, and Terence and Bett Spargo, Lizzie's parents, led their tearful children away.

Josh Spargo, Hannah's seventeen-year-old brother, who had a stubborn and quarrelsome disposition like their father, was next on the scene. He stood in front of Rufus

Kittow and glared at the small-bodied old fisherman who stank of sweat and whisky. Josh held out his muscular arms.

'Give my sister to me,' he hissed, his dark Spargo eyes glittering dangerously. 'Whatever happened here is bound to be the fault of your grandson. We should hound the pair of you out of the village before you cause any more trouble.'

The Methodist minister, the Reverend David Skewes, had come down from the Manse. His presence stopped a flow of similar sentiments from the array of grim faces but he did not reprimand Josh, for he was not a hypocrite. Rufus Kittow was known for being light-fingered and the other fishermen knew where the blame usually rightfully lay when any of their gear went missing.

At home, Hannah was helped by her older sister, Sarah, to wash and dry herself and put on her nightdress. Sarah said little but patted Hannah sympathetically before tucking her up in the bed they shared and leaving the room. Sarah knew what Hannah could expect the instant their father came home.

Her hair damp on the hard pillow, Hannah lay shivering and fearful, overwhelmed with loneliness and guilt for the trouble she and the others were in, feeling that somehow she should have stopped the boat trip. Time passed and the doctor arrived. She couldn't bear Leah's screams as he tended to her and she got out of bed, squeezed past the other double bed in the room, which Leah and Naomi used, and peeped out of the window.

Women and children were milling in groups, no doubt talking about the incident that had shattered the Sabbath's peace and praying the other children would return home safely; the men had gone to the little beach to see what they could do to help.

The village was set on a steep hill, flanked by sloping fields. At the bottom of Porthkilt Hill, close to the cobbled slipway, an underground, fast-moving stream emerged and flowed into the sea. It separated the village into two unequal parts. Hannah lived on the smaller side, called the dark side because Cliffside Cottage and the few other dwellings there were nestled in under the shade of the cliff for a large part of the day, and it was also the side Roscarrock was on. The other side of the stream was the heart of the village, with a greater number of homes rising in close tiers, and vying for space among them a few shops, the chapel, pub, post office, bakehouse, workplaces and quay. Hannah longed to run outside, away from the torment of Leah's agony, to dash across the long slab of granite that bridged the stream and tear back along the cliff path to Hidden Beach and see what was happening there.

She looked the few yards away to where the Kittows' shabby cottage stood. She could hardly bear to imagine the cries that would come from there when Rufus punished Daniel. Fred's cottage was next to the Kittows' and Hannah prayed her father had saved him.

A bleak feeling invaded her heart and ran down into the pit of her stomach as the bedroom door opened and someone came into the room. Even without the telltale disapproving sniff, Hannah knew who it was. She turned slowly to face her paternal grandmother who lived with the family.

Hannah said nothing. It never paid for her to speak first to Constance Spargo.

She looked into the bony face with its thin, bitter lips,

sunken cheeks, a high, aloof brow, and the beady dark eyes that seemed to penetrate her being every time they were cast upon her. Constance Spargo loomed over her, tall and stiff-backed, dressed in the musty, black, Edwardian clothes she had worn since her husband had drowned in a fishing accident down off the Wolf Rock.

'You have scarred your sister for life.' It was issued like a judge passing sentence, in a voice that sounded as if the woman's throat was parched and cracking.

Scalding tears of guilt seared Hannah's eyes. With difficulty she kept them in check and remained quiet. Leah wailed as the doctor put another stitch into her face, a pitiful sound that rose and rose. Hannah clapped her hands over her ears.

Constance Spargo flew across the room and ripped her hands away and clutched them cruelly tight. 'Listen to her. You did that. I don't know how your father is going to pay for the doctor. Are you satisfied now?'

There was another scream. It had come from a different person, someone outside. Hannah and her grandmother looked out of the window. It had come from deep within the soul of Hetty Gunn. She screamed again and howled and raised her hands to heaven, running across the quay like someone demented.

'No! No! Not my baby!'

Jake Gunn caught up with his wife and gathering her imploring arms into his body led her away to their cottage, followed by a wake of women like sea birds chasing a laden lugger. They would stay long after Jake had done what he could to comfort Hetty.

Prim came into the bedroom, tears coursing a path down her chubby pink face. 'Poor Hetty, she'll never get over it.' She joined them at the window and watched as the other men strode on gravely, branching off for their homes. Fred was being carried across the bridge by his father. Mitch, with a tear-streaked face, was holding his friend's hand and talking rapidly to raise his spirits, and perhaps his own.

'Y-you mean Eileen has dr-drowned?' Hannah got out through her constricted throat, and she knew this boded ill for her in more ways than one.

Constance Spargo placed a spread-eagled hand on her flat breast and made a sound as if she was stifling a fit of crying, but Hannah could see what looked like joy on her face.

Prim nodded and sniffed into her hanky. Hannah leaned against her, seeking comfort from her ample body. Prim led her to her bed, then said in a choked voice, 'Thank God none of mine were taken. Mother-in-law, have you any idea where Edwin is? He's not in his bed. I hope he hasn't wandered off again after his nap.'

Hannah gasped and looked at her mother with fear widening her eyes.

Before Prim could take in the significance of this there was a thundering of heavy feet up the stairs and the door was flung back.

'I'll tell you where your son is!' snarled Jeff Spargo, glaring at Hannah as if all the hatred of the world was in his eyes.

Hannah edged back to the window. Jeff leapt towards her, his finger pointed agitatedly. 'He's at the bottom of the sea, that's where he is, Prim Spargo. That's where Edwin is. Dead! And it's all her fault.'

'How can you say that?' Prim cried.

'She had Edwin on her lap. She should have saved his

skin before her own. She talked Kittow into letting the boy go with them.'

Terrified of the venom in her father's handsome features, Hannah edged along the wall, not stopping until she could go no further and her arm was pressed against the wardrobe. She put her back to the ancient wood and scratched at it with splayed fingers, wishing desperately that the mahogany would re-form itself into a tree and swallow her up in its trunk.

'I always said she would bring disaster on this family and now my words have come true.' Constance Spargo uttered each word precisely, gloatingly to Hannah's ears, as if the death of her grandson was something she could be triumphant about.

Prim clutched her full bosom and stared in horror as Jeff advanced on the petrified girl.

Hannah attempted to speak but the words refused to form.

'It was your fault,' Jeff raged, smashing a hand across her face. 'You've got no right to be here. Just because your mother is soft and—'

'Jeff, don't!' Prim screeched, hurling herself at him and trying to pull him away.

'It's time she knew the truth,' Constance said contemptuously.

'Not this way,' Prim wailed, fighting with her husband whose giant hands were reaching for Hannah.

Jeff threw Prim off him as if she was no more than a piece of fluff on his clothes.

Hannah's heart felt as if it was about to burst. She shook in terror as one of Jeff's raised fists headed for her face. She sank to the floor, blubbering like an imbecile for mercy, holding up her arms to protect herself in what she knew would be a vain effort.

Jeff smashed his fist into the wardrobe, splintering the wood and bloodying his knuckles. Then he reached down and grasped one of Hannah's arms and pulled her to him. He slapped her face again and again, harder and harder, his breathing violent and tortured.

Suddenly he was yanked away from her. Daniel plunged his fist into Jeff's jaw and, taken completely by surprise, he was hurled back towards the window, momentarily winded.

Daniel put himself between Hannah and her shocked and furious father. His young face was as dark and fierce as a raging storm. 'I swear if you ever raise your hand to her again I'll bloody kill you!'

Jeff gathered his great strength together and wiped his hand across his split lip.

Afraid he was coming after Hannah again, Prim begged desperately, 'Get her out of here, Daniel.'

Jeff had bunched his fist and was about to stride forward but halted at his wife's plea. Then he grinned, stretching his wide lips back to their fullest extent. And now he was gloating. Constance came to stand at his side, her fingers interlaced in front of her thin, bony body. Two judges about to pronounce a terrible sentence.

'That's right, Daniel Kittow, take the young bitch out of here for good.' Jeff turned his hate-filled gaze on Hannah. 'You've no right to be here, girl. You're no Spargo.'

Prim raised her hands to beseech the two at the window, but was ignored.

Through tight, cruel lips, Constance added, 'That's right, you don't belong here, you never have.'

Prim collapsed on one of the beds and wept for the two children she had lost this day.

Unable to speak, too weak to walk, Hannah leaned against Daniel's chest as he lifted her up into his arms. He plodded down the stairs and carried her away from the Spargo cottage.

Chapter 1

Hannah stood at the bottom of a small grave and gazed down dejectedly at the granite headstone.

EDWIN SPARGO
DIED 1926
AGED 3 YEARS
Beloved Son of Jeffrey and Primrose

Edwin had been dead for ten years and was buried in Gorran churchyard, four miles from Porthellis.

His body had been washed ashore further along the south Cornish coast, in Mounts Bay, a week after he'd drowned. Jeff Spargo had grieved publicly for the child who had most favoured his looks, raving about his great loss and getting drunk until the villagers, who had been outraged by his treatment of Hannah, lost their last scrap of sympathy for him, removing it to Daniel; after all, he was only a child and it had been a prank that had turned into a tragic accident.

To earn the money for Edwin's headstone, Jeff had worked the family lugger like a madman, making the crew go out in weather conditions that kept the sensible and less courageous at home. He weeded the grave and kept

23

it free of the lichen that flourished in the clear, sea-fresh air. He cut the grass and tended a small flowering shrub he had planted at the foot. Hannah had another brother and sister buried in the churchyard, on top of her grandfather; their names were recorded, Martin and Julie, but not their age or date of death; they had been still-born, of not much importance to her father, her aunt had told her.

On the day of the drownings, Daniel had taken Hannah, sobbing and shivering in her nightdress, her face bruised and swollen, across the bridge to the sunny side of Porthellis, to Janet Rouse, Prim's elder sister. Janet, an outspoken woman who recognised cruelty when she saw it, had immediately marched off to Cliffside Cottage and demanded an explanation. Prim had begged Jeff to give himself time to cool off and allow Hannah home but he had shouted that if she ever set foot over his threshold again he would walk out for good. Janet had called him a vicious bully, an un-Christian brute who had no right to step inside the chapel for more reason than one. With that she had declared that Hannah was welcome to live with her from now on and that the Rouses would treat her kindly. Vowing never to darken Jeff Spargo's door again until he had apologised to Hannah and mended his wicked ways, she had stormed out. Since that day, neither the Rouses nor Hannah had crossed the bridge to the dark side of Porthellis.

Jeff had sent word that Hannah must not attend Edwin's funeral, with the added warning that she must stay away from the grave. But today he wouldn't discover her here; he was at the wedding reception following her cousin's Lizzie's wedding.

Hannah had attended the small family marriage ceremony in the Wesleyan chapel, but outside, while the photographs were being taken, she had been confronted by her father. He had cut a striking figure in his navy blue suit and blue and grey striped tie, his thick black hair falling in its natural waves, but his manner as usual had been hostile.

'She's lucky t'be getting married at all,' he'd said accusingly, jerking his fine head in the direction of the radiant bride. 'She survived the day you killed your little brother.'

Hannah had not had the chance to respond. Janet Rouse, always protectively close at her side when her brother-in-law was about, had hissed at him, 'She did not kill Edwin, Jeff Spargo, and you very well know it. This is a happy occasion, leave her be.'

To Hannah's growing horror, Constance had pitched in. 'What's she doing here? She's not family! Tell her to go, Jeffrey.'

Hannah had turned away, as she'd done every time her father had assailed her in the last ten years. She wanted to defend herself and say she was sorry about Edwin, she wanted her father's heart to melt and retract the hateful things he'd said to her and welcome her back to the family, but she knew that would never be and was always too hurt to speak.

She thought she knew why he and her grandmother had always hated her. Her aunt had fended off her questions, only saying she had been a surprise baby, but what other reason could there be than that she wasn't Jeff Spargo's daughter? Her mother must have had an affair, which accounted for her fairness when all the Spargos were dark. Prim came to the Rouses' house as often as she could to see Hannah, sometimes bringing a little gift, but although she was warm and loving, she was obviously uncomfortable and Hannah couldn't bring herself to ask her for the truth. She often wondered who her real father was – she'd probably never know; if he lived in the village, Jeff or Constance would have made it known. A few people in the village had muttered about her being born 'the wrong side of the blanket' and Matt Penney's mother had said that she owed her fair beauty to being 'left by the small people'.

Since the day she had been thrown out of her home, Hannah had been unable to cry and now the heavy bleak emotion that stopped her from pleading with her father was upon her again. A strong hand touched her arm. It was her brother, Mitch. He smiled wanly at her and turned on his father and grandmother.

'Aunty Janet's right. This isn't the time or place and you know you're both being unfair.' Mitch often spoke up for Hannah and she had the comfort of knowing that her brothers and sisters, except for Josh, had not turned against her.

Constance ruffled her widow's weeds and tossed her head in disdain. In a less public place Mitch would have received the back of his father's hand; Hannah knew he would be treated to it later and she felt disheartened. If she went on to the reception, Mitch and the others would associate with her and there would be many a quarrel as a result; Jeff would even storm at Sarah and Naomi who were now married to village fishermen and had their own homes. In the end her mother would suffer the most; it was known that Jeff occasionally hit her. Hannah didn't want to risk that or have Lizzie's big day ruined. After giving Mitch a look of gratitude, she told Janet she wouldn't go on to Lizzie's house.

'Never mind him,' Janet said in a huff, taking her arm. 'If he don't like it, let him be the one to go elsewhere.'

'No, I've made up my mind,' Hannah said firmly, pulling away. 'You explain to Lizzie for me. I'm sure she'll understand and I'd rather be on my own.'

Hannah had glanced up at the sky, a habit inbred in those who depended on good weather conditions to make their living. It would stay hot and fine all day and she couldn't bear the thought of being stuck indoors. She walked quickly down to her home in Quayside Street; like all the streets in Porthellis, it could hardly be called a street at all, being no more than a narrow cobbled thoroughfare which a single vehicle had difficulty squeezing through. She had changed into work-a-day clothes and, borrowing Jowan's bicycle, had taken a route that avoided the wedding party. She'd had no specific destination in mind and had turned right at the top of Porthkilt Hill, weaving along the narrow, twisting lanes until she'd reached Gorran Churchtown. Resting the bicycle against the wall of the Anglican churchyard where generations of villagers were buried, irrespective of their beliefs, she had felt drawn to Edwin's grave.

Hannah always felt sad that she couldn't put flowers on it. Sometimes the unfairness of it was too much for her and she was filled with frustration and a little bitterness. She whispered goodbye to Edwin, asking him to forgive her, then moved away to gaze up at the sky for the answers that would free her soul. She rested her arm on the 250–year-old headstone belonging to Jeremiah Jago, unafraid that he would rise and haunt her for taking the liberty. It wasn't the dead who could hurt her. Taking off her wide-brimmed straw hat, she welcomed the fresh breeze which tugged at her glossy, shoulder-length blonde hair.

To lift her spirits, she melted away from her surroundings and dreamed of adventures on the high seas. Indeed, in the plain grey dress she was wearing her outward form seemed to merge with the large Norman church behind her. She could have been a statue set there by a sculptor who had an empathy for the lost and bewildered, tall, slender, in perfect proportion from her wide brow and high cheekbones to her shapely legs and sandalled feet. The proud lift of her graceful shoulders did not betray the sadness and grief that lurked behind her blue eyes which mirrored the colour of the summer sea.

The sea couldn't be seen from here, but somewhere out on the swelling and dipping mass of water, riding the waves free and unencumbered, were Daniel and Rufus Kittow on their lugger, the *Sunrise*, crewed and jointly owned by Matt Penney and Fred Jose's father Curly; Fred made up the crew. She wished she was with them, that the superstition it was unlucky to have women on board a working boat would be set aside and she could earn her living as they did. Hannah's next choice would have been to work in the carpenter's shop or bark house but that was also a male preserve, or to be a net-maker like Sarah and Naomi, but her Aunt Janet's heart had been set on her following her own trade, a seamstress. By hand or sewing machine they made and altered garments, curtains and bed linen, and produced the most exquisite embroidery and lace. Janet Rouse had built up a reputation for excellence and one of her customers was Mrs Feena Opie, the lady of Roscarrock. Hannah had produced a matching set of table runners for her only the week before. Hannah hadn't 'taken a peek' at Roscarrock in years but she would have loved to have delivered her work herself and seen inside the mysterious building; she might even have met the old lady who was said to have turned rather strange and was a virtual recluse, but the whole transaction was conducted by post. Hannah enjoyed making small things when she could take them outside and work on them, but in the main she felt stifled.

She was not totally sad, however. She had a good home where she felt wanted and she was pleased for Lizzie who had just married John Jacobs, a young widower. Lizzie adored John and he was attracted to Lizzie's vivacious nature, which the rowing boat tragedy had done little to dampen, an attribute his three motherless children needed while he was out at sea, now that his own mother had also passed on. Hannah would be free to visit their home, next to the pub, any time she liked. And Hannah had a special friend in Daniel. Jeff Spargo had been true to his word and forbidden his children to speak to Daniel, but the Rouses had put no such restraint on Hannah. She saw him every day when he was not out at sea.

It was near the end of July and all that week the fishermen had been preparing for the coming pilchard drive. Although their lot had improved since the poverty-stricken days before the Great War, fear of want drove the fishermen on to work hard for their families. They took nothing for granted and saw survival and full tables as a blessing, living and working to the rhythms of the seasons, the foibles of the weather, watching the sky and conditions of the tides and the 'likes' out in the bay.

The crew of the *Sunrise* had worked like beavers to tar her sides, scrape and rile the mast; they had seen to the cabin, picked out her name, number and moulding in white paint and topped up her fuel tanks. Now they were putting her through her paces. When the *Sunrise* returned, before Daniel made his way to the pub, he would tell Hannah how well the boat had ridden the waves, whether she favoured the port or starboard side this time out, how the engines sounded, every fine detail until Hannah burned with envy.

Hannah wended her way through the churchyard. There was no one else to remember here. Eileen Gunn's body had never been found. Hetty had slipped into a deep depression and died three months later of some mysterious malady; pining for her child, Constance Spargo had pontificated around the village, 'and we all know who to blame for that!' Jake had been killed in a freak accident two years later, apparently falling to the bottom of the cliff at its highest point near Roscarrock property. No one believed it was an accident; he'd had nothing left to live for. He was buried on top of Hetty. Still believing she should have at least stopped the girls going out in the *Wynne* on that fateful day, Hannah had never forgiven herself for what had happened to the Gunns' daughter; they would not want her looking at their last resting place. Jeff and Constance Spargo's accusations could not make her feel any worse about the family's fate.

Returning home quietly, she put Jowan's bicycle away and headed for Hidden Beach. The tragedy had not stopped her going there; it was one of her favourite places and it was on its shore that she usually remembered Edwin and Eileen. Janet, thoughtful and understanding, aware how much the sewing frustrated her, would not mind if she stayed out for the rest of the day, and Hannah intended to keep away from the village until after the wedding festivities were over.

With most people at work, and a wedding to gawp at for others, she was not expecting to find anyone on the beach and was surprised to see a man standing on the shoreline. She had taken off her sandals and was carrying them in one hand but the man, a stranger to her, was wearing good leather shoes and the sea was lapping over them. He was completely motionless, like a statue, the way she had been in the churchyard.

Annoyed at not being alone, she crept back the way she had come. She would walk further along the cliff path and sit in a sheltered, grassy nook somewhere. Before she put her sandals back on to climb up the rocky incline, she glanced once more at the man. He had not moved and seemed completely unaware that a wave, much stronger and higher than its passive predecessors, was bearing down on him. He would be soaked.

Shouting to warn him, Hannah ran towards him. She was too late to save the man's legs and trousers and he was so shocked at the sudden wetting he would have stumbled if she hadn't reached him in time to steady him.

'Oh dear, oh, I say, how silly of me,' he said, walking backwards with a sheepish expression on his face. 'I am indebted to you, young lady.' He was wearing a safari hat and swept it off to salute her.

'I'm sorry I was too late to save you from a soaking,' Hannah said, staring unashamedly at him.

He had the most interesting face she had ever seen. He was aged about forty-five and his skin was the colour and texture of the sand. There were deep wrinkles round his eyes, etched down his full, rounded cheeks, and gathering round his softly formed mouth which seemed impossibly small. His hair-line had receded halfway back over the crown of his head, leaving a dull and fuzzy fringe sticking out over big, pixie-shaped ears. Tiny darting grey eyes were topped by thin arched brows, and a small cleft chin dropped away abruptly to a long thin neck. His nose protruded over a wide moustache which was neatly combed to each side. His shirt, sleeveless pullover and trousers were good quality but not worn at all tidily, his black and red spotted bow tie was askew and looked like a large butterfly perched on his neck. He was more than interesting, he was peculiar.

When they were on dry sand they stopped walking and he looked down guiltily at Hannah's feet and the hem of her skirt. 'I do hope you haven't got too wet on my account.' He spoke well, telling of privilege and a good education.

'No, I'm fine,' Hannah assured him.

He was at a loss now, blushing and blustering. 'I-I am most grateful to you, Miss, um, ah . . .?'

'Spargo, Hannah Spargo. I live in Porthellis, the fishing village on the other side of the large grey rock stretching out in the sea.'

'Pleased to meet you, Miss Spargo,' he replied, a little more at ease now, and he offered a hand that was surprisingly grimy, the nails ragged and blackened. 'I'm Patrick Opie. I live at Roscarrock.'

'The big house!' Hannah gasped, forgetting for a moment to shake his hand. Seeing one of the three Opies who lived up on the cliff was as rare as hen's teeth. It was the first time for her in her twenty years. She had assumed he was a holidaymaker and had found his way here by chance. She stared at him even more closely, forgetting it was bad manners.

'That's correct. I rarely venture out of its grounds, preferring my own company. But I've viewed this little beach from my telescope many times and today I took it into my head to come down here and memorise it in every fine detail. I've got an excellent photographic memory, you know. I'm going to paint it. I was so absorbed in what I was doing I didn't notice the tide stealing up on me. It's a beautiful little place, isn't it? I dare say you come here often.'

Hannah was surprised he was so chatty. She thought one of the elusive Opies would have scuttled away back into their own private world by now.

'I love it,' she said emphatically.

Patrick Opie looked as if he was about to speak; he hesitated and blushed. Hannah had the feeling he wanted to ask her something personal but she was totally unprepared for his next question.

'Tell me, Miss Spargo, would you happen to be looking for a position?'

'A position?' Hannah raised her fair brows. What a curious thing to ask a stranger.

'Yes, that's right, a job. Roscarrock's housekeeper is about to leave us to care for her elderly father. Mrs Opie, my great-aunt, who owns Roscarrock, has charged me, unfortunately,' he grinned shyly, 'with the task of finding a replacement. It's live in, of course. Mrs Opie says the new housekeeper must be quite young so she's unlikely to have elderly parents to worry about and is not about to get married.' Patrick Opie looked at Hannah quizzically. 'I hope you don't mind me asking you but even on such a short acquaintance I think you'd fit the bill quite nicely and it would be a lot off my mind. You're not about to get married, are you?'

Hannah was astonished by his forthrightness and if he hadn't sounded so serious she would have laughed.

Keeping a straight face, she replied, 'No, Mr Opie, I am quite unattached, and I am employed as a seamstress which I intend to remain. In fact I have done work for Mrs Opie.'

'Oh, really?' He lowered his pinprick eyes, his expression mournful, like a rejected puppy. 'Mrs Opie would find you eminently suitable, I'm sure. You're strong and quick-thinking – I've just benefited from that – and you're very kind to have troubled yourself for a complete stranger.'

'I'm sorry, Mr Opie.' He looked so lost and defeated, the task his great-aunt had given him evidently a bother to him, Hannah truly was sorry to disappoint him.

'Oh, well, never mind,' he rallied and smiled at her; Hannah thought it made him look a kind man. 'If you change your mind or would just like to know more, Miss Spargo, perhaps to see if you would like us, do send me a little note and I'll reply with the necessary arrangements for an interview.'

Hannah felt honoured by this strange man's request. 'Thank you for considering me, Mr Opie,' she said politely.

'Yes, right then. I'd better be going.' He swung his over-long, thin arms about for a few moments as if he wasn't sure which direction he should take. 'I shall be hoping to hear from you in the very near future. A very good afternoon to you, Miss Spargo.'

Hannah said goodbye to Patrick Opie then sat down on the warm sand. He had given her a lot to think about. Aunty Janet would be astounded at the news. She would pump her for every detail, then repeat every rumour she'd heard about Roscarrock and be on tenterhooks to tell her menfolk when they came in for supper. Jowan would be avidly interested, he had heard that Roscarrock was filled with books and he would beg her to take the job and borrow some for him. He had been a fisherman since his fifteenth birthday but had ambitions of becoming an astronomer. He was saving up out of his meagre wages to go to college and pass examinations. Working out the position of the boats by the stars was probably all he would achieve in that direction, Hannah thought sadly. His younger brother, Ned, whose lameness did little to mar his excellence as a fisherman, was a sparky youth with a penchant for shocking people, particularly by poking them with his walking stick. He would say Patrick Opie's proposition was a bloody, sodding cheek as they'd only just met, and Uncle Roy would say, 'Ummm, that's nice, my handsome,' without really listening or realising his son had sworn again, and go back to snoozing in his chair.

It was Daniel's reaction she was most looking forward to. They shared most of their thoughts and secrets and now she had something to impress him with for a change.

Chapter 2

Daniel Kittow was standing, sure-footed, like a sentinel, in the prow of the *Sunrise*. He was proud of the forty-foot lugger and none had matched her during the lugger racing in Feast Week last month. Other crews possessed a better spirit of comradeship but few the skill and intuitions of the *Sunrise*'s fishermen, particularly her skipper, Rufus Kittow. The boat had been crafted locally two years ago in Mitchell's boatyard at Portmellon. Her frame was oak and pitch pine, her bow-fronted, teak-topped wheelhouse nearly high enough to accommodate Daniel's six foot, two inch, muscular frame. She carried a boom mizzen and a lug sail, was equipped with two diesel engines and strong canvas sails made on the quayfront of Porthellis, and her cabin provided accommodation for five and had a coal stove with a chimney. The boat hadn't been fished many seasons but seemed to possess similar characteristics to Daniel, swift-moving, rebellious, independent, able to soar over the wildest seas with youthful enthusiasm. Daniel had bought into the lugger partly with money from his share of the fishing profits and partly through some unlawful sidelines he had been running.

They were sailing downcoast and he was mesmerised once again by the beauty of the vast stretch of the Channel and the scalloped coastline where sleepy little coves nestled between magnificent headlands. He watched the green-tinged, long-beaked dark shapes of three shags perched on Gull Rock, their wings outstretched like old men wearing cloaks as they dried their feathers. When he got a peaceful moment like this, with just the healthy chug of the boat's engine and whistle of the wind in his ears, when his head wasn't filled with casting nets or throwing line, the size of the catch and profit margins, it gave him a lift like nothing else could; Hannah would understand how he felt.

The wheelhouse had room for four men at a time and Matt Penney left Rufus Kittow, Fred and Curly Jose there to take the opportunity to approach Daniel. Matt noted the deep concentration on Daniel's rugged face; they had done fairly well at the ray pits during the last few weeks and he assumed his workmate was looking forward to the hunt for pilchards. He waited for him to look his way before he spoke.

'What's up?' Daniel said, taking the last puff of the cigarette he had forgotten to smoke and tossing the butt into the sea.

Matt's serious expression provoked another question. 'Granfer hasn't said something to offend you again, has he? I'm afraid he had a skinful again last night.'

'No. Besides, I've got used to your grandfather's foul language – well, most of it, and I say the odd bad word myself. No, it's nothing like that.'

Daniel studied Matt. He was a picture of embarrassment. 'What then?' He teased Matt a little, indulging in the banter that often passed between them when Rufus wasn't about to add a prurient tone to it. 'Can't see what you're worried about. We've all agreed that the boat's

38

ready for the pilchard drive. You been asked to read a lesson in chapel again and worried about those long names? If it's advice on your runner beans you're after, don't ask me, I'm no gardener.'

A wash of red that rivalled the colour of Daniel's glossy mane spread up Matt's neck and disappeared under his thick earth-brown hair, but his gaze was penetrating as he turned it on Daniel. 'It's about Hannah.'

'Hannah? Why? Has her father been threatening her again? Why can't the bastard just leave her alone? He turned the maid out of her home, isn't that enough?'

Daniel's heated reaction wasn't at all how Matt wanted the conversation to go. Daniel was fiercely protective of Hannah. One day Jeff Spargo would be well and truly thumped, deservedly so, and it would be most unpleasant; Daniel could be very hard. He had nearly broken Rufus's arm when he'd tried to take his belt to him on the day of the boat tragedy and Matt had observed that the old man seemed a little wary of him at times.

Matt went on doggedly, 'I've been thinking of asking Hannah out, have been for a long time, but I don't want to step on your toes. You and her are very close. Would you mind telling me how close you are, Danny? If it's leading to something permanent then I apologise and you have my word I shall bow out gracefully and Hannah need never know.'

Astounded at this announcement, Daniel gaped at Matt. He was only four years older than he was, but for a 28–year-old man he seemed to Daniel to be much older, with something of a middle-aged outlook on life. He lived with his widowed mother in Cobble Street and when not working went nowhere but chapel or up the steep hill of the village to tend his beloved allotment. Alcohol had never been known to pass his lips and he was often quiet and serious, appearing to slip into a kind of melancholy at times. When Rufus was at his bawdiest he made fun of Matt's apparent uninterest in women, sniggering that he must still be a virgin and speculating that he might prefer men. Matt had been hurt and offended but he'd never retaliated, just ignored the old man and went about his business on the lugger. This had earned him the respect of the rest of the crew and the old man's taunts were becoming fewer. Daniel had never been given to ponder about what went on inside another's head. He had taken Matt's reserved nature for granted, but he knew from local gossip that the women hereabouts considered him a good catch.

'I had no idea you had a fancy for Hannah,' he said sternly.

'So you do mind,' Matt returned.

'Hannah and I are friends, in a way I s'pose you could say best mates. Nothing's going on between us like that and anyway I'm not the marrying kind, although if I was I would only consider marrying Hannah.' Daniel looked out at the small frolicking waves disappearing fast under the boat. He said to the sea, rather than to Matt, 'I s'pose she'll want to get married one day. Women usually do.' He knew that well enough. He had dallied with the younger females of Porthellis and further afield a long time before his own age of consent and most of them had hoped it would lead to marriage. He felt a strange despondency sweep over him, as if he was about to lose something very special and deeply rooted in him. 'If Hannah wants to go out with you, then good luck to both of you, Matt. But,' he paused heavily on the last word, because for all Matt's apparent respectability, he was still a man, 'forget yourself and try anything on her and I'll break your bleddy neck!'

At last Matt smiled, the warm and gentle smile that rarely lit his strong intelligent features but was distinctively his. 'That's all I wanted to know. Thanks, Danny.'

Before Daniel could say anything more, Fred Jose came up to them on tottering legs. His sea legs were not very sound, in fact they were the most unsteady in Porthellis and the village was waiting with grim expectancy for him to cause a mishap aboard the *Sunrise*. The weathering of the face and build-up of muscle that was quickly acquired by every other fisherman had passed Fred by. He was as pale and scrawny as he had been as a boy. His nose had been broken by Mitch Spargo's flailing hand on the day they had been thrown out of the *Wynne* and it made him look a little more manly – hard and quarrelsome to an unobservant stranger – but he was still a coward, inclined to panic easily. He worked as hard as the others when conditions were good to fair but was only tolerated as a crew member for Curly's sake; Curly had partnered Rufus for over thirty years and was a very able engineer.

'Dad wants to know how you think she's running,' Fred said, wiping spray from his face and clinging to the greenheart rail that topped the twenty-inch bulwarks.

Daniel and Matt turned and gave the thumbs up to the *Sunrise*'s other two partners. With a satisfied expression Rufus rammed his dirty pipe between his blackened teeth and Curly turned the wheel for home; they wouldn't waste the fuel.

Daniel looked up to check that the mizzen and fore mizzens were blowing to the best advantage. They were. It was fine weather and the wind was blowing hard in the sails. The blue and white lugger was parting the waters like a hot knife through butter, dominant, self-assured, the mistress today. Daniel could have stayed out at sea for hours yet.

Most people in Porthellis simply tapped on a neighbour's back door and entered the house with a cheery greeting. Janet Rouse, still upset that Hannah had felt she must leave the wedding, was forced to answer a persistent knocking on the front door that evening, even though it was left open to let in the cool breeze and she had called out many times, 'Come in.' She grumpily put aside her sewing, took off the floral pinny over her brown and white spotted cotton dress and checked the seams of her fawn lisle stockings.

'Oh, it's you, Matt,' she said, hastily putting on a welcoming smile. 'Why didn't you come in? Didn't you hear me calling? If you want any of the men they're down on the beach seeing to the boat.' Janet frowned, puzzled. Matt would have seen her menfolk on his way here. 'Oh, I see.' And Janet did see, even without the help of her thick-rimmed glasses. Matt Penney was not wearing the old jersey and faded trousers she'd seen him in when the *Sunrise* had been taken out. He had changed into a new white shirt and his second best trousers, his shoes were polished like mirrors and his hair was slicked back. Janet instinctively smoothed her own short plain hair and gave Matt a toothy smile. 'Come inside, Matt, no need for 'ee to stand on the doorstep. You're in luck, she came in just ten minutes ago.'

Matt ducked under the doorway and took the two deep, well-scrubbed, blue-stone steps down into the narrow passage and followed Janet to her kitchen. The moment his feet touched the rope rug in the middle of the chunky, serviceable furniture, where the makings of a half-finished dress lay on the table, Janet excused herself and left the room. Matt went to the small oblong mirror hanging on a nail near the sink and swiftly taking a comb out of his trouser pocket nervously neatened his hair again. The Rouses' fat, molly-coddled ginger cat, which Ned had unimaginatively named Ginger, watched him curiously from its basket at the hearth, and he crouched down and stroked it, making it purr loudly. Petting the cat helped to slow down the furious beating of his heart. He had noticed Hannah long before womanhood had touched her, attracted to her quiet spirit and noting how being turned out of her rightful home had not embittered her. To Matt she was as lovely as a spring morning and he'd watched her grow up, waiting patiently for the right moment to make his feelings known to her.

Janet called up the stairs. 'Hannah! Can you come down now, dear? There's someone here to see you.'

As usual Hannah had come in looking like a grubby child, her dress damp from sea water with sand sticking to it, her hair windblown, and after a light-hearted chiding from Janet she had gone to her little room to freshen up before she helped with the supper.

Janet was greatly excited at Matt being here to see Hannah. She approved of him. The fact that he owned a fourth of the *Sunrise* and was rumoured to have a bit put by, that he was intelligent and had done well on the scholarship he had won to St Austell Grammar School meant he unwittingly provoked envy in the village. But Janet liked him because he was quiet and steady and had lovely manners. His cottage, left to him by his father and high up on the cliff near the Manse with the better properties, had plenty of room for him to take a wife and rear a family. His mother was a good soul and would take kindly to having another woman in her home. Having taken on the responsibility of Hannah, Janet was keen to see her make a good marriage. She was disturbed at the amount of time Hannah spent with Daniel; she rather liked Daniel even though he had many of his grandfather's undesirable ways, he had been Hannah's rescuer and Janet was indebted to him for that, but she couldn't see that any woman would have a secure future with him. Matt, however, could give Hannah the confidence she needed.

'On my way,' Hannah shouted back. She was peeved that someone should want her now. She had washed and changed her dress and pinned back her hair ready for the sewing she would have to catch up on after supper. She was looking forward to telling her aunt about her encounter with Mr Patrick Opie. Then a thought made her push her dainty bare feet into her best shoes and rush down the stairs like a mad hound. Perhaps it was Mr Patrick Opie who had come to see her.

'Who is it?' she demanded of her aunt in a stage whisper before she reached the bottom step.

'It's Matt Penney. Why did you come down like a herd of elephants?' Janet asked in her bright and breezy way, delighted at the thought there might already be something going on between Hannah and Matt and he was expected. She watched her niece's face closely and was disappointed to see it take on a baffled frown.

'What's he want with me?'

'Go find out for yourself,' Janet said, pushing her towards the kitchen door. When she had catapulted Hannah into the room, she followed but didn't stay, going to the back door and muttering about seeing to her washing on the line. She didn't go to the line but stayed on the step with one ear flapping at the door which she had left slightly ajar.

Matt straightened up from the cat and smiled softly at Hannah.

Hannah didn't notice. She was worried at why he wanted to see her. 'Hello, Matt. Daniel's all right, isn't he? He didn't fall off the *Sunrise* or something?'

His smile dimmed. Daniel saw her as a friend, but how did she see him? He smiled again, wider; his reserved character disguised the fact that he never gave up on anything easily. He moved closer to her. 'I haven't come about anything like that, Hannah. No, please listen, I haven't got a car to take you to the pictures and I never go to the pub so I can't ask you out for a drink, but I'm wondering if you'd like to take a walk along the cliff path with me – now.'

'What for?' Hannah asked, completely nonplussed.

Janet barged back into the room, her features alive with intent. She knew Matt would need some help. Hannah saw men only in terms of friends or relatives. 'For a bit of company, dear, of course. A bit more fresh air will do you good. I've been working you too hard lately.'

Hannah thought her aunt had taken leave of her senses. 'But the supper—'

'I'll see to that.' Janet advanced on her.

'I was going to meet Dan—' Janet gave her such a hard nudge Hannah was thrust three steps backwards. Her aunt was making urgent sidelong expressions with her eyes, as if she was hinting at something... Finally it dawned on her what she was up to, and why Matt was here.

Looking over Janet's shoulder, for the second time that

day she stared blatantly at a man. She had never thought of romance before, she had been too absorbed in coming to terms with her father and grandmother's hatred of her, in stealing moments to speak to her brothers and sisters and looking forward to her mother's next forbidden visit to be bothered with that sort of thing. Like most of the villagers, she had taken Matt for granted as the quiet, serious-minded man he seemed to be. Now, although she had seen him throughout every year of her life, she took in all his physical details. He was about six feet tall and naturally lean, with the muscular build born of years of hard work. His hair was the warm brown of newly turned earth, inclined to curl about his ears and on his strong brow. His eyes were his most striking feature, wide and as black as coal, and they were steadily returning her frank appraisal. There was an intense stillness about him. Hannah knew women saw him as a challenge. It was a shock to realise he was a very good-looking man; an even greater one that he was interested in her.

While she had been staring at Matt, Janet had been busy. Hannah felt something being put in her hand. 'What's this?' She gazed at the small canvas bag as if she hadn't seen such a thing before.

'You haven't had a cup of tea yet so I've packed a flask and a couple of sandwiches for you both. That'll keep you going till supper. Off you go then, the pair of you. I don't want you under my feet. I'm very busy.'

Before Hannah could say another word, she and Matt were being bustled out of the back door. Matt shot Janet a look of gratitude then took the bag from Hannah's hand. Without a glance at Matt, Hannah quickly changed into her sandy sandals which she'd left beside the door-step. She walked through the back yard ahead of him but he moved forward to open the brown-painted wooden gate for her then stepped back to let her lead the way again. Feeling silly, Hannah thanked him then followed the narrow alley that led past the next three tiers of dwellings. Without thinking she headed towards the cliff path on the dark side of the village, where she had just come from. Matt stayed close. She was grateful her aunt had not shoved them out through the front door; that would have required them to walk along beside the quay and through the heart of the village. Nevertheless, they were seen by a few people who stopped and eyed them curiously and bid them good evening with a variety of stupid or knowing looks on their faces. Hannah knew that before they came back it would be all over Porthellis that she and Matt Penney were walking out together. She prayed they wouldn't come across her father.

Matt didn't speak and walked beside her as they climbed higher and higher until finally they scrambled up the last steep stretch of worn ground to the cliff path. He scaled it first then offered his hand to help Hannah up. She had made the journey hundreds of times, quickly and easily, without thinking about it, but made no protest. Matt's hand was as big and calloused as Daniel's. When they were on the path she pulled hers away.

'Where would you like to go, Hannah?' Matt said, searching her face.

'I don't mind. I went down to Hidden Beach earlier.' Her eyes were fastened on Roscarrock. From here a third of the house could be seen through the trees of the small wood. Having been offered a position there she had a sudden longing to see more of it. 'We'll carry on this way.'

They walked on, not talking, looking down on Porthellis, the beach, the seaweed-strewn rocks that stretched out in irregular lines to meet and be covered by the sea when the tide came in. On the landward side of the path, huge clumps of gorse and wire fencing protected livestock and fields of grain. A herd of rough-hided black heifers, with one solitary tan-coloured beast, stopped browsing to stare at them. Further inland, on the horizon, silent clay hills, called Cornish mountains, reared up in the St Austell area. On the coastal side the cliff fell away steeply, the rock concealed by sweeps of fern and banks of hawthorn bushes. Ivy sought to choke the growth and the few wind-swept trees. Sorrel, dandelions and primrose leaves grew in clumps and a wren flitted on a stubby tree which was covered with lichen like a second skin.

Occasionally there was a big hump of rock to climb over or the path narrowed and dipped sharply, and as they got nearer to Roscarrock land there was a stone stile in a hedge to climb over. Each time, Matt sought Hannah's hand to help her up and down, each time holding her hand a moment longer than necessary. There was no access to the cliff running along the bottom of Roscarrock and walkers had to make a wide detour inland. Roscarrock was enclosed by a wall of herringbone slates interspersed with foliage and small wind-bent trees.

'Let's climb over the wall and sit on the other side,' Hannah suggested. 'We shouldn't be seen.' She thought about Patrick Opie's telescope but decided it was unlikely he would be looking out across this quiet corner of his great-aunt's land.

Matt was happy with that; they wouldn't be seen by anyone who happened to be coming along the path. Hannah smiled to herself when he backtracked a short distance to find easy access and helped her up and over the wall.

The ground here was more overgrown than Hannah remembered. She led the way out of the undergrowth until they had a perfect view of Roscarrock House. She stopped and stared at it for some minutes.

Matt nudged her arm to remind her she hadn't come alone.

'Oh, sorry. I've always been fascinated by the house.'

'Shall we sit down?' He pointed to a smooth patch of springy grass.

Hannah nodded and took the bag from Matt. She hadn't had a drink since before Lizzie's wedding and was extremely thirsty. As she pulled the cork out of the flask and poured herself a cup of her aunt's strong stewed tea, Matt sat down close at her side, facing her. He watched her with pleasure. This close she noticed he had a tiny scar on the point of his chin.

Draining the cup, she shuddered. 'Aunty Janet makes tea brave enough to face the fiercest storm.' She met Matt's searching eyes. 'Would you like some?'

'Yes please.'

He took the refilled cup from her hand and she pulled out the sandwiches and offered him one. They were thick cut and filled with wedges of cheddar cheese. She ate hers quickly; she was ravenously hungry.

He broke his in half and chewed slowly. 'Mmm, tasty bread. Your aunt's?'

'No, mine actually.'

'I thought you'd be a good cook,' he smiled at her.

So he'd been thinking about her, had he, weighing up her attributes as a housewife?

'Did you enjoy the wedding?' Matt asked.

'Yes,' she replied soberly, not wanting to talk about it. She looked again at the big house. 'Did you ever take a peep at Roscarrock as a boy, Matt?'

'Yes. I got as far as the walled garden once. A man with a gun very nearly discovered me. Frightened the life out of me. I never went in so far again.'

Hannah looked at him with awe and gave an unfeminine whistle. 'Crumbs, that's even further than Daniel. What do you think the man had a gun for? He wasn't after intruders, was he? Do you think he would have shot you?'

Matt grinned, much amused. Hannah had an innocent quality about her that he found enchanting. 'No, he looked like he was about to shoot rabbits. I saw some on the lawn.'

'Did you ever hear the screams?'

'Believe all that, do you? Vengeful ghosts, the headless smuggler, the wronged mistress, a dog trapped eternally down a well?'

'Yes. Don't you?' she asked incredulously. 'And the smuggler isn't headless.'

'I think the rumours grew over the years as each generation added to them to make them more frightening. Anyway, whatever the smuggler's head was like, Hannah,' he said shaking crumbs off his hand and putting the flask cup down, then looking deeply into her eyes, 'I bet it wasn't as beautiful as yours.'

'Matt!'

'What?'

'I didn't expect you to come out with something like that.'

'Do you mind, Hannah?'

She could hardly take in the things that had happened

to her today. She had seen and talked to one of the elusive Opies, had even touched Patrick Opie. He had offered her a job at Roscarrock, a place only a handful of villagers had ever been inside and none in recent times – the staff were employed from further afield. A few minutes after arriving home, this man had turned up, out of the blue, asking her out. She didn't have the experience to know if a walk along the cliff path was romantic or not, but thinking about it she didn't mind his attention; in fact she was flattered to have been singled out by one of the eligible bachelors of the village.

She held his steady gaze. 'No, I don't.'

He moved in closer and surprised her again. He took her face gently in his hands and brushed his lips tenderly over hers. Hannah blinked. Of course, this was what usually happened next, according to the few love stories she had read. Butterflies agitated inside her and she mourned the loss of her sisters' closeness to share this sort of experience with.

Daniel always kissed her cheek on her birthday, when he usually had a little gift for her, and he often put his arm round her shoulders. Occasionally she had leaned against him as they'd sat chatting. This was different. Matt was different. His hands felt different now as they slid caressingly down her neck, along her arms, round her waist and he pulled her into his body. She didn't have time to ponder any more. He kissed her again, and her lips parted like buds unfolding in the heat of the sun under his light movements. Something wonderfully new and very welcome stirred inside her and grew into a delicious strong sensation. He was very gentle, and as she put her arms round his neck he increased the pressure of his mouth until she thought her feelings would soar and run out of control. Becoming a little disturbed, Hannah pulled her arms down, and sensitive to her retreat Matt ended the kiss.

He didn't release his firm hold and snuggled her against his chest, placing his chin on the top of her head. Hannah listened to his heart beating. It sounded very fast and she thought he must surely hear hers racing. She had enjoyed her first full kiss, but some half-remembered advice from Aunty Janet about how she should behave when alone with a man ran through her mind. She told herself she would have to be careful about how Matt had made her feel.

Matt slowly ran his fingers through her hair. He put a peck on the crown of her head. 'If I can get hold of a car would you like to go to the pictures? I'm sure my uncle in Gorran Haven would lend me his.'

'I'd love to go. I've never been to the pictures before. I've only been outside the village once or twice. I've been further out at sea than I have been on land.' She tilted her head to look up at him. 'Can we keep it quiet? My father might try to make trouble for you.'

'Never mind him. I'm not afraid of Jeff Spargo,' Matt said as if he had something sour in his mouth. 'You don't have to answer to him, Hannah.'

'I'm still under twenty-one, Matt. Besides, when he gets nasty with me he makes life difficult for the rest of my family.'

'We were seen leaving the village. He probably knows that we're together now,' he pointed out.

'I'd forgotten that,' she said in a small voice, imagining his cutting remarks or the insults he would hurl at her bedroom window the next time he got drunk. Her only comfort was that the villagers didn't believe she was 'a curse on Porthellis' or a 'whore like your mother'. If they believed she was a 'vile little bastard', they nonetheless treated her with respect, mostly with affection.

'Don't worry,' Matt said tenderly. 'You were bound to have a sweetheart one day. He'll just have to get used to it.'

Hannah thought Matt calling himself her sweetheart was presumptuous of him but she didn't object when he lifted her face and kissed her again.

Chapter 3

Prim Spargo put an earthenware pitcher down on the ground and looked about anxiously before slipping into her sister's house by the back door. Janet was at the kitchen table, unwrapping a parcel of fabric she'd ordered by post, voiles in pastel shades, a length of blue silk and one of lightweight tweed.

'Got some orders?' Prim asked, feeling under the cosy of the big brown and fawn teapot standing on the range, finding the pot hot and pouring out two cups of tea.

Janet nodded, then gathered up the parcel and put it on a chair. 'Mrs Vercoe wants a dress made up for her little granddaughter and old Miss Peters a skirt. I'm glad you've come now, Hannah's taken Mr Nunn's mending up to him.'

The two women sat at the table and Prim got straight to the reason why she was here. 'Is she all right? Sarah said you wanted to see me about Hannah. I'm sorry about Jeff and Mother-in-law. Nothing I say stops them from ostracising her.'

'No need for you to apologise on their behalf,' Janet said, leaning closer. 'It's not about they. This is something entirely different. I got a big shock last night.'

'About Matt Penney, you mean? It was all round the

village before the wedding tea was over that he'd called here for her. It caused just as much talk. Surely you don't object to Matt? He could be the best thing that's ever happened to Hannah.'

'No, no,' Janet replied impatiently. 'It's something Hannah told us after supper. She came across Mr Patrick Opie on Hidden Beach yesterday and, well, I can hardly believe this, he asked her if she wanted a job at Roscarrock, as housekeeper. He said Mrs Opie would find her suitable.'

'Her! What's she want with my Hannah?' Prim uttered scornfully, getting up and pacing the floor.

'Don't get excited, Prim. Of course Hannah told Mr Opie she wouldn't take the job. I sent Sarah to you because I thought you ought to know, that's all. With a bit of luck Hannah'll soon be married to Matt and settled down.'

'Is she keen on him then?' Prim said, returning to her chair.

'He's going to take her to the pictures if his uncle will let him borrie his car,' Janet smiled.

Prim breathed a little easier. 'Thank the Lord for that. Tell her I'm very pleased for her.' She gulped down her tea. 'I've got to go or Mother-in-law will wonder where I am. I'm s'posed to be at the pump.' A look of intense worry passed over her angular face. 'I hope Hannah doesn't tell too many people about Mr Opie's offer. I don't want Jeff to hear about it.'

Sarah had stayed in Cliffside Cottage to help Leah make bread, then she would take it to the bakehouse for her sister, to spare her the short journey across the bridge to River Street. Leah had withdrawn into a shell owing to her face being scarred in the tragedy. It was a hard task to get her outside the door and she had refused to go to Lizzie's wedding. The doctor who had stitched the wound had done an excellent job and the scar wasn't as obvious as Leah though it was; it had faded as she had grown and did little to mar her small round face, but she couldn't be convinced and hid away behind wide-rimmed glasses which she didn't really need and she arranged her black hair so it fell over her right cheek.

Every time Sarah looked at her she did so sadly; she knew Leah felt ashamed about Edwin and Eileen's deaths and that she deserved the scar as punishment for her part in the prank.

'Mitch said Father and Gran were horrible to Hannah again yesterday,' Leah said in the small whispery voice she had cultivated to draw as little attention as possible to herself.

'They were,' Sarah whispered back, afraid their grand-mother, who never did any work about the cottage, was indulging in her habit of listening behind doors.

Leah decided the dough hadn't risen enough and re-covered it with the tea towel. 'Poor Hannah, I haven't seen her for ages.'

'Well, things are looking up for her with Matt Penney interested in her now, and you won't see her if you never go out,' Sarah said sternly. 'When the men are off on the drive next week, come to my house on Thursday after-noon. I've invited Hannah, and Naomi will be there with little Sam. We'll have some fun, all sisters together like we were in the old days.'

'I don't know . . .'

'Oh, come on, Leah. You can't stay shut up in here all

your life. You're seventeen years old and haven't done anything since leaving school.'

'I'm happy as I am.'

'No, you're not. If you could just brave the world—' Sarah broke off. There were tears in her sister's dark eyes and she hated upsetting Leah. She hugged her. 'Well, at least think about coming next week, eh?'

Leah nodded and took off her glasses to wipe her eyes. She sprinkled the table with flour ready for the kneading, a sad, dejected little figure. Sarah hadn't been going to say anything about her message for Prim but she decided to get Leah interested in some tasty news.

'Here, you know Aunty Janet asked me to tell Mother she wanted to see her?'

The excited quiver in Sarah's voice made Leah look up expectantly.

'I think I know what it's about. My Arch overheard Hannah talking to Daniel last night. Well, Hannah met someone quite unexpectedly yesterday afternoon. Mr Patrick Opie! Can you believe it?' Sarah realised she was being loud and lowered her voice. 'And more exciting than that, he offered her a job at the big house, as house-keeper or something. Can you imagine working in that place? I'd be too scared of the ghosts, and they who live there are said to be awful strange.'

'What did Hannah say to him?' Leah gasped in wonder. She'd always longed to see inside Roscarrock and often daydreamed about what it was like. From tales handed down, it was said to be full of jewels and fine ornaments, ornate and beautiful furnishings and had chandeliers. Leah didn't know what a chandelier was but it sounded grand. She wasn't particularly scared by the eerie rumours. 'She's a bit young to be asked to be a house-keeper, isn't she?'

As the two sisters chatted on, Constance Spargo took her ear away from the other side of the back kitchen door. A smirk played about her cruel, thin lips.

That night Jeff looked at Prim with a twinkle in his eye and she gave him her duty in their lumpy double bed. It was something she hated because she loathed him, but if she refused he would sulk for days and take it out on the children and look to insult Hannah.

At sixteen years old, Prim had fallen for his handsome face and silver tongue, married him against everyone's advice and regretted it almost at once. Janet had often urged her to leave him and get away from his spiteful mother. Jeff hadn't been particularly hostile to Hannah until Constance had put her bitter tongue to work to stir him up against the fair-haired baby. But there had been nowhere for Prim to go with the children and such was Jeff's nature he would only have followed her and made trouble. She had coped with his arrogant and bullying ways but finding out he was going with other women had been humiliating. He flaunted his long-term association with the pub landlady, Maggie Curnow; he had been with her on the day of the tragedy, had probably seen the children leaving the quay in the *Wynne* and guessed where they were going. It explained why he had been first on the scene at Hidden Beach. His cruelty to Hannah, throwing her out of the house, had made Prim wish him dead.

Prim lay still and gritted her teeth, hoping her passivity would one day succeed in making him keep his attentions to his mistress. He was proud of his great virility and she knew he boasted to himself that he could keep his women 'happy'. After Edwin's death he had availed himself of her feverishly, hoping another son would be conceived. He had taken no interest in the sickly daughter who had been born and died on the same day eleven months later. Prim had never forgiven him for not allowing tiny Alice May to be buried on top of Edwin; in fact her last baby had no memorial at all.

When Jeff gave his final grunt and rolled off her, Prim immediately turned away. She was tired and desperate for sleep. Jeff clutched her arm and pulled her back. Sometimes he picked this time to give orders for the family, orders she was expected to see carried out.

'Haven't you got something to tell me?' he demanded gruffly.

Prim was glad he hadn't insisted the oil lamp be kept on and could see her face. Dear God, please don't let it be over what Janet told me, she prayed silently. 'What about?'

'That little bitch across the stream.' He pinned Prim down. 'Why didn't you tell me she was offered a job at Roscarrock?'

'I-I didn't think you'd be interested.'

'Liar! You know I've never wanted her in Porthellis. You flaunted her in my home for ten years and then passed her on to your sister for the next ten. Up there she'd be out of the way for most of the time. I want her to take the job. You see that she does.'

Prim struggled to sit up but he was too strong. 'You can't want Hannah to go there, you can't!'

'Oh, but I do. Anywhere would be better than having her in the village, and as Mother's always said, she belongs there.'

'But Jeff—'

'But nothing, woman.' He pinched her cheek until she yelped. 'When I get back from the first week of the pilchard drive she had better not be still living with your bloody sister or I'll make you and her more sorry than you could ever imagine.'

On Sunday in chapel, Janet ushered Roy, Jowan and Ned into their usual pew then sat down quickly next to Ned before Hannah could, leaving the mystified girl to sit down nearest the aisle. Ned usually sat at the end of the pew to accommodate his walking stick. There was space for one more in the pew and when Matt sat next to her a minute later, Hannah knew what her aunt had been up to. Leaving his mother's side for the first time amounted to nothing short of announcing their engagement. Janet nudged Hannah and looked round her to smile at Matt, who was looking a picture of elegance in a new navy blue suit, the colour favoured among the local men, but his had been tailored and was a cut above the rest. Hannah nudged her aunt back, hard, and gritted her teeth as she heard the sudden rush of whispering behind raised hymn books. She refused to look at Matt and kept her flushed face down. She'd have something to say to her aunt when the service was over.

Halfway through the second hymn, Hannah wondered what Mrs Penney thought of her son's desertion. The high-busted middle-aged lady, in an olive-green summer coat and black hat decorated with a sumptuous feather, was in the pew opposite, and when Hannah caught her eye, Mrs Penney smiled benevolently at her. Matt's mother obviously approved of his choice. Hannah suspected she and Aunty Janet had put their heads together;

her own mother's best wishes had been passed on to her. Hannah felt she was being surrounded and manipulated. She knew a moment of panic and wanted to run outside to Daniel who was probably wandering about somewhere, free as a bird, planning his last day's entertainment before the fleet left tomorrow for several weeks' hard work.

When the service ended, and it seemed three times longer than normal, Hannah stayed leaning forward as if still praying, waiting for Matt to go. Janet coughed and prodded her. Matt waited patiently. People looked their way as they filed out quietly into the bright sunshine. Hannah capitulated and looked at Matt. He smiled, warm and deep, then winked. Despite her earlier feelings of withdrawal, rebellion and resentment, she couldn't stay vexed with him. She took his proffered arm and walked out with him. It was flattering to have a man pursue you, and when he had humour, it was less threatening. Janet fell into step with Mrs Penney and Hannah overheard where she was expected to have her tea today.

The Rouses and the Penneys parted company and Janet held Hannah's arm and watched Matt escort his mother up the hill to their cottage.

'You'll love Seaview Cottage,' Janet said smugly. 'It's got rooms leading into rooms and no noisy cellar underneath like ours.'

'Aunty Janet, don't get carried away. You won't be measuring me for a wedding dress yet, you know,' Hannah chided her.

Janet was unrepentant. 'He's the right man for you or I'll eat Uncle Roy's mouldy old hat.'

Hannah saw Daniel at the end of the quay and trotted off to him. The unattached girls were parading in their Sunday finery to impress the young men. Daniel whipped away his appreciative eyes and came to meet her.

'What's all this about you and Matt sitting together in chapel?' he teased her. 'Practically about to make the arrangements with the minister, from what I've heard.'

Hannah shot a hard stare at the other girls, who she was sure were talking about her, and biffed his arm. 'Don't be silly.'

'Not true you're going up the hill to his place for tea then?'

'Oh, shut up, Danny Kittow, or I'll never speak to you again.'

Daniel rolled his splendid blue eyes. 'I'd never be that lucky. Seriously though, me girl, is he moving too fast for you? I'll have a word with him.'

'No, don't you dare,' she replied hastily and Daniel raised his strong brows and she blushed. 'Well, it's not Matt's fault, it's Aunty Janet and Mrs Penney pushing things along.'

Daniel put his arm round her waist and led her back along the quay, down the steps and on to the beach, away from the others, carrying her shoes for her. 'So, am I right in thinking you like Matt a little bit?'

'He's good company,' she said noncommittally.

'He told me he's going to take you to the pictures the first chance he gets. Could've been next week if it weren't for the drive. 'Tis strange,' he sighed.

'What is?'

'You walking out with someone. You sort of belong to me . . .' he blushed. 'You know what I mean.'

Hannah stopped walking and faced him. 'We'll always be close friends, Danny.'

He chuffed her chin. 'Always, Hannah Spargo.'

'What are you doing with that no-good bastard!'

At the sudden shout Hannah froze.

Jeff Spargo had sold a ship in a bottle for a good price to a holidaymaker and had spent it all on beer. He was still drunk from the night before and was lurching towards them. 'Isn't one man good enough for you?'

People taking a breath of air before dinner were outraged but hastened to watch and listen.

'Get away from us,' Daniel snarled, putting himself protectively in front of Hannah.

'Has your wretched mother spoken to 'ee yet?' Jeff hurled at Hannah.

Hannah took a step away from Daniel, her heart pounding, and shook her head. Daniel had tightened his massive hands into fists and she knew he was itching to thump her father, Sabbath or not.

'The bitch! I told her to tell you to take that job at Roscarrock. I don't want you living here any longer. If you're not gone soon I'll make you and your dear mother suffer like nothing on earth, you hear me?'

Hannah found her voice to answer her father's venom. 'I hear you.'

'Good. See that you do as I say.'

Jeff spat on the sand and Daniel made to run at him. Hannah clutched his shirt and held on grimly. 'Don't, he's not worth it, Danny.'

Turning shakily, Jeff stumbled off back to the pub.

Hannah was close to tears but as usual they would not come. Daniel held her gently. 'I swear I'll do for that wretched swine one day,' he said vehemently. Hannah was quiet, a quietness Daniel knew signalled she was seriously considering something. 'You're not going to take any notice of him? Listen, me girl, he's all mouth. You should let me warn him off and I promise that he and that old crone his mother will never bother you again. And don't forget my views on Patrick Opie's offer. I reckon he could be a dirty old man and you wouldn't be safe with him.'

Hannah pulled herself away from him. 'I-I have to go, Danny. I'll see you off tomorrow.'

Daniel watched her until she disappeared inside the Rouse house then he strode up to Seaview Cottage. He and Matt went into the garden. He offered Matt a cigarette and when they were both lit up he led the way to the end wall because Mrs Penney was watching them curiously from the kitchen window.

'Jeff Spargo had another go at Hannah a few moments ago,' Daniel said grimly, blowing smoke into the air.

Matt thought he had come about the boat and his easygoing expression turned thunderous. 'It's time it was stopped,' he muttered under his breath.

'Glad you think like me. He'll be nearly legless when he leaves Maggie Curnow's arms tonight. I'd put him in bed for a while but it would be better for Hannah if he goes on the drive tomorrow. A bleddy good fright will have to do for now.'

'Leave it to me,' Matt said.

'No, Hannah's been my friend too long for me to step aside. Spargo will be more afraid of me than you, but you can come with me if you like.'

'Just tell me when.'

'That's agreed then.'

Matt was attentive at the tea table but retained his natural quietness and Hannah was glad there was no forced sparkling talk. She had little appetite but to please Mrs Penney she ate two ham sandwiches, a slice of yeast

cake stuffed with sultanas, and a generous helping of
blackcurrant tart smothered with cream.

Mrs Penney was proud of her home and when they left
the table she showed Hannah over the two-storey building. Hannah had always thought the cottage an attractive
building, tiled as it was nearly to the ground in grey slate,
but she was fascinated that inside it rambled in every
direction, with rooms, as Janet had said, leading into
other rooms and not separated by a passage downstairs
or a landing upstairs. There was the luxury of an indoor
lavatory. Hannah admired the mahogany rail of the spiral
staircase and the red and blue carpet which ran down the
middle of the stairs. Mrs Penney let her peep into her
own small, neat bedroom, and on the floor above made
a point of expounding on the good points of a large
double bedroom with a clear view across the sea.

'Your home is lovely, Mrs Penney,' Hannah said as they
descended the stairs.

'Thank you, Hannah. Now I must wash up the dishes
before the evening service.'

'Let me help you.'

'A guest in my house never touches the dishes,' Mrs
Penney said brightly. 'You go into the parlour, dear, and
talk to Matt.'

Matt sprang up from the black, horsehair couch and
Mrs Penney closed the door on them. 'I was afraid Mum
would keep you all to herself, she likes a good natter.
Come and sit down.'

Hannah went to the window first. The cottage afforded
an unobstructed view all the way down to the harbour.
There were a few children on the quay. Were they discuss-
ing, as she, Daniel and the others had, ten years ago,
what to do to liven up the peaceful afternoon? Reminded

of the tragedy, she shivered and went to Matt.

He looked into her eyes; their blueness had no sparkle and she seemed dejected. He wrapped his arms round her and she leaned into him. 'Are you all right, Hannah?'

'Yes, I'm fine,' she lied and smiled up at him. 'It was kind of your mother to invite me to tea and show me over the house.'

Placing a tender kiss on her cheek, he eased her down to sit beside him on the couch. 'I hope she didn't show you my room. It's like a pigsty. Mum's always nagging me to be tidier.'

'You don't strike me as an untidy person,' she said thoughtfully.

Grinning boyishly, he ran the tip of his finger along her chin. 'You might be pleasantly surprised if you take the trouble to find out all you can about me.'

Capturing his light-heartedness, she laughed. 'I think you're probably right.'

Hannah had never seen eyes as dark as his, but they deepened and glinted even more as he moved to kiss her. She gave him her lips but gently pushed him away a few seconds later.

'What if your mother came in?'

'She won't,' he said confidently, and he gathered her in as close as he could and kissed her with passion.

Hannah responded, but very soon it wasn't being discovered like this by his mother that worried her. Matt's kisses aroused her in a way she found exciting but disconcerting. She snuggled into his shoulder and he caressed her hair, lifting it with his fingers, sniffing it, kissing it. Hannah knew of Daniel's reputation with women; mothers gathered in their young, unattached daughters like hens did their chicks if he cast his eyes in their direction. No one had suspected that there were hidden sensual depths under Matt Penney's stolid exterior.

She glanced round the room and saw evidence of the Penneys' relative wealth. There was electric lighting in most houses but here the fitments were enhanced with charming fringed shades. Most of the villagers only used electricity downstairs and economised by using brass oil lamps upstairs but Hannah didn't recall seeing any here. The floor was carpeted and had Turkish rugs on it; there was an upright piano, tall china vases with fresh flowers in them, and in a bow-fronted glass cabinet there were what looked like good pieces of porcelain. Mrs Penney had been a sea captain's daughter and had brought some of these fine things to the marriage, and having had only one child it had been easier for her and her late husband to make ends meet. Hannah liked this room; it was cosy and comfortable. She felt sleepy and thought it would be nice to doze in Matt's arms.

'I'll have to go soon, to get ready for chapel.' She wanted to go before his closeness disturbed her again.

'I wish we had more time to be together,' he murmured.

On another Sunday evening they might have decided to forgo chapel, but no one would miss tonight's service when prayers would be said to the Almighty for the safety of the fleet in the long weeks ahead on the pilchard drive, when the men would be home only at the weekend.

'Next Saturday seems a long time away,' he went on mournfully.

'I wish I could come with you,' Hannah said, words she had often repeated enviously to Daniel.

Matt took it another way. 'Oh, darling.' He crushed his

lips over hers, overwhelming and alarming her, and he didn't seem to notice when she pushed his face away.

'I've really got to go, Matt.'

He let her go reluctantly. 'I'll walk you home.'

'No, no, Matt. I-I have to call in at my sister Naomi's on the way. I want to see Samuel, my little nephew, before he's put to bed.'

Matt studied her flushed face for some moments, his expression unreadable. He said, 'Next weekend can't come too quickly for me.'

She knew he wanted her to reciprocate the sentiment but she could only stroke his arm and force a small smile. 'I'll go and say goodbye to your mother.'

She didn't go to her sister's tiny cottage in Chapel Road; she would see a lot of Naomi and Sarah and her cousin Lizzie in the next few weeks while their menfolk were away. Not wanting to face a barrage of questions from Janet about the tea, she went in through the front door and crept upstairs to her room. At the long, small-paned window she gazed out to sea, trying to calm her muddled brain. Between them, Matt and her father had pulled her, quite ruthlessly in their own ways, in different directions.

It was Jeff Spargo's ultimatum that gave her the most to think about.

At midnight, when everyone else in Porthellis was in their beds, Daniel and Matt were hiding in the shadows, waiting for Jeff Spargo to leave the Ship Inn. At last he appeared, on shaky legs; he mumbled something to Maggie on the doorstep of the tiny drinking establishment and when she had shut the door, the two younger men barred his way.

Jeff hurled a vile oath at them. 'Get out of my way or I'll kick your bleddy heads in.'

'You're not up to it, Spargo,' Daniel growled between clenched teeth. 'You're only good at terrorising innocent women.'

'And we've come to tell you it's time you stopped,' Matt hissed down Jeff's ear.

'Go to hell, the pair of you.'

Daniel reached out and clutched Jeff's collar. 'Leave Hannah alone, understand? If you hurt her just one more time, either me or Matt will see to it that you'll bitterly regret it.'

Jeff tried to back away from Daniel but it only brought him into contact with Matt's broad chest.

'We're deadly serious, Spargo,' Matt whispered, and the threat cut the night air like a carving knife.

Daniel gave Jeff a humiliating shaking and pushed him aside. 'Keep your mouth shut from now on where Hannah's concerned.'

'Or you'll get this,' and Matt thumped his fist into the palm of his other hand.

Jeff hit the pub wall and grabbed at the deep windowsill to keep his balance. It was some moments before he realised Daniel and Matt had gone and he was alone. Gathering his wits together, he headed for home, but when he shuffled into Squeeze-guts Alley at the side of the pub, a fist hit him in the face with the force of a sledgehammer.

At the crack of dawn the fishermen of Porthellis kissed their womenfolk goodbye and headed for the quay to the rows of luggers waiting on the full tide. When the three Rouse men had gone, Hannah ran up to her room and pulled back the white lace curtains to watch from her window. The men didn't like being seen off on the quay and the women kept out of the way as the men went to and from the sea.

Daniel and Matt were striding along together, heads up, faces alight at the prospect of the week's challenge ahead, their 'allowance bags' in their hands. Rufus followed them, lighting his grubby pipe, his scrawny legs looking steadier the closer they got to the *Sunrise*. Bringing up the rear was the affable Curly Jose, his cap set well back on his grey cropped hair, and at his side a whey-faced Fred. Hannah was certain he'd be leaning over the side bringing up his breakfast as soon as they left the harbour.

As they approached the Rouses' house, Daniel and Matt looked up at her window together. Daniel waved and smiled, as he always did. Matt waved and smiled in exactly the same way, friendly and casual. Hannah waved back and they were gone. She watched their broad backs, shoulders working, hands flexing, dressed like all the fishermen in blue dungarees, light brown fishing smocks and thigh-length boots turned down at the knee. Hannah's heart sank a little. Yesterday Matt had been her 'sweetheart', this morning he was one of the men. Had she imagined his possessiveness of her? Was he really, along with his mother and her aunt, pushing her into matrimony with him?

She caught sight of her father heading for the Spargo lugger, the *Misty*, eight years older and not so well furbished as the *Sunrise*. She stepped back and hid behind the curtain. Jeff Spargo had an ugly bruise on his cheek and he looked in a foul mood. The *Misty* was the last lugger in a row berthed three abreast, and he turned and scowled up at her window before making to climb over the other two boats with Mitch and Josh, and Lizzie's father Terence. His face was full of hate. Then he swung round to Daniel and Matt who were watching him keenly and shook his fist at them. The two younger men exchanged looks then climbed aboard the *Sunrise*.

Hannah retreated to her bed. What did it mean? Had Daniel finally warned her father off and had Matt been involved? That would only drive her father to more subtle ways of tormenting her and her family. She felt sick to her stomach. She knew Jeff would do as he threatened if she continued to live in Porthellis. With that and Matt's unexpected behaviour, making her unsure of the feelings he had stirred inside her, she had a burning desire to get away and make a life elsewhere.

Pulling open the little drawer of her bedside table she took out the box of good quality white stationery she had received one Christmas. She'd had little reason to write to anyone before, but now, summoning up her courage, she settled in front of her dressing table and wrote to Mr Patrick Opie.

Chapter 4

Hannah was certain Mr Opie would reply; he had seemed too polite to ignore her letter even if the position of housekeeper had been filled. She made sure she was outside the house to meet the postman every morning, and two days later, whistling cheerfully, he put a thick white envelope into her hand with an almost illegible script bearing her name and address.

Hannah wanted to run upstairs and open it immediately but Janet called her inside for breakfast. Janet was always desperately lonely the first few days her menfolk sailed off and it would have been mean to keep her waiting. It was an hour later, with the dishes washed and dried, before Hannah could slip up to her room to open the letter. She did so carefully and took out a sheet of white paper which smelled faintly of perfume. Hannah raised her brows; it must be Mrs Opie's stationery. Would it say what she hoped? Since she had decided to ask for an interview, the prospect of starting a whole new way of life had turned into a strong desire.

My dear Miss Spargo,

  I was delighted to hear from you. Would you kindly come to Roscarrock on Wednesday afternoon, at two thirty, for an interview with Mrs Opie. I shall meet you at the front door. I do hope this will be convenient to you. If not, do write and suggest a time yourself.

The signature was a splash of ink but she could just make out P. J. Opie.

The appointment was for this afternoon! For a moment Hannah was thrown into a dither and her heart hammered in her chest. What would she say about herself to Mrs Opie? Would Mrs Opie find her as suitable as her great-nephew had thought? Would the house's ghosts reach out and terrify her? Then more down-to-earth concerns came to mind. What should she wear? How should she do her hair?

First things first, she told herself firmly. She had to tell Janet before deciding anything. Steeling herself for an argument, because she was determined at least to go up to Roscarrock and see what the position on offer was like, she padded downstairs.

'Aunty Janet, I've got something to tell you.'

'Have you, dear?' Janet said, looking up from the piece of blue silk she was cutting out round a pattern. 'About Matt, is it? I've noticed you've been rather quiet since he went.'

Hannah took a deep breath and got straight to the point. 'It's nothing to do with Matt. It's about Mr Patrick Opie's offer as housekeeper at Roscarrock. I wrote to him saying I'd like to consider it and he's replied, asking me to go up there this afternoon.'

'But why? You can't possibly be serious!' Janet was very nearly shrieking. She loved Hannah as if she was the daughter she'd always wanted. Losing her to Matt or some other young fisherman would be hard but at least she would still be in the village, able to keep her company sometimes when the menfolk were at sea. For her to take a job that would mean being away for most of the time, and *there* of all places, was unthinkable. 'You don't know what you're saying, Hannah. What about Matt? What about your mother? What about me? Do you want cream on your pilchards, is that it?' she ended with a sarcastic snap, her eyes filling with tears.

'But Aunty Janet,' Hannah pleaded, sorry she had upset her aunt, 'it's Mother I'm thinking about, and the rest of the family. Father's threatened that he'll make trouble for us if I don't take the job, he wants me out of the village. I'll still see you and Matt. I'm bound to have time off and I'll go to chapel, no one will ever stop me doing that, and anyway, I don't know if I'll take the job for certain. I just want to see what it'll be like. And,' Hannah tried to soften her aunt with a sunny smile, 'I'll get to see inside Roscarrock and I'll be able to tell you what it's like.'

'I don't care about that,' Janet said weakly, sitting down as if all her energy had left her. 'You can't go there, Hannah, you just can't.'

There was something about Janet's vehemence that alerted Hannah; she hadn't forgotten her father and her grandmother's words that 'she belonged there' at Roscarrock.

Hannah tilted her chin and her eyes blazed in the way they occasionally did when she demanded forthright answers. 'Why are you so dead against me going to Roscarrock? Because of the rumours? Or something else? Do you know something about the place that I don't?'

'I know nothing,' Janet murmured piteously, seeing her exclamations had made Hannah more determined to go for the interview. 'I just don't want to lose you, that's all.'

Hannah put her arms round Janet and kissed her cheek. 'You won't ever lose me, Aunty. I shall always be grateful to you for taking me in and I shall always love you, Uncle Roy, Jowan and Ned.'

Not one to be down for long, Janet brushed away her tears and stood up. 'Right, if I can't get you to change your mind then you can go upstairs and take your best dress out of the wardrobe and your best shoes and hat. Then wash your hair and I'll pin it up for you. I'm not letting you go up there unless you're immaculately turned out.'

Hannah hoped to slip out of the village without being seen and provoking speculation about where she was going in her smart clothes. She was wearing a semi-fitted cream linen dress with decorative saddle stitching, long cream rayon cardigan with embroidery at the wrists and collar, brown felt hat with self-trimming, worn at an angle, and she carried a handbag. She didn't actually own a handbag, having no use for one, but Janet had insisted she take hers, a smart brown leather bag Roy had bought her on their tenth wedding anniversary.

Luck was not on Hannah's side. The men in the bark house and lofts stopped singing to the rhythm of their work as they saw her walk past. They asked her where she was going and when they saw they weren't going to get an answer, they called out their appreciation of her 'well-turned ankles'. Then she got waylaid by a group of seven retired old men, armed with pipe and walking stick, clad in shiny trousers, old sweaters, peaked caps or woolly hats, who were on their way down to the wooden seat placed on the quayside in a sheltered spot specially for them to indulge in their daily cogitation of the world and things closer to home. None of them asked her any pointed questions but Hannah knew she would be on their agenda today.

It took a lot longer to reach Roscarrock by road than stealing up to its boundaries over the cliff. As Hannah reached the top of the village hill and turned into the narrow lane, her nerve almost failed her and she nearly spun round and ran home. Her father's threats carried her along the lane, which was little more than an arm's length wide in some places. Gradually her tummy settled, and rising to the fore was the youthful sense of excitement and adventure she had suppressed since the day of the boat accident. Marching long-leggedly along the two miles of twists and bends of Turn-A-Penny Lane, praying she wouldn't come across a motorised vehicle or a farm cart and have to climb the hedge to let it pass and risk her appearance, she took off her white cotton gloves and plucked grasses from the hedge. She glanced down often to avoid ruts and dusty patches marring her only pair of high-heeled shoes. They were quite old and well worn but they were comfortable; at least she didn't have the worry of arriving with blistered or swollen feet. When she got close to the entrance of Hemmick Farm she had a hard task picking a clean path through the cowpats deposited by Henry Teague's small herd of cattle.

The lane finally curved round a long sharp bend where some of the few drivers brave enough to take this route to reach Porthellis rather than the wider road had come a cropper. Hannah saw fresh skid marks and the hedge was battered. She nipped on smartly and soon she was on the road.

In a wide break in the hedge was Roscarrock's gateway.

She stopped and looked at the granite posts which had once supported a pair of gates, now long gone. The silent stones gave her no clue as to what she would find if she walked between them; there was only one way to discover that and that was to walk up to the house and meet Patrick Opie. To dispel a niggle of apprehension, she reminded herself of his kindly character, that she was here of her own free will.

Hannah put her gloves back on and slipped through the gap, wondering what the gates had been like and why they had not been replaced.

The ground rose slowly with the gradient of the cliff and soon she was looking up at the side of the house she had peeped at with Matt the week before. In front of the house a wide lawn was sheltered by the small wood which gave way to the cliff and then the sea; a little further upcoast was the wide, rounded protrusion of the Dodman. She felt light-hearted, didn't understand why but was grateful for it, and her steps quickened. If any servants appeared, a groundsman perhaps, and challenged her, she would make it clear that she had a right to be here, she was invited and, more than that, she thought a trifle smugly, sought after.

The driveway was five hundred yards long and curved round lazily until it reached the front of the house. Hannah felt none of the foreboding of her childhood and thought Matt was probably right to scoff at the rumours. There were four tall windows downstairs and five upstairs, and windows in the attic. One upstairs room had a balcony. Two rows of chimneys stood at either end. Wisteria climbed the walls and tall trees, cedar, ash, sycamore and oak, grew behind the house, giving it a friendly frame.

True to his word, Patrick Opie was waiting for her in

the shade of the porch. When he saw her he bounded down the six wide stone steps. They had railings on each side with purple heather and broom growing through them – Hannah could smell the broom's pineapple scent. He was dressed in the same clothes, again slightly dishevelled, as when she had met him on Hidden Beach.

'Ah, Miss Spargo, there you are. A few minutes early too, how kind. You must be parched after your long and dusty walk. Do come inside and I shall take you up to my great-aunt and bring you a glass of refreshing lemonade.'

It was a very hot day and Hannah was extremely thirsty. 'Thank you, Mr Opie,' she said, shaking his hand before he whisked her up the steps and inside the house. She did not see the woman watching her from the first-floor balcony window.

Hannah held her breath before crossing the threshold through a heavy four-inch thick door. The house smelled of a combination of age, history, flowers, and the fresh salt air wafting in behind them. She wasn't disappointed in what she saw; in fact everything far outstripped her imagination. Standing on the thick plum-coloured carpet in the hall she gazed at a long, ornate, marble-topped side table where at one end stood a tall tapering green plant in a colourful bowl and at the other lay a small silver tray for calling cards. Between them were various ornaments in ivory and jade.

Upholstered chairs, some leather with studs, all with cabriole legs, were placed at regular intervals and mirrors and paintings adorned the walls in plaster picture bays. One mirror in particular caught Hannah's attention. Its glass was round and convex, enclosed in an ebony reeded frame with gilt foliage top and bottom. A more modern addition was a curiously twisting umbrella and coat stand. On opposite sides of the hall were two white doors with cornices but quite different intricate patterns carved on them. Hannah hoped Leah would venture out to see her at Sarah's house tomorrow so she could tell her all about this at first-hand. A long-case clock with a shell carved block front chimed the half hour, but Hannah was so absorbed she didn't hear it.

Patrick Opie could see she was awestruck. 'The mouldings and furniture in the house are mostly Georgian and Victorian – you'll see quite a variety in the house,' he said.

'It's lovely,' she breathed, looking up at the ceiling which had an exquisite cornice of plaster foliage. It made her feel totally cut down to size. She was extremely nervous about meeting Mrs Opie.

There were no servants about and Mr Opie headed towards the stairs. 'This way, Miss Spargo, if you please. My great-aunt will receive you in her suite of rooms.'

Hannah dutifully trotted after him. The stairs were carpeted and wide enough for them to walk side by side with room for two more. Flanked by the wrought-iron balustrade, they climbed eight steps and were on a large square landing. Hannah remarked on the beautiful arched window, which looked out on the back courtyard where she could see a cottage and stables.

'The window is Queen Anne,' Patrick Opie said with gusto and Hannah could tell he was very proud of the house. 'It's older than the house itself which was built round it. I'll tell you all about the place, it has a fascinating history.'

He carried on talking as they turned and climbed another eight steps, at the top of which a narrow flight of steps led presumably to the attic rooms, and a wide corridor gave on to rooms to left and right.

'The big manor house that stood originally on the site in the seventeenth century crumbled and was pulled down in the mid-eighteenth century. The house you see now retains some of its features but was built on smaller and more simple lines by the owners – they were mining speculators called Rosevear and loosely connected to the Robartes family. Their fortune dwindled as the mining industry petered out and they gradually relinquished much of the surrounding land and Porthellis. My great-aunt's father-in-law, Hector Baden Opie, bought the property for a song in eighteen ninety-four. My Great-Uncle Redvers was killed in the war. I'm the son of Great-Uncle Redvers' nephew Michael Opie.'

They were at the end of the corridor in front of double doors and Mr Opie tapped on them, grinned shyly at Hannah, and entered.

Hannah held her breath and her insides knotted.

'Miss Spargo for you, Great-Aunt Feena,' he said gaily and motioned Hannah to follow him.

Feena Opie was standing sedately in the middle of the room. It was a sitting room and every inch a woman's room with a more modern touch than what Hannah had so far seen. Everything was beautiful and tasteful; the wallcovering alone was worth looking at, Hannah thought, an oyster-pink background with blue and pink roses and large leaves hiding behind masses of paintings of every size and shape. The curtains were extravagantly styled with swags, tassels and rosettes, and rich rugs covered the oak floor. Silver-framed photographs vied for space on the mantelpiece with ornaments and vases of flowers; the whole room seemed to be filled with flowers.

Hannah noted sculpted flowers under glass domes similar to those she had seen on graves in the churchyard. There were two other doors in the room, one leading to the balcony, the other she assumed to a bedroom.

Hannah had taken it all in at a glance then kept her eyes pinned on Mrs Opie who dismissed her nephew with a flick of her hand. When he had closed the door, she beckoned Hannah to her.

'Good afternoon, Miss Spargo. You seem a little surprised.'

Hannah gulped and was horribly embarrassed to realise she had been staring. 'I-I'm sorry, Mrs Opie. I thought you'd be . . . um, I mean, I . . .'

Mrs Opie smiled. 'I think you're trying to say you thought I'd be much older. I'm afraid it's Mr Patrick's fault. He has the tiresome habit of calling everyone by their correct title or their relationship to himself. I would prefer he simply called me Aunt, but there it is. My mother had me late in life, you see, and Mr Patrick's mother had him at a very young age, so we are more of an age to be aunt and nephew. Do take off your hat, your cardigan too if you are hot, Miss Spargo. I'm afraid Mr Patrick is not any good at formalities.'

Hannah forced a nervous smile, put her handbag down on a chair with padded arms and a heart-shaped back and taking off her hat placed it on top of her bag.

'Has Mr Patrick offered you refreshment?' Mrs Opie asked, smiling lightly, and Hannah felt the lady was looking her over closely.

'Yes, yes, he has, lemonade.'

'Good. Shall we sit out on the balcony? It's quite cool out there and there is a magnificent view of the sea.'

'Yes, that would be lovely.' Hannah hoped her reply

hadn't come out as stilted as it sounded.

Mrs Opie turned slowly and walked to the door leading to the balcony. She had a decided limp on the left side. Even so, Hannah marvelled at her elegant carriage as she followed her. Everything about Mrs Opie was perfectly poised and sophisticated. She was slender, tall and straight despite her limp, wearing a classic, tailored, linen dress with deep pleats, and court shoes. Her grey hair was chicly parted on one side and waved close to her head. Hannah had expected her to be in her late seventies at least but Mrs Opie looked to be in her early sixties. Her face was expertly made-up, a little wrinkled and rather puffy, but there were hints she had once been a very handsome woman.

At the door, Mrs Opie took the gold-topped walking stick propped against it. On the balcony were three plush padded chairs with parasols attached to the backs, situated round a circular conservatory table. Mrs Opie sat in the first chair and put her left foot up on a footstool and invited Hannah to sit beside her. Before Hannah could exclaim at the splendid sea view, a ball of white fur in the third chair suddenly came to life and a small dog, no bigger than the average cat, gave a little yap and jumped on to Hannah's lap.

'Oh! Who are you? Aren't you lovely?' she laughed, stroking the excited creature's silky head.

'Pogo, you are a bad boy,' Mrs Opie chided light-heartedly. 'I hope you don't mind, Miss Spargo. Pogo is very curious and absolutely loves being spoiled. He's a Pomeranian.'

'He's sweet,' Hannah said, thinking that Daniel would call the dog a piece of nonsense and disclaim its right to be called a dog at all.

Patrick Opie came out on the balcony with a tray. 'Here we are, ladies. My favourite recipe and I've added plenty of ice.' He put two tumblers, a glass jug of lemonade and two napkins on the table. 'Drink it before it gets warm. And,' he sounded pleased with himself, 'some of my very own brandysnaps, filled with thick cream. Eat them before they melt.'

As suddenly as he had appeared, Patrick Opie was gone. Mrs Opie smiled after him. 'He's very sweet,' she said fondly, deliberately echoing Hannah's comment about the dog, and Hannah laughed. Patrick Opie was as pleasant as he had first seemed and she was warming to his great-aunt by the moment.

Mrs Opie poured out the lemonade. 'I think we'll thrash out the details about the position of housekeeper first, Miss Spargo, and then I'll ring for Mr Patrick to show you over the house. As you can see, I'm not very good on my legs, it's arthritis of the hip, and I spend a lot of my time up here. I have a wheelchair to get about the grounds and sometimes I am foolish enough to allow Mr Patrick to wheel me around his beloved gardens. I must warn you he'll probably want to drag you all over them before you go. He has two passions, gardening and cooking. It's all he does, and since he came here to live I haven't had to employ either.'

'I see.' Hannah didn't see, she thought it rather strange, a gentleman doing the work of two servants.

'I've had to let my housekeeper go because her father took a turn for the worse and his need was greater than mine. First of all, Miss Spargo, let me assure you that you will have absolutely no skivvying to do. I have a maid who does the laundry, cleaning, looks after the fires, that sort of thing. Her name is Angie Miller, she's quiet and middle-aged, and after she's finished her work she likes to go up to her room. You won't have any trouble from her.'

It wasn't lost on Hannah that Mrs Opie was talking as if she had agreed to take the job.

'You will be required to make sure things are running smoothly, to order goods from the tradesmen and check their prices, to decide when a room needs spring-cleaning, the chimneys sweeping, if repairs of any kind are needed and so on. And the linen, of course. There is a modern sewing machine in the linen room. You are a seamstress, I understand, and I have some of your and your aunt's work in the house.'

'Yes, Mrs Opie. I noticed some lacework of mine on a table in your sitting room.'

'Isn't it nice,' Mrs Opie paused, 'that you and I already have a connection? One other little job I'd like you to do. Mr Patrick for some obscure reason quite forgets to water the indoor plants, so if you wouldn't mind, Hannah.'

So I'm Hannah now, Hannah thought wryly as she sipped her lemonade. She was in no doubt Mrs Opie was used to getting her own way.

'Your room will overlook the sea – I have a feeling you have a fondness for the sea. Your meals, clothes and shoes will be supplied, also toiletries. I like to look after my staff. You may wear a little jewellery, but please nothing too flashy. Your pay will be one pound, one and sixpence a week with an annual review. You will have two half days off a week, you can choose them on regular days or move them about, as long as I know what you're doing, and all day Sunday off, when I'm sure you'll want to go to chapel and spend the day with your family. Mr Patrick and I occasionally attend Gorran Church and you'd be welcome to join us. There is a bicycle in the stables you may use so you won't have the walk back and forth to the village. If you go out in the evening, I'd like you to be in by ten o'clock. Mr Patrick locks up at ten fifteen. If there is a special occasion, I'm sure we can accommodate you. Do you happen to have a boy friend, Hannah?'

Hannah didn't know how to answer that.

Mrs Opie eyed her keenly. 'You seem uncertain. Is someone becoming special to you?'

Hannah thought it was none of Mrs Opie's business. She said blandly, 'He's just a friend.'

That must have satisfied the lady, for next she said, 'Your family may call on you occasionally as long as they don't keep you from your duties. Tell me a little about your family, Hannah.'

'They are all involved with the fishing industry. I have two brothers and three sisters.' Hannah flushed as she admitted she lived with her aunt. 'The family home is rather crowded, you see,' she offered as a reason.

Mrs Opie smiled and handed her the plate of brandy-snaps. Pogo jumped about on Hannah's lap and tried to filch the one she took. Mrs Opie tapped his snout. 'No, Pogo, bad dog.' The dog looked crestfallen but after a whining grumble, settled down to sleep on Hannah's lap.

When the brandysnaps were eaten, Mrs Opie delicately wiped her fingers on her napkin. 'I'm sure you won't find it too much for you here. Roscarrock is a family home. Have you any comments or questions, Hannah?'

'Well, I've never worked in service before but your terms sound very generous. I particularly like the fact that my family can visit me.' Now she was talking as if she'd accepted the job. 'Does anyone else live here?'

'My grandson, Mr Gregory Opie. He's not here all the

time. He's an author and playwright and is often away researching his projects. He's currently in London. When he's here, he spends most of his time in the library which he's turned into a study.' Hannah had a vision of another Patrick Opie, a dried up, rather eccentric bachelor, shutting himself away to write. Mrs Opie smiled graciously. 'You'll find us no trouble, Hannah.' She rang a little silver bell. 'Mr Patrick will come and show you around now, then come back to me and we'll make the final arrangements.'

'If I decide to take the position, Mrs Opie,' Hannah said, finding her independence as she lifted Pogo on to his own chair and stood up.

Mrs Opie looked at her sideways. 'Of course.'

Patrick Opie showed her a guest bedroom on the first floor, which was richly furnished and smelled faintly of mothballs, then he took her up the servants' back stairs to the linen room. Hannah gingerly touched the sewing machine; her aunt would love to own this model. If she took the job, perhaps she could keep up her sewing and continue to contribute to her foster family's funds.

Next they went down to the drawing room. Hannah was astounded and wished Leah was with her. The marble fireplace could only be described as magnificent, its plaster decoration reaching nearly to the high ceiling. It had intricate patterns of grapes and leaves, garlands and tassels and, most intriguing of all, a face in the centre under the mantelshelf.

'It's in memory of a dead relative of the previous owners,' Patrick Opie explained.

On the mantelshelf were a bracket clock and porcelain figures of eighteenth-century lovers and lute-playing shepherdesses.

The ceiling, which seemed very far away, was decorated with symmetrical plasterwork and a huge cut-glass chandelier hung from the centre. The deep windowsills held potted greenery and a satinwood grand piano stood in the corner behind the door. A gramophone sat on a small square mahogany table with cabriole legs and ball and claw feet. A dado rail ran round the four walls between contrasting designs of flock wallpaper. The bays were painted with country scenes, seascapes and vases of flowers.

The next room, the dining room, had four small chandeliers and a huge rectangular mahogany table and twelve chairs. This ceiling had a moulded arabesque design.

'The sideboard was made in the second half of the eighteenth century and the two things that look like urns at either end are actually knife holders,' Patrick Opie said.

'It's all so beautiful,' Hannah marvelled, studying the back rail with candle holders, and the fluted designs on the serving table. Hannah was captivated by the house and its contents, and drawn to the job of housekeeper in it. The two Opies she had met seemed perfectly charming. As Patrick Opie led the way down the narrow, uneven, servants' stairs to the kitchen to enthuse over what he saw as his own private domain, Hannah knew she couldn't turn down the offer to work here at Roscarrock.

Chapter 5

Aboard the *Sunrise*, as the sun sank in the west on Wednesday evening, Matt stared intently at the water.

'Take a look at this, Granfer,' he said quietly, using the name all the crew applied to their dirty-faced skipper. 'It looks dark and oily, just right, wouldn't you say?'

Rufus nodded. The condition of the water meant it was a good place to shoot the nets and with any luck they'd have a catch as large as the last two nights.

Daniel, alert and ready as always, picked up the headrope of the first net. He glanced round to make sure Matt had made his way to the leech, then the two of them skilfully began to shoot the nets, twenty of them, each one a hundred and twenty yards long. Fred enviously watched their swift, rhythmic movements. The white buff of the first net curved out in a low arc from Daniel's hand and hit the water with a dull splash, while Matt steered. Every five fathoms along the headrope, Daniel used his muscular arms to jerk a coble – bunches of twenty-five corks secured together and attached to the headrope by a three-fathom stop – and send it spinning on to the water. Every now and again he glanced astern, pulling the headrope straight, before nodding to Curly in the wheelhouse to give the lugger a 'kick-ahead'.

When the last net was shot, Matt took the spring rope and secured it forward. Curly switched off the fuel and the engine died after a splutter or two and all was silent. There was an expectancy in the air. Hopefully, in a couple of hours' time they would be hauling in a bumper crop of pilchards.

The men were in thoughtful mood, watching the light of the hurricane lamp which was fitted to a dan buoy on the white buff of the flotter net, the first to be shot, so they could spot its whereabouts if the wind changed. They hoped the hurricane lamp wouldn't go out. All watched except for Fred who was feeling nervous. He'd have to shoot the nets tomorrow with Rufus and if he made a botch of it the old man would threaten to throw him in for shark bait. Sharks haunted the pilchard nets and Fred was frightened of the very thought of them. Ten years ago when he'd been tossed out of Rufus's tosher, he'd been convinced a shark would eat him.

The wind was fresh and the mizzen sail flapped and creaked with the swaying of the boat. Daniel and Matt lit cigarettes then passed the packet and box of matches to Rufus. Rufus put a fag between his ragged lips and shook the box at Fred.

'I don't smoke, Granfer,' Fred reminded him.

'Of course, I fergot,' Rufus sneered, taking a half-eaten meat and pickle sandwich he'd been saving out of the fold of his sea-boot. 'Makes 'ee feel sick, don't it?'

Fred turned away miserably and stood alone, not in the way Matt did, content with his own thoughts and company, but horribly, wretchedly alone. Fred didn't have a friend in the world. All of Porthellis knew of his coward-ice on the day the *Wynne* had capsized. Even Mitch had hardly spoken a word to him since the day of the tragedy.

After a while Fred took refuge in the warm galley to make mugs of tea and fresh sandwiches.

Curly stayed in the wheelhouse, attending to the instruments, and the three other men stood in the bows, puffing smoke into the darkening, salt-laden damp air, listening patiently. Time passed. They heard the unmistakable splash of a fish turning. Glanced at one another. It was followed by a flurry of water, sounding like a running stream – music to a seasoned fisherman's ear.

There was another good sign. Gulls were settling on the nets, then flapping up heavily into the air and dropping down again further along the nets. Their mirrs intermittently filled the great space of sea and air, each too intent on its own feeding prospects to become quarrelsome with its neighbour.

There was nothing more the men could do for an hour or so. Rufus took his tea and food from Fred and joined Curly in the wheelhouse. Fred left Daniel and Matt in the bows and went back to the galley.

'Half a week gone already,' Daniel said conversationally, taking a long deep breath of fresh air into his lungs and massaging his broad chest as if to energise the rest of his body.

'A good start,' Matt replied matter-of-factly, chewing on a cheese sandwich, remembering fondly when he had eaten one with Hannah.

'Missing her, are you?'

'I take it you mean my mother?'

'You can be an awkward sod when you've a mind to be, Matt Penney,' Daniel returned, but he was grinning. 'I didn't mean Mrs Wallis Simpson either. Do you think the King will marry her?'

'I don't know and I don't much care.' Matt took a gulp

from his mug, his eyes on the distant lights of another boat. 'Yes, I'm missing Hannah.'

'You want to be careful,' Daniel joked. 'She might have her wedding dress all stitched and ready for when you get back.'

'She'd make me the happiest man in the world if she did.'

Matt had spoken with such depth, a catch in his throat, that Daniel moved so he could see his face in the lantern light strung up on the mast. 'Are you in love with her?'

Matt turned his head towards Daniel. 'Yes. Hannah's a woman for marrying, for looking after, not for messing around with.'

Making a face, Daniel drained his mug, ate his last morsel and said thoughtfully, 'You're right, it's never crossed my mind to mess around with her. You're an odd mixture, Matt. For years you've kept your feelings hidden, then you declare your intentions in a matter of days.' Daniel tapped his arm. 'I meant what I said, mind. No trying anything with her.'

Matt breathed deeply, just that, but Daniel knew he was being told to mind his own business.

Daniel glanced along the length of nets, stretched out and lit up like a celestial path by the moonlight. He was waiting patiently for the moment to start hauling in the nets yet itching to get on with it at the same time. 'So, what do you think about Hannah being offered that job? Damned strange thing, if you ask me.'

A dark look passed over Matt's stern features. He didn't like it one bit that Hannah had confided something to Daniel and not to him. 'What job?' he asked harshly, standing stiff and straight.

'Don't you know about that?' Daniel replied, deliberately being tactless. Since Matt's interest in Hannah, he had found himself feeling quite possessive about her. He spun out the tale to show just how much she'd told him. 'It happened on the day of Lizzie's wedding, the day you first asked me about Hannah. Jeff Spargo insulted her at the wedding and she left, first to visit Edwin's grave – her father won't let her go there, you know, she visits it in secret – then she went to Hidden Beach. Strange thing was, someone you'd never think to find there was already there. Patrick Opie from Roscarrock, and he offered her the job of housekeeper up at the house. Just like that! Well, I told her I was worried he might be after her. They're a funny lot up there, haven't had anything to do with the village for years, so why the sudden interest in her? And why was he on Hidden Beach anyway? Said he was looking about because he wants to paint it. Sounds a likely story to me. Hannah told him she already had a job, he left and that was that,' Daniel paused dramatically, 'until . . .'

'Yes?' Matt demanded, his face full of shadows.

'When Spargo was nasty to her last Sunday, he spat out that he knew about Patrick Opie and the job and he told her she must take it and get out of the village or he'd make terrible trouble for her.'

'And that's when you came up to me and suggested we frighten him off, but you didn't tell me everything,' Matt commented sourly. 'And?'

'Well, nothing really,' Daniel said, casually lighting another cigarette, 'except I got the idea she was seriously thinking about Opie's offer.'

Matt held out his hand. Daniel offered him his cigarette packet. 'Your mug,' Matt said gravely. 'I'll take it back to the galley with mine.'

Daniel watched him walk away, soon a dark looming profile. He felt a louse for what he had said, then shrugged it off and grinned.

Matt was seething. He knew Daniel had been taunting him but that didn't really concern him. Obviously he didn't mean very much yet to Hannah, and although he consoled himself that she'd responded warmly to his kisses, he was worried about his noncommittal goodbye wave to her on Monday morning. He hadn't wanted to spend the week having to put up with Rufus's vulgar mouth. If he'd blown her a kiss and made his feelings obvious, Rufus would probably have made lewd remarks and Matt didn't want to quarrel with him. Now he hoped Hannah hadn't taken his restraint as lack of interest. He slipped into a morose silence.

At the end of the hour, Rufus went up to the prow and, lying back on the spring rope, with Daniel's help he began to pull the lugger up to the nets. The old man wanted to take a look. If the net closest to the boat contained pilchards, there would be plenty in the outer nets. Rufus gave a satisfied grunt as they caught sight of the silvery fish.

The men rapidly pulled up their heavy, leather sea boots, donned their long yellow oilskins and took up their positions, As one by one the nets came up over the roller, the gulls hovered like a great white mass, shrieking just out of reach, swooping when a shimmering fish fell from the net into the sea. The men worked with great skill and swiftness to get the pilchards smacking and squelching into the fish berth, those caught in the mesh quickly freed with dexterous flicks of the wrist. They had to fend off the troublesome, clamorous birds with yells and missiles.

It was laborious work and over three hours later they

were still at it, but they were not tiring, not even Fred who, in the excitement of the big catch, a heavy 'splat', had forgotten all his fears. There was at least another three hours' work to be done before they could rest.

'Make a fisherman out of un yet!' Rufus yelled to Curly, at the same time tossing him a small medicine bottle that had come up in the net for Curly's collection.

Their hands, toughened to a leathery texture, didn't feel the needle-sharp bones and spurs of the pilchards. As they stowed the leech of one net they hauled in the next, and the next, until they got to the eleventh one and Matt felt a vicious tug on the net.

'Shark!' he called out.

Fred froze. Daniel patted his shoulder and threw a nine-inch hook attached to a chain and baited with a large mackerel over the side. Then he fastened a bucket to the line that ran from the chain to the mizzen mast. A few minutes later the bucket gave a metallic clang as the shark took the bait and the chain was pulled taut. Fred headed for the cabin. Daniel pulled in the chain, bracing himself against the lugger's stern.

The blue shark he hauled in was six feet long and weighed about one hundred and eighty pounds. Matt stunned it with a heavy weight as its head appeared over the transom, cut its throat to retrieve the hook, and watched grimly as the shark fell back into the sea. As they hauled up the net they saw the black space where the shark had torn the mesh and stolen their fish.

The rest of the night they worked unhampered. When Fred rejoined them, no one said anything, their silence more humiliating than any scornful remark. As time went on they slowed a little as muscles tired, backs ached, and breathing became a little heavier. They worked in a concentrated silence, eager to get the job done. When the last white buff had been lifted aboard, the stars had disappeared and dawn was streaking the sky, the fish berth was deep in pilchards, and the fishermen were exhausted but pleased. They had made good money tonight and looked forward to a huge fry-up for breakfast.

Now the work was over, most of the gulls had deserted them and only a few persistent ones remained. Matt looked up and saluted them with a nod; he could be persistent too.

He turned his gaze north-east towards the Wolf Rock which towered an awesome one hundred and ten feet above the sea. The place had got its name from the sound of the water that had howled like a wolf through the holes in it, until wreckers had filled them up to stop it warning ships of the danger of circling tides. Pilchards could be found in plenty for several miles around it. It provided six weeks to two months' livelihood to the fishermen of Porthellis, and fleets came also from Plymouth, Looe and Polperro, Newlyn and Mousehole, St Ives, Newquay and Padstow, and Porthellis's near neighbour Mevagissey. A few boats were still about, but many had gone on to Newlyn to sell their catch.

As the *Sunrise*, too, got underway for Newlyn, her crew knew that after the long journey there was more hard work in store, with around nineteen thousand pilchards to unload, the lugger to wash down and the next night's fishing to prepare for. It would be long past midday before they could get their heads down, and four hours later they would be heading out again. Daniel was as quiet as the others at the prospect but he had a smile of anticipation on his handsome face. It wasn't one of the five bunks in the lugger he was planning to sleep in.

Chapter 6

When Hannah got home, Prim was there and Hannah could see she was set on a confrontation.

'How did it go then?' she asked in a bitter tone before Hannah had even kicked off her high heels.

'It's a beautiful place,' Hannah said with the enthusiasm she had carried away from Roscarrock. She glanced at her aunt but Janet looked down and carried on with her sewing; this was between mother and daughter as far as she was concerned, and Prim had the right to probe and argue in this instance.

'What happened, I mean,' Prim said tartly.

Hannah felt guilty; in a decision as big as this she should have found a way to consult her mother first. 'I-I'm taking the job, Mum.'

Prim put a hand under Hannah's chin, making her look into her sad eyes. 'Hannah, if I never ask you to do anything for me for the rest of my life, will you send word to Mrs Opie and tell her you've changed your mind?'

This was so unlike her quiet, downtrodden mother that Hannah was taken aback. 'But I want to give it a try, Mum,' she pleaded. 'It'll be a good opportunity for me to do something different. And Father's demanded that I take it.' Hannah never thought the day would come when she would unashamedly use his cruelty to further her cause, but her desire to live and work in the magnificent house, to get to know the enigmatic people there, burned in her breast. 'It's only for a month's trial to see if it works out. I might be home soon.'

'Home,' Prim muttered, as if the simple word hurt her. 'I'm not worried about what your father does, Hannah,' she implored. 'You've put up with him all these years, don't let his drunken talk drive you out of the village now. And what about Matt? Your future could lie with him if you let it. Hannah, for goodness sake, don't take that job.'

'But it's just a job, Mum. I don't understand what all the fuss is about. I won't be going far away and I'll be able to come home often and go to chapel every week. Mrs Opie's said my family can visit me there. Just think what it could do for Leah if she could be tempted to go up there. She's always been fascinated by Roscarrock.'

'I'm not concerned with Leah!' Prim snapped.

'Prim,' Janet said in a voice edged with warning.

Prim visibly checked herself.

'There is something, isn't there?' Hannah got up and gripped her mother's arm. 'Something about Roscarrock that concerns me. Grandmother said I belong there. What is it?'

Prim pushed her hand away. 'There's nothing. I'm going now, but let me tell you this, Hannah Spargo, if you go to that place you'll break my heart.' And Prim swept out of the house, tears running down her face.

Hannah was stunned. She turned to Janet. 'What did she mean?'

Her face pinched and white, Janet replied, 'I hope you'll never find out, Hannah, truly I do.'

Janet wouldn't be drawn any further and Hannah tried to push away the feeling that somehow she had betrayed both her mother and her aunt.

Mrs Opie wanted her to start next Monday and it was arranged that she should take her things to the big house on Sunday afternoon, have tea and supper there and settle in. Mrs Opie had assured her that she would only be expected to take on her duties a little at a time, as she got used to the house.

Hannah spent the end of the week finishing off the sewing she had started and packing her clothes and few belongings. She wondered what Daniel would say, and pictured him drawing in his bold features in disapproval. They had often talked of adventure, what they would like to do with their lives, had fantasised wildly over the years, but she was sure he wouldn't like her doing this. Hannah couldn't see that she would be at risk in any way with the courteous Patrick Opie.

The *Sunrise* left the fishing grounds in the early hours of Saturday morning and made all speed for Newlyn. Their last catch of the week was not a big one, forty-two thousand pilchards. While the others salted and hauled the nets on to the foredeck, Rufus collected the week's wages at the merchant's office. He paid the harbour dues, a shilling in the pound, deducted the fuel and grocery expenses, leaving a profit of fifty-nine pounds and two shillings. It was divided into seven parts, one for each crew member (a slightly smaller share for Fred), one for the nets and one for the boat. When the *Sunrise* was washed down, they left it at its weekend berth with the other vessels not local to Newlyn and Mousehole and took the bus and train home; it took less time and was a more economical way to get to and from the fishing grounds during the pilchard drive. Rufus and Daniel, having no family back at Porthellis, often stayed the weekend at Newlyn and chose this to be one of them.

Matt did not say goodbye to Daniel and walked off curtly with Curly and Fred to catch the bus to Penzance.

'What's the matter with 'e?' Rufus said, screwing up his ugly face and scratching at his food-laden, itchy beard. 'Think he'd 'ave a spring in 'is step now 'e's off t'see 'is maid. I would, Hannah's a lovely creature. He 'aven't gone off 'er already, 'ave 'e?'

'Don't know, Granfer,' Daniel fibbed.

Twenty-five men from Porthellis and sixty Mevagissey men crowded on to the train at Penzance. Matt ignored Jeff Spargo, who was in a belligerent mood because the *Misty* had only made forty-seven pounds, and took a seat in a dusty carriage next to Jowan. The two young fishermen discussed the fortunes of the week and expressed the hope that they'd have a weekend of fine weather after the terrible rain on Thursday night.

'I want to put some time in on the allotment,' Matt said quietly, settling back against the hard seat as if to relax. He closed his eyes.

'Eh?' Jowan nudged him, but couldn't make him open his eyes, 'Be down our house the first chance you get, won't you? With a bunch of flowers for Hannah?'

'I'm tired, Jo', Matt murmured. 'Might as well catch up on some sleep now.'

All the fishermen were bone-weary. They'd get home, eat a welcome hot meal, and usually sleep for a few hours before pursuing other interests, but they always found time for their womenfolk. Matt wasn't inclined to talk much but he had sounded totally uninterested in Hannah.

Jowan pondered on this as the train rattled out of the station and the majestic castle which topped St Michael's Mount out in the clear blue waters of Mounts Bay came into view. Hannah had responded well to Matt's sudden courtship and Jowan, inexperienced in matters of the heart, wondered if she was going to be let down just as suddenly. It was an uneasy thought. Jowan hated it when Hannah was upset; the terrible memory of the day when Daniel had brought her to the house was never far from his mind. He had gladly given up his bedroom and moved in with Ned, and apart from wishing he could be an astronomer, his biggest wish in life was for Hannah to find happiness.

'I hope you aren't dallying with Hannah's affections,' Jowan said sternly, making his father, Ned, Uncle Terence and cousin Morley look his way. 'She's like a sister to me.'

Matt's eyes flicked open and he fidgeted about, embarrassed to find himself being glared at by five of Hannah's male kinsfolk. 'I feel the same way as you all do about her,' he mumbled. 'I just don't want to talk about it, it's private.'

Satisfied with that, the men resumed their chatter. Matt sank down in his seat and returned to his private thoughts.

Jowan kissed his mother, and after she had fussed over him and moved on to Ned and Roy, he kissed and hugged Hannah tightly.

'You had a good week then?' she said, holding his shoulders, looking into his young and weather-beaten face. 'What about the *Sunrise*?'

'Did better than the rest of us. Daniel's staying at Newlyn.'

'Ooh,' she pouted. 'I wanted to talk to him.'

'Matt's home,' Jowan said, looking intently at her. 'He seemed very quiet, a bit down in the dumps. Is everything all right between you? Do you think Daniel could be jealous of him? I noticed they parted on bad terms.'

Hannah didn't answer. Daniel and Matt had been friends for years; what could have come between them?

Janet gave her a clue. Tapping her on the shoulder, she said stoutly, 'Have you been telling things to Daniel and leaving Matt out? You have something to tell him now, and it would be better coming from your mouth and not someone else's. I think he has the right to know.'

'What're you talking about, Mother?' Roy said, looking longingly at the range from where the tantalising smell of meat and potato pie with vegetables reached him.

'I'll tell you men later,' Janet said, bustling towards the dresser and taking down plates. 'Have a quick wash.' She looked at Hannah who was covered with a guilty flush. 'Well, young lady?'

'I agree with you, Aunty. Keep my dinner warm, please.' She slipped out the back door before her uncle could ask another question.

Hannah knocked loudly on the front door of Seaview Cottage. Mrs Penney opened it and looked at her curiously, raising her brows. Hannah felt guilty again; she hadn't called on Mrs Penney once during the week. At the least it was bad manners, at worst a snub to the mother of the man it was taken for granted was courting her. Mrs Penney would have heard she had taken the job at Roscarrock and must be wondering what it meant for her son.

'Hello, Mrs Penney. Could I have a word with Matt, please?'

'He's in the bath.' Mrs Penney, dressed in a plain dress with a frilled collar and apron, made no move to invite her in.

'I'd rather not have to come back,' Hannah said, edging her foot towards the doorstep. 'It's important.'

'You'd best come in and wait for him in that case, Hannah.' Mrs Penney moved aside and showed Hannah into her parlour. 'I'll tell him you're here then bring you in a cup of tea.'

'Oh, d-don't put yourself to any trouble,' Hannah stammered.

Mrs Penney merely smiled and withdrew.

Hannah walked about the room, looking at things without taking in what they were. She felt as awkward as an insecure child. The parlour which had been cosy when she had been here with Matt last Sunday seemed cold.

She was wearing a sleeveless blouse and cotton skirt and was rubbing her bare arms when Mrs Penney came in with a tray of tea.

'Sit down, Hannah. Matt will be along presently.'

She sat in a winged armchair near the window and watched silently as Mrs Penney set the tray down on a small pedestal table and poured the tea. She was using what looked like her best china.

'Thank you,' Hannah said, dismayed that it came out gruffly owing to a lump in her throat.

'Would you excuse me if I attend to Matt's dinner?' Mrs Penney said politely.

'No, of course not, please do. I'm sorry if I've interrupted you.'

Mrs Penney walked to the door then turned and considered Hannah for a few moments. Hannah knew she wanted to say something but, looking slightly regretful, she smiled and closed the door.

Trying to work out what she would say to Matt, Hannah let the tea go cold, then not wanting to offend Mrs Penney she drank it down and put the cup and saucer on the tray. She watched the regulator clock on the wall tick away five long minutes. She twiddled her thumbs, she picked at the pocket of her skirt, she crossed and uncrossed her legs. Another five minutes passed and seemed like an hour. She listened for Matt coming down the stairs but could only hear the occasional indecipherable sound of his mother in the kitchen. Would Mrs Penney mind if the meal was ready and she kept Matt from it?

Her stomach was knotting up more painfully than when she arrived at Roscarrock for the interview with Mrs Opie. She got up and looked out of the window. There was no one in sight. Everybody else in the village was probably sitting down to eat, despondent if their men hadn't earned a good week's money but rejoicing that they'd come home safely. She thought of Lizzie throwing herself into John's arms. How would she have reacted if she'd seen Matt walking down the village hill after getting off the bus from St Austell?

'Hello, Hannah.'

She jumped and spun round. She hadn't heard Matt open the door and come in. She had thought little about him all week, but now she was actually facing him her heart leapt and her feelings ran amok; what they were exactly she didn't know. He had closed the door but had not moved away from it. She took several steps towards him. He was wearing an open neck white shirt, the sleeves rolled up above the elbows. The muscles on his forearms bulged and there were little nicks on his hands and wrists from handling the pilchards. He had shaved and his hair was wet and curling, very dark and combed back from his face, making him look younger. He smelled wonderful, of soap and salt and himself.

She had never felt so shy in all her life. 'Hello, Matt . . . I wanted to see you right away . . . I have something to tell you.'

His dark eyes seemed to penetrate her mind. 'I think I know what you're going to say.'

'I take it Daniel told you I was offered a job at Roscarrock?'

'He did.'

'I didn't mention it to you, Matt,' and Hannah was speaking rapidly now, the words spilling out of her mouth and running into each other, 'because I didn't take it seriously.'

She saw Matt swallow hard. 'But you are now?'

'I-I have actually been up to Roscarrock and have taken the job.'

Very calmly, he said, 'Are you sure you've thought this through, Hannah? The Opies are an unknown quantity, you don't know what you may be letting yourself in for. I've been thinking about it, you get a lot of time to think when you're not hauling in the fish out at sea. Why does a man who's never set foot in Porthellis suddenly offer a job to a woman he's never met before? It doesn't make sense. I don't like it. Patrick Opie's only lived at Roscarrock for five years. No one knows anything about him.'

'But I've met Mr Patrick twice and Mrs Opie, Matt,' she appealed to him. 'They seem really pleasant. The terms of my work are very generous. I won't be locked away and I can have visitors up there.'

His tanned features took on the intense look she was

becoming familiar with. 'You don't have to go there, Hannah, not because of your father. I'll look after you. I'd never treat you badly. You'd be happy living here with Mum, she'd never interfere. I know you like your freedom. You could wander the cliffs and beaches and visit your family as much as you liked, they'd be welcome here anytime. I'm asking you to marry me, Hannah. I love you.'

Hannah was thunderstruck. 'Oh Matt . . .'

He clenched his fists. 'I can tell from that what your answer is.'

Hannah put her fingers to her lips and glanced at the floor before meeting his eyes again. 'It's too soon for us . . .'

Matt sighed and shook his head. 'So where does this leave us, Hannah?'

She gazed at him. It was too soon in their relationship to marry him, but she didn't like the thought of not being close to him.

'The same as before, I hope.' She surprised herself by dashing across the floor, taking his big rough hand and kissing the back of it. 'Please don't be angry with me, Matt.'

He pulled her into his arms and held her as close as he could. 'I'm not angry with you, darling, I never will be.' Gently gripping a handful of her hair, he breathed, 'Dear Lord, you frightened me. I thought it was all over between us before we'd hardly begun.'

Hannah sought his mouth as hungrily as he did hers, sliding her arms up over his chest and clamping them round his neck. She pressed herself against him and when he finally took his lips away he nuzzled her neck, making her tingle deliciously. They kissed long and hard again, then laughed because they were both out of breath.

'When are you going to start at Roscarrock?' he said, caressing her back, arms and shoulders, kissing the palm of her hand.

'On Monday. I'm moving in tomorrow.'

'No, you can't,' he protested mildly. 'I won't see you.'

'That's another reason why I'm here. I need help to carry my things up there. I want you to come with me, then we can spend more time together after chapel and you'll see Roscarrock for yourself.' It was a lie, she had intended to ask Jowan to go with her, partly in the hope of reassuring Janet.

'It'll be my pleasure,' Matt murmured, kissing her lips. 'And I want you all to myself for the rest of today.' He opened the door and called out, 'Mum, have you cooked plenty of dinner?'

Mrs Penney came out of the kitchen and plodded along the passage. Her face broke into a king-sized grin when she saw the couple with their arms wrapped round each other. 'Of course, dear. Why?'

'Because Hannah's joining us.' And Matt put a possessive kiss on the top of her head.

Chapter 7

After dropping a bag of washing into the home of one of his women friends and promising to give her some of his time in the coming week, Daniel walked up the steep hill of Trewarveneth Street. He entered a large dreary boarding house with grimy upstairs bay windows and was immediately set upon by a large, hostile looking dog. Daniel only laughed and the moment the brown and black hound recognised him it changed its long throaty growls to excited whimpers and jumped up, putting its two front paws high on his chest.

'Hello, Scamp. Missed me, have you?' Daniel ruffled the dog's floppy ears then pushed it away. Scamp followed him along the dark narrow passage to the door at the end, their feet making plodding and scratching noises on the lino floor.

As Daniel opened the door, Scamp burst through and a harsh voice shouted, 'Who's let the bleddy dog in here again? Oh, 'tis you, Danny. Long time no see. You got something for me?'

Wilfred Hickey, a man in his mid-forties who had retired early from fishing owing to a bad back, got up from the kitchen table where he had just finished a meal of fried fish. Of average build, he could be as hard as he looked, with a sneering mouth, bent nose, tight pale eyes, and a head of thick white hair combed back from a widow's peak. He had little respect for anything or anyone, except people like Daniel, who helped finance his living.

After a struggle, Daniel got Scamp back into the passage and closed the door on him. Then, taking a package, flat and square, out of his allowance bag, he passed it to Wilfred.

Wilfred didn't open it or ask what was inside it. He slipped it inside a pocket of his jacket hanging on the back of his chair. 'Sit down, boy. Where did you get it?' he asked, referring to the package.

'From someone further upcoast. He said my share should be worth twenty pounds.'

'Fair enough.' Wilfred never doubted Daniel's word, and he knew he would be sorry if he did. 'I'll get it for you later. Right?'

'Right.'

Daniel helped himself to a mug of tea from the teapot on the table.

'Viv gone out, has she?' he said, looking round the depressing surroundings. It smelled of grease and condensation, and damp marks stretched across the ceiling which hadn't seen a lick of paint for years. The curtains were bleached of all colour and the furniture was old and ugly; Wilfred had bought it for next to nothing from a dealer. Nothing matched and the table, too big for the room, was set awkwardly against a cupboard.

'Just popped out to the greengrocer's. Shouldn't be long now.'

Daniel smiled, his sea-blue eyes lighting up. 'If I ask her nicely, p'raps she'll cook me a hot dinner.'

Wilfred wasn't interested. He put his jacket on and made for the back door. 'I'm off to meet my contact. See you later, boy.'

Daniel nodded goodbye and waited patiently.

Ten minutes later a girl came through the back door carrying a laden basket. He jumped up and took it from her.

'Danny! I had a feeling we'd see you today. I said the very same thing to Dad. He gone out and left you all alone? Miserable sod. He's got no manners.'

'Never mind.' Daniel squeezed her arm and put the basket on the table. 'I stayed here to ask you out for a bite to eat, Viv.'

'What for?' Viv said, glancing at him as she began putting her shopping away. She had to pull the table out to put a can of paraffin in the cupboard. Daniel pushed it back.

'To celebrate your birthday. I remembered out fishing that I'd missed it.' Leaning against the stone sink he took his time admiring Wilfred Hickey's sixteen-year-old stepdaughter. Wilfred made some good money from time to time but he was too hard-hearted to give any to Viv to spend on clothes. She was wearing down-at-heel shoes and an ill-fitting floral dress, but with his practised eye Daniel knew that underneath she had a wonderful figure to match her long shapely legs and pretty pale face. Her long, shiny auburn hair, which she always wore swept up, showed off her graceful neck.

'I don't expect you to remember my birthday, Danny,' she said, her hazel eyes on him as she reached for the teapot to make a fresh brew. Her gently curving cheeks had gone a little pink. 'I've already eaten. I'll slap a bit of bacon in the pan if you're hungry.'

Grinning at her, he seated himself at the table. 'I'll take you out for a walk later then. I knew you wouldn't see me starve. You're a sweetheart. Throw in a couple of eggs too, will you?'

When he'd eaten the meal, which included several doorsteps of bread and two slices of Viv's apple pie, washed down with a couple of mugs of tea, he stretched his arms in satisfaction and turned his eyes on her again. She had her back to him at the sink where she was peeling vegetables for tomorrow's Sunday dinner for the lodgers, humming softly to herself. She had a sweet singing voice for which she was known throughout Newlyn, sometimes earning a few pence for herself in the pub where she washed dishes. She'd had a hard life, caring for Wilfred and putting up with his surly and dishonest ways, cooking and cleaning for the five boarders in the house, coarse individuals whom Wilfred usually had to chase up for the rent. Daniel knew she couldn't read or write. Brought up in rough conditions, she had a temper and could swear like a man but, unlike her mother whose loose life had contributed to her early death, Viv was sweet and innocent, qualities that had drawn Daniel to her when he'd first noticed her growing up.

He came to stand behind her. 'I knew you wouldn't want to go out and eat so I got a little present for you.'

Viv dropped the knife and looked over her shoulder at him. Her mouth was agape. She had rarely had presents in her life, never on her birthday. 'You didn't have to do that, Danny.' Her face was vibrant.

'It's nothing special,' he said, feigning coyness. 'Just a little something I saw I thought would suit you.'

Viv watched as he took a small parcel, wrapped in brown paper, out of his bag. She stared at him but didn't take it, as if she was afraid it would disappear in a puff of smoke.

'Dry your hands then,' he smiled with all his charm.

She dried her hands on her apron, took the parcel and looked at him, her eyes shining like a child's. 'Thank you, Danny.'

Her hands were shaking and she had difficulty tearing off the paper. When she saw the two tortoiseshell combs she let the paper fall to the floor. 'They're beautiful! Oh, Danny, thank you. I've always wanted something like this to put in my hair.'

He dropped his head and she obliged him with a kiss on the cheek. 'Put them in and see what they look like.'

'I'll have to go up to my room and look in my mirror.' And she rushed excitedly from the room.

Upstairs in her cramped, damp attic room Viv picked up the small hand mirror, the only pretty possession she owned and all that was left to remind her of her mother, and moved to the light of the tiny dormer window to arrange the combs in her hair. Her heart was beating at twice its normal speed and her soul was full of hope. Viv had adored Daniel from adolescence and she'd wished and prayed that one day he would look further than the older women he associated with and notice her. Could this be the start of something wonderful? She longed to be a fisherman's wife and get away from this crumbling house, the drudgery and stultifying life.

A noise made her look towards the door. Daniel was standing in the doorway, smiling. 'You look beautiful, Viv, but then that's easy because you are beautiful.'

'Do you really think so?' She thought her heart would burst with excitement.

'Absolutely beautiful,' he breathed huskily.

He moved up to her. She was radiant and he could feel the warmth emanating from her. Putting his hand on the side of her face, he gazed into her eyes. 'Can I kiss you properly, Viv?'

Unable to speak, she nodded.

He took the mirror from her and put it on the chair at the side of her narrow bed. Then he kissed her gently, revelling in her tenderness. Keeping the kiss short, he wrapped her in his arms. Stroking the thistledown softness of her neck, he murmured, 'You mean a lot to me, Viv. I've thought of nothing else but you all week. If we hadn't been so busy I would have come to see you on Monday but Granfer insisted I stay close to the boat. You're very special to me, darling.'

'Really?' Viv's face was pressed against his chest. She hadn't felt the comfort of anyone's arms round her in years, and never a man's, having fiercely discouraged the lewd approaches from the lodgers and roughnecks in the pub. It was the most marvellous feeling on earth. 'I – I've liked you for ages, Danny.'

'That's wonderful.'

He raised her face to kiss her again but she spoke. 'Can I tell Dad?'

'Tell him what?' He kissed her forehead, running his wide mouth all the way down to her neck.

'That there's something between us.' She was in a state of agitation, as if a motor was running inside her.

'No,' he said, his handsome features becoming stern for a moment. 'Let's keep it our secret for a while. It will be more special that way.'

He claimed her lips again, coaxing them apart, gradually pushing her back until he had her sitting on the bed. His hands were beginning to wander when Viv gently eased herself away from him. 'I've got work to do, Danny. Dad will be mad if I haven't got everything finished before I go to the pub.'

'All right, sweetheart. Let's stay up here alone for a little longer then I'll give you a hand and we'll walk to the pub together.'

The Crown was situated in Fore Street overlooking the harbour. Viv felt proud to be holding on to Daniel's arm as he walked her to the back entrance. He planted a kiss on her cheek and went round to the front door and entered the bar. Viv had to clear up the landlord's family's tea dishes, prepare their Sunday vegetables and wash glasses and clean out ashtrays all evening.

Fay Dunn, the landlady, popped into the kitchen at eight o'clock. 'You ready to give us a song, my handsome?' she said cheerily in her loud voice, handing Viv her seven and sixpence week's wages. 'The pilchard drive got off to a good start. Reckon there'll be a few sentimental souls ready to part with a bob or two tonight.'

'I'll be right there, Fay,' Viv replied, smiling happily as she untied her apron. She took the combs Daniel had given her out of her shapeless summer coat pocket and tidied her hair before inserting them into it. She had heard Daniel's laugh a moment ago and she would sing specially for him tonight.

A cheer went up from the regulars in the bar when she appeared and Daniel, sitting at a table with Mitch Spargo who had also stayed in Newlyn, raised his full pint of beer to her. Viv smiled back, then mounting the stool that was always put out for her, she sang a collection of favourite Cornish songs, ending with 'Trelawney' which the drinkers entered into with gusto. Several pennies and two sixpences were tossed gaily at her and Viv gave a little bow and thanked the crowd. Daniel pressed half a crown into her hand as he helped her down off the stool.

'I'll walk you home at closing time,' he whispered in her ear.

Clutching her handful of money, Viv made her way through the tightly packed tables to the kitchen. She always had to look out for those who were a little drunk or lecherous and this time a foreign sailor stretched out his hand and patted her bottom. Usually she swore at anybody who was over-familiar but she was too happy to worry about it tonight and moved on quickly.

Suddenly there was a yelp. She turned to see Daniel twisting the sailor's arm back. 'Keep your hands to yourself, you dirty bastard, or I'll break your bloody neck,' he snarled.

The sailor nodded meekly. There was something frighteningly violent about the expression on the young fisherman's face.

Mitch envied Daniel his hardness. Mitch wasn't afraid of a fight but this particular sailor was known for wielding a knife in times of conflict. And Mitch envied Daniel's easy ability with women. He had noticed Viv before and had considered trying to get to know her. Apart from the odd spark of temper, she seemed the quiet, hard-working, decent sort he liked. He was two years older than she was but looked more mature, but it seemed that Daniel always stepped in first when he fancied a woman. Mitch usually ended up making do with one of the tarts who plied their trade in this pub, but it didn't satisfy all his needs, there was no love and affection in it. Still, it was much better than going home and hearing the bedsprings jerking in the next room as his rotten father had his poor mother again.

Now in a melancholy mood, Mitch took to thinking about Hannah. He couldn't stomach the way his father treated her. He made a fist and massaged it, feeling again the satisfaction as it had rammed into his father's face in Squeeze-guts Alley. He had done it for Hannah, for all the blame and injustice heaped on her by Jeff. Mitch had never had the courage to admit what had really happened on the *Wynne* that day, and the beaten look in Hannah's eyes when Jeff had confronted her at Lizzie's wedding had been the last straw.

A heavily made-up woman who had serviced Mitch before sat down beside him, put her hand on his thigh and asked him to buy her a drink.

'It'll be my pleasure,' Mitch said tonelessly. The *Misty* hadn't had as many good catches of pilchards as the other boats but he had enough earnings in his pocket not to be lonely for a while tonight. He went to the bar to buy the drinks, thinking that if his hate for his father kept growing, one day he might even be driven to kill him.

Daniel had followed Viv to the kitchen. 'You had no need to do that, Danny,' she said, referring to the sailor. 'I can manage his type.'

'No one touches my girl like that,' he said vehemently and Viv was as proud as punch to hear it.

Daniel bought fish and chips, a rare treat for Viv, as they strolled back to the boarding house. Darkness had spread its fingers, making gloomy corners and shadows among the boats on the still water and in the quiet streets but Viv didn't notice, she had never felt happier in her life.

There was no one in the boarding house, everybody

went out on Saturday night. Wilfred never said where he went or what time he would be back and Viv never asked.

After letting Scamp out into the back yard for a short while, Viv hung her coat up behind the back kitchen door. She felt shy to be alone with Daniel now. 'Would you like a cup of tea, Danny?'

'I'd rather have a kiss,' he murmured and took her in his arms. Moments later, as he held her close, he said, 'Why don't we go up to your room? It'll be nice and cosy and we won't have to worry about anyone coming in and interrupting us.'

'No one's likely to,' she pointed out.

'But it's not very comfortable in here, not even an armchair we can cuddle up on, and there's no sitting room with the boarders taking every bit of space.'

'I don't know,' she tossed her head uncertainly. 'Dad wouldn't like it.'

'He'll never know, will he? Don't worry, sweetheart, if he comes home suddenly I can creep out like a cat, no one will ever know I've been here.'

Viv disentangled herself from his clinging arms to let Scamp in and gave him a bowl of fresh water. She watched the dog as it lapped thirstily, knowing Daniel was watching her. He raised an eyebrow and grinned disarmingly when she turned back to him.

'Just for a little while, Viv.'

It was the loving expression on his handsome face that made her decide to throw all caution to the wind. Putting Scamp in his station at the front door, Daniel followed her upstairs. He sat on the bed and held out his arms to her.

His kisses were different now, demanding, persistent,

explorative. Viv felt his hands caressing her, gradually moving to more intimate places until he was lifting her skirt. She pushed it down and he kissed her more fiercely. She felt his hand on the top of her leg.

'Don't touch me there, Danny.'

'It's all right, sweetheart. I won't hurt you. You're very special to me, you know that, don't you?'

He had moved so they were lying on the bed and suddenly he was on top of her.

'What are you doing? I want to sit up.'

He ignored the panic in her voice. 'It's all right, Viv, don't worry.'

She felt a terrible pain tearing inside her. 'Ahhh! Don't, Danny. Stop!'

'Relax, Viv, you'll be fine in a minute. Hold me tight.'

She clutched his shirt collar with one hand, the bed-cover with the other. He didn't stop hurting her until he made some strange noises and was no longer rising over her. He got off her and shakily she pushed down her dress. Her inner body was sore and she was horribly wet. She cried.

Daniel lay on his side, panting a little, and pulled her round to him. He kissed her forehead, damp with perspiration. 'Don't worry, sweetheart. It'll be better next time. You'll enjoy it.'

'Next time?' she wept in anguish. 'We shouldn't have done it, Danny. It's wicked. You'll get me into trouble.'

'Trust me, Viv.' He gently stroked her cheeks, wiping away her tears. 'There's nothing wrong in making love, it's the best way a man and woman have of showing they care for each other.' He gazed into her eyes. 'You do care for me?'

'Oh, yes, Danny.' She clung to him.

'Happier now?'

'Yes, Danny.' It wasn't altogether the truth.

'Good girl.' He rolled on to his back keeping his arms lightly about her.

Viv placed her face against his chest, eyes stinging as fresh tears came at her hurt and humiliation, but a hope grew that it would lead to a wonderful new future.

Daniel closed his eyes and relived the delicious moments as he'd taken her.

Chapter 8

Janet was a little less troubled at the prospect of Hannah leaving home after she had brought Matt home for supper on Saturday evening and Janet had seen how the couple were absorbed in each other. Jowan, Ned and Uncle Roy had grave reservations but wished her luck, demanding that they be told all about her first week at Roscarrock immediately they got home next weekend. Prim hadn't come round but Hannah hoped she would change her mind if things worked out well for her at the big house.

Hannah was both apprehensive and light-hearted as she walked to Roscarrock with Matt. He was carrying the big leather suitcase Mrs Penney had loaned her. It was packed with most of her belongings. 'Is that heavy?' she asked as they neared the end of Turn-A-Penny Lane.

'No, darling,' he smiled mischievously. 'It's not nearly as heavy as a net full of pilchards.'

'You men,' she laughed, and she had laughed a lot with Matt in the past two days, 'are so proud of your muscles. Danny loves to show his off to the girls.'

'Well, I'm only interested in one girl. You.'

'You'll tell him I've taken the job?'

'I won't forget,' he promised, and he'd make it plain to Daniel Kittow that Hannah was well and truly his girl.

Their little tête-à-têtes would have to stop.

At the gateway of Roscarrock, Matt put the suitcase down and took the bag from her hands. She looked at him curiously. 'I want to say goodbye to you properly,' he explained. 'We won't get the chance at the house.'

Willingly, Hannah spent five minutes in his arms. 'Good job I'm not wearing lipstick, it would be all over you.' She pecked his strong chin. 'How did you get that little scar there, Matt?'

He looked away and Hannah was sure he was embarrassed. 'I – I don't remember. We'd better go on, I suppose,' he added reluctantly.

He looked all about as they made their way down the long drive which had not a weed in sight. 'The gardens are well kept.' He admired the trimmed lawns, and the shrubs, four of which were shaped into birds, something Hannah had not noticed on her first visit.

'Mr Patrick tends the gardens,' she said, thinking it was going to be a pleasure walking round them.

Matt glanced at her sideways. 'Perhaps he'll give me a part-time job, I'd be able to see more of you then.'

'I have the feeling Mr Patrick likes to do everything himself.'

When they arrived at the front of the house, Hannah looked up at Mrs Opie's balcony. There was no sign of her or of Pogo.

Hannah told Matt she was to enter by the front door. Sounding as if he had a gulp in his throat, he murmured, 'I'll carry the suitcase up the steps for you.'

Hannah followed him. He used the brass door knocker. Several moments later, Hannah clutched his arm, whispering like a nervous child, 'Mrs Opie said if no one was about I was to just walk in and go up to her suite of rooms.'

'Are you sure?' he whispered back. 'What about the housemaid?'

'I don't know, perhaps she has the afternoon off. We'd better go in. We can't stand about here all day.'

Matt gingerly tried the door handle. The door opened and he ushered Hannah past him to step over the threshold first. He put the suitcase down beside her in the hall.

Looking up at the high, decorated ceiling, at the plush furniture in the hallway and the exquisite moulding on the doors, Matt was awestruck. 'I can see why you're attracted to this place,' he said, his voice low. 'It's absolutely beautiful. Are you sure you'll be all right here, Hannah?'

'Yes,' she said quietly, but she was jittery and didn't want him to go.

There was no one about so they embraced and had one last quick kiss. 'You will be careful at sea, darling?' She searched his face anxiously.

He nodded. 'I'll come down to your aunt's next Saturday afternoon as soon as I can, right?'

She nodded.

With one last squeeze of her hand, he left.

Hannah rushed after him and waved goodbye at the top of the steps, savouring the sight of his proudly held dark head, his long-legged stride, his arms swinging loosely at his sides. At the curve in the drive he turned and waved and then he was out of sight. Dropping her hand, gathering her composure, she went back inside the house and mounted the stairs to Mrs Opie's rooms.

'Come in, Hannah,' Mrs Opie called out to her tap on the door.

Hannah went in and found her new employer was out on the balcony. 'Good afternoon, Mrs Opie.'

'Come here, Hannah. I saw the young man who came with you. Is he one of your brothers?'

Hannah didn't know how to describe Matt to Mrs Opie; last time she was here she had told her she had no boy friend. After a moment's hesitation, she answered, 'He's a close friend.'

Mrs Opie looked at her keenly. 'The friend you mentioned?'

'Well, no, another friend.' Looking up the drive, Hannah was glad the trees hid the gateway or Mrs Opie might have seen her and Matt kissing.

'You're a very lucky young lady to have so many friends, but then I'm certain you are a very nice person and deserve them.' Despite her stiff leg, Mrs Opie whirled round gracefully. 'Now, Hannah, I want you to feel at home straightaway so I'll show you to your room and you can settle in. Pass me my walking stick, please. If you're wondering where Pogo is, Mr Patrick is taking him for his afternoon walk through the woods. Perhaps you'd like to take Pogo sometimes.'

'I'd love to,' Hannah said, passing her the gold-topped cane.

Mrs Opie walked astonishingly quickly down the corridor and stopped at the room at the opposite end to hers. She opened the door. 'Here you are, Hannah. In you go. Tell me what you think.'

Hannah disobeyed one of her first orders by hesitating. 'But I thought . . .'

'You'd be up in the servants' quarters?' Mrs Opie

smiled graciously. 'Miss Benson had a nice little room at the back of the house but I promised you a room overlooking the sea, remember? I rarely have guests and it seems a shame not to use my lovely rooms. Now, in you go.'

Pink-faced, and hoping Mrs Opie hadn't thought her cheeky, Hannah did as she was bid. She looked, gasped, clasped her hands together under her chin, everything else in her life at that moment quite forgotten. The room was nearly as spacious as Mrs Opie's sitting room and contained a double wardrobe, dressing table, stool, chest of drawers, tallboy, bedside cabinets and a double four-poster bed. The bed had damask curtains and bedspread, and plump pillows. Hannah had seen a similar bed in the room Patrick Opie had shown her but she'd never dreamt she would actually sleep in one herself. There were table lamps and lace runners and a bowl of red roses. Hannah could see herself in a cheval mirror with curved and reeded legs. Brass sconces on the walls held tall white candles. The oak floorboards were covered with opulent Turkish rugs, and fluffy pink towels, a face cloth and bar of soap complemented the pedestal sink. The long window reached nearly from floor to ceiling, its curtains held in the centre by tie-backs with gold tassels. There was a little round table in front of the window and two comfortable-looking small armchairs on either side of it.

The room was the size of all the downstairs rooms put together in some of the cottages in Porthellis. She would have more drawers and space than she could possibly need to put her things in and on. She was being given her own private place, a place to dream in. It would be wonderful if Aunty Janet and her sisters could come here and take tea with her, especially Leah. But now she must stop gawping and give her attention to Mrs Opie.

'I . . . I . . . it's wonderful! Oh, thank you, Mrs Opie.'

'I thought you'd be pleased.'

Hannah felt she could almost kiss the woman. 'Pleased? I'm . . .'

'Speechless?' Mrs Opie laughed, a pleasant tinkling sound. 'Why don't you fetch your things and put them away then pop down to the kitchen and make yourself some tea. Angie Miller has left out everything you will need and something for your tea and supper. I promised you there would be no duties today and I meant it. You may please yourself what you do with the rest of the day. You may wander the gardens and woods freely.'

Hannah was looking at some dresses lying on the bed.

'Those are your uniforms,' Mrs Opie explained. 'I ordered them from Haskey's of St Austell. As you can see, there are two different styles of dresses so you won't get fed up wearing the same thing every day and there are different sizes to try on.' Mrs Opie pointed with her stick. 'There are your shoes. Again in different sizes for you to try. Wrap up the things that do not fit you and I'll have them sent back.'

Hannah's eyes had followed the stick. 'They're lovely.' She hadn't expected to be provided with such pretty, fashionable clothes and there were pairs of dainty flat shoes and high heels. She was overwhelmed and her face was bright pink with excitement. She felt like a very lucky child on Christmas morning.

Mrs Opie looked as if she was delighted with Hannah's joy. 'You may wear your hair down if you like, it's very pretty, as long as you keep it tidy. Now I'll leave you to it and see you in my rooms at eight o'clock in the morning when you can bring up my breakfast tray which Angie

Miller prepares – she does the breakfasts. Then we can discuss your duties for the day. If you want to discuss anything with me before, Hannah, please don't be shy about coming to see me. I won't be going down to dinner tonight, I shall be in my rooms.'

'Thank you, Mrs Opie,' Hannah said evenly, finding her composure. 'I'm sure I'll be fine until tomorrow.'

'Enjoy your day, Hannah.' And Mrs Opie departed to her own rooms.

Hannah kicked off her dusty shoes and padding to the window sat down in one of the armchairs, quite overcome by the kindness shown her. One of the first things she'd do when she got back to Porthellis would be to dispel the rumours about the people living here being odd.

Hannah was up with the dawn next morning, and after saying a prayer for Matt, Daniel and the menfolk of her family, including her father, to have a safe and prosperous week at sea, she put on one of her new dresses. Hannah couldn't help admiring herself in the mirror, knowing Aunty Janet would approve of the design and cut. Made in a mixture of linen and cotton, in a royal blue print that accentuated her lovely eyes, it fell gently from a belted waist and was shaped delicately at the bust. There was a big pocket in the skirt. She put on the flat shoes in case she'd be running up and down the stairs a lot. Deciding she would wear her hair down, she pinned it back from her face.

She made her bed, which she had found wonderfully comfortable; she'd had to thump her feather bed at home to distribute the feathers evenly. She tidied up the sink and towels and went to the window for a long look at the sea. The wash of the waves and the wind sounded different up here. The sea was distant, muffled and low, but with the house being up on the cliff the wind was stronger and would no doubt whistle and howl on stormy days. Whatever the weather, she had a panoramic view she would enjoy every day. She could see the Dodman with its towering cross erected by Christians at the end of the last century and all of Veryan Bay. Looking closer to home, she saw the tops of the cliffs falling away either side of Porthellis. Down on the lawn directly in front of her was the giant oak tree; she mused that it could possibly tell many a wonderful tale from the times when horse and carriage had drawn up in front of the house until the present day.

Hannah was ready to start her first full day but felt shy at meeting Angie Miller who hadn't been about anywhere yesterday. Squaring her shoulders, she went downstairs to the kitchen.

At the three-burner black Cornish range, its maker's name, Oatey & Martin, Wadebridge, prominently displayed, was a short, dumpy woman in a long pink dress, white starched cap and apron, and large feet in hefty black shoes. She didn't hear Hannah enter the kitchen. She was stirring a pot and Hannah could smell porridge cooking.

'Ahem,' she said, to announce her presence.

The woman dropped the wooden spoon in the pot and whipped round.

'I'm sorry I startled you,' Hannah apologised. 'I'm Hannah Spargo. I'm starting here today as housekeeper. You must be Angie Miller.' She put out her hand. 'I'm very pleased to meet you.'

Angie Miller's middle-aged face relaxed a little. She bobbed an awkward curtsy and wiping her podgy hand on her apron shook Hannah's hand, then snatched hers away. 'P-pleased to m-meet you, Miss S-Spargo.'

'I'm terribly nervous,' Hannah said with a sunny smile, in the hope it would ease the other woman's nervousness of her. 'I don't know what to do first.'

'Breakfast,' Angie blurted out, fiddling with a tea towel drying on the brass rail over the range. 'Have breakfast. Mr Patrick said for me to give 'ee breakfast when 'ee came down.'

Hannah knew she couldn't offer to do her own, it would upset the natural hierarchy of the house which she was sure Angie was accustomed to and felt safe with. 'Where shall I sit?'

'In the servants' hall next door,' Angie replied.

Hannah knew where it was, a small room situated behind the kitchen at the back of the house. Patrick Opie had showed her it on the day of the interview. She went through and as there was no one senior to her on the staff she sat in the Windsor chair at the head of the table. Angie plodded in on her flat feet a few moments later, having changed her apron.

'What will 'ee have, Miss Spargo? Bacon 'n' egg? I like a bit of porridge ev'ry day meself. The fruit on the sideboard is fer the servants.' While she was speaking, careful not to look Hannah in the eye, she put condiments, marmalade, jam, cutlery and napkins on the table from the dresser.

Instinct told Hannah that Angie felt at home with direct orders. 'I'll have some porridge followed by bacon and eggs, please.'

It was too hot for porridge, but as Angie liked it Hannah thought it would help to forge a friendship with her and by the shy smile that broke out on Angie's ruddy features it seemed she had done the right thing.

When Angie had gone back to the kitchen, Hannah wandered about the room. There was a wall clock with a large octagonal face by the comfortable fireside and Patrick Opie had told her it would be her duty to wind it and keep it synchronised with the one in the kitchen. 'An essential for good time-keeping in the old days but we don't run a strictly tight ship here,' he'd added.

Hannah opened the outside door and stood on the top of four high granite steps. Across the cobbled yard was the cottage where the coachman had lived and the stables. Both seemed empty and Hannah thought it a shame there weren't any horses here; she'd always wanted to learn to ride. The cottage was bigger than any in the village, a size the fishermen's wives could only dream of living in. She'd investigate them later. Mr Patrick had told her there was a disused dovecote with a chapel door but she couldn't see it from here. Yesterday she had strolled through the gardens at the side of the house and carried on over the overgrown grass to the boundary hedge. She'd sat at the spot where she and Matt had first kissed – it seemed so long ago now.

'M-Miss Spargo?'

'Coming, Angie.'

Sitting down at the table with an apologetic smile, she had toast and butter and a tea tray put in front of her. Hannah could see that she would eat alone. Janet had told her a bit about what it was like to be in service, that servants could be more snobbish than their masters, that everyone was expected to keep their place. House-keepers didn't usually sit down with housemaids but Angie's abject shyness would have forbidden it anyway.

The porridge and fried meal were delicious and as Angie gathered up the crockery, she asked, 'Do 'ee want anything else, Miss Spargo?'

'No, thank you,' Hannah said, rising and feeling something of a lady being waited on like this. 'You don't have to call me Miss Spargo. I don't mind you calling me Hannah.'

It was a mistake and threw Angie into a dither. Hannah was immediately sorry. 'Well, if you'd rather call me Miss Spargo that's fine by me.'

'I could call 'ee just Miss if you'd rather,' Angie said, screwing up her face as if it had taken a lot of concentration to come up with the suggestion.

'That's better, sounds less formal.' And that settled her relationship with Angie Miller. Hannah was sure they'd get along well when Angie was used to her. She marvelled that she had been a little scared of meeting Angie. Everyone in this house was kind and friendly.

It was too early to take up Mrs Opie's breakfast tray and so as not to distract Angie she put on a businesslike face and left the kitchen as if she had something pressing to do. She looked around the wash-house, trying to feel like a housekeeper by checking on the cleanliness of things but feeling as if she was snooping on Angie. There was a washing machine and a wringing machine, a box mangle, an ironing stove, a drying closet with sliding racks, a towel horse and overhead drying rails. A long ironing table was fitted under the window which looked out on railings at the side of the house. Everything was spick-and-span.

She went up to the ground floor and stood back out of Angie's way where she couldn't be seen as the house-maid came up the narrow flight of steps and took some dishes into the dining room, obviously for Patrick Opie's breakfast.

The door across from the drawing room was locked and Hannah pondered what was inside. The library? A games room with snooker table? At that moment Patrick Opie, wearing a comfortable old cardigan, sprang down the stairs as sprightly and awkwardly as a youth.

'Ah, Miss Spargo. Good morning to you. I hope you slept well.'

'I did, Mr Opie, thank you.'

He rubbed his hands vigorously together, a habit of his. 'Splendid, splendid. I say, you look most charming. You will save a little energy to take a look round the walled garden this afternoon? I assure you you'll be amazed at what I have growing in there, sheltered place and all that.'

'I shall look forward to it,' Hannah said truthfully. She wanted to see all the gardens and she felt comfortable in Patrick Opie's company.

'Have you had your breakfast?'

'Yes, thank you.'

'Good, good.' He glanced at his pocket watch which instead of hanging from a chain in his shirt pocket was stuffed in his trouser pocket. 'Six fifty-five.' He grinned. 'Up early, eh? A little too soon for Great-Aunt Feena's tray. You must have a lie-in tomorrow. Well, must get on, lots to do today. Hope you like pigeon, that's what we're having for luncheon.' With a final rub at his hands he bounded off, then stopped and turned at the dining room door. 'By the way, my nephew, Mr Gregory, uses that room for his writing. Always keeps it locked. Can't bear his papers and things being touched. I should give that room a wide berth if I were you.'

Hannah was left to ponder when she would make Mr Gregory Opie's acquaintance. To the left of the room was a portrait of a young man in medieval clothes. He didn't look as if he belonged to the era. His hair was short and very fair, his eyes were a stony grey and his face, although far from unattractive, was stern and rather gloomy. Hannah didn't like the portrait, feeling it ruined the friendly atmosphere of Roscarrock.

Chapter 9

'Everything all right with Hannah?' Daniel asked Matt as he climbed aboard the *Sunrise* that same morning in clean overalls and jersey, with Fred and Curly Jose.

Matt looked at his red-headed workmate. 'Everything's all right between Hannah and me.' It was said like a challenge and Daniel answered in the same manner.

'Is that so?'

The two men hauled the nets off the foredeck and didn't speak again until the lugger had cleared the Runnel Stone buoy and was closing in on the Wolf Rock. A strong south-easterly wind roughened the surf and sent it beating and pounding on the base of the Wolf, throwing sheets of spray up its mighty column. The Atlantic was surging in on the starboard side and the boat was rolling heavily. It was going to be a hard night, and while it made Fred fear for his life it matched Matt and Daniel's sparring mood.

As they got ready to shoot the nets, Matt suddenly said above the din of the sea, 'Hannah took the job at Roscarrock.'

'What?' Daniel shouted, but not because he hadn't heard Matt.

'She moved in yesterday. I carried her things up there for her.'

'I hope she knows what she's doing,' Daniel muttered, then got on with his work. He felt cut to the quick that Hannah had done something so decisive without consulting him first, but of course he had stayed at Newlyn.

Rufus settled the watch and Daniel and Matt found themselves taking their two-hour rest together. The cabin stank of drying oilskins, remnants of fish, and Rufus's socks. Matt searched Fred's bunk in case Rufus had played one of his cruel tricks on Fred and left crab claws, dog ends or chewed food under the blanket for the nervous young fisherman to lie on. The bunk was clean. With mugs of tea and pilchard pies Mrs Penney had made for all the crew, he and Daniel sat crossed-legged on the bunks, eating, drinking, occasionally glancing at each other.

Finally Daniel said, 'Did she want to speak to me about it?'

'Yes.' Then the intense stare came into Matt's eyes. 'But she's got me to talk to now.'

'You're a possessive bugger, aren't you? It's up to Hannah who she speaks to.'

The subject was closed as far as Matt was concerned. He'd made his position clear and he would do anything necessary to pursue it. Finishing his pie, he brushed the crumbs off his jersey and lay back with his hands under his head. He didn't want to quarrel with Daniel; hostility on a working boat could be dangerous and there were times when a fisherman's life depended on his workmates' total concentration.

'Did you have a good weekend, Danny?'

Daniel grinned broadly. 'I did, one of the best.'

He felt again Viv's satin-soft skin, her firm untried body, revelling that his had been her first touch, her first time. He'd tried to repeat the delicious experience on Sunday but she'd refused to go upstairs or allow anything past kissing and cuddling. He shrugged his massive shoulders, leaving Matt to wonder why the dismissive movement went with what was obviously a sweet memory. If Viv was always ready and willing for him, Daniel mused, it wouldn't be long before she'd be talking of marriage and settling down. He'd try again though, she was far too tasty a peach to let slip too easily out of his grasp.

He gazed across at Matt. He was perfectly relaxed with his eyes closed. He looked peaceful and contented. The lugger rolled heavily and gave a sickening lurch before righting itself. Matt calmly put out a hand to stop himself being flung off the bunk. Daniel knew now that beneath that cool exterior lay a spirit as hard as rock – but rocks could be broken.

Leah Spargo was glad the menfolk were gone for another week. Life was much easier without them around, particularly her father and Josh who had inherited many of his bad traits. Both men were foul-mouthed and, as well as boasting about his conquests, Josh had a habit which disgusted Leah; peeping in on her as she dressed and undressed. It was a pity they couldn't take the old harridan, her grandmother, with them. Constance Spargo spent most of her waking day picking fault with everything she and Prim did.

Leah regretted not going to Sarah's house last week and saying goodbye to Hannah before she'd left to start her new life. Prim wasn't saying much but Naomi had told her that Hannah was still seeing Matt. Leah envied her fair-haired sister. Hannah had got away from Porthellis, to a place Leah would love to enter, and she had a handsome boy friend. Leah did not expect to be courted and fall in love. Who would want a girl with a scar on her face? Her family never stopped pointing out that a man might well take an interest in her if she would only steel herself to venture further than the washing line outside. Leah didn't believe their assertions that her long black hair and dainty figure made her attractive.

'Mooning around again, maid?' Constance said in a grumbling voice, coming up behind her as she stripped Josh's bed of sheets, which like most of the bed linen in Porthellis were made of flour bags stitched together. They were white now from the constant boiling but still retained the telltale lettering to mark their origin. 'You won't get the washing in the copper till midday at this rate.'

'Sorry, Gran. I'll do your room next.'

'Make sure you tuck my bed in properly this time. I hardly had a wink of sleep last night I was so uncomfortable. And my windowsill wants wiping and the chamber pot washing out.' They didn't. Constance's room was spotless because it was given the most attention.

'Yes, Gran.' Leah gave a hearty sigh of relief when her grandmother shuffled out of the room to pester her mother, taking her mouldy smell with her. 'Silly old bag,' she said under her breath. 'Should do it herself rather than moaning at me.' Then she took to wondering again what Hannah was doing at Roscarrock.

During the morning Janet Rouse walked up to Chapel Street with Miss Peters' new skirt.

'Come in, wipe your feet, shut home the door, pull fore a chair,' the tiny old lady said, fixing Janet with her fierce eyes. Her pure white hair was tied up in a bun on top of her head and a few white whiskers stood out on her sharp chin. No one could work out her exact age, only that she was past eighty and seemed to have been in the village for ever. 'Took your time finishing it. The maid said she was going to bring it to me at the end of last week.'

'I'm sorry, Miss Peters, but things got held up with Hannah leaving.' Janet thought she might as well mention her niece, she wouldn't get out of the little whitewashed cottage without being interrogated.

Miss Peters took the tweed skirt out of its wrappings and held it up against herself. After some humming and hawing she started peeling off her clothes to try it on. 'Some funny business, if you ask me,' she said, handing her long black cardigan to Janet. 'Hannah being asked to work up there. They've never had much to do with we down here and they haven't employed no one from the village for nigh on twenty year. Tell her to call on me when she comes home. I want to hear all about Roscarrock.'

'I will, Miss Peters,' Janet said, taking the old lady's cross-over pinny to add to the cardigan lying over her arm. 'I miss her already. It's so quiet with just the cat for company.'

'Course you miss her. You half reared her. Did a good job, by all accounts. I see she's kept the good sense to go on with Matt Penney. Wonder how long this fancy new job will last. Matt might want to put a ring on her finger.'

'I hope so,' Janet said, trying to hide her fears and worries for Hannah.

Miss Peters struggled out of her dress, refusing Janet's offer of help with the hooks at the back, adding indignantly, 'I've dressed myself for over eighty years!' She stood in her slippers and white flannelette petticoat, her long drawers peeping out at the bottom. She looked like a wizened old fairy and Janet turned her head to hide a smile.

Miss Peters put on the new skirt and smoothed it down over her hipless shape. She peered at her reflection in the shiny bottom of a copper frying pan hanging up by the fireside, then turned the skirt round to study the pleat at the back and looked at the hem. She nodded and Janet knew she was satisfied.

'How much?' Miss Peters asked curtly, her eyes straying somewhat menacingly to the table where the whip she always kept by her lay. She was as tough as old boots and people said the reason she had the whip wasn't so much to protect her diminutive self as to satisfy a natural mean streak.

'With the material, labour and trimmings, its four shillings and tuppence.'

'Will you take four shillings?'

Janet appeared thoughtful, a little game she always played with Miss Peters who liked to haggle over the price. She wouldn't be happy until at least a farthing was knocked off. 'Oh, very well, four shillings it is then, seeing as it's you.'

Miss Peters took off the skirt, got dressed again and fetched her purse from a cupboard. She counted out four shillings in sixpences and pennies and pressed them into Janet's hand. 'A job well done, Janet. I'll wear it next Sunday when I'm entertaining the visiting preacher to dinner and tea. Will 'ee stay for a cup of tea?'

Janet usually declined because she was busy, but without Hannah in the house it felt cold and empty, as if an early winter had spread its gloom through the rooms. 'I'd love one, Miss Peters.'

Mrs Opie expressed her approval of Hannah's appearance as she carried the breakfast tray with the morning post and newspapers into her bedroom. Hannah glanced at a photograph of a woman on the bedside cabinet; aged about forty, she was standing in front of a pyramid holding the reins of a camel.

'That's my late daughter, Stephanie,' Mrs Opie said sadly. 'She died last year in Egypt. I saw little of her over the years. She was always off somewhere exploring the world.'

'I'm sorry,' Hannah said.

'I mustn't be too sad, she had a good life.' As Mrs Opie ate her breakfast in bed, she asked Hannah to take certain clothes out of the wardrobe and chest of drawers and fetch a pair of shoes from the closet.

'Miss Benson used to do it for me,' she explained. 'It saves me having to be on my bad leg for too long.'

Hannah made a mistake with the dress but when the chosen ensemble for the day was ready for her, Mrs Opie climbed carefully out of bed and limped in her nightgown to an armchair by the window. She beckoned Hannah to join her, and sitting up very straight in a high-backed chair Hannah listened to her instructions for the day.

'Here you are, the tools of your office, so to speak.' Mrs Opie handed her a small bunch of keys.

'Thank you, Mrs Opie,' Hannah said, turning the keys over and over in her hands and feeling very important.

'You'll soon learn which key belongs to which door, although very few are locked. This being Monday it's laundry day. If you go to the linen room you can lay out the clean linen on the table for Angie. She'll change the beds and do the washing and ironing and carry it back to the linen room for you to put away later in the week. Miss Benson has kindly left instructions about which linen is used for which bedroom. When you've done that you can liaise with Mr Patrick in the kitchen who will tell you if anything needs to be ordered from the tradesmen for the pantry and so on. There is no telephone here, I've never felt the need to have one. Miss Benson used the servants' hall to write out the orders. You'll find stationery, pens and the addresses you'll need in one of the drawers in the dresser. Mr Patrick will see to it if the orders need posting but usually they are given to the delivery boys. Do you think you can manage that, Hannah?'

'I'm sure I can.' It sounded simple enough. With Angie Miller doing the hard labour, Hannah wondered if there was going to be enough work to keep her occupied each day.

Mrs Opie looked down on the gardens, basking already under a benevolent hot sun. 'It's a lovely day. I think I'll go outside for the morning. When you've finished, perhaps you'll come upstairs and help me down.'

'Certainly, Mrs Opie,' Hannah smiled, rising and putting the keys in her pocket. It seemed she had the run of the house. She'd enjoy trying out the keys. When no one was around perhaps she'd take a sly peek into Gregory Opie's study.

Patrick Opie told Hannah what groceries would be needed and when she had written to the butcher, the baker and the grocer she pinned the orders up on a board in the servants' hall to be handed to the tradesmen's delivery boys on the days they called at the house. The butcher's boy would come at midday today and Hannah made a mental note to be in the kitchen at the time. Miss Benson had made her job much easier by leaving details of all that was required in the house and their prices, plus a few helpful tips, such as, 'Watch the baker's boy, he's likely to nibble the goods. The garden shop tries to leave Mr Patrick's orders at the house; insist they are put in the shed.'

Mrs Opie took Hannah's arm for support as she came down the two flights of stairs and into the hall. Hannah thought she looked perfect in this setting, elegant and regal in a floral, georgette, two-piece dress topped with a matching cardigan, her head perfectly poised in a large picture hat.

'Now, my dear, will you be good enough to go to the cupboard at the side of the stairs. You'll find a garden chair, an easel, canvas, palette, brushes and paints. Carry them outside and leave them at the bottom of the steps. I'll choose a place to sit when I'm outside.'

Hannah was beginning to realise she would be at Mrs Opie's beck and call a lot but she didn't mind, it was a joy to be close to this gracious woman. The cupboard had a low door and Hannah found that if she lowered her head she could step inside it and straighten up; it was the size of a small room. All manner of things were stored in here. The painting equipment was in one corner. Mrs Opie waited in the hall as she trotted back and forth with it. Then she helped Mrs Opie down the stone steps.

Putting her well-manicured hand under her chin, Mrs Opie debated where to sit. 'On the lawn here in front of

the house I think, Hannah. In the shade of the oak tree.
I'd like to paint the house on such a glorious day.'

'Do you want a pot of water, Mrs Opie?' Hannah asked
when her mistress was settled and the painting equipment
set up.

Mrs Opie smiled at her. 'Bless you, but no, dear. I'm
painting in oils.'

Hannah blushed, feeling silly.

Mrs Opie was viewing her critically. 'You're such a
pretty girl, you have lovely eyes and hair and you hold
yourself so well. You'd make a good subject for canvas.'

Feeling this an honour, Hannah said, 'Thank you. Mr
Patrick told me that he likes to paint too.'

'You must be mistaken,' Mrs Opie said, sizing the house
with the wood of a brush. 'I'm the only one who paints
in this household. Now will you do just one more little
job for me? Fetch a glass and a jug of lemonade and the
little white table in the cupboard to put them on. Then
after all the running around I've made you do, you must
have a break and some refreshment. I'll go in at twelve
o'clock to get ready for luncheon, if you would be kind
enough to come for me then.'

There was a frown creasing Hannah's face as she went
off to get the lemonade and table. Patrick Opie had told
her on Hidden Beach that he painted and indeed was
planning to paint the beach.

Why had he lied?

Chapter 10

Hannah slipped quickly across the corridor from the bathroom to her room in her nightdress, smelling of lily of the valley and feeling pampered thanks to the toiletries Mrs Opie had provided for her. This was the third night she would climb into the big bed and she felt she was living in the lap of luxury. The food Patrick Opie cooked, which she and Angie Miller had at lunch and dinner, Hannah in the servants' hall and Angie eating after she had finished, was delicious. Many dishes, like smoked haddock soufflé and raspberry sorbet, she had never even heard of before. There seemed to be no end to Mrs Opie's kindness and Hannah felt a loyalty towards her as if she had worked at Roscarrock for years.

This morning, after she had re-sewn the hem of one of Patrick Opie's sheets, she'd asked Mrs Opie if she would mind if she put the sewing machine to her own use. Mrs Opie had replied that she could do as she liked with it, adding, 'If you make anything pretty, dear, I'd love to see it.' And when she took an afternoon tea tray into the drawing room, Mrs Opie asked her if she played cards.

'Yes, Mrs Opie, my Uncle Roy taught me many games

and I often played with him and my cousins, Jowan and Ned.'

'Would you care to play something with me later?'

'I'd love to,' and Mrs Opie had smiled at her eagerness. After dinner Hannah lifted the walnut card table across to the fireplace in the drawing room and unfolded the legs and top which had sections for counters cut away in the polished surface. They played rummy and seven-card whist until ten o'clock, winning an equal amount of games, then she helped Mrs Opie upstairs.

'Good night, Hannah,' Mrs Opie said at her door. 'I must teach you how to play bridge and perhaps when Mr Gregory returns home I'll talk him into playing with us and Mr Patrick.'

There hadn't been a minute when Hannah had been bored and she sat up against her pillows now and picked up the newspapers which the Opies had finished with. There were tasty snippets about the King and Mrs Wallis Simpson, and more serious news from Europe where Adolf Hitler's troops were continually on the move. Hannah preferred the gossip and fashion pages; she felt sheltered and too far away from the outside world to feel threatened.

As she put aside the *Telegraph* and picked up *The Times*, she heard a noise. She wasn't sure where it was coming from but it was definitely inside the house. The noise, like low thuds, stopped and she went back to her reading. There was a photographed report of a grand house in Sussex, several times bigger than Roscarrock, and she pulled the page out to put aside for Leah who was interested in that sort of thing. The noise came again. Hannah listened. It sounded like someone plodding along the corridor.

Getting out of bed, she put her ear to the door, wondering if Mrs Opie wanted her or was taking a walk to stretch her arthritic leg. Hannah knew her mistress sometimes walked round her rooms to keep the joint supple. There was a dull thump and fearful that Mrs Opie had fallen over, Hannah opened the door and peered outside. She could see no one in the gloom. Then came another noise, something she couldn't define. She crept along the corridor and listened outside Mrs Opie's rooms. She could hear her happily talking nonsense to Pogo; nothing was amiss with her. Hannah walked on and looked out of the window on the north side of the house. There was little to be seen except the tall trees swaying gauntly in the wind under the dark, cloudy, night sky. Hannah shivered and gooseflesh crept up her arms and back.

Turning tail, she sped back to her room on silent feet and closed the door. She got into bed and snuggled down under the covers to get warm. A moment later she smiled at herself. Before this she had been eager to see Daniel and tell him Roscarrock was quiet and peaceful. What would he say if he knew she had suddenly become spooked?

Patrick Opie kept imploring her to visit the walled garden and the following afternoon Hannah made her way there, full of anticipation. If the lawns and gardens he kept in immaculate condition were anything to go by, she was in for a treat. The large square red-brick garden was set a little distance from the house, its walls high and made of cob, their tops thatched. Hannah walked through the small built-in gardener's room first, another of Mr Patrick's domains, and was amazed to see the floor was a mosaic of pebbles and shells sunk in mortar. Two initials were scratched out in front of the opposite door, JJ – Jeremiah Jago, she presumed.

As she stepped through the door she found herself in another world, so different and so beautiful she held her breath, expecting fairies to flutter in front of her on tiny gauze wings and welcome her to their land. Against all four walls was a profusion of shrubs and flowers of every variety and a carnival of colour: carnations, dahlias, roses, lavender, deutzias, heather, sweetpeas on cane supports, clematis scaling two of the walls. Hannah tiptoed along the red-brick paths separating the beds, breathing in the heady scents, keeping company with the bees busy about their work making a friendly drone.

In the centre of the garden was the bubble fountain Mr Patrick had told her he'd built himself from scratch. Hannah could see why he was proud of it. It was spectacular, the silver-clear water spouting five feet in the air, spraying outwards and down over the pebbles set in mortar at the bottom. The kitchen garden was at the furthest corner with a wheel herb garden, the 'spokes' separated by red-brick walks to give easy access for gathering. The scent of the herbs under the warm sun was as powerful as the flowers. There was also a fruit garden of strawberry beds and raspberry, blackberry, loganberry, greengage, blackcurrant and redcurrant bushes, and the biggest rhubarb she had ever seen.

Patrick Opie, wearing earthy old clothes and his battered gardening straw hat, was hard at work in the kitchen garden. Hannah approached him quietly because he was talking out loud. He was laying shallots out on the ground.

'There you are, my beauties, you've done me proud this year. We'll have the finest pickled onions this winter, and I'll earn a shilling or two in the local shops to help pay my keep. You'll dry out nicely today, the sun's just right, not too hot for you. I've got your nets all ready to hang you up in the shed. When I've finished with you I shall earth up the celery again then pick some penny royal and thyme for the kitchen.'

Hannah interrupted his monologue by gently clearing her throat.

Patrick Opie swivelled his head round on his long neck. 'Ah, Miss Spargo, how kind of you to come.' He stood up, quite unconscious that he had been overheard talking to the shallots. 'Got your sunhat on, good, good, must take care of your lovely complexion.'

'The garden is more beautiful than I imagined, Mr Patrick,' she said, and saw his eyes light up with pleasure.

'I'm so glad you think so. Now,' he rubbed at his unruly moustache, 'what shall I show you first? Ah, yes, I know, the Victorian beds. You'll love them, I'm sure.'

He led the way to the long beds situated against the south wall. 'These are what I call my Victorian selection. You see? I have polyanthus, sunflowers, lilies, poppies, moss roses, stocks, speedwell, rockets, pinks, valerian, lupins, mignonettes.'

'They are beautiful. You've obviously put a lot of hard work into the garden,' Hannah congratulated him and breathed in the mixture of intoxicating scents.

'It's a labour of love. Everything was terribly overgrown when I first came here to live five years ago, after my wife died.'

She looked at him curiously; she would never have taken him as a once married man.

'I'm grateful to Great-Aunt Feena for allowing me to do it. I had nothing left, you see, when I came back to England from Africa, no wife, no home, no money.' Suddenly realising he had given away a lot of personal information, Patrick Opie turned as scarlet as the poppies. 'O-dear me, I've never told anyone that before. I trust you will be discreet, Miss Spargo.'

'You have my word, Mr Patrick,' she answered in solemn tones, and his confidence in her made the feeling that she belonged here at Roscarrock grow. Her grandmother, too, had said she belonged here, Hannah thought, putting it aside to rest in her heart, not caring what the old woman had meant.

'Well, then, yes, what was I saying? How would you like to pick some everlasting flowers for me? Then perhaps you'd like to tie them in bunches and hang them upside down in the shed.'

Half an hour later he joined her in the large wooden shed which was built outside the walled garden on its south-facing side. 'Don't be afraid to tie the twine fairly tightly,' he said. 'The stems won't break. It's cool, dry and airy in here, they'll dry out nicely.'

'You have everything in order, Mr Patrick,' she observed, nodding at the neat rows of tools on the walls.

'It's the best way to work, so I've found,' he smiled, making the rounded cheeks in his peculiarly ugly face puff out like a hamster's. He took a bunch of flowers from her and hung it up high over their heads on a hook.

Hannah gazed upwards. 'They're so pretty, I love their texture which looks brittle yet is so strong.'

'Be careful, Hannah,' Patrick Opie wagged a mock warning finger. 'If you get a feel for gardening you could end up becoming a fanatic like me.'

Hannah knew it was time to wash and change and get back to her indoor duties, but there was something Mr

Patrick might be able to tell her. 'Mr Patrick, you know a lot about the history of Roscarrock. Would you happen to know if the initials in the gardener's room floor belong to Jeremiah Jago?'

'Ah, old Jago, who wails and moans on nights bearing a full moon and other occasions. He was gardener here in the eighteenth century and died in seventeen eighty-six. Apparently he was a handsome fellow, a favourite of the lady of the manor house and she paid for a headstone for him.'

'Do you know why he haunts the place?'

'Mr Gregory found some writing about him in an old journal in the library. It seems he was involved in smuggling and used to hide the contraband about the property, such as in the stables. He used to creep along the tunnel—'

'You mean there's a tunnel leading from Roscarrock?' Hannah squealed, letting her youthful exuberance get the better of her.

'Oh, yes, a secret tunnel, no less. It was built during the civil war to hide treasure and gold from Cromwell's troops.'

'Where is it?' she asked excitedly.

'I'm afraid my great-aunt had it blocked up for safety's sake years ago. It came out halfway down the cliff. One had to climb the rest of the way down to the beach, a precarious journey, by all accounts. Anyway, as I was saying, Jeremiah Jago brought contraband up the tunnel to sell later when the coast was clear. One night he quarrelled with one of the smugglers who suspected him of cheating him of his share of the ill-gotten gains and followed him to his living quarters. There was a violent fight which spilled over on to the lawn in front of the house and both were killed, the smuggler of a broken neck when he was hurled against the oak tree, Jeremiah two days later of a ruptured spleen, so he vents his spleen up on the cliffs, you might say.'

'So there is truth in the old rumours, although it was always thought in the village that one of the Bodinnicks killed him,' Hannah said thoughtfully. 'No wonder people say the big house is haunted.'

'It is,' Patrick said matter-of-factly, putting a drop of oil on a pair of shears.

'What?' Hannah returned in a small voice, remembering the footsteps she had heard last night.

'Oh, nothing to be alarmed about, it's only rumours.'

'But you said—'

'Must get on, lots to do,' Patrick Opie said cheerfully, ending the conversation.

Chapter 11

On Saturday afternoon Viv Hickey went down to the north pier at Newlyn and searched for the *Sunrise* amongst the rows of moored luggers. After the intimacy she had shared with Daniel last week, her adoration for him making her overlook the fact that he had more or less forced himself on her, she had taken it for granted he would come to see her at the boarding house. When there was no sign of him by four o'clock, she decided to look for him.

She was dressed in her best outfit, which was third-hand but not as shabby as the rest of her clothes, and she had left off her hat to display the combs Daniel had given her. As she tried to read the names of the boats, she wished her mother had not kept her away from school so often to work in the boarding house. She felt conspicuous wandering about the harbour; few women went there, and those that did were usually morally loose. She only had a rough idea what the Kittow lugger looked like.

Mitch Spargo had just left the *Misty* and was watching her. He tidied his dark hair with his fingers, straightened his jersey, threw back his broad shoulders and went up to her.

'Hello, are you looking for someone?'

'Yes, the *Sunrise*,' she replied, not paying him much attention.

'You've passed it. It's two rows back, the boat nearest the pier.'

'Silly me,' Viv coloured, hoping this man whom she recognised as one of Daniel's acquaintances did not realise she could not read. She gave her attention to two young gulls fighting over a titbit a few yards away.

'Are you looking for someone in particular?' Mitch asked, putting his foot up on an iron mooring cleat, hoping to keep her talking.

'Yes, Daniel Kittow. Do you know where he is?'

'He's gone home for the weekend.'

'Oh.' Her face dropped.

Mitch's hopes rose. He was greatly attracted to Viv Hickey. With Daniel out of the way, he might just stand a chance.

'He wanted to check over his cottage, make sure all's well. I've heard you singing in the Crown,' he went on. 'You've got a lovely voice. I really enjoy listening to you. I'm Mitch Spargo. I live in Porthellis too but as I've no wife or girl friend there I usually stay over at Newlyn for the weekend. I believe your name's Viv.'

'That's right,' she said tightly, turning back towards the town, her head downcast. Now she had at least another week to wait before seeing Daniel again. She realised Mitch Spargo was walking at her side.

'Did Daniel leave a message for me with you?'

'No, nothing.' Mitch plucked up his courage. 'I was thinking, would you like to—'

'I have to get on,' Viv said sharply, in no mood for company or conversation, certainly not another man's approaches. 'Thanks for the information.'

Mitch stood alone and dejected on the pier but told himself he must take a leaf out of Matt's book and not give up on a woman he was interested in. No doubt Viv would sing in the pub tonight and she might let him walk her home.

Hannah had Saturday afternoon off and was on her way home, eager to impart all the news of her first week at Roscarrock. Daniel was waiting for her at the top of Porthkilt Hill. She waved to him and speeded up her steps. He tossed his cigarette away and ran to her, lifted her high in the air, swung her round and round then let her fall giddily into his arms. They were both laughing with sheer delight.

He kissed her cheeks again and again, finally planting a firm kiss on her lips.

'Goodness,' she laughed breathlessly, hugging him, 'what a greeting. Oh, Danny, I've had such a wonderful week. I've got lots to tell you.'

'First tell me if you missed me.' He gazed deeply into her sparkling blue eyes.

'Of course I did. I always miss you when you're away.'

Putting his arm round her, he held her close as they started down the hill. 'I couldn't believe it when I heard you'd taken the job. So you like it at Roscarrock then?'

'It's such a beautiful place, Danny. It's not at all creepy – well, just a tiny little bit, but there's nothing to be afraid of. The Opies and Angie Miller, the maid, are very kind to me. I feel as if I've worked there for ages. Did Matt tell you I'd taken the job? How is he?'

'All right, I s'pose,' Daniel said, looking her up and down and seeing the lovely young woman his workmate and partner had fallen for. 'Was a moody bugger most of the week. Can't make him out some of the time.'

'Matt was moody? I wonder why. He was in very good spirits the last time I saw him.'

'Never mind him. Tell me all about Roscarrock.'

Hannah filled him in on everything from the size of the rooms and their contents, her own room, Mrs Opie's wonderful clothes and her painting – omitting Patrick Opie's lie – to the week's delicious menus, the ominous looking picture beside Gregory Opie's study and Mr Patrick's beautiful gardens.

'You have to call him Mr Patrick?' Daniel exclaimed. 'It's archaic.'

'It sounds friendlier than Mr Opie and that would be confusing when Gregory Opie comes home,' she said, keeping her eyes on Daniel. She had looked forward to the familiar sights and smells of the village again, the bark house, bakehouse, carpenter's shop, net machines and the sea at close quarters but she was so taken up with Daniel she didn't notice them at all.

'Well, it sounds like paradise up there. I'm glad for you, Hannah. You deserve it.' He kissed her cheek again. 'Hope it makes your old man happy too. So you haven't met the third Opie yet?'

'No, but I soon will. Mrs Opie is expecting him down from Oxford any day now. He's been researching for a stage play there. I hope he's as nice as she and Mr Patrick are.'

'He can't fail to like you, me girl.' Daniel hugged her.

They had reached the houses fronting the quay and Hannah started forward at seeing Janet, Roy, Jowan and Ned outside the house waiting for her, but Daniel kept her in his grip. Matt was with them.

Janet left the group and pulled her niece away from

Daniel. Unperturbed, Hannah kissed Janet's warm cheek. Janet took off her glasses and wiped them on her apron, a sign that she was displeased, then she glared at Daniel.

He grinned broadly. 'I'll see you later, Hannah.'

'She'll be busy all weekend,' Janet snorted, propelling Hannah towards the menfolk.

Hannah knew she had made a mistake, forgetting Matt would be here to meet her, but she ignored the niggle of guilt and kissed her uncle and two cousins, then gave Matt a lingering embrace. He crushed her to him and his lips were persistent on hers.

'Well, then, let's not stand out here giving the village something to talk about. Get inside and I'll make the tea,' Janet declared.

When they were all sitting round the kitchen table, Hannah repeated everything she had told Daniel, ending by telling Janet that Mrs Opie had said she could use the sewing machine to continue her previous work.

'That's very kind of her, I'm sure, but you've got enough to do,' Janet said importantly. Hannah could tell that despite her misgivings her aunt was proud of her new position and that she was getting on so well; if she could soothe Prim's feelings about it, her happiness would be complete.

'But I've got plenty of free time, Aunty,' Hannah assured her. 'I'm not exactly rushed off my feet and I bet you've got more work than you can manage.'

'In that case I'll sort out something to take back with you. Well, I'm sure Matt doesn't want to sit in here all day. There's two hours till teatime. Why don't the pair of you go for a walk or something?'

Although Matt hadn't taken his eyes off Hannah, he had said very little. They made their way up towards the cliff path and he didn't take her hand until they were tramping the narrow path out of sight of the village.

'Where do you want to go?' he asked quietly.

'How about Hidden Beach? You can just about see it from certain windows in the big house.' She squeezed his hand to show she was glad to be with him. 'Did you have a good week, Matt?'

'Not bad.'

'When are you going to work on your allotment?'

'This evening, after I've seen you back to Roscarrock. Why?'

'Just wondering. You'd love the gardens at Roscarrock, Matt, especially the walled garden. When I've been there a bit longer I could ask Mr Patrick if you can look over them. I'm sure he wouldn't mind. He's so proud of all he's done. Would you like to?'

'Yes, anything that would bring me closer to you.'

Matt held back the gorse bushes that hid the way to the beach so she could slip past them and they walked without speaking on to the dark golden sand. Three small children were playing on the shore and after waving to the couple they went back to their game. Matt led the way to the rocks and sat down with his back against them.

Hannah knelt down in front of him. 'Matt, you're difficult to hold a conversation with today. Is anything wrong? Danny said you were moody all week.'

He reached forward and pulled her into his arms, speaking over her lips. 'I don't like seeing you close to him like that and I don't like you talking to him about me. Actually I haven't been moody, he's just a damned troublemaker.'

'Danny is not!' she protested, struggling to free herself. 'You're just jealous.'

'Too damned right I'm jealous,' he said angrily. 'You're my girl. That's agreed by both of us, remember? Would you like it if you saw me armed up with another woman for all the village to gawp at?'

'No, I suppose not.'

She turned her head to the shore and was relieved that the children, probably annoyed they hadn't got the beach to themselves any more, had gone. The tension went out of Matt's hands and he held her gently. No longer his prisoner, Hannah allowed her body to sink against his. 'I don't like it when you get so intense, Matt.'

'Sorry, darling, but it was hard wanting to be with you so much. You may have had a good week but it dragged like a year to me. Then seeing you like that . . .'

'I'm sorry, Matt.'

They kissed and Hannah felt his hands sliding over her, caressing her, then as he nestled his mouth hungrily in her neck, one hand crept over her breast. She pushed it away and put her burning cheek to his chest. He cuddled her tightly and didn't try to get familiar again.

Hannah had been too absorbed to think much about Matt in the last week but she considered her relationship with him now. They had only spent a few hours together during their three-week courtship but Hannah felt she was beginning to sift through his unreadable exterior. He could be moody, there was no mistaking that, but she didn't really mind. A thrill shot through her when she realised he could probably be every bit as ruthless as Daniel and she knew that under his apparent calmness, his passions ran as high as the seas.

She looked at him. He smiled and squeezed her possessively. Hannah was beset with mixed emotions. She wanted to continue as his girl friend and she wanted to stay close friends with Daniel, feeling she had the right to do so, but if she tried to have both, there would inevitably be friction.

Daniel was up on the cliffs further upcoast that afternoon. He was looking down on Gorran Haven, a fishing village famous for crabbing. A man who did not bear the stamp of a fisherman scrambled up to meet him. Both men looked furtively about then the man, small, pale and foxlike, passed Daniel a fat parcel which he put inside the canvas bag slung over his shoulder.

'My cut?' Daniel asked, lighting a cigarette and offering the man the packet of Player's Weights.

'A good haul this time, thirty-five quid.' The man took a cigarette and lit it off Daniel's.

'Fine,' Daniel handed the man an envelope. 'I'm glad to hear things are so good at St Austell.'

The man stuffed the envelope in his jacket pocket without looking in it. He trusted Daniel not to cheat him. 'You sure it's safe?'

'Yeah, I pass on goods from all over, my contact's good. I'll shift this as soon as I get the chance,' Daniel blew smoke in the air, his face grim, 'but no one would dare go through my things on the boat.'

'Nice doing business with you. I'll be in touch.' And the foxy little man took himself off down the cliff and into a waiting van.

Leah Spargo made a rare appearance in chapel that Sunday. The desire to see Hannah had overcome her fear of being seen out with her scarred face. Hiding under a large brown felt hat, she sat at the back. When the service was over, she made a beeline for Hannah who, snatching a few words with Prim, had not realised she was there, but Leah was waylaid by the Reverend David Skewes who good-naturedly admonished her for her poor attendance. When she managed to wriggle free from him, Hannah was walking up the hill with Matt and Mrs Penney for dinner.

'Hannah, wait for me,' Leah shouted, hanging on to her hat.

'Leah!' Hannah's heart went out to her little sister, remembering how she had shouted to her and the children in Rufus Kittow's tosher to stop for her and Edwin ten years ago. She pulled her arm from Matt's and ran down the hill towards her. She hugged Leah and they both started talking at once.

'I hear you like it at Roscarrock.'

'You must come up and see me. I'm allowed to have family visits. You'll love the house and Mrs Opie's dear little dog. I've got a lovely room and we could have tea there together.'

'Leah!' The shout echoed furiously over the cove. 'What're you wasting your time talking to that bitch for? Get home at once.' It was their father.

Hannah choked down a painful gulp and Leah turned tail and ran. Matt stormed towards Jeff Spargo and did not stop despite his mother calling after him. Hannah, Mrs Penney and others who were in the vicinity watched horrified as Matt clutched Jeff by the collar and rammed him against the wall of a house.

'You may not want her as your daughter, Spargo, but she's my girl. Make one more remark like that and I'll spread your bloody rotten face all over Porthellis.'

'Stop it, Matt!' Hannah shouted.

'Matt, leave him be,' Mrs Penney appealed in a wail.

'It's Sunday. Remember where you've just come from.'

Jeff wasn't strong enough to push Matt off him but he spat in his face. Enraged, Matt shook him and slammed his head against the wall. It was John Jacobs, Lizzie's husband, who intervened.

'He's not worth it, Matt. He may hate Hannah but everyone in Porthellis despises him for it, including his own family, all except his spiteful mother.' John pulled on Matt's stranglehold. 'Come on now, leave him go like your mother and Hannah said.'

Matt conceded to the quiet argument. He let Jeff go with a violent shove and the older man fell to the ground. Matt wiped the spittle off his face and walked to Hannah who was as pale as sea foam. She turned on shaky legs and walked on with Mrs Penney. By this time Leah had scurried all the way home and had shut herself in her room.

Hannah was quiet as Matt walked her back to Roscarrock in the evening.

'Don't stay angry with me, Hannah,' Matt appealed as they closed in on the gateway of the big house. 'We won't see each other all week and it's unlucky with me going to sea.' He looked about for some iron to touch to ward off bad luck.

'I didn't know you could be like that,' she muttered, adding another passion to the list she'd made on the beach. She took his arm at last.

'Like what, for goodness sake? I was only standing up for you.' He sounded genuinely surprised.

'There was no need to be violent.'

'Violent?' He was amazed. 'Huh! I bet you wouldn't have minded if Daniel had smacked your old man against that wall.'

'That's not true, although I'd have expected it more of him than you. Did you hit my father the day before the pilchard drive started? I noticed his face was bruised.'

'No, I did not.' He stopped walking and took her by the shoulders. 'Do you want Jeff Spargo to go on calling you vile names for the rest of your life? Well, I don't. Asking him to stop wouldn't do any good and the only thing he understands is what I did to him. I can't stand anyone hurting you, Hannah. I'd never hit a woman and he hits your mother, don't forget. What do you think poor Leah's had to put up with for the rest of the day? And just for speaking to you.'

'I just don't—'

'For goodness sake, the man's a bastard!' Matt was getting exasperated.

Hannah was furious. 'If you're going to swear and shout at me, Matt Penney, you can leave me here. I don't want you to walk on any further.'

Matt's heart sank. He knew he had gone too far. Jeff Spargo was still her father.

Sighing, he dropped his arms. 'I'm sorry, I didn't mean to upset you, Hannah. I'll see you next week.'

Hannah accepted a goodbye kiss from him but there was no warm reciprocation on her part.

Chapter 12

Hannah took her next afternoons off on Wednesday and Friday. She wanted to avoid another confrontation with her father, and she thought it might be best if she saw less of Matt. His possessiveness was beginning to make her feel uncomfortable. Janet and Prim weren't pleased, accusing her of playing with Matt's feelings, but it gave her more time to see Sarah, Naomi and Lizzie. On the Friday, Sarah rounded up the young women to meet at her house. Hannah was delighted that Leah came too.

'Did Father gave you a hard time last Sunday?' Hannah asked her.

'He said he'd thrash me if I ever spoke to you again,' Leah replied, wincing at the memory of the tongue-lashing, pitted with obscene language, she'd received from Jeff. She hadn't told anyone he'd smacked her face three times.

'Well, he can't do anything when he's out at sea,' Sarah said brightly, passing round the teapot and a plate of scones. 'We can enjoy ourselves now.'

They plied Hannah with questions about Roscarrock and she happily gave them every detail. 'I particularly like the nursery. It's style is late Victorian, so Mr Patrick told me, and there's furniture, crockery and cutlery small enough for children to use, including a dear little rocking chair. There are even tiny ornaments on the mantelpiece. The cradle has rockers and there's a matching one for dolls, and a rocking horse on wheels and a Noah's ark which they'd love to have in Sunday School. I like the doll's house best, it has miniature furniture just like in the house and Victorian dressed dolls.'

'I'd love to see it,' Leah said dreamily.

Hannah was telling them the true tale of Jeremiah Jago's death when Lizzie suddenly sprang up with even more energy than usual and, white as a sheet, pushed her youngest stepchild into Hannah's arms and rushed outside.

Sarah and Naomi exchanged knowing glances.

'What's the matter with Lizzie?' Hannah asked. 'I didn't scare her, did I?'

'She's running to the closet. John Jacobs has fathered another,' Sarah said, reaching out to stop his two eldest children from tearing round her spotless kitchen.

'Oh, I see. When's it going to be your turn, Sarah?'

'Arch and I are working on it,' she answered with a mischievous glint in her dark Spargo eyes.

Leah had gone quiet. She felt she would never be able to join in talk about husbands and babies. Hannah noticed her melancholy.

'Have you thought any more about coming up to Roscarrock, Leah?'

'I-I'd love to but how can I get away?' she said in a panicky voice. 'Grandmother will tell Father and Mother doesn't want any of us to go there.'

'Don't keep making excuses, Leah. You can say you're here with me,' Sarah said stoutly. 'Grandma rarely ventures across the bridge, she and Mother will never know. And it'll do you good.'

'Go on, Leah,' Naomi urged. 'You know you'll love it and it will be worth the risk. You'll never get a better chance to see inside the big house.'

Leah looked at her sisters' expectant faces. 'I'll think about it,' she promised, not wanting to be the centre of attention.

Lizzie came back from the lavatory clutching her stomach. 'Ohhh, how long does this sickness go on for?'

'As long as you're capable of childbearing,' Naomi said wryly, nursing her son at her breast. 'Look at how many of us Mother had.'

Lizzie rolled her eyes. 'Don't say that,' she groaned, making the others laugh.

'When's Mitch coming home?' Hannah asked. 'I haven't seen him for ages.'

'He's taken a fancy to a girl at Newlyn, so Josh said,' Leah informed her.

'Really? Looks like he'll be the next one to settle down then.'

'What about you and Matt?' Sarah asked in a forthright manner. 'You're some lucky maid to land he.'

Hannah disappointed her sisters and cousin. 'I've got no plans to marry yet.'

Hannah got back to Roscarrock at six o'clock. A fierce wind was thrashing through the trees and dark clouds were forming overhead and she managed to get inside the house just before a heavy shower of rain. The vestibule and hallway were dark and gloomy, the atmosphere heavy and stuffy. She felt a tiny prickle of apprehension. As she passed the portrait of the stern-faced medieval man, she tried not to look at it, but as always her eyes drifted that way. He looked sullen in the dusky light.

There was a sound on the stairs and turning her head Hannah made to bid Patrick Opie a good evening.

But it wasn't Patrick Opie. It was a much taller man, younger, leanly built with short blond hair. It was the ghost of the man in the portrait and he was coming straight at her.

Hannah shrieked and clamped her hands over her mouth. She tried to back away but her legs wouldn't move, she was petrified with fear.

He came closer and closer until he was standing inches away from her. Hannah thought her pounding heart would explode inside her.

'What's the matter with you?' the man said tersely. Strangely, there seemed to be a look of shock on his face too.

A ghost that talked. What could Hannah say to him? Please don't hurt me, ran through her mind.

'Well?' the ghost demanded haughtily. When still she did not speak, he went on in the same vein, 'Are you Hannah Spargo? My grandmother's new housekeeper?'

Grandmother? The terrible truth dawned on Hannah and she wished the floor would open up and swallow her. The ghost – the man – was Gregory Opie.

Taking her hands from her face, she stammered, 'I-I'm s-sorry. I th-thought you were a ghost.'

'A ghost?' He sounded scathing. 'A ghost of whom?'

With a tremulous finger she pointed at the portrait. 'Him,' she squeaked, never feeling more foolish in all her life. 'You look just like him.'

Gregory Opie made an impatient face. 'That *is* me.'

'Oh!'

'I was in a university drama,' he explained as if she was

the stupidest person on earth. 'My grandmother thought the costume suited me and talked me into sitting for her. It was years ago.'

Now she had the chance to study him, Hannah could see he was a few years older than in the painting, in his mid-twenties, and she realised he was wearing smart but casual modern clothes.

With a great effort she spoke normally. 'I'm sorry, Mr Opie. Yes, I am Hannah Spargo.'

'I'm glad we've settled that.' He held out his hand and clasped hers in a firm handshake. 'I'm going to my study. I don't wish to be disturbed until dinner, understand?'

'Yes, sir,' she answered feebly, feeling like a gauche schoolgirl.

Rushing upstairs to her room she leaned her back heavily against the door. She didn't know whether to laugh or cry. One thing was certain, putting aside his intolerant manner, and the fact that he was younger and rather better looking than she'd expected, she had taken an instant dislike to Gregory Opie.

She heard three tinkles of Mrs Opie's bell and hastily tidying her appearance in the cheval mirror hurried to her mistress's rooms.

'Hannah, my dear,' Mrs Opie began from her seat at her desk, 'Good heavens! Are you well? You look as if you have a fever.' She beckoned Hannah closer.

'I've just had a very embarrassing moment, Mrs Opie,' Hannah said, and she told her about meeting her grandson.

Feena Opie gave a hearty laugh. She took Hannah's hand. 'Dear me, I bet Mr Gregory didn't know what to make of you. I'd love to have witnessed it, he can be quite pompous at times – it comes from mixing with academics.

You would have seen his motorcar outside the house but I insist he parks it round at the back. Don't worry, my dear, he'll spend most of his time shut away inside his study.'

Hannah was pleased to be reminded of that.

Mrs Opie glanced out of the window; the rain was hammering against the panes like hailstones. 'I'll get Mr Patrick to take Pogo for his walk this evening. I'm not having you going out in that.'

Hannah would have said she didn't mind, that she'd never found even the harshest weather a bother to her, but she had learned that although Mrs Opie was very kind, when she had made up her mind she never changed it. Pogo heard the word 'walk' and sprang off his chair and performed an excited little dance at Hannah's feet. She picked him up and stroked his silky white coat.

'Angie's just brought me up some tea. Would you like some, Hannah?'

'Yes, please.'

Mrs Opie led the way to the other side of the room, overlooking the front of the house, where a tray had been put on a small round table. There were two teacups on it. Hannah put Pogo down on a cushion in the window seat.

'What sort of afternoon did you have?' Mrs Opie asked, pouring the tea.

Hannah was always delighted that her employer seemed to take a genuine interest in her. 'I spent it at my sister Sarah's house. My sisters Naomi and Leah joined us and my cousin Lizzie.'

'Naomi's the one with the baby, isn't she? It must be nice having a large family even though you lived with your aunt. What does Leah do? Has she got employment?'

'No, she stays at home and helps Mother with the housework. She's very shy and rarely goes out.'

'Oh, why is that?'

'Her face was scarred in an accident as a child. It's made her feel ugly and ashamed, which is a pity because she's quite pretty and she has no reason to feel any blame.'

Mrs Opie was gazing steadily at Hannah and asked carefully, 'Blamed for what, Hannah?'

Hannah looked down at her lap. It was difficult to talk even now after all these years, but she felt able to confide in Mrs Opie. 'There was an accident, it wasn't anyone's fault really, a group of us children went out in a boat, it tipped up and . . . and my little brother and one of the girls were drowned. My father blamed me . . . and he turned me out. That's why I lived at my aunty's.'

'That doesn't seem at all fair. Why did he take such a hard line with you?'

'He's always hated me . . .' Hannah coloured, but Mrs Opie might as well know the truth. She hoped it wouldn't change her position here. 'I'm not his daughter, you see. That's why I'm fair and my brothers and sisters are dark.'

Getting up, Mrs Opie put her hands gently on Hannah's shoulders. 'I'm sorry, my dear, it must have been painful for you talking about it.' She brushed a tress of hair away from Hannah's face. 'Never mind, you've got a new life here now and I hope you'll always be happy. If there's anything I can do for you, Hannah, please don't hesitate to ask.'

Hannah felt a surge of emotion and for the first time in years tears fell from her eyes. She felt she'd had a weighty burden lifted from her. For a moment she could have put her head on Mrs Opie's shoulder. 'It's very kind of you,' she sniffed.

Resuming her seat, Mrs Opie said with a sunny smile, 'Occasionally when he's here, when we can drag him out of his study, Mr Patrick and I eat together with Mr Gregory. How would you like to join us for luncheon on Sunday?'

'Well, I . . . I . . .' Hannah was at a loss. It was not usual for a servant to eat with the family and she felt the invitation was a great honour. It would mean she wouldn't see Matt until the afternoon, but that was no bad thing, she decided.

'Do say yes. Mr Patrick is so very fond of you and he'd be delighted to have you taste his roast lamb and mint jelly. You can send word to your aunt not to expect you till later via one of the delivery boys.'

The words were out of her mouth before she knew it. 'I'd love to, thank you, Mrs Opie.'

When Hannah went back to her own room, Feena Opie returned to her desk. She lifted a journal out from under her stationery and opened it at the place where she had last written, last Sunday evening: '*Hannah enjoys her days off but is always eager to come back.*' She drew a careful pencil line under the entry then taking her silver fountain pen filled in the day's date underneath it, and wrote in large flowing letters: '*Jeff Spargo has a lot to answer for and I'll make sure he does.*'

The *Sunrise* had a tremendous catch on Monday night. The news quickly spread round Newlyn and the quay was soon crowded with people – ship's chandlers, rope makers, innkeepers, the odd housewife – come to watch the landing; a couple of holidaymakers eagerly taking photographs were squeezed out of the way. Dozens of gulls with alert greedy eyes jostled for position up on the market roof. Four 'slingers', old retired fishermen, were employed by the crew to help count the pilchards into maunds, the two-handled, close-woven baskets which were slung down from the long quayside by the foreman.

Viv Hickey heard about it from one of the boarders. Wilfred was out so she stole to the quay too; she knew there was no chance of a word with Daniel but if he saw her he might give her a wink or quick wave and she'd know if she was still special to him. Mitch was one of those watching and he opened up a conversation with her.

'Be all day, they will, with a catch that size,' he said loudly over the screeching of the excited gulls.

'It's one of the biggest seen here for a long time,' she answered, hoping that Daniel had left a message with him for her today.

'Time they finish they'll only have an hour to get their heads down.'

'Yes, I suppose so,' she murmured miserably. She had been aching to know exactly what she meant to the powerfully built, red-haired fisherman and was jealous to see hers weren't the only female eyes lingering on him.

'Could I take you for a cup of tea?' Mitch ventured, crossing his fingers behind his back.

Viv considered it for a few moments. Mitch Spargo might be able to tell her about Daniel's life at Porthellis, whether he had a girl there, but if Daniel saw her going off with him he might get the wrong idea.

'No, I'd better get back to work.' To keep Mitch friendly, she added pleasantly, 'But if you want a meal in Newlyn any time, I cook dinner and tea for a shilling at the boarding house up Trewarveneth Street. Just let me know.'

She left after one last sad look at Daniel's straining back.

Mitch thrust out his chest, content that he seemed to be getting somewhere with Viv at last.

Onlookers moved on and were replaced by others until fifteen wagon loads, over three hundred maunds, were carried away to be salted in vats; a lot of the fish would be sold on the Continent, with two hundred of every ten thousand fish given to the merchant. At a pound a thousand, the hard night's labour made ninety pounds, a very handsome sum. Congratulations abounded but the *Sunrise*'s crew would keep their celebrating until the weekend – if their luck held.

Even Daniel's muscles were aching by this time, but the deck had to be scrubbed down with chloride of lime to kill off green algae and the cabin cleaned, and he did this with Fred while Matt had the easier job of slipping ashore to replenish the food store. Rufus repaired shark holes in the net and Curly saw to the all-important job of tending the engines and fetching fuel and fresh water. The first man to finish would start cooking a meal.

The next night's fortune went the other way and the maund of fish they caught did not even cover their expenses. Daniel was bitterly disappointed but it gave him time to take his package to Wilfred Hickey and make a good sum of money that way. He could tell by Viv's shining face she was pleased to see him and he hoped Wilfred, who was lounging by the hearth in his stockinged feet, would soon send her out of the room on some pretext so he could hand over the goods burning a hole in his allowance bag. Wilfred would then leave at once to see his contact and Daniel would have plenty of time to talk Viv into making the short journey upstairs with him to her room; he even had a plausible excuse ready.

Viv had to answer a knock at the front door and when she came back Daniel was alone. 'Where's Dad gone?' she asked.

'Had to see someone, he said.'

'Got a card game, I expect, the lazy swine,' she said grimly. Wilfred didn't work and the boarding house made only a small profit but he was usually in funds through his fast hand at the card tables – so Viv believed.

'Come here, Viv,' Daniel said with an engaging smile from his chair at the table.

Taking off her apron, Viv stood shyly in front of him. He lifted her slight form onto his lap and caressed her hair with gentle fingertips.

'Seems like an eternity since we've been together,' he said.

'I've missed you terribly, Danny,' she breathed, hugging his neck. 'Will you have to go home this weekend?'

'That rather depends on you,' he kissed the tip of her nose. 'On how welcome you make me feel.' His voice had dropped to a husky tone and he sought her lips and kissed her deeply. Then he took something out of his trouser pocket. 'This is for you, sweetheart.'

'Another present?' Her hazel eyes widened in amazement.

'I don't want you to open it here, someone might come in. It's private and personal and special just between us.'

'Let's go out for a walk then.'

'I need some sleep, darling. I've got another hard night in front of me.'

Doubt flickered through her mind. 'There's only my room.'

'You can open it up there, then perhaps you'll let me

sleep for an hour on your bed and wake me up with a cup of tea, eh?'

It sounded innocent enough.

She was absolutely thrilled with her present, a paste brooch in the shape of a fish. It was to remind her of him when he couldn't be with her, Daniel said meaningfully.

It was nearly an hour later, with burning cheeks and a sense of shame mingling with the hope in her tender heart, that Viv left her room and Daniel settled down to sleep.

Chapter 13

Hannah kept out of Gregory Opie's way until the Sunday luncheon. The few times their paths crossed he hardly spoke, seeming preoccupied; Mr Patrick told her he was writing a play for the London stage. She wondered if he was naturally unfriendly, had appalling manners or simply considered her beneath his notice.

She helped Angie lay the dining room table and carry the hot dishes up from the kitchen.

'What do you think of me eating in here, Angie?' She felt guilty that Angie hadn't been invited to eat as well and didn't want the maid-of-all-work to think she was getting above her station.

Angie looked vacant for a moment. 'I think 'tis a honour for 'ee, miss, but I wouldn't like t'eat at same table as Mr Greg'ry.'

'Oh, why not?'

'He d'have some terrible temper when he's roused. Shouts like billy'o.'

'Thanks for telling me.' Hannah wished she hadn't asked. She was very nervous as she took her place at the table.

She had taken great care with her appearance, wearing a dress she had made herself modelled on one of Mrs

Opie's, with a square yoke and buttons on the short sleeves. She tied a turquoise floral silk scarf round her neck. She was wearing the only jewellery she owned, a string of black beads and a dainty gilt bracelet Janet had given her on her last birthday, and had put on a little make-up and arranged her hair on the crown of her head.

'My word,' Mr Patrick's eyes twinkled the instant they fell on her. 'You look absolutely charming, doesn't she, Gregory?'

Greg Opie twisted his head round from the sideboard where he was opening a bottle of red wine. He eyed Hannah up and down in a way that made her feel uneasy, it was a distinctly male gaze, the way Daniel looked when he was carnally interested in a woman. 'Very pretty,' he said blandly, turning away, but she thought the disinterest in his voice was forced.

The men were formally dressed in suits, although Mr Patrick's was old-fashioned and crumpled, and Mrs Opie wore a flowing silk day dress and pearls. She fascinated Hannah with talk of her youth spent among famous actors, actresses and leading socialites in London. 'I seem to have turned into something of a country bumpkin since I was widowed,' she laughed. 'It would be good to see some of my old friends again.'

Hannah wondered why she didn't invite them here but thought such a question too presumptuous.

Mr Patrick rabbited on about his tomatoes and planting the winter greens. No one listened but he didn't seem to notice.

Greg Opie stared at Hannah throughout the meal. 'Have you lived in Porthellis all your life, Hannah?' he asked the instant the first course was served.

'Yes,' she replied, wishing he wouldn't speak to her

178

because she wanted to concentrate on putting the food into her mouth and chewing it properly.

'Your father is a fisherman, I take it, or is involved in the industry?'

'He's a fisherman.' She nearly choked on a mouthful of wine.

During the roast lamb, as he topped up her wine glass, he said, 'What made you decide to take the job here?'

She was becoming more and more embarrassed by his probings. 'I-I thought it would be a good opportunity for me.'

Greg eyed his grandmother who dropped her eyes for a moment. 'I've been teaching Hannah to play bridge, Greg,' she said. 'Perhaps we could have a game later.'

'Not today,' he said gruffly. 'I'm too busy.'

Hannah thought he had finished his inquisition but as she put the last spoonful of chocolate dessert in her mouth, he said forcefully, 'I must congratulate you, Hannah. You've fitted in here very well.'

'Oh, do stop, Greg,' Mrs Opie said impatiently, throwing her napkin down. 'Leave Hannah alone. You're verging on bad manners.'

'Sorry, Grandma Fee,' he replied. He did not apologise to Hannah, even though the unappeased look on his grandmother's face suggested she thought he ought to.

'Shall we take coffee in the drawing room, Hannah?' she said. Patrick rushed to pull back her chair. 'We'll leave the men to finish the wine.'

Greg stood up as Hannah followed Mrs Opie's example, his sharp grey eyes once more rooted on her face. Hannah was offended.

When the women had left the room, Greg told his cousin to shut the door.

'I want to get on,' Patrick protested, wringing his hands. 'Got lots to do.'

'Sit down a minute. I want to say something.'

Patrick was too civil to consider arguing. He sat down next to Greg as the younger man helped himself to the last of the wine.

'Did Grandmother advertise the position of house-keeper, Pat?'

'No, she'd heard about Hannah for some reason and asked me to approach her and offer her the position. It was a devil of a job to arrange it, I can tell you.' Patrick frowned. 'Don't you like Hannah?'

'That's not the point,' Greg said impatiently. 'Doesn't she remind you of someone?'

'No.' Patrick scratched his head vaguely, as if it would conjure up the memory Greg was implying he should have. 'Can't say she does. Who do you think she looks like?'

'Oh, no one,' and Greg clammed up. Patrick had something of a runaway tongue and on reflection probably couldn't be trusted to keep mum about what was going through Greg's mind. When Patrick had left, Greg let the wine get warm between the palms of his hands as he thought about Hannah. Even though he spent most of his time in his study he had noticed his grandmother called constantly for her company, to accompany her round the grounds, to listen to the wireless or have cosy little discussions.

Through the window Greg saw Hannah taking Pogo for a walk. He confronted his grandmother in the drawing room. His face was alive with eager questions but before he could open his mouth, she said assertively, 'Don't ask me, Greg. I'm not prepared to say a word for now.'

He went to the study and rooted about in the cupboards until he came across what he was looking for, some photograph albums. He searched through them until he came to pictures of two young people, a brother and sister standing in front of the house. The man was his father who had been killed with his mother in a boating accident when he was a boy. The woman was his late Aunt Stephanie, an unmarried adventuress. It had nearly broken his grandmother's heart when she had died. Hannah Spargo bore a striking resemblance to her.

Matt spent the afternoon in his allotment, half-heartedly hoeing and weeding the neat rows of vegetables. He looked down sullenly at the empty spaces where his mother had pulled salad vegetables, praying that he wasn't going to be left with an empty heart. He was certain Hannah had changed her afternoon off and hadn't put in an appearance so far today to avoid him because she was still angry about his threats to Jeff Spargo.

Matt's feelings for Hannah had deepened and he loved her with a passion that astonished even him, but he knew things had moved too fast for her and he cursed himself for letting his hands stray over her on Hidden Beach. Hannah was a decent woman and she also had an independent streak which would bolt at being tied down too soon. He would have to cool his ardour, in every way, if he was going to keep her.

He toiled on, sweating under the hot sun, until finally he gave in to exhaustion and sat on the ground with his back against a wheelbarrow, fearing Hannah wouldn't come down to the village at all today.

Hannah was actually on her way to see him, going over in her mind how she was going to tell him she wanted to end their present relationship, that she wanted some time and space to sort out her feelings for him. Living and working at Roscarrock had altered the natural course of their courtship; she didn't think about him or miss him as much as she thought she ought to and his forwardness and over-possessiveness was making her feel trapped. And his venom towards her father alarmed her.

His head was bowed over his knees when she arrived at his side. 'Your mother told me you were up here. She asked me to give you this.' She held out a bottle of Coca-Cola, keeping an expressionless face.

'Thank you, Hannah,' he said softly, shading his eyes with his hand, 'You've saved my life.'

'Your mother also asked me to tell you not to work so hard.' She didn't have the courage to plunge in with her speech until he gave her an opening. 'I've heard about the good week you had, except for Tuesday night.'

Hannah did not seem at all concerned about him personally and Matt's heart was heavy. He swigged a mouthful of Coca-Cola, letting it cool his parched throat. He'd have to box clever or he'd be out in the cold. 'I think Mother's right. I've worn myself out. How are the gardens at Roscarrock? Does Mr Patrick let you help him?'

Hannah was surprised Matt hadn't got up and tried to kiss her and she was taken aback by his question. 'Um, no, he only lets me put crumbs on the bird table.'

'You must be getting used to living there now. You've done a good job dispelling the rumours. The children are no longer afraid with you there and they don't play "taking a peep" any more; it's got no glamour now. It's easy to see you enjoy your new life.'

'I do. I've met Gregory Opie now.'

'What's he like then? As nice as the others?'

'He's horrible,' Hannah said, happy to chat about her favourite topic, Roscarrock and the people who lived there. She sat down beside Matt. 'He's got terrible manners and I think he's an arrogant snob. I'm glad he doesn't live there all the time.'

'I don't expect he'll stay stuck away down here for long. Must miss his friends – university types, I expect. I was going to college or university once.' He'd try to get her interested in a different aspect of himself.

'Of course, you went to grammar school. Why didn't you go on with your education?'

'For three different reasons. My father asked me to look after Mother just before he died and I didn't like to leave her. I had no strong ambition and felt I wouldn't fit into an academic world. And, the main reason, the call of the sea was too strong for me to ignore.'

'I know what you mean. I couldn't bear not to be near the sea for even a whole day.' Hannah cast her eyes on the sea; it was flat calm with a glassy surface at the moment, hiding its ever-present dangers. When it was rough she 'concentrated' to bring the men safely home. She turned to Matt and explained why she had not seen him earlier today.

'You mean you ate in the dining room with the family?' he exclaimed, sounding suitably impressed. 'All posh with napkins and wine? Weren't you nervous?'

'I was quite nervous. I only had a few sips of wine, I was afraid it would go to my head. It was delicious and so was the food. Mr Patrick made roast lamb with honey spread over it and a lovely mint jelly.'

'You'll have to tell Mother how to cook it.' He was testing her mood with him.

'Yes,' Hannah agreed, unable to bring herself to tell

him what was on her mind. 'Are you going to carry on working here?'

'No, I've had enough,' he said, getting to his feet. 'I'll come back this evening and water the plants when the sun's gone down.' He didn't want her to feel pressurised but he could not suddenly refrain from being good-mannered. Offering his earthy hand to help her up, he gave hers a small affectionate squeeze and then let it go.

'Matt, I haven't seen much of Aunty Janet today. I'll have to have tea with her.'

He nodded. Her restrained manner told him that if he protested he'd end up regretting it. 'Mother's expecting me. I'd better get cleaned up. I'm feeling very tired. After tea I think I'll have a lie-down. I'll see you next weekend, then?'

He couldn't hide the hope in his voice or on his face. It made him seem vulnerable and Hannah felt a huge surge of warmth for him. She smiled and nodded.

Matt felt he had to risk kissing her. He didn't want them to fall into a casual relationship like the one she had with Daniel. He held out his arms and bent his head. Hannah did not move but when his lips touched hers they responded as if they had a will of their own. There was something about Matt's kisses she found hard to resist.

They walked down through the village, arm in arm, more polite than close, but it fooled all who saw them. Matt left Hannah at the Rouses' house with a peck on the cheek and a fond farewell. She told him to be careful at sea, afraid if she didn't something terrible would happen to him.

Chapter 14

For the next few weeks Hannah's life fell into a comfortable pattern. Sometimes she took Saturday afternoon off, other times she didn't. She continued her private chats with Daniel and valued his friendship more than ever; he was very attentive and took everything she said and did seriously. She knew Matt didn't like it but he did not object. He sat next to her at chapel, they occasionally had meals in each other's homes, they went for walks. They talked, but of nothing personal; they kissed but not passionately. Matt had brought up the subject of borrowing his uncle's car to go to the pictures but she had sidestepped the issue. Hannah couldn't work out how she really felt about him; part of her hoped his feelings for her would peter out and he would put an end to their courtship himself.

''Tis time you stopped seeing Daniel Kittow,' Prim would grumble when they were gathered at Janet or Sarah's house, and she would refuse to eat the cakes and buns Hannah bought at the bakehouse with her wages. 'The man's no good. He won't make no woman a decent husband, he's up to his neck in fishy things and I don't mean what he pulls out of the sea. He don't do nothing openly. He was seen recently skulking up on the cliffs with a man called Ken Blee from St Austell who's been to prison for thieving, it was in the papers. It's not fair on Matt. He's a fool to let you go on like it.' And her mother always ended with a plea to her to leave Roscarrock.

'I wish you'd tell me what you have against the place, Mum,' Hannah said each time. 'If you would only give me a good reason then perhaps I'd think about it.'

Prim's eyes would fill with tears and all she'd add was another plea that Hannah be careful, saying ominously that Hannah might find two of the Opies friendly, but they were only friendly to *her*. It bothered Hannah, and so did Daniel's mixing with shady characters, but she put it to the back of her mind.

The villagers took it for granted that she and Matt were a couple and occasionally she had to ward off questions about an engagement.

'When are you going to make the announcement?' Miss Peters asked as with many others they decorated the chapel for Harvest Festival.

'You asked me that at the Sunday School anniversary tea party,' Hannah replied, making to escape up a ladder to put a couple of mackerel in the nets the caretaker had draped over the gallery.

'And you never answered me then,' Miss Peters huffed indignantly. 'Leave they fish. Let the men do it. 'Tisn't ladylike climbing about putting your drawers on display. Help me put these apples round the vegetables in the windows.'

Sighing in resignation, Hannah handed the fish to the Sunday School superintendent and took the basket of pollies – sweet yellow apples – from Miss Peters. The formidable old woman led the way to a window at the back of the chapel.

Hannah took a long satisfying sniff of the air. 'Doesn't it smell wonderful in here with all the fruit and vegetables?'

'Don't change the subject.' Miss Peters skilfully placed the apples in a pleasing display with the red and green ones already arranged beside two huge marrows. 'Well, when are you getting married?'

'We haven't talked about it,' Hannah whispered because the ears of two women arranging vases of russet, golden and red chrysanthemums at a nearby table were wagging.

'Why not?'

'We just haven't.'

Miss Peters stared at her for so long Hannah felt she could read her deepest thoughts. 'I don't know what else you want out of life, Hannah Spargo. You may like it at Roscarrock, but let me tell you this, there's nothing more worth having for you than Matt Penney. I hope one day you'll see it, for your own sake.'

When she wasn't either sewing for Janet or looking over the gardens with Patrick Opie, Hannah spent much of her free time wandering through the small woods which were teeming with wildlife. She saw moths and butterflies, crows, pigeons and a woodpecker, scurrying insects on the mossy floor, a creamy coloured stoat and rabbits by the dozen and once she was treated to the rare sight in daylight of an old badger whose quiet, ambling character reminded her of Mr Patrick.

She was beginning to re-establish the overgrown path running through the woods to the cliff which towered seventy feet above the sea, Hidden Beach and Porthellis.

She'd tried many times to find the blocked up entrance of the tunnel Patrick Opie had mentioned, but with no success. She assumed it must be overgrown with grass, ferns, gorse or hawthorn. She gave up looking for it and instead would pick a spot to sit and watch everything below. She couldn't make out who all the small figures down in the village were but guessed it was from here that Patrick Opie had spied the beach through his telescope and chanced upon her going there the day he'd offered her the job. She decided to save up for some binoculars.

One sunny day Mrs Opie told her to put on her best hat because Mr Gregory was going to take them to St Austell in his motorcar. Hannah sat on the thick upholstered back seat in the year-old, four-door, black and cream Railton saloon beside Mrs Opie and listened as Mrs Opie and Mr Gregory chatted. They obviously had a great affection for each other but Hannah hadn't grown to like him and was dismayed to learn he was going to be at Roscarrock until after Christmas. He seemed to take little interest in her and she knew she had been wrong to fear he was going to bother her in the way gentlemen sometimes did their female staff, but there were occasions she caught him staring at her, as if he was trying to work out something puzzling.

Greg pushed his grandmother through St Austell's streets in her wheelchair, heading first for a bookshop. As he looked at volumes with unpronounceable names, Mrs Opie bought a copy of an epic novel that was sweeping the country and America. Hannah was astonished and delighted when Mrs Opie presented it to her over tea that evening. She read *Gone With The Wind* quickly, enjoying every word of the tempestuous Southern beauty Scarlett

O'Hara's troubled life and adventures in the American Civil War. She left it with Sarah to pass on secretly to Leah and was waiting to hear if her shy younger sister had enjoyed it.

When Angie Miller was taken poorly with a stomach upset and took to her bed for the first time in five years, Hannah climbed up to the servants' quarters with a glass and jug of fresh water to see how she was faring. Hannah had not been up here before; she'd wanted to, but had felt she would be trespassing on Angie who was even shyer than Leah.

The short landing branched off to left and right, presumably for male and female servants, and Hannah wasn't sure where to find Angie's room. She tried left, tapping on the first door and opening it slowly. It was an empty room, more spacious than Hannah had imagined a servant's room would be, with two bare iron bedsteads and some furniture, of better quality than she and her sisters had shared at Cliffside Cottage. The ceiling sloped sharply and there were huge black beams running across the floor. The other two rooms were also empty and Hannah walked across the landing. On the side of the landing facing the front of the house a small door opened on to the roof. Beside it was a window which gave a marvellous view of the sea. She tried the attic door but it was locked. The next room was a bathroom, small and basic but a luxury to anyone who did not have one at home.

She found Angie in the last room on this side of the landing. As Hannah entered, she sat up in bed in a flannelette nightdress buttoned up to her neck, her hair covered in a black hairnet. She looked very ill but she managed a shy grin. 'Sorry about this, miss.'

'Don't be silly, Angie,' Hannah said kindly, stepping over the black beams that ran across this room too and setting the jug down on the small square nightstand by the bed. 'You can't help being ill. You must have plenty of rest and recover properly before trying to get out of bed.'

'But I was going to do the ironing this afternoon.'

'I will do that,' Hannah said firmly. 'Could you take a drink of water? It's the best way to help the germs pass through you.'

Hannah filled the glass and Angie took a few sips before falling back with a reeling head on the pillows.

'Thank you, miss,' she said when her head had cleared. 'I keep running to the toilet but at least I've stopped being sick.'

'That's good,' Hannah said, wondering how servants had managed in the past before the bathroom had been fitted on this floor.

'You've got it lovely in here, Angie,' she added, looking round the room. Colourful hessian mats covered the bare boards and there were pictures of country scenes and Bible texts on the wall. A few cheap plaster ornaments were dotted about and wooden-framed photographs rested on a large oak chest of drawers. There was also a wardrobe and a built-in cupboard with butterfly hinges. Hannah hoped Angie wouldn't feel it an intrusion as she studied the old brown photos of various groups of people. 'Are these your family?'

'They're all me family, they lived at Portscatho. My dad was a fisherman, he drowned when his boat sunk in a storm just before I came here. My mum died two year later, she weren't never very strong and 'twas thought she never got over Dad's death. My brother Tommy died of cancer soon after and my aunty and uncle moved upcountry. I got no one left now.'

'I'm sorry, Angie,' Hannah said, thinking how lucky she was having so many in her family, even if two hated her.

'Aw, don't you go being sorry for me, miss. I'm happy just so long as I can stay here.'

'Well, I'm sure Mrs Opie could never do without you, Angie,' Hannah smiled. 'Now I'd better leave you to get some rest. I'll check on you in a couple of hours.'

As she got to the door, Angie said, 'Miss?'

'Yes, Angie?'

'You aren't going to leave here soon, are you?'

'No. What makes you think that?'

Angie blushed, adding to her high colour. 'I thought p'raps you might go and get married. You have a young man, I know, and the butcher's boy said he's some good-looking and you're really smitten with him. I-I don't want you to go yet.'

'Don't worry, Angie,' Hannah smiled in reassurance. 'If I do get married it won't be for a very long time.'

After that, Hannah couldn't get Matt out of her mind, no matter how hard she tried.

Towards the end of September the pilchards moved out towards the Isles of Scilly and while many of the fleets returned to their home ports, the Porthellis luggers joined the hardy Mevagissey fishermen to chase the fish. The drive would last one more week then the boats would come home to prepare for the dogfish season. The fishermen would be at home during the day but out most of the night then; they got up at three in the morning to go hunting for dogfish.

Leah knew that when the boats came home at the end of the week she'd have no chance to go to Roscarrock for a very long time. She'd told herself she would go there the second week Hannah had left to live in, but each time she'd come near to setting out along the narrow lanes that hadn't seen her feet since childhood, she'd convinced herself with a good argument why she should not. She was upstairs in her bedroom, sitting and dreaming. Constance scorned her need to be alone for long periods, calling it unnatural, but Leah found a measure of peace and contentment in her own little world where she could pretend she had a perfect face and a man like Rhett Butler from *Gone With The Wind* would one day come and sweep her off her feet. It helped her forget her recurring nightmare of Eileen Gunn's remains rising up from the seabed to get her and it helped her forget her guilt that if she hadn't insisted on squeezing herself and Edwin into the boat it might have stayed upright, he and Eileen would still be here today and Hannah would not have been thrown out of her home.

She had read *Gone With The Wind* again and again and felt guilty about keeping it so long. It was hidden under old toys in the bottom of the wardrobe and Leah knew she ought to sneak it out of the house and take it to Sarah's. At the weekend her father had either been too tired to care what she was doing or spent most of his time at the pub, but if he saw the book he would tear it up, and there was always the possibility her grandmother's snooping might uncover it. It was Thursday afternoon and Hannah had taken her afternoon off yesterday, so she would be at Roscarrock now. Constance was snoozing in her chair and Prim was out; this could be her last chance to smuggle the book out of the house.

Taking the book out of the wardrobe, still in its paper bag, she hid it under her cardigan. Stealthily descending the stairs, pulling her over-sized hat down firmly over her head, she slipped out the front door, careful not to let it bang in the wind. She was over the bridge in a trice, and as usual ignored everyone who greeted her, not wanting to look them in the face, until she reached Sarah's cosy little house in River Street.

Sarah was not at home. Everything was neat and tidy, no cooking utensils or flour on the table to say she had taken bread or pies to the bakehouse, nothing to give a clue as to where she had gone. Leah waited half an hour. She considered leaving the book on the table, but she couldn't risk her mother popping in and discovering it; Prim would be upset that Hannah was receiving gifts from the lady whose name she refused to have mentioned in the house. It wasn't like her to bear malice but Leah understood how hard it had been for her, first to have had Hannah fostered by Aunty Janet and now to have another woman housing her and showering her with kindness.

Leah thought about leaving the book in a drawer for Sarah to find but that seemed such a cowardly and ungrateful thing to do. She could take it to Roscarrock, of course, but she baulked at the thought. She ran the flat of her hand over the paper bag. Scarlett O'Hara wouldn't have been scared to be seen if she had been scarred all over her body; she would have gone anywhere, any time she wanted. Inspired by the book's heroine, Leah hid the book in her cardigan again, took a last look out of the window to see if Sarah was on her way home, then left the house to start up the village hill.

When she had passed all the shops and houses and turned into the lane, she relaxed and enjoyed the exercise.

The further she walked between the blackberried hedges, the more a sense of freedom overtook her and she realised she had been living in a prison of her own making. And she felt excited. She was going to see Roscarrock close up at last; more than that, she was going to see inside it. Hannah must have felt this way when she'd made the journey for the interview.

A partridge suddenly flew out of the hedge letting out its loud grating 'kirr-ic' call. Leah watched with startled eyes as the brown and chestnut bird disappeared over the opposite hedge of Hemmick Farm. 'You frightened me out of my wits, stupid bird,' she breathed, her hand pressed against her hammering heart. But it hadn't frightened her enough to send her scurrying home.

Leah arrived at the gateway of Roscarrock and took the book out of her cardigan; no need for secrecy now and it gave her a ready excuse if she was challenged as to why she was here. Butterflies formed in her tummy and she told herself not to be nervous. There were only five people at Roscarrock, one was her sister and one a simple maid. She walked on, but her steps slowed, stopped, started again, and repeated the pattern. She was arguing with herself. Mrs Opie might have said Hannah's family were welcome but perhaps Hannah was supposed to make arrangements with the lady first. Hannah hadn't said so though. Leah was horribly aware of the clothes she was wearing. Her dress was old and faded, cardigan stretched hopelessly out of shape, shoes flat and scuffed. Her long black hair was flowing free and tangled by the wind. Leah never bothered about her appearance. Would Hannah be ashamed of her?

The moment she got a full view of the house, all her misgivings were overridden by the desire to look around inside it. She sped on, taking in the magnificent gardens, the green of the trees and shrubs changing to rich yellows, reds and browns with the approaching autumn, marvelling at the height and girth of the oak trees on the lawn, looking in wonder at the house itself. It didn't seem creepy or bleak, but grand and majestic.

She took the narrower path that branched off round to the back of the house but suddenly Hannah was tearing down the front steps towards her.

'Leah! You came after all! Oh, I'm so glad.' Hannah grabbed and kissed her in a bear hug.

'Careful,' she protested, afraid Hannah's exuberance would alert one of the Opies to her presence. 'You'll bend the book. I've brought it back.'

Hannah didn't seem to hear. Hauling Leah along by the arm, she trilled, 'Come inside. You won't believe what you'll see.'

'Shouldn't I go in by the back door?' Leah asked doubtfully.

'No, I never do unless I've got muddy feet.'

Linking her arm through her younger sister's, Hannah pulled her through the door, then tilted Leah's hat back from her face. 'Well, what do you think?'

Leah's mouth was wide open but she was speechless. Hannah let her go and watched as Leah's eyes, underneath her big round glasses, travelled from floor to ceiling and up the first flight of stairs. Leah crept forward and gingerly touched an upholstered armchair. 'Fancy actually sitting on something like this.'

'See that painting?' Hannah said, pointing at the wall. 'That's Mr Gregory, the man I thought was a ghost.'

'Is he in there?' Leah whispered in awe, knowing from

Hannah's tales that the study was next to this particular painting.

'Yes, but he rarely comes out until mealtimes.'

'Will you get into trouble with me being here, Hannah? Am I stopping you from working?'

'I was just going to water the house plants. You can come with me and I'll show you over the house at the same time. Then I'm going to take Pogo for a walk and you'll be able to see more of the gardens.'

'Won't they mind? The Opies?'

'Not at all,' Hannah smiled confidently. 'As long as we don't go near their private quarters.'

'You are lucky, Hannah,' Leah said as Hannah led the way down to the kitchen to fetch water. 'I wish I could work here.'

Hannah started on the upstairs' plants so Leah could see her room first. 'We'll take tea up here later.' She put on a high-faluting voice. 'Like two grand ladies.'

'Aw, you're some lucky,' Leah repeated, fingering the soft silky bedcover wistfully. She only had coarse blankets at home and because her father had sold the ones on the other bed in her room, she still had to lay her coat over the bed in winter to keep warm. At the basin she smelled the lily-of-the-valley soap.

'I've got plenty,' Hannah said. 'I'll give you a bar to take home.'

'Better not, Dad or Gran would smell it and there'd be hell to pay.'

As they walked down the corridor to water the plants in the north window, Leah tapped Hannah's arm and whispered, 'Do you still hear those ghostly footsteps at night?'

'Yes, now and again, but I daren't leave my room to

see what they might be with Mr Gregory sleeping in the room next to the bathroom. I'm afraid he might see me.'

There was the tinkling of a bell. Leah drew in her breath. 'What's that?'

Hannah pointed to the door that led to her employer's suite of rooms. 'It's Mrs Opie ringing for me. You go back downstairs and wait for me in the drawing room, that's the door opposite the study. I don't expect she'll keep me long.'

'I don't know,' Leah muttered worriedly. 'Perhaps I'd better go.'

'Don't do that, you'll be all right. Mr Patrick won't come in from the garden for hours and Angie is up in her room. Go on, I'll join you shortly.'

Leah obeyed, still full of doubt. Hannah went in to Mrs Opie. She was in the sitting room, painting a still life of fruit and cheese on a cheeseboard.

'Did I hear you talking to someone, Hannah?' she asked, mixing colours on the palette and filling in a grape.

'Yes, it's my younger sister Leah. It's all right for her to be here, isn't it? It's not stopping my work.'

'Of course it's all right, dear.' Mrs Opie smiled graciously. 'You may take some time off and catch up later if you like. Bring a tea tray in here. I'd like to meet Leah.'

Hannah hesitated.

Mrs Opie raised a curved eyebrow. 'Is something wrong?'

'I hope you don't think me rude or ungrateful, Mrs Opie, but the thing is, Leah is terribly shy.'

'Of course, the scar. Well, never mind, perhaps another time. She may call any time she likes.'

Hannah thanked her and hastened down the stairs to

tell Leah that Mrs Opie had invited her to take tea with her.

Feena Opie set aside her paintbrush and smiled with satisfaction. She'd had no idea who the shabbily dressed girl walking up the drive was until she'd looked up at the house and Feena had seen her resemblance to Jeff Spargo. She had Hannah. With a little time and trouble, she'd take a daughter away from Jeff Spargo that he wanted.

Leah looked around the drawing room with childish delight, standing in the middle of the carpet, too afraid to touch anything; simply being here among the many beautiful things was enough. The grand piano captured most of her attention. The shiny wood was decorated with medallions depicting mythical creatures she'd seen in a book at school, the stool was gilt-edged and had curved legs. Clutching her hands in front of her, she went up to it. She took off her glasses for a closer look. What would the piano sound like? A heavenly choir, she thought. It inspired her to hum the hymn 'All Things Bright and Beautiful'.

'Who are you?' a voice said at the door.

Leah nearly leapt out of her skin. She spun round guiltily. A tall, fair-haired man stood with his hands on his hips, gazing at her intently. It was Hannah's 'ghost'. 'I . . . I didn't touch it.'

'I didn't say you did,' Greg Opie replied, coming closer. 'I asked you who you are.'

Leah backed away, turning her face in fear he would see her scar. 'I'm . . . Leah Spargo, Hannah's sister . . . It's all right for me to be here . . .' she got out in halting tones. 'Mrs Opie said Hannah could have family visit her.'

Greg Opie advanced on her like a bird of prey. 'Keep

still, I'm not going to eat you. So you're Hannah's sister? How interesting. Take off your hat, you don't need it indoors.'

It didn't occur to Leah that she didn't have to obey him; he had made her feel like an intruder and she found him intimidating. She pulled off the hat and held it tightly in both hands with her glasses, keeping her face turned. He was right in front of her. She couldn't retreat any further because her back was against a sofa. Greg crooked his head to see her face and she dropped her chin.

'Why are you afraid to look at me?' he demanded.

Leah was on the verge of tears. 'I . . . I want to go.'

'Don't be silly. I've told you I'm not going to eat you and I'm sorry I startled you. You were looking at the piano. Do you play?'

'N-no, sir,' and Leah briefly gave him eye contact. He was grinning and she felt foolish. He put out his hand.

'I'm Greg Opie. Pleased to meet you, Miss Leah Spargo.'

Leah thought she would die. She had never shaken the hand of anyone more important than the minister before. Timidly she put her hand in his. His grip was firm, smooth and cool.

'We're introduced now so it's all right to look at me,' he said.

Leah knew she couldn't keep her head down. Slowly she raised her chin and, with her face crimson, braced herself for the expected expression of horror as he saw her scar. He seemed to devour her every feature, but he kept smiling.

'You and Hannah are both pretty but you're not at all alike.'

Leah stared at him. Pretty! Did he call me pretty?

'Has Hannah been showing you over the house?'

'Yes, but Mrs Opie rang for her,' Leah answered with a little more confidence.

'Is there anything in particular you'd like to see?'

'Yes,' Leah admitted. 'A chandelier.'

Greg pointed to the ceiling. 'Up there, the lighting.'

Leah gazed up, utterly awestruck. 'It's more beautiful than the stars,' she breathed.

'Well, I think the Almighty might argue about that but they are rather splendid.'

Hannah entered the room and was surprised to see her sister and Greg Opie looking up, Leah with her head bare, glasses off, black hair cascading like a waterfall down her back, seemingly quite at home. Greg saw her first.

'Hannah, I was looking for you or Angie to make me some coffee when I heard someone in here. I'm pleased to have made your charming sister's acquaintance.'

'I'll make the coffee for you, Mr Gregory,' Hannah said, wondering what he could have said to Leah to put her at her ease.

'Five minutes then,' he said, and after a small smile at Leah he left the two girls alone.

'I've never seen anything as wonderful, as beautiful, as gorgeous in all my life as the drawing room,' Leah enthused as she sat on a stool at the kitchen table and watched Hannah making tea and coffee. And she had something to boast about for the first time in years. 'He called me charming.'

'I know,' Hannah smiled. 'I've never heard him compliment anyone before, not even Mr Patrick on his cooking.'

'And,' Leah said dramatically to get Hannah's attention again, 'he called me pretty.'

'Did he?' Hannah said, wondering with a niggle of worry why Greg Opie had said that. Putting some cream biscuits on a plate, she went on emphatically, 'Well, you are pretty. You've been told often enough.'

Leah ran her finger down her right cheek. 'He didn't seem to notice my scar.'

'That's because it hardly shows. You've been told that often enough too. It's just a thin white mark.'

'Oh, Hannah,' Leah said with all her heart. 'I wish I could work here.'

'Well, you never know, perhaps Mrs Opie will decide she needs more servants one day.'

Leah put her chin in her hands and fell into a daydream about just that.

Upstairs, Mrs Opie was thinking about the very same thing.

Chapter 15

There was a strong south-easterly gale the first Sunday of October and although the wind dropped the next day the sea was riding too high to go out safely for the second week's dogfishing. Daniel used it to his advantage to go up to Roscarrock. He had bought Hannah a birthday present and he didn't want to wait until she took time off. He approached Roscarrock over the back fields and stood under the swaying trees behind the house, hoping to catch sight of her.

A few minutes earlier there had been a fierce shower of rain and his coat was dripping wet, but although there was still a drizzle, the wind allowed a watery sun occasionally to blink through the dark clouds. Daniel's gamble paid off; a short time later he heard Hannah's voice as she came round the back of the house under a large black umbrella with a small white dog on a lead.

'Mind the puddles, Pogo, you won't like getting your little paws wet,' she said in a cooing voice.

'Fancy talking to the silly little creature like that,' Daniel said as he stepped out from the trees.

'Ohh!' Hannah tilted back the umbrella, her face white. 'Danny, you nearly frightened the life out of me. What are you doing here?'

'I've come to wish you happy birthday,' he laughed. Pogo yapped and snapped round his feet. Daniel picked him up and stroked his head. Pogo's aggression vanished and he licked Daniel's chin.

Hannah frowned at him and glanced around to see if they were being watched. 'You didn't have to make a special journey. I'm down in the village tomorrow afternoon.'

'Can't fish in this weather, me girl, so I thought I might as well come up here and give you your present.' He was looking at her admiringly. 'What have you done to yourself? You look beautiful.'

'Thank you.' Hannah turned her head from side to side. Her blonde hair was gently waved from the parting to her shoulders. 'Mrs Opie's having her hair styled today, she has a hairdresser call at the house. It was a lovely surprise when she said I was having my hair done first as a birthday treat.'

'You look good enough to eat.' And he licked his lips as if he meant it literally. 'Is there somewhere quiet we can go so I can give you my present?'

'We could go in the stable. Pogo can run about in there to get his exercise.'

Inside the stable, which was whitewashed and empty except for some bales of straw and a few pieces of horses' tack on the walls, Hannah let Pogo off the lead and he trotted about to sniff the surroundings. Daniel sat down on a bale and beckoned Hannah to sit beside her. He took a prettily wrapped parcel out of his pocket and put it in her hands.

She looked at him and smiled. 'Thank you, Danny. It's very thoughtful of you.'

'I hope you like it, I took a long time choosing it.

Twenty-one years is a special birthday.'

Hannah unwrapped the parcel and was amazed to see it contained a sheer, pure silk white nightdress. It had shoestring straps and a low cutaway back and front. 'Daniel, it's beautiful,' she gasped. She would never have believed he could choose such a feminine, intimate gift. Then again, maybe he could.

'There's something else,' he said, placing a small, wrapped shape on the nightdress.

Hannah widened her eyes at him and opened the second gift eagerly. She snapped open a jeweller's box and stared at an oval silver locket with a delicate scroll design on it. 'Oh, Danny,' she was overwhelmed. 'I don't know what to say.'

'I don't want another thank you. How about a kiss?' he said huskily.

Hannah squeezed against him, hugged his neck and firmly kissed both his cheeks. 'Thank you, they are the best presents I've ever had. I'll treasure them always.'

Daniel put his arms round her and gently brushing her hair away from her face kissed her cheek then put a soft, lingering kiss on her lips. 'You mean more to me than just a friend, Hannah.'

'I know, Danny,' she said, turning her head to see what Pogo was doing. He was chewing on a piece of discarded string.

Daniel pulled her back to face him. 'I don't think you do, Hannah. You're very special to me.' He gazed into her eyes, smiled beguilingly, then looked at her lips. His voice dropped another tone. 'Do you understand?'

Hannah held her breath. She understood. She was mesmerised as he put his mouth over hers and pressed and explored tenderly. She was aware Daniel had an overt male attractiveness, was strong and desirable, but it had never crossed her mind that he would be anything more to her than a very close friend. She'd had his arms about her many times but not crushed to him like this, with his lips seeking a totally different response from her. It was good and she wanted more.

Carefully putting her gifts beside her on the bale, she wrapped her arms round his neck and returned his kiss. He held her tighter and she felt the warm roughness of his mouth probing behind her ears, down her neck and back to her lips again.

He held her hands and smiled into her eyes. 'I think I love you, Hannah.'

She was stunned. 'Danny . . . I . . .'

'Don't say anything now. I know I've taken you by surprise but I can't go on any longer ignoring my feelings for you. I know I've said many times I'd never settle down but I think of nothing but you day and night, darling.'

Pogo started yapping to be let out and collecting her wits, Hannah pushed Daniel away and stood up. She knew her face was on fire and her mind was whirling in confusion. 'I . . . I have to go, Danny. Mrs Opie will wonder why I'm taking so long.'

Standing beside her, he took her face in his hands. 'All I'm asking is that you think about what I've said, Hannah. And think about us.'

'I will,' she breathed, picking up Pogo's lead and calling to him. 'Thanks for the presents, Danny.'

Before they left the stables he took her in his arms again and kissed her soundly. He held her chin in his cupped hand. 'If we fish tomorrow, try not to leave the village before the boats come back in.'

Outside, the wind was whipping up and a shower of

rain threatened. Putting the locket into her pocket and securing the nightdress inside her coat, Hannah put up the umbrella to protect her hair. She blushed scarlet as Greg Opie appeared in front of them on his way to his car. He glanced at Hannah then eyed Daniel curiously.

'Oh, Mr Gregory, this is a friend of mine from the village, Daniel Kittow,' she explained hastily. 'He came here to give me a birthday present. He's just going.'

'I see.' Greg stared at her a moment, making Hannah feel she had committed a crime. She was sure her face gave away what she and Daniel had been doing. 'I didn't realise it was your birthday, Hannah. Many happy returns.' He turned to Daniel. 'I'm on my way to St Austell, Kittow. I'll give you a lift to Porthellis.'

Daniel would have preferred to walk but seeing that Greg Opie was younger and better looking than Hannah's dislike of him had led him to believe, he grasped the opportunity to get to know something of the other man. 'Thank you, Mr Opie.' He smiled warmly at Hannah. 'I'll see you tomorrow, hopefully. 'Bye, Hannah.'

Hannah watched the two men walk away then hurried indoors. Now Daniel had been seen she'd have to tell Mrs Opie about him coming here and the reason why, but before she took Pogo back to Mrs Opie's rooms she put the nightdress away in her room. The gift was too personal to show anyone.

'Have you and Hannah got something going?' Greg said, as he carefully manoeuvred the saloon along the muddy lanes, overhanging wet foliage smacking the sides of the car.

'Yes,' Daniel glared sideways at him, an edge of warning in his voice. He crossed two of his fingers and put them under Greg's nose. 'We're as close as that, if you get my meaning.'

'Hannah's very lovely but you have no competition from me, Kittow,' Greg said harshly, not liking the fisherman's tone. 'I admit to being a little curious about Hannah though. Why did she live with her aunt and uncle?'

'That's Hannah's business. Are you sure you aren't interested in her? I won't let anyone come between us.'

Tension crackled in the car. They had reached the end of Turn-A-Penny Lane. Greg slowed down and stopped, keeping the engine running. 'I'm not a liar, Kittow. I'm sure you won't mind walking from here.'

'Thanks for the lift. It was very kind of you,' Daniel muttered sarcastically, getting out of the car. Feeling he had put the toff in his place, he grinned sardonically as he strode off for the village.

Vexed that he hadn't got very far with the surly young villager, and left with an uneasy feeling about him, Greg took another turning to continue his journey.

At the house, the hairdresser had gone and Mrs Opie had a tray of tea and fancy biscuits ready for Hannah.

'Thank you, Hannah. Put Pogo up on his chair by the fire,' she said, looking at the box in Hannah's hand. 'What have you got there, dear?'

Hannah showed her mistress the locket. 'It's a birthday present from a friend. He came up from the village to give it to me.'

Mrs Opie touched the locket with a fingertip. 'It's lovely, how kind of him. Is he the dark-haired young man who carried your suitcase here?'

Hannah was awash with colour again. 'Um, no, that was Matt. It was Daniel who gave me the locket.'

'Are you walking out with either of them?' Mrs Opie asked, passing her a cup of tea.

Hannah put it down on the table. 'No, well, I mean I'm supposed to be going out with Matt, but I . . .' She couldn't continue. Daniel's sudden appearance, his gifts and his kisses, the declaration that he thought he loved her, had made her even more confused about Matt.

'But you're not really sure you want to be?' Mrs Opie ventured.

Hannah nodded.

'The locket looks expensive and it's a very personal gift. It must be flattering to have two men romantically interested in you, but you are very young, Hannah. I wouldn't like to see you tying yourself down. You are an excellent housekeeper and you've also been a good companion to me. You're bright and intelligent and could do well.' Mrs Opie patted her hand. 'You're perfectly fine as you are, wouldn't you say?'

'Oh, yes, Mrs Opie, my first loyalty lies with you,' Hannah said quickly, and as the words tumbled out of her mouth she knew it was the truth.

Mrs Opie smiled and took the locket out of its box. 'I'm very glad to hear it.' She moved to Hannah and fastened the locket round her neck then stroked her hair. 'You are so pretty, Hannah. Let the young men wait.'

As they sipped their tea, Hannah could tell Mrs Opie had something else to say. 'I'm going to ask Mr Gregory to teach you how to drive then I shall get a motorcar and we'll be able to travel anywhere we like. Would you like that, Hannah?'

'It would be brilliant,' Hannah grinned excitedly, copying one of Mr Patrick's phrases. 'I don't think there's a woman in the village who can drive a car, not even the minister's wife.'

'There's another matter I'd like to discuss with you. I've been thinking about Angie Miller. She's not getting any younger and it seems unfair to allow her to carry on with her present workload. I won't have you helping her, it's not a housekeeper's responsibility and anyway I couldn't spare you. I'm thinking of engaging a maid to train under Angie, someone like her, quiet and dutiful. I was wondering if your sister, Leah, would like the job.'

'Leah would love to take it but I don't think my father would allow her,' Hannah said, sad that while her father had forced her here, her younger sister's dream could not come true.

'Well, you mention it to Leah and give her time to think about it. I'll leave the job open for a while before I advertise it. Now,' she smiled broadly, 'when you leave here, go down to the kitchen, dear. Mr Patrick has a surprise for you.'

There was a storm in the night and the fishing boats were kept battened down in the cove for a second day. Hannah was buffeted like a sock on a washing line as she cycled to Porthellis, the hedges giving little shelter from the forceful wind. She didn't go straight to Quayside Street or seek out Daniel, but propped the bicycle outside Seaview Cottage's back door, tapped on it and walked in to find Matt and Mrs Penny in the kitchen. Hannah was curious to see if Matt had a birthday present for her.

He was heartened to see her. He had been cleaning his sea boots and hastily put them away and washed his hands. He kissed Hannah's cheek and gave his mother a meaningful look.

'Well, I think I'll pop out and see how old Mr Nunn is. He's got a cold on his chest. Can't be too careful at his age and he'll be glad of the company.'

'Take him some of this, Mrs Penney,' Hannah said, putting the cake tin she had with her on the table. Matt and his mother watched as she took off the lid. 'Mr Patrick made me a lovely cake for my birthday and I've brought some with me to share out.'

'He did a good job,' Mrs Penny said, much impressed, fetching a knife. 'It must have cost a fortune to make, a dark fruit cake with royal icing and pink piping.'

'And there were twenty-one candles on it,' Hannah said proudly.

Matt took the opportunity to kiss her in congratulation. Hannah cut him a large slice of cake when Mrs Penney had gone. 'So you enjoyed your birthday then?' he said, popping a piece into his mouth. 'Take off your hat and coat.' He sighed inwardly when she did; he had been afraid she'd rush away.

'It was wonderful. I had my hair done by Mrs Opie's hairdresser as her treat. You wouldn't think so now,' she said, pulling on a windswept tress.

'It still looks beautiful, but then it always does.' Matt sat down by the fireside. He wanted to take her in his arms and kiss her long and hungrily but he never showed her the extent of his love and affection since she'd cooled towards him.

Hannah joined him at the fireside, eating cake on the rug at his feet. 'Shame about the weather. The men with young families must be getting worried about their loss of earnings.'

'Can't be helped,' Matt said philosophically.

'The wind will have blown your allotment around.'

'Yes.'

'Want some more cake?'

'No, save some for your family.'

'I'll leave a slice for your mother.'

'She'll like that.'

This is silly, Hannah thought. Has he got a present for me or not? Then she felt guilty. She hadn't been treating Matt much like a girlfriend should and sometimes she had been cold and offhand with him. How dare she hope he'd bought her a present.

Matt did have a present for her but was worried what her reaction would be. He wanted to give her jewellery but feared she'd see it as too personal, that he was trying to lay claim to her. Without thinking, he caressed her hair and was instantly afraid he'd regret his action, but she didn't shy away from him as lately she sometimes had. Encouraged, he said, 'I've got something for you.'

'Oh?' She turned and looked up at him.

'For your birthday. It's nothing much . . .'

Matt went to a cupboard and took out a large paper bag. He hadn't wrapped up the gift properly, again to try not to make her feel pressured.

Out of the bag Hannah pulled a musical jewellery box made in dark golden wood, exquisitely carved, and decorated in red and blue paint. 'Oh, Matt, it's lovely,' she exclaimed, and reached up to kiss his cheek. She put the box on the table, opened the lid and watched enchanted as a ballerina on a spring turned round to the tune of 'The Blue Danube'.

Matt took a chance. Winding his arms round her waist, he kissed the top of her head. Hannah leaned against him and put her hands over his. His heart lurched and he was hopeful their estrangement was over. He turned her round to claim a full kiss and saw something shining round her neck.

He lifted the locket. 'Goodness, this must have cost an arm and a leg. Did Mrs Opie give it to you?'

'N-no . . . it was Daniel.'

Matt's eyes became darker and intense, a cold glint in them. He let the locket fall from his finger. 'When?'

'Yesterday. He came up to Roscarrock.'

Matt spun round from her and stuffed his hands into his pockets.

'Matt—'

'Well, at least you've got something to put your locket in now,' he uttered coldly.

'Matt,' she began again.

'Don't say anything more, Hannah, just take your ruddy birthday cake and go.'

Putting her hat and coat on quickly, she gathered up the cake tin and made for the door. The strains of the jewellery box she'd left on the table wound down and stopped.

Chapter 16

The Porthellis fleet put to sea in the early hours of Wednesday. The sky was empty with angry splashes of grey, as if the stormy weather had washed and boiled it but had failed to take out its sulky stains. The fishermen muttered every phrase they knew to ward off ill fortune as they headed south-west of the Dodman.

On the *Misty*, Mitch sharpened his knife until it was sharp enough to shave with and sliced pilchards into five or six pieces for bait. He threw salt over the bait while his father and Uncle Terence gazed anxiously at the sea and sky for signs of a gathering storm or a descending fog, knowing from years of experience that conditions could quickly worsen.

An hour and three-quarters out, Jeff called to Josh in the wheelhouse to bring the bows of the lugger due east and ventured a trial shoot over the churning waters, something that was always done after poor weather, to see if there were any dogfish about. Jeff shot a line of two hundred hooks in one dextrous movement, curving it through the salt-laden air, clearing a hook swiftly if it looked as if it would foul. It took a steady arm and wasn't for the indecisive. They waited half an hour, watching and praying for the telltale grey-green shapes of spur-dogfish but saw nothing but oily rags thrown over-board by another boat. When they hauled in the line they found no fish. Jeff cursed and Josh opened up *Misty*'s engines. Mitch had thought it too early to try the line, all the other luggers had sailed on nearly out of sight, but he kept his counsel.

'Keep her heading up into the tide,' Jeff shouted at Josh. He took a cigarette from his nephew, Morley, and as he lit up he glared at the rest of the crew. 'We'll have to go out Saturday to catch up on lost time and money.'

Mitch nodded sombrely and where necessary rebaited the hooks on the line that had been shot. There had been no need for his father to make that statement, all the boats would go out at the weekend; Jeff Spargo was being quarrelsome owing to a splitting headache courtesy of a hangover. Mitch had known on Sunday night when the gale had breached the cove that his hopes of going down to Newlyn to see Viv the following Saturday were lost. He had taken meals at the boarding house, as she had offered, but the moment he paid his shilling she made it clear that she wanted him to leave.

The last time Mitch had seen Viv was two weeks ago at the end of the pilchard drive and she had been tired and angry. 'Stop bleddy moaning to me,' he'd heard her shrieking in the passage at one of the lodgers. 'You ungrateful sodding swine. I do my best. You don't pay the rent most weeks anyway. If you don't like it, bugger off somewhere else!'

The lodger, a ferret-faced man, none too clean, had been about to shout back when Mitch had opened the kitchen door. The lodger took one look at him and slammed out of the front door.

'Come and sit down, Viv,' Mitch had said kindly. 'I'll make you a cup of tea.'

'Don't be silly,' she retorted irritably, pushing unceremoniously past him. 'You pay for your meals and drink.'

'I don't mind, really.'

Viv flopped down on a chair, tears in her eyes.

'Were you hoping to see Daniel?' He had noticed her getting more and more grouchy at Daniel's non-appearance. Mitch wished he could tell her that Daniel was with a tarty blonde who'd been waiting for him near the quay, but he didn't want to sound like a telltale.

'I don't think Daniel cares for me,' she said forlornly.

'I care for you, Viv.' He knelt beside her, taking her small rough hands in his. 'Why not give me a chance instead?'

'Oh, stop it, Mitch.' She snatched her hands away. 'Don't be kind to me or you'll make me cry.'

'What's the matter?' He tried a different approach. 'Are you feeling poorly? You look tired and pale.'

She looked into his eyes for a moment then raised her hands despairingly. 'It's everything, it's this place, I hate it. It's such a dump. No matter how hard I try I can't keep it nice and no one appreciates all my work. I'm so tired, so fed up. I thought I had a future with Daniel, but he . . . he . . .' She couldn't finish and burst into tears.

Mitch put his hand gently on the back of her head and she leaned forward and sobbed on his shoulder. Mitch had thought he was in with a chance at last and had written four letters after they'd brought the boat home, but there had been no reply. He felt despondent and was on a short fuse today. He wished he could get far away from his father whom he was beginning to hate with all his heart.

Jeff had been watching him. 'Look at un,' he said scathingly to Morley. 'Bloody lovesick now he can't see that red-headed Hickey maid at Newlyn.'

Mitch gave his father a murderous look and Morley interjected hastily, 'I don't blame him, Uncle Jeff, she's a sweet little thing.'

'Yah,' Jeff spat on the deck. 'Was a sweet little thing, you mean. Daniel Kittow's being getting his leg over that one.'

Mitch made to rear at his father but Terence grasped his arm. 'Ignore him,' he whispered harshly. 'There's more important things at stake than your love life.'

Mitch felt like tossing his father into the cold, surging sea but he clamped his mouth tight and moved to the other end of the boat.

Josh steered slowly back to the first dan and the rest of the crew went for their crib.

'Hope we don't hit hitchy ground,' Terence said conversationally in the cabin as he opened his crib tin.

'Not bloody heavy cake again,' Jeff scowled as he unpacked his allowance. 'Stupid cow, can't she get anything right? I told her to put in yeast or seed cake for a sodding change. What have I got to do? Bake it myself?'

Terence Spargo had never had the guts to stand up to his elder brother. If he didn't agree with one of Jeff's heated statements he scarpered quickly, doing so now by taking his food and a mug of tea up to Josh in the wheelhouse. Like a puppy, Morley followed him, not wanting to hear the ranting and raving his uncle subjected them to when he was in one of his foul moods.

'Don't talk about Mother like that,' Mitch growled angrily the moment he and his father were alone.

'Mind your bleddy lip,' Jeff hurled at him, then clutched his pounding head; he cursed Maggie Curnow for refilling his tankard too many times last night then complaining because he couldn't 'perform'. He'd have to sort her out. 'Bleddy women, they're all useless bitches. Your sister's just as bad, always mooning about the house with her head in the clouds. Going off her bleddy head, if you ask me.'

'But Leah's beginning to come out of herself,' Mitch protested. He hated the fact that his father never had a good word for any woman in the family except his cantankerous grandmother. 'She quite often goes to Sarah's, Naomi's or Aunty Janet's these days.'

'Don't mention that cow to me.' Jeff tore off a chunk of cheese, stuffed it in his mouth, spitting out crumbs as he continued his abuse. 'Pity I couldn't turn her out of the village along with the bitch who lived with her.'

Suddenly Mitch could stand it no longer. 'For goodness sake!' He slammed his fist on the table between them. 'Stop going on and on about Hannah. She's your daughter, how can you go on treating her like this? She's your own flesh and blood. It's evil, you've got no bloody right to say those things about her. You're a cruel and rotten bloody swine!'

Jeff rushed round the table and grasping Mitch by the throat thrust him back against the bunks. 'How dare you speak to me like that, you young bastard! She killed your little brother, or have you forgotten that?'

Hearing the furious voices, Terence and Morley darted back into the cabin, closely followed by Josh. Alarmed by the violent rage on his brother's face, Terence shouted at him, 'Let him go, Jeff, you're choking him.'

'Choking him? I gave him life and I'll bleddy well kill him for what he just said to me.'

Finding strength in his anger, Mitch threw his father

off him. Jeff's back hit the table with a sickening thump and he crumpled to the cabin floor.

'It wasn't Hannah!' Mitch screamed at the top of his voice, shaking from head to foot, totally out of control. 'We all could have been to blame that day, we all wanted to go out in the *Wynne*. But it was me! It was my fault the boat turned over and Edwin was drowned. I did it. It wasn't Hannah! It wasn't her fault and you had no right to blame her all these years.'

Jeff had clambered to his feet and with his hands outstretched, his face as dark as thunder, he went again for Mitch's throat. Terence and Morley pounced on him and with Josh's help the three men managed to hold Jeff off.

Glaring into his father's black eyes, Mitch went on, 'We were in the boat and me and Fred Jose were larking around, pulling Eileen and Hannah's hair. Then I suggested we put itching powder down their backs. It made the girls jump up in pain and that's when the boat became unsteady and turned over. It was my fault entirely. If I hadn't started the prank we would all have got safely to Hidden Beach and then Daniel was going to make the girls and Edwin walk home, there would have been no accident and Edwin and Eileen would be alive today.'

'Why didn't you say so before?' Jeff accused him, still struggling to get out of the others' combined grasp. 'Are you a coward, boy?'

'No, I'm not a coward but I'm afraid of you, Father. All your children are, even Josh. You've brought us up by bullying and threatening us. As a twelve-year-old boy I was afraid that if you could beat Hannah and throw her out of the house, what would you have done to me?' Mitch's eyes narrowed to slits and he raised his chin and pointed at Jeff. 'But now I wish I'd spoken up all those years ago and laid the guilt of the accident at my own door and your dreadful behaviour to Hannah at yours. You had no reason to blame her, you just picked on her as you have done all her life. You're a totally evil man and I hate you and Grandmother both. If you don't mend your wicked ways you'll both deserve to burn in Hell for your cruelty. And before you throw me out of the house, I've made up my mind I'm going. The minute I step off this boat I'm packing my bags and I'll be out of Porthellis for good.'

Jeff Spargo looked as if a tornado had hit him. For a moment his body sagged as if all his strength had left him, then his face contorted in pain and began to turn blue. He clutched his chest. 'C-can't breathe . . .'

'Quick, cut the lines free and head back for shore,' Terence shouted fearfully. 'He's having a heart attack.'

Chapter 17

'How's Jeff?' Janet asked Prim when they met at the village pump.

The cast-iron pump, which stood out in the middle of the village like a monument, was a meeting place for the women to chat and there were several concerned faces turned towards Prim.

'A bit better than he was three days ago when it happened,' she answered, shivering as an icy blast of wind swept over them, throwing up grit and sand. 'The doctor said he was very lucky, it was only a mild heart attack.'

'He'll have to be careful though,' one woman said, pulling her headscarf on more securely. 'Have to give up drinking and smoking. One attack can lead easily to another.'

'I know, Mrs Trebilcock,' Prim said. There was a strange look of wonder on her chubby face. 'Funny thing is, he's taken quietly to his bed and hasn't even asked for a cigarette. S'pose he will when he's feeling better.' Prim shrugged dismissively, making her thick winter coat climb up to her ears. 'But if he wants to smoke and take a drink there's not much I can do about it.'

The other women nodded understandingly, no one but

his mother had ever been able to tell Jeff Spargo what to do.

Bett Spargo said tartly, 'It cost them all their line and hooks. 'Tis going to be hard to find the money to replace them. He'd better look out if he wants to keep my man and boy's partnership on the *Misty*. Terence and Morley have had enough of his domineering ways. If he goes on like he did before, they'll sell up and fish with someone else.'

'Good for them,' Prim said quietly, and the other women could see she meant it. Some pondered on precisely how heartbroken Primrose Spargo would have been if her husband had died of the heart attack.

'It's given them something to gossip about,' Janet said as she walked part of the way back with Prim, leaving the other women to close round Bett who was filling them in on all the details of what had occurred on the *Misty*. 'Though there was no need for Bett to be sharp about the lost line. The *Prudence* lost her nets on the pilchard drive; it's a fact of life, boats are always losing equipment.'

'I don't care what those women think but in Bett's place I'd feel the same way. At least Jeff now knows exactly how the accident happened ten years ago. He can't blame Hannah for it any more.'

'Do you think it will make any difference to his treatment of her?'

'Shouldn't think so, but he has been unusually quiet. Must have realised how close he came to seeing the Almighty. What worries me is Mitch threatening to leave home. He says he's only staying to help out until Jeff's well enough to go back on the boat, then he's going for good.'

'Poor Mitch, he's such a good boy. I know he caused

the accident but he was a child back then and it was ages ago. There's no good turning against he or Fred Jose. It won't bring Edwin or Eileen back. Is Jeff insisting Mitch goes, like he did Hannah?'

'I don't know, he won't talk about it. Mother-in-law says the boat can't spare Mitch but she's only worried about her bread not being buttered.'

'If you could just get rid of she,' Janet said vehemently. 'She's the cause of all your trouble.'

'Aye, the bitch, as if I should say the word. Jeff wouldn't have turned against Hannah if it wasn't for her. Pity someone doesn't ill-wish her,' Prim said wearily. 'I would myself but no doubt the trouble would only come back on me and I've had enough for a lifetime.'

'Well, you know what our mum used to say, the tide doesn't go out unless it comes back in again.'

They were at the bridge leading to the dark side of Porthellis. Before Prim put a foot on the granite, she asked, 'Have you seen Hannah this week?'

'No, and she said she might not come home for a while to avoid seeing Matt. I don't know what happened between they two but it quite ruined her birthday.'

'Such a shame.' Prim shook her head sadly. 'Matt's one of the pleasantest young men I've ever known. I don't think he's at fault. I blame Feena Opie. I reckon she's been filling Hannah's head with fancy ideas. Having her eating at her table indeed, and what does Hannah need to learn to drive for? It's ridiculous! My worries are coming true. That woman is getting her clutches into our little girl, Janet, and there isn't a darned thing we can do about it.' Prim sniffed to hold back a rush of tears. 'We'll see less and less of Hannah in the future and then not at all, you mark my words.'

Janet stroked her sister's arm comfortingly. 'Oh no she won't, even if I have to march up there and remind Hannah who her family are. Prim . . .' Janet hesitated. She knew Leah had slipped off to Roscarrock and she'd been about to suggest allowing her to go there again to check on Hannah, but Prim harboured strong feelings against Feena Opie.

'What?' Prim said.

'Chin up, that's all.'

There was no sign of Hannah the next Sunday and in the afternoon, while her family were relaxing and Mitch had gone off somewhere to be alone, Leah said she was going for a walk. It was quite a long walk because she went to Roscarrock.

Greg Opie looked up from his work in the study and saw the girl in her shabby brown coat, grimly holding on to her huge hat in the blustery wind, hesitatingly approaching the front door. Grabbing his jacket off the back of his chair, he rushed outside to meet her.

'Miss Spargo, do you want to come in?' he said, sounding almost as jovial as Patrick.

'Well, I . . .' Leah wasn't wearing her glasses and kept her eyes on the gravelly ground. Greg Opie had managed to put her at her ease with him, when he'd come across her in the drawing room a few weeks ago, but she still felt intimidated by him. 'I-I came because Hannah hasn't been down to the village. Me and my aunt were wondering if she was all right.'

Greg smiled at her. 'Hannah has a cold, actually, and is resting in bed.'

'Oh, I see. Will you tell her I called? I'd better get off.'

'Nonsense,' Greg said, taking her by the arm before

she could escape. 'You've walked all the way here on a bitterly cold day to see your sister and see her you shall. Come inside and warm up, then you can go up to her room.'

'Thank you, Mr Opie,' she murmured.

As Greg shut the front door behind them, Mrs Opie called out from the drawing room, 'Who is it, dear?'

Smiling first at Leah, Greg popped his fair head round the door. 'It's Miss Leah Spargo, Grandma Fee. She's come to see Hannah.'

Leah waited nervously by the door. Would Mrs Opie think she was taking a liberty? Hannah had told her about the job offer, but she did not believe Mrs Opie encouraged visitors.

'Has she walked here, Greg?'

'Yes, Grandma, she's quite frozen. I was just about to—'

'The poor girl. Bring her in here by the fire, Greg.'

Greg made a face at his grandmother but did as she said. He beckoned to Leah. She took a step backwards and shook her head. 'Don't worry,' he whispered, taking her by the hand. 'My grandmother won't eat you.'

Feena Opie was sitting on a sofa at a right angle to the blazing log fire crackling under the magnificent mantelpiece. Her little white dog was on her lap. She put a book down at her side. Pogo looked at the two people who'd come into the room then dropped his head on his mistress's lap and went back to sleep.

'Do come in, Leah,' Feena said in a soft, motherly voice. 'How kind of you to come to see Hannah. Were you worried about her? Has Mr Gregory explained she has a cold and is resting in her room?'

'Y-yes, ma'am, M-Mrs Opie,' Leah stuttered in the

doorway, not sure whether she ought to curtsy. Mrs Opie was wearing a tailored georgette dress and her pearls and to Leah looked as elegant as the pictures she had seen of the Queen.

'Bring Leah over by the fire, Gregory. We must get her warmed through or we shall have two girls with colds.'

Greg was still holding her hand and he escorted her across the room. 'Give me your hat and coat, Leah,' he said.

Leah didn't mind this order too much. She was wearing her best dress which was in much better condition than the coat and she had taken pains to twist her long hair neatly at the nape of her neck. Greg watched her as she pulled out a long hatpin and took off the hat, removed her black and white striped woollen gloves which she stuffed in a coat pocket, and undid the three big scratched buttons of her coat and slipped it off. Feena noticed his interest and she wasn't amused. Despite her scar, Leah Spargo was a pretty young girl with dazzling dark eyes and wind-kissed cheeks. Greg, who was a loner by nature, had no time for the confident, cultured, socialising women of his own class and he had been attracted to Leah Spargo's type before. Doubtless he would have made a play for Hannah if he hadn't been harbouring suspicions about her.

Greg took the garments from Leah, put them aside and before Feena could make the offer he told Leah to sit on the sofa opposite her.

'I'll look after Leah, Greg,' Feena said in a dismissive tone. 'I'm sure you'd rather get back to your work. You have a deadline to meet.'

Greg gave her a dark look. So his grandmother had realised his motives for inviting Leah into the house; if it had been anyone else, he would have left them to freeze on the doorstep. Never mind, he was sure Leah would appreciate the drive home in a warm car.

Leah was very nervous at the thought of being left alone with Mrs Opie and didn't want him to go. Greg turned his back on his grandmother and smiled warmly at her. Leah smiled back, it made her feel braver. When he had gone, Leah saw Mrs Opie regarding her and she blushed.

'There's no need to feel uncomfortable, Leah,' Mrs Opie said softly. 'Hannah is perfectly at home working here. Did she by any chance mention there is work for you in the house if you desire it?'

'Yes, Mrs Opie,' Leah replied shyly, in her whispery voice. ''Tis very good of you to think of me, but neither my father nor my mother will let me work away from home, specially to live in.' Leah thought it best to lie.

'I only require a little extra help, someone to relieve the maid of some of her duties. Living in is not necessary. Perhaps you would consider two afternoons a week.'

Deep in thought, Leah stared down at her lap. This could just work, if Lizzie, Sarah or Naomi would say she was with them. They were all pregnant and she was often at one of their houses these days helping them out. She'd have to hope she wasn't seen coming and going but the villagers were used to her wandering about now, and the roads were usually quiet.

Feena could see she was making up her mind. 'Why don't you talk to Hannah about it? It might help you decide. Then we could discuss it again before you go.'

'No.' Leah brought her head up sharply, her eyes bright and shining. 'I mean, that will be all right, I'm sure. I'd like to work here two afternoons a week.'

'Good. I expect your mother will need you more on Mondays and at the end of the week. Tuesdays and Wednesdays will suit nicely, one thirty until four thirty. Your pay will be a shilling an hour and a uniform will be provided.' Feena was sure Leah was going to work here by subterfuge. 'You may change into it when you arrive if you like. You will train under Angie Miller but of course you will be answerable to Hannah. You'll have no problem with that, I take it?'

'Oh no, Mrs Opie. Me and Hannah have always got on. I'll do everything she says, honest I will.'

Mrs Opie smiled to herself, Leah was so childlike. How had Jeff Spargo managed to sire such a sweet and gentle person? She showed none of the undercurrents of passion that Feena had discerned in Hannah.

'That's all settled then. Now, Leah, before you go upstairs to see Hannah, perhaps you could throw some light on something for me. Hannah has been very unhappy since the last time she went down to the village. Do you know why?'

Hannah woke up from a troubled nap and hauled herself up groggily to sit against the pillow. She was hot, feverish and slightly dizzy, her head ached, her throat was sore and dry, her eyes were stinging and watering and her nightdress was soaked in perspiration. She felt dreadful but was glad she had a genuine excuse not to go home. She'd ask the butcher's boy tomorrow to send word to Janet, or get Angie to if she was no better. Mrs Opie had packed her off to bed yesterday morning, saying she would send for the doctor if the cold 'went down on her chest'. Hannah coughed, a dry barking sound which hurt her throat and she prayed the cold wouldn't worsen.

She looked at the dark grey sky through the window. It was miserable weather and matched her mood completely. She didn't like herself much at this moment. How could I have hurt Matt like that? she asked herself wretchedly for the umpteenth time. He didn't deserve it. She should have been honest with him. Honest? Difficult when she wasn't sure even now what she felt about him.

Daniel had met her when she'd walked away from Seaview Cottage. He was the last person she had wanted to see.

'What's up, darling?' he'd asked, bending over the bicycle and kissing her cheek. 'Your face is like a boiled lobster's.'

'Oh, don't, Danny,' she appealed to him, walking quickly down the hill.

'You've just come from the Penneys' cottage. Have you ended it with Matt?'

Hannah didn't like the jubilant gleam in his eyes. 'No, he ended it with me. I don't want to talk about it. It was horrible. I've treated Matt badly.'

Daniel took the bicycle from her and put it on his other side so they were walking close together. 'Had to happen. You weren't right for each other. He'll get over it.'

'You won't crow over him, will you, Danny? I've seen the antagonism between the pair of you. Promise me?'

'I promise, darling. Matt's a good workmate and partner. I respect him. I won't say a word to him.' Daniel half meant it now things were working out the way he wanted. 'I'll let him find out about us in due course.'

Hannah shook her head. 'No, Danny. There is no us. I'm all confused right now and need time to think.'

'Fine, I'll be waiting. You'll soon realise it's me you need. Till then we'll go on as before.'

She wouldn't let him kiss her again and had stayed in the house at Quayside Street for the rest of the day until she'd left for Roscarrock, not going to chapel in the evening because she couldn't face the tittering when Matt sat next to his mother and not her. Janet told her, with an accusing expression, that Matt hadn't gone to chapel either and that Mrs Penney considered the rift nothing more than a lovers' tiff.

'I hope it blows over,' Janet had added impatiently. 'It will if you've got any sense.'

Hannah wished Matt had not turned away from her when she'd told him Daniel had given her the locket. Her dreams were now filled with hideous or agonised expressions distorting his handsome face. She had taken the locket off before going inside her aunt's house and it was now in its box, wrapped up in a large handkerchief in the top drawer of the dressing table. Hannah didn't know where or when she'd wear it again. Daniel would be disappointed but she didn't want to have to explain it to anyone else. In fact, her association with Daniel, whatever footing it turned out to be on, would be best conducted secretly in future.

The bedroom door opened and she saw a tray being brought through. 'Oh, Angie,' she croaked. 'I told you not to bother— Leah!'

Leah walked into the room with a big grin on her face and Mrs Opie followed her. Pogo shot across the room and leapt on to the bed.

'I came to see how you were, Hannah, and Mrs Opie let me make us some tea,' Leah said brightly.

'And I've brought you some more aspirin, dear,' Mrs Opie said. 'Pogo, off the bed.' She shooed the dog on to the floor then felt Hannah's fevered brow. 'You poor thing. You're burning up. Leah, find a clean nightdress for Hannah and help her to wash and get comfortable.'

Mrs Opie stroked Hannah's damp hair away from her face as Leah put the tray down and hunted about in the chest of drawers. 'There's some of Mr Patrick's hot honey and lemon on the tray to soothe your throat and a jar of menthol to rub on your chest and back. Come along now, drink your tea and take the aspirin and you'll feel a little better.'

'You're very kind,' Hannah said, feeling cosseted. It struck her then that although her father and grandmother had been cruel to her she was used to this treatment. Her mother and Aunt Janet had always fussed over her. Hannah swallowed two aspirins and the honey and lemon then slowly sipped her tea. Mrs Opie watched her intently, a matronly smile on her face, and Hannah hoped she wasn't going to stay in the room while she washed and changed her nightdress. That would be embarrassing.

When she put the teacup down, Mrs Opie took her leave. 'Leah has got a lot to tell you. I'll leave you to chat. Don't tire her out, Leah.'

'She's wonderful, isn't she?' Leah said when they were alone. 'I was quite scared at first when Mr Greg took me into the drawing room to her.'

'You saw him too, did you?'

'He let me in,' Leah trilled as she came towards the bed holding a cotton, long-sleeved nightdress.

'What?' Hannah exclaimed, threatening her recently soothed throat. 'You mean he actually got off his backside and came to the door? He usually lets a caller wait ages for Angie or lets Mr Patrick be dragged away from what he's doing rather than answer it himself.'

Hannah pushed the covers away and let Leah help her

take off the sweaty nightdress. 'He came outside to meet me,' Leah said, generously soaping the flannel and passing it to Hannah.

'Did he now?' Hannah muttered suspiciously. Just what was Mr Gregory's game? She hoped he didn't have the sort of designs on Leah she had once thought she was in for herself.

Leah helped her dry herself with the fluffy towels, dusted her with talcum powder, rubbed in the menthol and put the clean nightdress over her head. She poured a second cup of tea for Hannah and one for herself then sat on the bed. 'You've got lovely bosoms, Hannah,' she remarked enviously, cupping her own small breasts. 'You're so feminine. Do you think mine will grow some more?'

'They might. I heard somewhere that the body doesn't stop growing until you're eighteen. You've got a few more months to go yet. Come on then, what's this news Mrs Opie said you've got to tell me?'

'First,' Leah sprang up and went to the chest of drawers, 'you can tell me where you got this.' She held the white silk nightdress against herself and studied her reflection in the mirror. 'It's very daring. Did Matt give it to you?'

'Put it away, Leah,' Hannah protested. She couldn't admit Daniel had given it to her. 'I bought it in St Austell out of my wages.'

'Caw, you're getting saucy. I'm going to buy some nice things out of my wages,' Leah said, putting the nightdress back in the drawer.

'What?'

'That's part of my news.' Leah danced back to the bed. 'I'm going to work here, Hannah. Mrs Opie wants me two afternoons a week. I'm going to ask Sarah, Naomi or Lizzie to say I'm with them.'

'It will be wonderful if it works out but you'll cop it if Father finds out.'

'Be worth it if I get in a few weeks first and save some money. And hopefully he might not be as furious as he usually is. He's gone very quiet since his heart attack.'

'What! When did this happen?'

Leah told her about the events on the *Misty* that had led to their father's illness.

'But why didn't someone tell me?'

'I wanted to come but Mother wouldn't hear of it. Father wasn't about to die, she said.'

Hannah sank back into the pillows. 'So it was Mitch and Fred who made me and Eileen leap up that day. I never could understand what burnt my back. Poor Mitch, no wonder he's stood up for me so many times against Father.'

'You don't feel bitter about him and Fred then?' Leah drank her tea and nibbled an almond biscuit.

'What would be the point? If he'd owned up and Father hadn't thrown me out, it probably would have been awful for me living with him and Grandmother all those years. I loved living with Aunty Janet and I might not have come here to live and work.' It was true, Hannah thought. I might not be happier now if my real father turned up to claim me and was a wonderful man. 'What sort of week did the boats have?'

'Very poor owing to the bad weather. None of them made up much for it on Saturday. The merchant's men weren't kept busy on the quay. One said it wasn't worth him sharpening his knife apparently.' Leah helped herself to another biscuit. 'Hannah, what happened between you and Matt?'

Hannah looked away and answered in a small voice, 'It just didn't work out, that's all. I don't want to talk about it, Leah.'

When Leah was standing in the vestibule in her hat, coat and gloves, Greg appeared in a long wool coat, trilby hat and driving gloves. 'I'm just off out, Leah. I'll give you a lift to the top of the village hill, if you like.'

'Oh,' was all she said, but Leah felt important as he took her through the back of the house and showed her into the front passenger seat.

'I've never been in a car before,' she said, holding on tightly to the seat as he drove down the drive.

'What, never?'

'There's only two or three cars in the village at any one time, and the Chellew brothers' motorbike and sidecar. My brothers and sisters have been on the charabanc outings but I haven't.'

'Why is that?' He turned out of the drive and glanced at her.

Leah hoped he wasn't looking at her scar. 'I preferred to stay at home.'

'You're rather like me. I like my own company. Will you be coming to Roscarrock again soon? It's good for Hannah to keep in touch with her family.'

'Actually I'm starting work there next week, Tuesday and Wednesday afternoons,' she said, her eyes glued to the hedges as they sped past.

'Really? I'm sure you'll be a great asset to us.' Greg was fascinated by her.

Chapter 18

The next three weeks' dogfishing went a lot better for all the local fleets. Things were quiet and efficient on the *Sunrise*, but every so often Daniel found himself studying Matt's perpetually stern face.

Daniel wanted Hannah, the desire burned in him, in a much much deeper way than when he'd planned to take Viv Hickey, and for a deeper reason. The few times he'd seen her since her cold he'd behaved in the same friendly way as before her birthday, but he didn't intend to be too backward about claiming her completely. When the work was finished today, he was going to brave another secret visit to Roscarrock in the hope of seeing her alone.

The line had been drifting for two hours and the crew were preparing to haul in the catch. Curly Jose kept the lugger stemming the tide as Rufus hauled in the line and Fred coiled it into the tubs. Daniel and Matt were sending the dogs sliding down into the net room which they were using as a fish berth, pressing the fish against an old piece of oilskin wrapped round their sea boots as they took out the hooks with one neat, rapid twist, careful to avoid the dogs' viciously sharp spurs on the foreside of their dorsal fins. Less attentive fishermen could end up with cut and blood-soaked wrists. The dogs, their grey, streamlined

bodies resembling tiny sharks, were rather sinister looking, with their flat underlying mouths and oily, unwinking
green eyes. Eyes as soulless as Matt's, Daniel ruminated,
glancing at him.

Matt was aware of the cocky blue eyes on him again
but did not pause in his work. The depth of his loneliness
was no one's business but his own, but Daniel Kittow
needn't think he had simply stepped aside to give him an
easy path to Hannah. Matt had thought it through. It had
been bad luck that he'd shown his feelings for Hannah at
the same time she'd gone to work at Roscarrock. She
loved her new life and it had thrown her feelings into
confusion, and Daniel had deliberately added to them.
Matt would give her time to sort out her feelings, then
he would approach her again, praying in the meantime
that she wouldn't be fooled by Daniel's interest. He just
wanted what he felt was being taken away from him and
Matt was sure there was only one thing on the arrogant
swine's mind. Matt had one small hope: when last he
had glimpsed Hannah she hadn't been wearing Daniel's
locket.

Fred, his mind only half on his task, was hopeful there
would be a serious altercation between Daniel and Matt,
so Rufus would have a reason to bawl them out for once.
Daniel was carefully removing a red gurnard from a hook
and Fred wished the vicious erect spines on the fish's
head and body would tear into his hand.

'Knock her out, you bastard!' Rufus suddenly shouted.
Fred hadn't realised he'd been coiling too tightly as he'd
watched Daniel. Daniel shook his head sardonically and
Fred, already in some distress at a painful boil on his
wrist rubbed up by his oilskins, vowed revenge. He was
fed up being seen as the fool on the boat. Everyone knew

Daniel Kittow was up to no good and Fred had spied him before secreting a package into his locker. Next time he did that, Fred would take a look at what was inside it.

In the late afternoon they were back at the quayside, Daniel and Matt throwing up the dogs on the deck from the fish berth. Matt glanced at the lace curtains of what had been Hannah's bedroom window. Was it one of her afternoons off? Daniel smirked to himself. He knew Hannah would not be in Porthellis today.

The catch numbered ninety-seven score of dogfish. The crew didn't hang about to watch the merchant's men gutting, swiping off spurs and tails, skinning the dogs on hooks to turn the fish into pink lengths of rock salmon for the fish and chip shops. They moored the boat, completed the baiting up, scrubbed down and covered the tubs with tarpaulin to protect the bait from rain and thieving gulls.

Daniel gulped down the quick meal of fried ray and mashed potatoes that Rufus tossed on the table then he bathed, shaved, scrubbed his teeth and changed into smart clothes. Rufus took no notice of him combing his hair and slapping aftershave on his wide jaw. Although he preferred the company of his whisky bottle nowadays, the old seafarer had been proud of the strong sex drive of his youth. Daniel was merely about to indulge in his favourite sport.

From his talks with Hannah, Daniel knew the routine at Roscarrock ran like clockwork. Dinner would be over, the maid would have completed her duties and gone up to her room, Gregory Opie would be in his study, Patrick Opie retired to plan his next day's gardening and cooking, Mrs Opie in the drawing room or her suite with her silly dog. Daniel hoped the old lady didn't want Hannah to play cards or keep her company tonight and he'd find her relaxing in the servants' hall.

Under the cover of darkness he crept along the gardens to the back of the house. It seemed his luck was in; there was a light on in the room over the granite steps. He tiptoed up the steps and tapped on the door. There was no answer. He tapped again. A lace curtain was pulled back and Hannah's lovely face appeared at the window. He waved to her.

She opened the door slowly. 'Daniel,' she whispered. 'What are you doing here at this time? There's nothing wrong, is there?'

'No,' he said, sweeping her aside and entering the cosy room where a hearty fire was burning. 'I just felt like seeing you.'

'But someone might see you. I'm only supposed to have family call on me.'

He looked at her with a twinkle in his eye. 'Is anyone likely to come in here?'

'No, but—'

'Does the old girl want you with her tonight?'

'No, Mrs Opie's got a headache and has gone to bed with a sleeping tablet.'

'Then we've got nothing to worry about, but if anyone catches me here we'll say I've called with some news about your old granny. Say she's poorly or something. Anyway, Mrs Opie is so pleased with you she's hardly likely to send you packing.'

'I don't know why you couldn't wait until tomorrow,' Hannah muttered, not at all pleased he was here. She liked to keep the two aspects of her life separate. 'It's my afternoon off.'

'But I only get to see you alone for a few minutes in

the evenings.' He put his red head to the side and grinned boyishly at her until finally she smiled back. 'That's better.' He stepped forward and kissed her cheeks. 'If you don't want to stay here and worry about me being seen, why don't we slip out to the cottage? You've got the key and you've said it's still furnished. We don't need a light, there's a full moon.'

Hannah didn't like it but she knew Daniel wouldn't be sent packing, and it was good to see him. 'All right then, but just for a little while.'

Hannah fetched her coat and they stole along to the cottage. As she unlocked the door, she whispered, 'We'll have to take our shoes off on the doormat or we'll leave footprints.'

This done, she led the way into the little parlour at the back of the cottage. The moon was shining through the window, illuminating the large, dark, cumbersome shapes of the furniture. Daniel closed the door. Hannah shivered. He took her by the hand and moved to the small settee.

'Sit down,' he breathed in her face. 'We'll cuddle up and get warm.'

Hannah sat down and pulled up her stockinged feet which were cold from the stone floor and covered them with her coat. Daniel sat close and wrapped his arm round her.

'This is cosy,' he said, breathing in the fresh feminine smell that was part of Hannah, something he had only recently noticed.

'How have the boats done this week?' she asked automatically. Like all those brought up in the closeknit community, she was concerned for all the families.

'All did pretty good as far as I could tell.' He caressed

241

her hair then touched the soft skin behind her ear.

'Did my father go out?'

'No, he hasn't got over the heart attack yet. Apparently the doctor has warned him to stay home for a while longer.'

'So Mitch is still at home?'

'Yes, but still threatening to leave.'

'I wish I had the chance to talk to him. I'll try and see him for a few minutes after chapel on Sunday.'

'I'll tell him you want to see him.'

'Thanks.'

'How's Leah getting on here?'

'She loves it, she and Angie are getting on well. I only hope she doesn't get found out. There'll be hell to pay.'

'Her secret's safe with me.'

'Good.'

'Nice like this, isn't it?'

Hannah took her head off his broad shoulder and gazed up at his face, shadowy in the moonlight. 'What are you up to, Daniel Kittow?'

'What do you mean?'

'Oh, don't try sounding innocent. I know you, remember? You don't do anything without a reason. Why are you here?'

'I wanted to be with you,' he protested. 'Isn't that reason enough? You know how special you are to me, Hannah.'

He was so good-looking in the silvery light, the bold planes and angles of his face set off to their best advantage, his thick hair turned a deep copper. The many women who had been so easily charmed by him would love to be this close to him. Hannah snuggled in closer; it was a good feeling.

'You're so beautiful, Hannah,' he said huskily, putting a light kiss on her chin. 'No longer the little girl I liked being with, but a beautiful, desirable woman.' He pulled her closer and put his mouth very tenderly over hers.

Hannah wasn't sure if she wanted this but after a moment she kissed him back. She enjoyed the physical contact. He parted her lips with his and gently explored inside her mouth.

'I could eat you,' he said, his voice throbbing, then he ran his lips searchingly down her neck.

Minutes later they were still kissing and Daniel put his hand inside her coat. Hannah felt his fingers undoing her cardigan buttons and straying to her breast. She allowed him to caress and knead. Then his lips became more persistent and his hand was sliding down inside her dress. Part of her wanted him to go on but she pulled herself from his kisses and clamped her hand round his wrist.

'Stop right now, Danny. I'm not ready for that sort of thing.'

'Okay, fair enough,' he murmured, his voice full of desire. 'I won't do anything you don't want me to.'

'I don't want things to move too fast between us,' she said, primly straightening her clothes.

'Fine by me. We'll carry on meeting secretly. It's more enjoyable this way.'

'I'm glad you understand. I'm just not ready to start again, not after . . . How is . . .'

'How is Matt? You don't have to feel guilty about him, darling. Actually, he seemed quite cheerful today.'

'Oh? Well, I'm glad of that.' She sat up straight, not sure he had told her the truth. 'I'd better go in, Danny, and don't forget you've got a very early start.'

He got up reluctantly and pulled her to her feet. When

they'd put their shoes back on, he held her intimately against him and kissed her with all the passion of his long experience of delighting women.

'I'll see you tomorrow when you can slip away from under your dear aunty's eagle eyes.'

'Danny, don't make a habit of coming here like this. I won't let anything spoil my good relationship with Mrs Opie.'

'I wouldn't expect you to, darling.' He hugged her so she couldn't see his disappointment.

When Hannah was back sitting in front of the fire, she relived her meeting with Daniel. It had been enjoyable, even rather exciting, but she felt troubled and couldn't work out why.

Chapter 19

The following morning the parish constable rode his bicycle up to Roscarrock. Hannah showed PC Douglas Burt, a fresh-faced young man, new on the job, up to Mrs Opie's rooms then out of the front door twenty minutes later.

'Thank you, miss,' he said as he put his helmet back on his close-cropped head. 'Would you mind giving me your name? I come from Camborne and I'd like to get to know the local people.'

'Hannah Spargo,' Hannah replied, beginning to close the door to shut out the cold draught beating about her legs.

He wrote her name down on a new page of his notebook and looked at her again from owlish eyes. 'Have you worked here long, Miss Spargo?'

'About four months, Constable Burt.'

He put the notebook and pencil into his breast pocket. 'Do you happen to go out of an evening?'

Hannah thought of her little excursion across the yard last night and wondered if he had come to warn the household about a prowler. 'Not off the property.'

'There's a dance at St Austell on Saturday night. Would

you be interested in coming with me, Miss Spargo? I can arrange transport.'

'What?' It took a few moments for Hannah to realise what he meant. 'I . . . no, no, I would not, Constable Burt.'

He seemed quite unperturbed and doffed his helmet. 'Good morning to you then, Miss Spargo.'

Hannah closed the door, thinking the policeman had a damned cheek. She went straight up to Mrs Opie as instructed and explained what had delayed her.

Feena Opie pursed her pink lipsticked mouth then smiled, partly amused, partly serious. 'You sound as if you aren't interested in young men at all, Hannah.'

'I'm not,' Hannah said fervently, sitting down to discuss the day's orders.

'Let's hope the dashing Constable Burt doesn't need to come back for a while. He came to warn us that some of the local wealthier houses have been broken into recently. A doctor's house at Mevagissey was burgled last night in the small hours. The thieves took silver and jewellery. I'm not overly concerned. They're unlikely to come here and we have two men in the house.'

'I hope no one was hurt.'

'No, the thieves are very professional, a syndicate, the police believe. If the house isn't empty they usually slip in and out without anyone noticing until the next morning. I promised the constable we'd keep our eyes open for anything or anyone unusual. Now, enough of that, we don't want to get anxious.' Mrs Opie thrust her shoulders forward slightly and peered directly into Hannah's eyes. 'Are you going down to the village this afternoon, my dear? There's a new play on the wireless this afternoon that I think you will like. We could listen to it together.'

Occasionally, Mrs Opie had an idea that kept Hannah from going home. Still fuming about the nerve of the young constable, Hannah didn't really want to see Daniel. 'I hadn't really thought what I'd do this afternoon, Mrs Opie,' she fibbed. 'I'd like to listen to the play.'

'Good.' Mrs Opie gently ruffled Pogo's silky white ears. 'Rain is forecast for this afternoon and it will save you a cold, wet journey. Besides,' she paused, 'your family could come to see you here. Why should you always have to go to them?'

At St Austell railway station Mitch jumped into the train for Penzance and was dismayed to see Daniel getting into the same carriage. Viv had seemed quite pleased to see him on the last two weekends but as usual had plied him with questions about Daniel. Mitch had hoped that if Daniel never showed up she'd eventually forget him.

'Surprised to see you, Mitch,' Daniel said, sitting opposite him and lighting a Player's Weight. 'Where are you off to then?'

'Same place as you, I expect,' Mitch answered gruffly, sliding down defeatedly in his seat.

Daniel took a few moments to think about it, then he grinned. 'No, same place but different people. I'm off to see Wilfred Hickey. Taken a fancy to Viv, have you? Course you have, bloody fool,' he scoffed at himself. 'I should have realised why you were going there for your meals during the pilchard drive.'

The train chuffed out of the station and Mitch's dark good looks brightened, but only slightly, Daniel noticed.

'Not going too well, eh?' He'd have to use this to his advantage because he didn't want Mitch in the boarding house while he handed his package over to Wilfred. 'Tell you what, mate. Give me a few minutes with her first and I'll put in a good word for you.'

Mitch didn't like the idea but he felt that only Daniel could purge the infatuation Viv had with him. 'Thanks, Danny.'

'I wish you good luck, mate. I won't be hanging about. I'm on the next train back.'

When they reached Newlyn, Mitch stood looking over the harbour as Daniel turned up Trewarveneth Street.

The instant Wilfred had gone out, Viv fell on Daniel. 'Oh, Danny, thank God you've come.' She clung to his arms and her eyes filled with tears. 'I'm in trouble. I've missed two months and I'm pregnant. I've been hoping desperately you'd come to see Dad. What am I going to do? Dad will throw me out.'

Daniel sighed irritably, pushing her hands away. 'There's no need to go on about it like this.' He ran his coarse hands through his hair, his mind ticking over. If he didn't need to call occasionally on Wilfred, he'd tell her to go to hell, she wouldn't be the first woman to bear a Kittow bastard. There was only one thing for it. 'Don't worry,' he said harshly, angered by the way her panic-stricken, hazel eyes were boring into him. 'I'll see you're fixed up.'

'What do you mean?' she wailed, pushing back her auburn hair which was hanging like rat's tails over her shoulders. She had been so worried she hadn't been taking care of her appearance. Fay Dunn in the pub had threatened to dismiss her if she didn't buck up. Viv had burst into a flood of tears. Fay had asked her what was the matter, and Viv had told her.

'The rotten bastard,' Fay stormed. 'You're a good girl, I know that. He must have forced you or as good as.

Well, there's only one thing you can do now. You'll have to tell him and get him to face up to his responsibilities, though I don't think you'll get very far from what I know about Daniel Kittow.'

This was what Viv was trying to do now.

Daniel sidestepped her as her imploring hands reached out to him again. He took out his wallet and counted out the notes inside it. 'I've got enough. I'll just slip out and see Aggie Crabb and arrange it. Don't worry, it'll all be over in a few hours.'

'What are you talking about, Danny?' Viv was getting hysterical. 'Can't we get married? Take me to Porthellis and I'll keep house for you and your grandfather. I'll be a good wife to you. I won't nag you or tie you down. Please, Danny, I'm desperate. You did this to me and you've got to do something about it.'

'That's what I'm trying to do, you silly bitch! Aggie Crabb will get rid of the kid for you. She's done it heaps of times. I know women who've been to her.'

'But I don't want to do that, Danny. I weren't brought up to go to church or chapel but I know it's wrong.' Viv tried to grab him but he thrust her away.

'You don't have any bloody choice! I don't want to marry you. You're nothing to me, and anyway I'm engaged to a girl in Porthellis.'

'Who?' Viv shrieked, hurling herself at him and pounding her fists on his chest. 'Who are you going to marry? I thought you loved me. You said I was special to you. You can't do this to me, Danny.'

Holding her at arm's length, he smacked her hard across the face. 'Shut up, you stupid little bitch! Her name is Hannah, not that it matters. I said I'm going to fix things up for you. You should be bloody grateful. It'll cost me a sodding packet.'

Viv held her stinging face and collapsed in tears. Fearful that Mitch would come in and witness what was going on, Daniel lifted her up and carried her to her room. He soaked the ragged flannel with cold water from the pitcher on the washstand and pulling her hands away from her face dabbed round her eyes.

'Come on, pull yourself together. Things haven't worked out as you wanted between us but when you've got rid of your problem there'll be other men. You can start again. A pretty girl like you won't have any trouble attracting a husband. I'm going now but I won't be long. Tidy your hair and wash your face. Stay here until I get back.'

Daniel met Mitch as he opened the door to the street. 'Sorry, mate, you're out of luck. Viv has gone to stay with a cousin for a few days.'

'Viv has never mentioned a cousin,' Mitch said, his spirits tumbling. 'Where's she gone exactly?'

'Wilfred didn't say. You might as well go home. I've got someone else to see for a few minutes. Why don't you go on to the Blue Anchor? I'll meet you there for a drink before we go home.' Daniel passed him half a crown. 'Get 'em in, mine's a bitter.'

Mitch took the money and shuffled off, his head down, to the pub on the waterfront.

Daniel walked on up the steep hill and made his way to an address in one of the back streets. He handed over ten pounds and was back in the boarding house in fifteen minutes.

Viv was on her feet, sniffing and snuffling as she pinned up her hair.

'Good girl, it's all arranged and paid for. You can go straight away.' He gave her the address. Then thrusting out his hand he took hold of Viv's quivering, bruised face. 'Don't let me down and I don't want to hear anything about this ever again, you hear? I don't want any trouble when I'm visiting Wilfred.'

Having conjured up a modicum of pride, she ripped his hand away. 'You've ruined my life, Daniel Kittow. You're a complete and utter bastard. I hate you.'

'Good, let's keep it that way. I hate women hanging around me.'

As he got to the door, Viv had a parting shot. 'Whoever this Hannah is, I pity her greatly.' She threw the hair combs and brooch he had given her at his feet.

A dark shadow passed over Daniel's face and for a moment she thought he was going to come back and hit her. He crushed his gifts under the heel of his shoe, pointed a warning finger at her and then he was gone.

It took Viv over an hour to summon up the courage to go to the address Daniel had given her; it was in a small part of the port that respectable people avoided. She put on her baggy coat and tied a large headscarf under her chin. She was trembling as she made her way through the narrow streets, her hands clamped tight in her pockets, her short ragged nails biting into her palms. When she got there she went numb, standing like a block of stone a few feet away, staring at the low black-painted door of a dismal cottage, terrified of what would happen to her if she stepped inside it. People passed by and stared curiously.

A rough looking man in ragged clothes, stinking of stale alcohol and sweat, asked her if she was lost.

'Yes, totally lost,' she murmured.

'Tell me who you're looking for, my luvver, and I might be able to help 'ee.' He moved in close and put his arm round her shoulders.

'Bugger off or I'll scream the sodding place down,' she spat at him.

Startled, the man didn't hang about.

Viv knew she couldn't stay here. She wasn't sure what an abortion entailed exactly but knew that after a short time in the cottage, some agonising pain and bleeding, her 'problem' would be over. No one but her and Daniel and Aggie Crabb would ever know, and neither of them would tell anyone about it – or worry that it could put her life at risk. She was terrified but it had to be done; there was no alternative.

She willed her legs to take her to the door. There was a crooked iron knocker on the flaking paint. She must act quickly; if someone saw her going in here they might guess her reason.

Viv's hand stretched up, as if in slow motion. She lifted the knocker, then a terrible longing came over her, hitting her like a freak wave, permeating her every sense and emotion. From the moment she'd realised she was in trouble she hadn't given one thought to the third person involved in her dilemma. Now it was as if her baby was begging to be allowed to live. Dropping the knocker, which clanked noisily against the door, she turned and fled.

Chapter 20

Hannah was having her tenth driving lesson. Knowing that Greg Opie begrudged the time it took him away from his writing, she was glad she was learning quickly. They were travelling home past the castellated outer wall of the castle of St Michael Caerhays and Hannah glanced at a big, brown, long-horned bull in a field near the beach on the opposite side of the road.

'Keep your eyes on the road,' Greg said sternly, 'or you'll put us in the ditch.'

'Sorry,' she said tightly. She was pleased to be learning to drive but would have preferred another instructor.

'Change down a gear to go up this hill.'

She did it expertly and Greg nodded his approval. 'You're a competent driver, Hannah. I'll tell Grandmother you can apply to take your driving test and she can buy herself a motorcar as soon as she likes.'

'Mrs Opie has already chosen one,' Hannah said, sweeping the car smoothly round a bend.

Greg said nothing. He was annoyed. This wasn't the first time Hannah had mentioned something he knew nothing about. He wasn't the sort of man to care about his position being usurped in his grandmother's life, and he didn't believe it would happen, but he was uneasy

about what the outcome of all this might be. His grandmother still refused to answer any of his questions. Did
she intend one day to tell Hannah, as Greg suspected it,
that she was her grandmother too?

'I've noticed you don't go down into the village as often
as you used to,' he said. 'Why is that?'

Hannah wanted to tell him it was none of his business
but that would have been rude. 'I've got Leah to tell me
the news twice a week.'

'She's settled in very well with us.' Greg liked talking
about Leah as much as he liked talking to her. Could he
get her somewhat hostile elder sister to open up about
her? 'I was wondering how she came by that scar on her
face. A childhood accident?'

'Yes.' Hannah frowned as she slowed down behind a
haycart. 'I hope you won't mention it to her, Mr Gregory.
She's rather sensitive about it.'

'I wouldn't dream of it.' Greg saw her knuckles whiten
as she gripped the steering wheel and he thought it wise
to keep quiet about Leah.

When Hannah pulled the car in smartly at the back
of Roscarrock, Patrick Opie opened the door
for her. Hannah thanked him and took off her
gloves.

'I say, you did that jolly well. You're a natural motorist,
Miss Spargo. What do you say, Gregory?'

'She hasn't put a scratch or mark on my old jalopy yet,
I'm happy to report.'

'Splendid, splendid.' Patrick sucked in his face in one
of the quizzical expressions he was apt to make. 'Great-
Aunt Feena will be pleased. I'm sure she sees you as
more than a good investment, Miss Spargo. Well, must
get on, lots to do.' He hurried off to the garden shed in

his ancient coat, floppy colourless hat and Wellington boots.

Hannah felt Greg's eyes on her. His gaze was unwavering. 'I'm sure my grandmother wouldn't part with you at any price,' he said and stalked off, leaving Hannah chewing over exactly what that cryptic statement had meant.

Later in the day, Angie Miller and Leah were sitting at the kitchen table, swathed in old aprons, armed with the cleaning rags and the Silvo, cleaning the dining room silver. Leah balanced a heavy knife on her hand and looked at the writing on the blade.

' "Sheffield," ' she read. 'Is that where this was made, Angie?' She was eager to learn everything about the house and what was in it.

'Ais, don't be afraid to rub on un hard,' Angie replied. She appreciated Leah's work and her quiet, pleasing character and was happy to pass a few words now and then. 'We'll do the set with ivory handles next, then the candlesticks and then the brasswork. I enjoy sitting here quietly and doing this.'

Someone was coming down the servants' stairs. It was a heavy step and they looked up, expecting to see Mr Patrick. Angie jumped up and nearly knocked over her chair when she saw it was Mr Gregory; she was totally in awe of him and he had never ventured below stairs before.

'Ah, Angie,' he said, smiling at Leah who had followed Angie's example and was on her feet, waiting to see if they were going to be told off for missing his bell ringing, 'I was turning out a few cupboards in the study and I'm making dust everywhere. Could someone come with a brush and duster?'

'Y-yes, sir,' Angie stammered.

'You look busy here,' Greg continued, unperturbed that

his presence was making colour creep up Angie's flat face. 'Perhaps Leah could come.'

Relieved that it wasn't her who had to go, Angie told Leah to fetch the relevant cleaning materials. Greg had gone when Leah came back from the broom cupboard. As she changed into her clean apron, Angie muttered, 'What's got into he? He only lets me go in there to clean out the grate and light the fire. You watch your step, Leah. Don't 'ee touch none of his precious papers.'

Leah wasn't particularly concerned as she tapped on the study door and entered the room. Mr Greg had always been nice to her and she was longing to see inside the study. She held her breath in amazement. Most of the walls were taken up by bookcases which were crammed full of heavy brown, black and maroon volumes decorated with gold leaf. Those that didn't reach down to the floor had cupboards underneath them and Greg was on his knees in front of one with items spread all over the floor. It was gloomy owing to a heavy shower of rain and he was illuminated by the firelight, giving his fair hair a golden sheen. With her fanciful nature, Leah likened him to the picture of the Angel Gabriel she'd seen in a book at Sunday School.

'Right, Leah,' he said, admiring again her trim figure in her pink dress and apron, a white frilled headband keeping her black hair off her dainty face, 'if you'll dust the things and pass them to me I'll put them back in the cupboard. I'll throw away the rubbish as we go.'

Kneeling down on the other side of the pile he'd made, Leah picked up a box containing a board game. She read the label as she dusted – Chinese Checkers – then handed it across to him.

'I haven't played this for years,' he said as he put it on

the top shelf of the cupboard. 'My father and mother were alive then and we always played something after dinner. Does your family play games, Leah?'

'Not very often,' she replied, marvelling again at how easy she found Mr Greg to talk to. 'My grandmother lives with us and she's a miserable old so-and-so and won't let us make any noise.'

'That's a shame.'

'What I'd really like to play . . .' She broke off, thinking he wouldn't be interested in her desires.

'Yes? Go on, Leah.'

Before speaking, she cleaned years of collected dust off a chocolate box, heavy, and not containing chocolates now, she supposed. 'Well, I've always wanted to play the piano. My Uncle Terence has one and he said he'd teach me, but when I asked my father if we could have one he told me not to be silly.' Jeff Spargo had said a lot more, including some choice swear words. 'We wouldn't have had the room when all my brothers and sisters lived at home but we could now,' she finished wistfully.

Greg's heart went out to her. His old university friends would find it incredible that a man of his background had become besotted with an ordinary village girl, a girl who'd had no experience of life and had simple ambitions. But it was Leah's innocence he was attracted to, her total honesty. Here was someone unspoiled by the world, by conventions and hypocrisy. If his grandmother knew he had inveigled her in here to be alone with him she'd be furious, and not just because they were worlds apart. He'd assured her that he had no designs on Leah's person, but if Leah misread him or became upset by his attention it could threaten his grandmother's very close relationship with Hannah.

'Perhaps one day I'll play for you, Leah.'

One of the last things to be put back in the cupboard was a small telescope. Greg changed his mind and threw it in the bin.

'Ohh . . .' The little moan was out of Leah's mouth before she knew it.

'What's the matter, Leah?'

'I . . . nothing, sir.'

'Don't be afraid to tell me,' he smiled at her, shuffling closer to her on his knees.

'Well, I was wondering, if you don't want that telescope . . .' she began bashfully.

'Yes?'

'Well, my cousin, Jowan, would like it, to look at the stars. He studies the stars at night.'

Greg took the telescope out of the waste paper basket and placed it in her hands. 'I don't think it will be any good for star-gazing but he's welcome to have it.' He rummaged around in the overflowing basket. 'I put something else in here you might like for yourself.' He took out a glass paperweight, domed in shape with pretty curling streaks of colour inside, like half a giant marble.

Leah took it from him as if she was being presented with a pot of gold. 'Thank you, Mr Greg.'

They cleaned out two more cupboards together and Greg gave her many a little treasure to take home: a jigsaw puzzle of the African jungle, an ornament of a bluetit with a tiny piece of its tail broken off, and a big box of postcards sent to him and late members of the Opie family from all round the world. Leah had never felt so excited in all her life. She was supposed to be at Lizzie's house today and would have to leave most of the things there until she could smuggle them home. She couldn't wait to peruse them at her leisure in her room.

She swept up the dust and debris left outside the cupboard doors, unaware that Greg was watching her intently. When she straightened up, she gazed at the titles of some of the books. He came and stood beside her.

'What are you looking for, Leah?'

'Oh, sorry sir, I'm forgetting myself. I'll get back to the kitchen.'

'I don't mind. Were you looking for something in particular?'

'A book on astronominy for my cousin.'

'Astronomy,' he corrected her gently. 'You'll never carry one of these big books home. I think I've a pocket book on the subject somewhere. I'll look it out for you and give it to you tomorrow.'

'Oh, thank you, Mr Greg. You are kind.'

Down in the kitchen, Angie had done the silver and was about to tackle the brass, when Hannah joined her. 'All alone, Angie? Where's Leah got to?'

'Oh, she's with Mr Gregory, miss,' Angie said, her tongue curled on her bottom lip as she vigorously rubbed a poker with the Brasso.

'Why?' Hannah asked, immediately disturbed.

'Mr Greg is turning out cupboards in the study, miss. He wanted Leah to clear up the dust behind un. Do 'ee want a pot of tea now?'

'No, thank you, Angie, you carry on. I'll go and see how Leah is getting on.' Hannah took the back stairs two at a time and ran to the study. She gave one hard rap on the door and went into the room. She wasn't amused to see Greg Opie standing very close to her younger sister, and gazing down at her, apparently engrossed with her.

'I've been looking for you, Leah,' she said in a formal

voice. 'The rain has stopped and Mrs Opie has said you can leave now before there's another shower.'

'That was kind of her.' Leah gathered up all the things she had been given and said at the door, 'Thank you, Mr Greg.'

'You're welcome, Leah,' he smiled.

'What are you going to do with them?' Hannah said, looking at the things clutched in Leah's arms as they returned downstairs. Hannah was carrying the laden waste paper basket.

'Mr Greg gave them to me.' Leah was suddenly worried. 'It was all right for me to take them, wasn't it? He was going to throw them away.'

'It's all right, don't worry,' Hannah returned, hating to see the disappointment on her face. Leah was so happy working here, but was Greg Opie about to ruin it for her? Hannah's worst fear was that he might try to seduce her. 'I'll give you a shopping bag to carry them home in. Be careful Father, Mum and Grandmother don't see them.'

'I will,' Leah said happily, changing into her own clothes in the servants' hall.

'Have you got your torch to light the way?' Hannah fussed. 'It'll be quite dark by the time you reach the village.'

Lea produced a small torch from her coat pocket and held it out for inspection. Hannah was struck by the childlike gesture. She saw Leah to the door, kissed her goodbye, then went straightaway to the study.

She knocked and this time, as she usually did, waited for Greg Opie to call, 'Come in.'

He was at the desk, reading by the light of the lamp. He didn't look up at her.

Hannah walked round the desk and put the empty waste paper basket down. 'I'd like a word with you, Mr Gregory.'

'I'm busy.'

'I'm not going until you hear me out,' she said stubbornly, raising her chin.

Smiling sardonically, he rose and faced her. 'Well? What's this about, as if I didn't already know.'

She met his stony grey eyes. 'I'll say this clearly, leave Leah alone.'

He folded his arms. 'I don't mean Leah any harm. I'm very fond of her.'

'Well, I don't trust you,' Hannah snapped, wanting to wipe the smug smile off his face. 'Leah is still a child. She's spent most of her life hiding away at home and hasn't had the chance to grow up like other girls her age. Your interest in her alone could do her an immense amount of harm if she develops a crush on you. You're her employer's grandson, there could never be anything between you. You should know better.'

'And what will you do if I tell you to go to hell?'

'I'll tell Mrs Opie and unfortunately Leah will be dismissed. I've noticed your grandmother doesn't like your unhealthy interest in Leah either. Leah will be terribly upset but I'd rather have that than leave her to fall into your clutches.'

'You do that and I'll tell my grandmother you've been meeting your lover in the cottage at night.'

'What?' Hannah gasped.

Greg warmed to his counterattack. 'I often take a walk around the grounds in the dark. It clears my mind and gives me inspiration to write. I saw you and Daniel Kittow going into the cottage and I noticed you were in there rather a long time. Time enough to—'

'Daniel and I are not lovers,' Hannah interrupted, her voice rising.

'Come now,' Greg sneered. 'Neither I nor my grandmother are that naive.'

'You can think what you damn well like, Greg Opie, but I'm telling you the truth.'

'And you can think what you damn well like, Hannah Spargo, about the way I feel for Leah. Just remember, you open your mouth and I shall open mine.'

Hannah knew he had her in a corner but she still had some fight left in her. 'I won't let you hurt Leah. I don't know what I'll do but I won't let you lay a finger on her.' She turned and stormed for the door.

'I'm surprised you keep such disreputable company, Hannah,' he said, stopping her in her tracks.

She whirled round. 'What do you mean?'

'I haven't kept up with many friends around here, but the Chief Constable happens to be the father of one of them. We all had lunch in St Austell the other day. The Chief Constable is worried about a spate of recent local burglaries. He doesn't like his friends and acquaintances being robbed. He brought up several names of suspects and one of them was your boy friend, Daniel Kittow.'

'But Daniel's not involved in the burglaries,' Hannah protested, sure of Daniel's innocence.

'Well, the police are convinced he's up to his neck in them somehow. He keeps company with known villains. Don't tell me you didn't know that.'

Hannah couldn't deny that all of Porthellis reckoned Daniel was involved in shady dealings.

'Can't think of anything to say?' Greg taunted her. 'Well, I suggest you tell your boy friend to keep his head down. And bear in mind, Hannah, that if my grand-mother knew that you had covertly entertained a villain on her property, it would be you who would be dismissed. And who knows, she might offer Leah your job in your place.'

Hannah had to get away from his taunts. She thrust open the door, closed it with a bang and ran, red-faced and horror-stricken up to her room. When she calmed down she went over everything Greg Opie had threatened her with. She wasn't too concerned about Daniel. He had been ducking and diving all his life and could look after himself. But if Greg Opie ever gave her the slightest reason to suspect he might violate Leah, she'd walk into Cliffside Cottage herself and tell her father that Leah had been working at Roscarrock.

Chapter 21

It was lashing down with rain but it didn't stop the redoubtable Miss Peters from venturing out. She was on her way to give Janet Rouse an order for a new nightgown and saw a small female figure standing alone, huddled on the quayside. She watched the figure keenly as she knocked on Janet's front door.

'Miss Peters,' Janet greeted her, surprised. 'Come in. Fancy you coming out on a day like this.'

'A drop of rain never hurt no one,' Miss Peters scoffed, shaking her little navy blue umbrella and stepping down into the passage. She promptly turned round and peeped out of the door. 'Who's she?'

'Who's who, Miss Peters?' Janet said, craning her head round the old woman.

'She along there. Gazing at the men unloading their catch. Must be mazed standing about leaking wet on a day like today. She don't look familiar to me.'

'Nor me.' Typical of the villagers' sense of hospitality, Janet added, 'I'll get Hannah to put her coat on and invite her inside.'

Janet closed the door and led the way to the kitchen. Miss Peters' shrewd eyes homed in on Hannah who was sitting sewing by the fire.

'So you've found your way back here, have 'ee?' she said accusingly. 'Haven't been to see me for ages. Getting above we in the village, are you, Hannah Spargo?'

'No, Miss Peters.' Hannah put her sewing aside. 'It's nice to see you. I'll make a fresh pot of tea.'

'Why didn't you come in by the back door?' Janet asked Miss Peters as she took her wet hat and coat. ''Tis much quicker.'

'And get my boots muddy as I walk through your yard? I'm not soft in the head, Janet Rouse. Don't forget to tell the maid to put her coat on.'

Hannah looked at her aunt curiously and Janet told her about the stranger on the quay. 'Ask her if she would like to come in by the fire and have a cup of tea. She must be waiting for one of the men. Some of the boats have nearly finished but she might welcome shelter for a while.'

Putting on her hat, coat and boots, and taking Janet's umbrella, Hannah braced herself to go outside. The stranger was still there, clutching a cloth bag which was soaking. Hannah hastened across the two hundred yards to reach her and put the umbrella over both their heads. The woman turned a startled wet face to her.

'Hello, my aunt lives just along the street there. We were wondering if you'd like to come inside out of the rain.' Hannah could see the stranger was younger than she was and had the saddest eyes she had ever seen.

'I-I'm waiting for someone,' the girl said through chattering teeth, pushing a lock of auburn hair in under her hat.

'You'll freeze if you stay here. You can watch the boats from my aunt's window if you like and then you won't miss who you're waiting for. We'll get you a cup of tea

266

to warm you up. I'm Hannah Spargo,' Hannah ended, inviting the girl to tell her her name.

The girl stared at her out of hazel-brown eyes which seemed too large for her small deathly-white face. 'I'd rather stay here.'

'What about your bag then? I could put it inside for you. Whatever's inside it must be soaked through.'

'I'm fine, there's no need to trouble yourself,' the girl said, her features tight and rather hostile now.

Hannah shrugged her shoulders. She had tried her best to help. If the girl wanted to stay here in the rain and risk getting pneumonia, that was her business.

At that moment there came the heavy thud of several pairs of sea boots and an outbreak of chatter as the fishermen who had been helping each other to complete the day's work in the awful conditions leapt ashore and started down the quay. They were a mass of yellow oil-skins. The girl lurched towards them.

Daniel, his head down as he lit a cigarette, walked in front with Matt and the rest of *Sunrise*'s crew. Hannah made to go home; her father was behind the men, he must have ventured outside to see what size *Misty*'s catch was. Rufus nudged Daniel and as he brought up his red head and saw the girl, he swore profusely. Hannah was shocked, not only by the profanity but by his ugly expression. The girl's small body started as she saw him and she ran back to Hannah, fear plain on her face. Daniel strode past but Matt stopped to speak to them.

'Is everything all right, Hannah?' He too had noticed the girl's distress.

'I don't know, Matt.' Hannah looked at the girl. 'Is something wrong?'

The girl didn't answer. She kept her eyes on the plodding fishermen, then suddenly she darted off.

Mitch saw her and ran to her. 'Viv! What are you doing here?' He was shocked by her gaunt appearance. He took her aside and spoke softly so he couldn't be overheard, 'What is it, Viv?'

'Oh, Mitch,' and tears formed in her eyes to compete with the rain streaking her face. 'Dad's thrown me out. I didn't know what to do. You once said if I ever needed help . . .'

'And I meant it,' Mitch said, putting his arm round her shoulders. 'I'll take you home. My mother will soon have you dry and comfortable and then you can tell me what this is all about.'

'I-I don't want to be a bother,' she sobbed.

'You won't be,' he promised her. 'Not one little bit.'

Jeff Spargo took his eyes off his son and the girl speaking to him and gave a hacking cough as he walked past Hannah and Matt. Hannah waited for the inevitable insult. He glared at her but said nothing; it seemed Leah was right when she'd said their father's brush with death had quietened him.

Hannah waited until all the fishermen had cleared the quay, then asked Matt, 'Do you know who she is?'

'She's a Newlyn girl. I've see her talking to Mitch on the quay.' He didn't mention he'd seen her waiting for Daniel.

'She must be the girl Mitch has been interested in. She looks as if she's in some sort of trouble.'

'You could be right, Hannah.' Matt had a good idea what the trouble was. Daniel had boasted about his conquest on the boat.

It was good to talk to Matt again. Hannah looked up at his handsome face, his dark eyes blinking as rain dripped off his sou'wester. 'How are you, Matt?'

'Oh, you know,' he shrugged his broad shoulders.

'I, um, I've been wanting to say sorry about . . . you know.'

'And I'm sorry I got shirty with you. I've still got your birthday present, if you want it.'

His gaze was fixed and unreadable. Hannah felt embarrassed. 'Um, yes, I would like to have it . . . I might pop in for it some time.'

'You'll be very welcome, Hannah,' he smiled softly. 'Well, we'd better not stay out here all day. I'll walk you to your aunt's door.'

They said goodbye and Matt was gone before Janet, who had been watching from a window, could fly to the door and invite him in. Miss Peters had grabbed her cardigan to stop her. 'Let 'em take it slowly,' she said. 'The worst thing you can do is rush 'em along.'

'What were you and Matt talking about?' Janet demanded the moment Hannah got back inside the door.

'Never mind that,' Miss Peters intruded. 'What does that girl want with your brother?'

Mitch hurried Viv over the granite bridge and into Cliffside Cottage before his father and Josh arrived home. Prim and Leah were laying the table for the men's hot meal and Constance was in her rocking chair beside the kitchen hearth. She shrieked in complaint at the sight of Mitch in his wet oilskins.

'What're 'ee thinking of, boy? Standing there like that, soaking the floor.'

Mitch had become decidedly rude and surly with his grandmother since the day he'd stood up to his father on the boat. 'Oh, never mind that, 'tisn't you who'll wipe it up. Mum, I've brought someone with me. This is Viv. She's soaked through. Have you got something for her to put on?'

Prim hadn't seen the girl hiding nervously behind Mitch and the moment she did she started clucking like a broody hen. 'Aw, you poor little soul. Leah, run upstairs and fetch something of yours for her to wear and a couple of towels. Take her into the parlour, Mitch. It's warm and cosy in there, your father was sitting by the fire until he was daft enough to go out.'

Viv kept her eyes on the ground, clutching her wet worldly possessions as Mitch struggled out of his oilskins and Prim helped him take his sea boots off. Before he could take Viv into the parlour, Constance trilled, 'Was your father following you? Benefit you looked after he instead of a complete stranger.'

'Viv is not a stranger to me and I'll thank you to keep a civil tongue in your head,' Mitch retorted. Gently taking Viv's arm he led her to the parlour. 'Take no notice of the old girl, she's so sour she curdles the milk.'

Viv was too cold and tired to take exception to Constance Spargo's spite. She let Mitch take the bag from her, pull off her coat and seat her beside the fire. He took off her saturated shoes. She gave him the faintest smile but he could see she was near to tears. Crouching before her, he took her frozen hands in his.

'Everything's going to be all right, Viv.'

Prim bustled in with the clothes and towels. She put a hand on Viv's shoulder. 'Good grief, my handsome, you're soaked through to the skin. I'll have to get you out of these things before you catch your death of cold. Out you go, Mitch, while I get Viv – that was her name, wasn't it – while I get her dry.'

'She came to see me, Mum,' he protested, unwilling to relinquish a moment of being with her.

'Maybe she did, my son, but she can't stay like this, can she? Don't worry, I won't ask her anything, I'll leave that to you. Leah's just bringing in a cup of tea for her then you can stay in here together for as long as you like. I'll keep some stew warm for the pair of you.' Prim eyed him critically. 'It wouldn't hurt you to get cleaned up yourself.'

Reluctantly, Mitch left the room and Leah came in with a cup of tea. Viv was trembling too much to drink it so Leah put it down in the hearth. She gave Viv a small encouraging smile, and not wanting to embarrass her slipped away quietly.

Viv sat still and unresponsive as Prim gently pulled off her hat and wrapped a towel round her hair.

'What a lovely colour your hair is, Viv,' Prim said cheerily. 'Now if you stand up, dear, I'll help you off with your dress.'

Numb from the cold and wet, her emotions trampled, Viv obeyed meekly. Prim quickly pulled off all her top clothes and was shocked by the bruises on the girl's body, but keeping her promise she asked no questions. Holding the other towel under her armpits, Viv took off her undergarments and Prim passed her the clothes Leah had supplied, which included her second best dress. When Viv was dressed, Prim eased her back on the chair and put the tea to her lips.

'Take a few sips, my handsome. It'll make you feel better.'

Viv sipped the tea then gave Prim her first response. 'Th-thank you, Mrs Spargo.'

'You're welcome, dear.' Prim rubbed her hair with the

towel then put it over her thin shoulders. 'Right then, I'll tell Mitch to come back in.'

Viv hung her head, afraid she was being a nuisance. 'Thank you.'

Mitch was waiting outside the door, having changed into dry clothes and splashed a flannel over his salt-encrusted face. Prim caught his arm. 'She's got bruises on her, Mitch.'

He sighed angrily. 'Poor girl, she's had a rotten life. I'll see what's happened.' He had a rough idea. Wilfred Hickey was a lazy swine, he relied on Viv to skivvy at the boarding house for him. There was only one reason why he would throw her out, and Mitch was sure it had something to do with Daniel Kittow.

Viv didn't raise her face as he came to her. He crouched down in front of her and took her hands. 'Tell me what's wrong, Viv.'

She looked fearfully at him. 'I-I'm in trouble, Mitch.'

'A baby?'

She nodded and tears ran down her face. 'D-Dad wouldn't let me keep it. I c-couldn't get rid of it and he told me to pack my bags and get out. I didn't know what to do then I thought of you. I had saved some money from my singing and I caught the buses and train here. I-I thought you might be able to help me.'

'Of course I'll help you, Viv.' He passed her a clean hanky. 'Did your stepfather hit you?'

'Yes, when we rowed about the baby. I told him, you see, hoping he'd understand and let me keep it.'

Mitch had a lump in his throat but he forced himself to talk normally. 'Was it Daniel Kittow who did this to you?'

'Y-yes,' she sobbed wretchedly and Mitch stroked her

272

wet hair. 'H-he got angry when I told him and he paid for me to get rid of the baby but I couldn't go through with it.'

'The bastard,' Mitch muttered under his breath. 'Well, never mind him. I'll look after you, Viv.'

'I th-thought he loved me, Mitch, or I wouldn't have l-let him do it. I didn't really want to do it anyway. I never liked it.'

Mitch sat on the arm of the chair and gathered her into his arms. 'Don't cry, Viv,' he said tenderly. 'The worst is over now. Everything is going to be all right.' He lifted her chin and looked into her eyes. 'Daniel Kittow may not want you but I do. I've loved you for ages. We can get married and I'll bring the baby up as mine. Even if it's got red hair it doesn't matter, people will think it's taking after you.'

Her tears stopped and she looked amazed. 'Y-you don't have to do that, Mitch. You'll be getting used goods.'

'I could never think of you like that, Viv. I know you're a decent girl. You can live here until we get married and as soon as I can find somewhere else we'll move out of the village. There's a boat at Portmellon interested in taking me on. I don't intend to spend the rest of my life living with my rotten father and evil grandmother, and we won't have to stay here and have that cocky swine living next door and ruining things for us.'

Viv could hardly dare to believe what she was hearing was true, that her problems were coming to an end and she would become a fisherman's wife after all. 'You mean it, Mitch?'

'I meant every single word, Viv.'

She could see the sincerity in his face and through a

fresh flood of tears she clung to him. 'Oh, Mitch, you're a good man.'

'And we'll have a good life together. I promise on my life, Viv.'

A few minutes later Mitch went through to the kitchen. Jeff and Josh were at the table finishing their meal. The three women looked at him expectantly.

Jeff gulped from his big mug and stared moodily over the rim. 'Well?'

'I've got Viv into trouble,' Mitch said boldly. 'We'll have to get married straightaway. Her stepfather's thrown her out. She'll have to stay here.'

'Gah,' Josh scoffed, looking at his brother as if he was the biggest fool on earth. 'It's not up to you. Daniel Kittow put that bastard in her belly.'

With a supreme effort, Mitch stayed calm. 'Kittow tried but Viv knew what he was like and she wasn't interested. It was me who did it. We fell in love and Viv gave herself to me. 'Tis my baby and I'm standing by my responsibilities.'

'Really, Mitch,' Prim said crossly. 'You should have known better. She's little more than a child and you're only a boy yourself. Was it her stepfather who hit her?'

'Yes, but I vow that no one will ever hurt her again.'

It had always been up to Jeff to say what went on under his roof but if he said Viv couldn't stay, he knew Mitch would walk out with her and he was needed on the *Misty*. 'She can sleep in Leah's room,' he said tersely. 'I'm not having any goings-on under my roof. You can go to your Uncle Terence and ask him if he can spare a couple of blankets for her. She can help your mother and sister round the house. I'm not having her sitting about on her backside all day, pregnant or not. You'll be out at sea all day tomorrow. I'll go up to the Manse and tell the minister your shame and set a date for the wedding.'

'Thank you, Father,' Mitch said, astonished he had given in without threats or a quarrel.

'Jeff, you can't mean it,' Constance exclaimed.

'I've said my piece, Mother,' he snarled, getting up from the table. 'If he's stupid enough to get the girl in the family way he can repent of it for the rest of his life. I'm getting changed and I'm off to the pub.'

Mitch and Prim exchanged jubilant looks. It was rare for Jeff to go against his mother's wishes. The best thing that had ever happened as far as they were concerned was Jeff's heart attack.

Chapter 22

When Jeff entered the Ship Inn, a small, dark building whose interior had been made to look something like an old packet ship, he was coughing into his hand. Daniel offered to buy him a drink.

'I'll have a drop of brandy for my throat,' Jeff said, shrugging out of his wet coat. 'Bleddy rain, in for the rest of the week by the look of it.'

Jeff usually drank at the bar with the regulars but Daniel wanted to talk privately and carried a glass of brandy and a pint to a quiet table, which was in fact an authentic water barrel.

'How are you feeling these days, Jeff?'

'Why?' Jeff took a swig of brandy. ''Tisn't like you to ask after someone.'

'I don't like to see a good fisherman down on his luck.'

'Huh!' Jeff said bitterly. 'They're managing all right without me. Been bringing in better catches. Maybe I should cling on to this bleddy cold.'

'I reckon they're missing you.' Daniel studied the other man. 'You got a visitor in your house, I see.'

'Oh, so that's why you've bought me this drink. You worried the maid who's brought trouble to Mitch should be laying it more rightly at your door?'

'No.' Daniel glanced about to see if they were being overheard.

'Mitch said you tried it on with Viv Hickey but you didn't get anywhere. That true? You were bragging you had her. He said he's the only man she's been with and he's the father. That true?'

Daniel sighed inwardly with relief. If Viv and Mitch had told the truth he would have denied it, but people would probably have believed them and it might have ruined his plans with Hannah. 'You know what it's like, Jeff. You try your hand but when a maid won't give over, sometimes you say she did anyway, partly to make you feel better, partly out of spite. I was concerned for young Viv, I've known her since she was a little maid. I knew what she and Mitch were up to. Is he going to do the right thing by her?'

'I'm going to see the minister tomorrow. Get 'em decently married before she's showing. Bloody idiot, he should have been more careful.' Jeff's mind seemed to wander for a moment. 'But there's always one that slips through the net.' He had said enough. 'I'm going to the bar. Thanks for the drink.'

Terence Spargo came into the pub and Daniel listened as the two brothers talked about the same thing.

'What does Prim think about it?' Terence asked.

'You know that silly cow. She likes taking in lame ducks and she's delighted to think she'll have a grandchild under her own roof, if she can get Mitch to stay.'

Daniel finished his pint feeling pleased with himself. The next time he went to Newlyn, to get his cut from Wilfred Hickey for the last package he had left with him, he'd call on Aggie Crabb and get his ten pounds back.

When Maggie Curnow called 'time', Daniel found he

was the last to drink up. He took his empty glass up to Maggie who was covering the pumps.

'They've all scuttled away home to their beds, Maggie,' he said, gazing at her generous bosom swelling against the thin silk of her blouse.

'I don't blame 'em on a night like tonight, Danny.' She eyed him provocatively. 'Even Jeff's deserted me.'

'That's a shame.'

'He don't let himself go since he was took bad.' She slunk round the bar, her strong perfume wafting towards Daniel. 'He's lost his virility.'

'You need someone younger and more able, Maggie.'

She ran her red-varnished fingertips up his arm, tweaked his collar and ran her tongue over her bottom lip. 'You got any idea who would fit the bill, Danny?'

Daniel smiled at her, pulled her to him and kissed her roundly. 'Lead the way, Maggie.'

Sometime later, as they lay naked in her bed, bodies glistening with sweat, listening to the howling wind beating round the pub, Maggie lit two cigarettes and passed one to him. 'Someone was asking about you today, Danny.'

'Oh, who was that?'

'The parish constable.'

Daniel drew in deeply on the cigarette and looked up at the ceiling. 'What did he say?'

'Asked me who you spoke to when you came into the pub and if you'd met any strangers here. He mentioned a man called Ken Blee. Course, I told him I'd never heard of him and what my customers did on my premises was their business. You been up to no good, Danny?'

Daniel turned on his side and looked over Maggie's voluptuous figure. 'Nothing that need concern you or PC

Plod.' He stubbed out his cigarette and did the same to hers. He wasn't the least bit disturbed. Ken Blee and his cohorts knew things were getting too close for comfort and were not planning to burgle any more houses for several months. Knowing that the police suspected he was involved in fencing the stolen goods, Daniel had stashed the jewellery from their last haul safely aboard the *Sunrise*.

Jeff wasn't up to satisfying Maggie Curnow but he took his pleasure from Prim. 'Do you believe it's Mitch's baby that girl is having?' he asked before she turned away from him.

'Mitch hung around Newlyn all through the pilchard drive and he's gone down there at the weekends. You can see he adores her. She seemed to be 'fraid to let him out of her sight after he'd announced the news. Course it's his baby.'

'People have been known to accept other's bastards.'

Prim knew the bitter statement referred to Hannah. There would never be a right time to bring up her name but Prim plunged in. 'Mitch wants Hannah to go to his wedding.'

'Well, she bloody can't.'

'It's Mitch's wedding.'

'If she goes then I won't.'

'You know the truth about the boat accident, Jeff,' Prim persisted. 'Hannah shouldn't be blamed for Edwin's death any more than the others.'

Jeff turned away. 'Leave it, woman.'

'It's Mitch's wedding. We can't afford to lose him. If you came round about Hannah, he might consider staying.'

Jeff said no more. Prim dropped off to sleep with a little hope warming her breast.

The next morning her hopes were dashed. After Leah and Viv had got up, Constance poked about in Leah's room. She didn't find anything she could complain about in the few things of Viv's that weren't drying out in the kitchen, but under Leah's bed she found the box of postcards Greg Opie had given her. Her shrivelled old face brimming with malice, she carried the box downstairs. Ignoring Viv's presence in the kitchen, she went straight in on the attack.

'Have you seen these, Jeffrey? What your daughter had hidden in her room? Where did she get these from?'

'You've got no right to go through my things,' Leah shouted furiously.

'Shut up!' Jeff snapped. He was in no mood for a female tussle; his mother caused one nearly every day. 'Where did you get them, Leah?'

She couldn't tell the truth but the lie she gave was little better. 'Hannah gave them to me.'

Prim had been ready to defend her daughter but now she snatched a handful of postcards out of the box. When she saw the Opie name and address she tossed them back in disgust. 'Why did Hannah give you this rubbish?'

'They weren't wanted at the big house and she thought I'd like to look at the pictures, that's all. They've been sent from all round the world.'

'Burn them, Jeffrey,' Constance hissed. 'We don't want nothing from there in the house.'

'No!' Leah screamed. 'Please, Dad, they aren't hurting anyone.'

'They're hurting me,' Jeff snarled, his head spinning as

281

shrill voices all arguing at once filled his head, making him feel disorientated. He threw the box and postcards into the fire and stood in the way so Leah couldn't whip them back out. 'Tell Hannah she's not to give you anything from there again.'

'It's not ruddy fair,' Leah wailed. 'I can't have anything nice in this house.'

'Are you going to let her speak to you like that, Jeffrey?' Constance bristled. 'I'd have got a smack 'cross the face if I'd spoken to my father like that.'

'Aw, shut up, Mother, for goodness sake!' Jeff exploded. 'You're always on about one of the children. Leave it be.' He swept out of the kitchen, slamming the door.

Viv trembled at the sink where she was washing the breakfast dishes and fervently hoped Mitch would not take long to find them somewhere else to live.

In the small hours a terrible choking wail woke up the inhabitants of Cliffside Cottage and many of those living on the dark side of the village. Jeff and Prim hurried out of bed to Constance's room.

'Jeffrey! I can't breathe.' Constance was sitting up in bed grasping her withered throat with both hands.

Prim turned on the electric light but the hideous contortion on her mother-in-law's face kept her away from the bed.

'Do something,' Jeff yelled, looking about helplessly.

Leah had joined them, shivering in her flannel nightdress. 'Pound on her back, Dad,' she suggested.

Constance held out one gnarled hand to her son. 'Jeffrey,' she implored. Her skin was purple and the noise coming from her throat was like the sea hissing and rattling as it was forced through a fissure in the cliff.

Jeff went to the bed and pushing his mother forward banged the flat of his hand on her bony back.

Josh and Mitch were peering round the door in their pyjamas. 'What's the matter with her?' Josh asked.

'She can't breathe,' Leah explained, shuddering as a terrible cry broke from their grandmother.

Viv, in her patched nightdress, the long cardigan she had borrowed from Leah over her shoulders, touched Mitch's back. He put his arm round her.

'What's that awful sound?' Viv whispered fearfully.

'It's my grandmother. She's been taken ill.'

'Is there something we can do?'

'Go downstairs and make some tea, I suppose. Will you help me?' Mitch did not want Viv to witness the gruesome scene inside the room.

'Yes, of course.'

'Josh, run and fetch the doctor,' Prim said urgently as Constance fought to breathe.

Josh had no wish to stay and watch his grandmother suffering and hastened away to the room he shared with Mitch to change into his clothes.

'You don't have to stay, Leah,' Prim said, pushing her daughter towards the door. 'Go downstairs with Mitch and Viv.'

Leah beat a hasty retreat. She found Viv searching for the tea caddy and took it down off the dresser for her. 'Sorry you have to put up with this on your second night here.'

'I've never heard anything like it, except . . .'

'Except what, my love?' Mitch said, unable to resist holding her comfortingly in his strong arms.

'Except when a lodger died one night. I'm sorry, I shouldn't have said anything.'

'What did he die of?' Leah asked, stoking the remains of the fire and putting on more coal to heat the kettle of water.

'The doctor said he must have ate something he was allergic to. I was glad he had eaten out that evening or I would have felt like I'd murdered him.'

'I shouldn't think it's anything like that,' Mitch said, hugging his sister too who was trembling with horror. 'Grandmother's old. It's more likely water on her lungs or something.'

There was a knocking on the door and Mitch answered it. It was Daniel and Fred Jose. 'What's going on?' Daniel asked. 'Sounds like someone's being murdered.'

'My grandmother has been taken ill,' Mitch said glaring icily at Daniel. 'She's frightened and in a lot of pain. I'm sorry if you were woken up.'

'Is there anything we can do?' Fred asked, shivering in a coat over his pyjamas, hoping the offer of help wouldn't be taken up. Constance Spargo's gasping cries were curdling his blood.

'No, nothing, thank you.' Mitch raised his eyes as another wail of anguish came from overhead. 'Except pray for her.'

The doctor arrived half an hour later and after an examination said there was nothing he could do. Constance's heart and lungs were failing and it was only a matter of time before she died. Josh was next sent to fetch the minister and his Uncle Terence. As Sarah, Naomi and Lizzie were pregnant, it was decided not to tell them until it was all over.

Jeff, Prim and Terence prepared to keep vigil with the Reverend Skewes; Bett Spargo despised her spiteful mother-in-law and had refused to get out of her warm bed. The four younger people, and Morley Spargo, stayed downstairs in the kitchen; Constance was making so much noise, weeping and wailing, gasping for breath, that if any of them had gone to bed they wouldn't have slept.

'You'd think she'd pass away quietly,' Morley observed, looking up at the ceiling.

'She's fighting it,' Leah said. It was four o'clock and she was making the umpteenth pot of tea.

'I hope I don't go like that,' Josh commented.

'We'll miss a day's fishing tomorrow,' Morley said. 'Pity she couldn't die on Sunday.'

'Aargh! J-Jeffrey, help me!' was heard from above.

'She can see the gates of Hell stretching out in front of her,' Mitch said dryly. 'If she doesn't make her peace she'll reap her just rewards.'

'Don't say things like that, Mitch,' Viv said, raising her head from his shoulder – they were huddled together on a chair. ''Tis wicked. I don't know much about religion but I know you have to be forgiving.'

'Sorry, my love.' He kissed her cheek, the first kiss he had given her. 'But she's been so evil over the years. She's never been kind to anyone. It was she who turned Father against Hannah. It's what Mother has always said.'

'Aye,' Morley said, 'my mother will be along later but she said she wasn't going to stay up all night.'

Josh was staring at Viv's middle. 'One life ends, another begins.' He wasn't convinced the child she was carrying was Mitch's. It occurred to him that he would probably have been in luck if he had taken the trip to the boarding house in Newlyn.

Two hours later Terence called them upstairs. 'It won't be long now. 'Tis time you came upstairs, but not your maid, Mitch, we don't want to risk her losing the baby.'

Left alone, Viv shivered even though the fire was burning heartily. Do I belong here? she asked herself. Mitch had left his jersey on the chair. Viv picked it up and wrapped it round herself. It smelled of fresh air, salt, a slight tang of fish and Mitch. She felt instantly warm and comforted.

Constance Spargo thrashed and howled on her bed for another ten minutes. 'Oh, God, help me. Oh, God, arrgh! No!' She was lying on her pillows and suddenly sat up straight. The Reverend Skewes stopped in mid-prayer and looked as shaken as the others. Constance opened her mouth wide, saliva flooded out, then she fell back dead.

Leah had been clinging to Mitch and she hid her face in his chest. Prim nudged Jeff and with a look of abject distaste he closed his mother's eyes. Then he began to cry.

'Oh, my poor mother,' he sobbed over and over.

Mitch gave voice to a sentiment all the others agreed with. 'Let's hope she's taken all her hatred with her.'

Chapter 23

Fred Jose glanced slyly out of the *Sunrise*'s cabin door. The boat's line had been shot and he had offered to prepare the crib. Rufus and Curly were in the wheelhouse, Matt and Daniel were smoking at opposite ends of the boat. It was unlikely anyone would come into the cabin for a few minutes and, sweating fearfully, Fred took his chance.

Daniel always left his and Rufus's crib boxes on the table and stashed his bag in his locker. Fred took out the bag and rooted about in it. There was a clean but unironed handkerchief, a packet of cigarettes and a thick package. His hand trembling, Fred undid a corner of the brown paper. There was something inside the package wrapped in cloth. He didn't dare undo the cloth but prodded the contents. A triumphant smile broke out on his weak features. He felt a small, hard object attached to a chain, almost certainly a necklace, and what he was sure was other jewellery too. Swiftly rewrapping the package, he thrust it back in the bag and into the cupboard and shut the door.

He returned to his job of making tea and putting the food boxes on the table. He couldn't wait for the day's work to be over when he would meet PC Douglas Burt as arranged. The young constable had questioned Fred, as he had Maggie Curnow, and had found Fred more forthcoming. Bitter at what he saw as his unfair treatment aboard the *Sunrise*, Fred had mentioned he had an idea Daniel kept things hidden aboard the boat; Daniel was adamant his personal items must never be touched. Now Fred had proof that would put the red-haired bastard in prison for months if not years.

Up on deck, Daniel tossed the butt of his cigarette into the swaying water and went up to Matt. He had been unnerved by Constance Spargo's noisy death last night and felt like talking about it.

'The tide's on the make today. Shame the *Misty* can't take advantage of it.'

Matt gazed at him. They didn't speak much nowadays and when they did he was wary of Daniel taunting him about Hannah. 'A lot has happened in the Spargo household in the last forty-eight hours,' he replied.

'You ever seen anyone die before, Matt?'

'Yes, my father.'

'Did he go peacefully?'

'Yes, thank the Lord.'

'Constance Spargo didn't.' Daniel shivered as he recalled her horrendous wailings. 'I didn't see it but I heard it, every moment of it. She went kicking and screaming and kept half the village awake. 'Twas bloody chilling. Hope I don't go like that when my time comes.'

'Depends on what you've got on your mind,' Matt said quietly.

Daniel looked at him. With Jeff Spargo talking in the pub last night about Mitch getting married, it was all round the village that it was going to be a rushed wedding. Did Matt suspect he was the father of Viv Hickey's baby?

He had seen Hannah speaking to Matt yesterday at the quay. Matt was considered honest and reliable, he never gossiped; if he voiced his suspicions to Hannah it was likely she'd believe him.

'A wedding in the family will help the Spargos get over the old lady's death,' he said. 'Mitch is a lucky bloke. Viv's a pretty little thing, a nice sort. I was hoping to get somewhere with her myself but she preferred Mitch.'

'I thought you did get what you wanted, Daniel,' Matt said coolly. 'You bragged about it often enough.'

Daniel's face darkened. 'You know how it is. I was just trying to live up to my reputation.'

'No, I don't know how it is,' Matt returned, his mouth tightening. 'It's something I would never do.'

Daniel glared at Matt, suddenly afraid that his crewmate could yet prove to be a threat. Things hadn't progressed with Hannah as well as he'd hoped, she kept him firmly at arm's length. 'Well, I've had enough of gallivanting around,' he said, determined to have the last word. 'I want to settle down and I've got just the right woman in mind.'

'Fred's calling,' Matt said stonily, not rising to the bait. 'The crib's ready.'

At the end of the morning they were pulling in a goodly number of dogs and with the tide ebbing strongly, Rufus called to change ends and work from their eastern dan. Daniel was desperately thirsty and slipped into the cabin to snatch a drink of water. He had the tin mug to his lips when the lugger rolled with the heave of the sea and his locker door flew open. Throwing the mug down he rushed to the locker and looked inside his bag. All seemed to be in order but someone must have opened the door because he was always careful to latch it properly. There was only one man shifty enough to search his property and he'd had ample opportunity this morning. Balling his fists, Daniel went on deck.

The rest of the crew were busy about their labour. Fred was pulling in the line as Matt unhooked the fish.

'Fred Jose,' Daniel thundered. 'I want a word with you, you bastard!'

The pure venom in his voice made Fred squeal and he let the heavy line fall back into the sea. Matt was unhooking a dog; the hook was ripped out of the fish's mouth and took with it the top of his right forefinger.

Matt howled in agony. He shook his hand and blood sprayed over his face and oilskins.

'Hold your hand still,' Rufus shouted at him, running towards him.

Fred was stunned at what he'd done. Rufus pushed him out of the way and he fell to the deck. When Rufus had wrapped a rag round Matt's hand he turned on Fred.

'You stupid, clumsy bastard!' he yelled. 'What's the bleeding matter with 'ee? You've ruined Matt's hand.' Rufus lashed out with his boot and Fred yelped as it hit him in the chest. 'I ought to throw you overboard for this.'

'It wasn't my fault,' Fred whimpered like an injured puppy, scrambling out of Rufus's reach. 'Daniel shouted at me. I was startled.'

'That's just a bleeding excuse.' Then Rufus boomed at his grandson, 'What's this all about?'

Daniel was frozen in shock.

Rufus hurled a vile oath at him. 'Don't just stand there or I'll throw you into the sea with that other no-good bastard!' Rufus's face looked fit to burst in fury. 'I'll have to get a new crew at this bleeding rate!'

Curly had run for the first-aid box and as he pushed past, Daniel came to his senses. 'My locker had been opened.' He pointed at Fred, who was still on the deck and had received another kick, this time from his disgusted father. 'It could only have been him.'

'Yes, it was me,' Fred shrieked like an indignant schoolboy. 'He's got stolen jewellery on board. I saw it in his bag. The moment we get ashore I'm going to tell the constable and he'll go to prison.'

For a moment the other three fishermen looked at Daniel in amazement, then Curly got on with binding up Matt's bleeding stump and Rufus advanced on Daniel.

'Whatever you've got, get rid of it. Throw it over the side. The police can't do nothing if they've got no proof. The rest of us never heard what that useless bastard said and,' he turned, putting his foot to Fred's throat, 'you never saw nothing, right?' Fred stared, terrified, and Rufus roared, 'Right?'

'Y-yes,' Fred nodded, choking and gagging.

Muttering angrily, Daniel went off to obey his grandfather's order.

'Can 'ee hold on another hour or so, boy?' Rufus asked, placing his hand on Matt's shoulder. The young fisherman was white and shaking. 'We got a good catch here and you're gonna need every penny we can get in case you're laid up.'

Matt grimaced as another wave of pain shot through his injured hand. 'I-I'll be all right, Granfer. I'll carry on working.'

'Good boy. Curly, take un to the cabin and make un a mug of sweet tea.'

Daniel had thrown his illegal package over the side and he met Matt and Curly at the cabin door. 'I'm sorry,

Matt.' There was no love lost between the two men but he didn't like to see Matt hurt in this way.

Matt glowered at him but said nothing.

When Curly left Matt sipping the tea in the cabin, Rufus was unhooking and Daniel coiling the line. Fred was sulking, angry that his plan to get even with Daniel had failed, shamefaced that it had partly caused Matt's injury.

'How is he?' Rufus asked the engineer.

'What do you think?' Curly said grimly and made his way to the wheelhouse.

Matt rejoined the crew and they carried on working until the last hook was up. They made for home without a word passing anyone's lips.

Chapter 24

Jeff Spargo refused to allow anyone to go to Roscarrock and inform Hannah of her grandmother's death and he insisted Leah stay at home and keep Viv company, so Hannah didn't learn about Constance's demise until the postman commiserated with her two days later. She asked Mrs Opie if she could go down to the village; she had already taken her two half days off that week.

'That explains why Leah did not turn up to do her work,' Feena Opie said. 'Of course you may go, Hannah, but are you sure you want to? From what I have gathered from Leah, your grandmother had no time for you at all. Your father won't welcome you at the house and there is nothing you can do.'

'I suppose you're right,' Hannah replied miserably. She didn't particularly mourn her grandmother's passing but it was one more family occasion she had missed. She made a mental note to tell Leah not to discuss the family's business with Mrs Opie. 'I won't be able to go to the funeral either but I would like to be in the village then. I'll take some time off when I know what day it is to be held, probably the day after tomorrow.'

'I am sorry about your family circumstances, Hannah.' Mrs Opie gazed at her closely. 'But never mind, you're happy here now, aren't you? There's something I want to discuss with you. I haven't been out of the house for years and I have a yearning to look up some of my old friends. I can't possibly manage on my own with Pogo and I couldn't bear to leave him behind. How would you like to come to London with me as my companion? We'll stay in a top hotel and it will give you an opportunity to see the sights.'

'I'd love to!' Hannah exclaimed.

'That's settled then. I'll see to the arrangements.'

'When will we be going?'

'There's no point in a delay. We should be able to set off straight after your grandmother's funeral.'

There was something Hannah was concerned about. Gregory Opie had finished his stage play, had taken it up to London and had come back a couple of days later saying he was going to start on his next novel. Without her and Mrs Opie here, Leah would be at his mercy. Mrs Opie had also thought of it.

'I won't require Leah while we're away. I'll pay her a retainer so she won't lose her wages. I'll give them to you and you can send them and a message to your sister Sarah's house for her.'

When Hannah went about her duties, Feena Opie made a list of the things she would take to London with her and the things she wanted to order for herself and Hannah. It was a long list, she was planning to keep Hannah away for several months.

That night Daniel turned up again at Roscarrock. Hannah reluctantly let him into the servants' hall. 'You shouldn't have come here, Danny. I've told you that Mr Gregory saw us going into the cottage and what he assumed we were doing in there.'

'I don't care what he thinks,' he said, sitting in the cosy armchair she had vacated. 'You hardly come down to the village these days and when you do you spend more time with your aunt than me. I thought we were friends, Hannah – more than that.'

Hannah didn't sit down. 'I'm sorry, Danny, but things have been awkward.'

'How?'

Hannah couldn't tell him the truth, that since talking to Matt she had no desire to see Daniel as a romantic partner. She was more attracted to Matt than to him, but she didn't want either of them; her life here held the greatest sway over her hopes for the future. 'I've been very busy,' she answered lamely.

'Well, you aren't busy now,' he said putting on a cheery voice. 'How about making us a cup of tea?'

'I can't. Mrs Opie hasn't given me permission to have friends here, only family,' she said firmly. 'Please, Danny, you must go.'

He took some moments before he got up and Hannah was reminded of how stubborn he could be. He came close to her, took her in his arms and tried to kiss her.

Hannah turned her head away. 'Don't, Danny.'

'Why not, for crying out loud?'

'Someone might come in.'

He gripped her tighter. 'I think you're lying. You've kissed me before. Why don't you want to any more?'

Hannah wrenched herself free. 'I'm sorry, Danny, but I don't want to be attached to anyone right now. I'm enjoying my new life here and that's all that's important to me.'

A dark shadow passed over his face. This was the first

time a woman had rejected his advances and he didn't like it. But Hannah really was special to him and his disappointment was immense. 'Is it because it's too soon after breaking up with Matt?'

'It's partly that,' she said to placate him; Daniel would argue all night if she didn't offer a crumb to salvage his pride. 'And partly the reason I gave you. Please, Danny, I'd thought we'd agreed to go back to the way we were. Can't we stay like that, at least for the time being?'

'If that's what you want,' he sighed, then forced himself to smile with his old familiar charm. 'You will seek me out when you're down in the village from now on and not avoid me?'

'I promise.' She returned his smile, seeing her boyhood friend in his handsome features and not the impatience and umbrage lurking behind them. 'But we'll still have to meet secretly. I don't want Aunty Janet nagging me.'

That suited Daniel. He pressed a hand on her shoulder. 'I'm glad we've sorted that out, me girl. I'd hate to think we couldn't always be friends. I suppose I'd better go then.' Before he left he kissed her cheek in a brotherly peck but was determined that somehow he would soon turn their relationship into something more intimate.

On the day of the funeral, wearing black even though she wasn't going to the chapel or churchyard, Hannah made her way to her Aunt Janet's house. She was pleased to see that Leah and the girl who had met Mitch on the quay were there; Hannah had been wondering what had happened between the mysterious stranger and her brother.

'This is Viv Hickey,' Leah proudly introduced the pale-faced, auburn-haired girl who had already become a close friend. 'She and Mitch are getting married.'

Hannah shook Viv's hand. 'I'm pleased to hear it, Viv. That's wonderful news.'

Janet was on her knees pulling dishes out of the cupboards of the kitchen dresser for the funeral tea, and she asked Leah to help her.

Viv felt rather shy to be left facing Mitch's only fairhaired sister who, because of her position at the big house, was considered a cut above the ordinary girls in the village. She rubbed her hands down the black dress she was wearing. It had belonged to Janet who had cut it down to size and restyled it for her, leaving two large pleats under the bust for when she grew in size with the baby. Viv had put her hair up and Mitch had bought her a new pair of shoes. She looked smart and pretty but felt shabby in Hannah's presence.

'Mitch has told me a lot about you,' she said quietly.

'I suppose he's told you why I won't be going to the funeral.'

'Yes, but he wants you to come to our wedding. He's going to ask his father to let you come.'

'It would be lovely if I could, Viv. Have you set the date?'

Viv blushed. 'It's two weeks on Saturday. It's quick because I'm pregnant.'

Hannah had an overwhelming desire to hug Viv and Viv was very surprised when she did. 'That's wonderful news. I'm so pleased for you both. Mitch will make a good father, he's been so kind to me since I was forced to leave home. Mother must be over the moon, she'll have three new grandchildren next year.'

'All the family have been very kind to me,' Viv said, which was true – apart from Josh who made her flesh crawl the way he sometimes ran his eyes over her body as if he was mentally undressing her. She stared at Hannah a moment. 'You and your sisters all have lovely names. Are there any other Hannahs in the village?'

'Only an old lady who died a few years ago.' Hannah was taken aback by the question but before she could ask why Viv asked, Leah came forward with an armful of dishes.

'Come on, Viv. We'd better get back. Mum will be waiting to put food on these plates.'

Viv took half of Leah's burden and made for the door. Leah whispered in Hannah's ear, 'Will you tell Mrs Opie I should be able to come back to work next week? She's not angry with me, is she?'

'I will and she's not,' Hannah replied in a whisper, opening and closing the door for the girls.

'I can't get over the change in that girl,' Janet said, referring to Leah. 'She's come out of her shell even more since Viv's been staying in the house. 'Tis a pity Mitch got the maid into trouble, but she seems a nice little soul, hard working and happy to oblige. Even your father seems to like her.'

'I wish he could learn to like me,' Hannah said wistfully, taking off her hat and coat and sitting down. She was going to stay here until her aunt got back from the funeral to tell her how everything went.

'Pity you're staying here all alone,' Janet said, putting on her best hat. 'I can't see it being a big funeral. Your grandmother wasn't well liked, but then she only had herself to blame for that. Most of the boats have put to sea.' Janet faced Hannah squarely. 'Of course Matt hasn't gone out with the *Sunrise*.'

'Why not?'

'Haven't you heard?' Janet took off her glasses and cleaned them furiously on her handkerchief in a disapproving manner. 'That's the trouble with you living up there, you might as well be in another part of the country,' she said shortly.

I soon will be, Hannah felt like saying, but in her aunt's present mood that piece of information was best kept until later, and she was impatient to learn about Matt. 'What's happened to Matt?'

'Last week he had his finger torn off on the boat. Carried on working, of course, as it looked like he wasn't going to bleed to death, but the wound became anguished and he's come over all whist. It was Fred Jose's fault, the stupid idiot. He let the line go without warning and it took Matt's finger off with it. Rufus says he won't have him on the boat again if there's one more incident.'

'Poor Matt,' Hannah said, suppressing a shudder. She was cross with Daniel for saying nothing to her about it.

'Poor Matt. Is that all you've got to say? It wouldn't hurt you to go up and see him. Betterfit you do that than sitting here on your own. Mrs Penney is going to the funeral so Matt might be glad of a bit of company.'

'Don't worry, Aunty Janet, I'll go and see Matt before the afternoon is over,' Hannah said wryly, but she was keen to see him.

She walked up to Seaview Cottage the moment she judged the funeral party would be inside the chapel. A harmony of Celtic voices was raised in singing 'Abide With Me' when she walked past. She tapped on the kitchen door of the Penneys' home and went in. The fire had been banked down in the range and there was a delicious smell of chicken broth. The table was set for two people, presumably for the evening meal. Matt wasn't

there. She crept along the passage, tapped on the door
of the parlour but he wasn't in there either. The house
seemed very quiet but Hannah doubted he had gone out
if he was too poorly to work. She climbed the stairs to
see if he was resting, calling his name; she felt something
of an intruder.

Matt was lying on top of his bed in his clothes, fast
asleep. A fire was burning in the hearth, and true to his
statement of several months ago, the room was exceed-
ingly untidy. Hannah went to the bed and gazed down
on him. His face was flushed and there was a slight
sweat on his forehead and in the well of his neck which
was revealed by his open shirt. His bandaged hand was
lying on his chest, the other hand gripping the wrist
protectively. He looked forlorn, a woeful expression on
his face, yet strongly masculine and very appealing. She
looked at his wide mouth. She had known those parted,
sensuous lips and she had enjoyed them. Daniel's kisses
had in no way compared to Matt's.

She tiptoed over discarded clothes and a pile of old
magazines on sailing he must have been browsing
through, intending to put a few lumps of coal on the fire
to keep it going then to put a chair near the bed and
watch over him until he woke up. As she put the chair
down she spied the jewellery box he had given her for
her birthday in an open drawer. She lifted it out and
ran her fingers over it. Now she had the chance to study
it she saw it was a perfect work of art. Made in solid,
dark golden wood, it was intricately carved round the
edges and the top was inlaid with a pattern of mother-
of-pearl. It was as splendid as anything she had seen in
Roscarrock. Matt must have chosen it with great care.
Carefully, she opened the lid and the ballerina twirled

and the music played. Hannah whirled round to see if it had woken Matt.

He stirred and opened his eyes. 'Hannah?'

'Hello, Matt,' she said softly. 'I'm sorry I woke you.'

He blinked and rubbed at an eye with his good hand. 'I thought I was dreaming for a moment.'

Hannah felt guilty to have been going through his things. She put the jewellery box back in the drawer.

'No, don't,' Matt said, pulling himself up into a sitting position. 'It's yours, Hannah. I want you to have it.'

'Thanks, Matt,' she said shyly, putting the jewellery box down on the bedside table to take with her when she left. She took off her hat and coat and sat down again. 'I only heard about your accident today. How are you feeling now? Can I get you a cup of tea or something?'

He took a sip of water from the glass on the table. 'My head's aching a bit and my finger, what's left of it, is very sore. I don't want anything, thank you. I hope you're not going for a while.'

'I'd like to stay and chat.' She was gazing intently at him and although she felt she was being silly, she wondered again how he had obtained the little scar on his chin. It was as good as anything to talk about. 'How did you get that scar on your chin, Matt? You must be able to remember.'

'Well, I don't.' He flushed and looked away.

Hannah thought there was a mystery here and, hoping she could get on a friendlier footing with him, she teased him. 'Oh, come on, I can see from your face you do remember. Was it through a childhood prank? Were you up to mischief?'

'No,' he said dismissively. 'It happened a long time ago.'

She leaned over him. 'What were you doing?'

'Nothing.'

'You must have been doing something,' she persisted, not sparing his discomfort.

'If you must know,' his dark eyes suddenly bore into hers, 'I fell out of bed and hit my chin on a washstand.'

'How on earth could you do a thing like that?' she laughed.

'I wasn't alone, there wasn't much room in the bed.'

Hannah's smile died. 'You mean you were with someone, a woman?'

'That's right.'

'Not in this bed?' Hannah asked indignantly.

'No, somewhere else.'

'Where? Who was she?'

'I don't think that's any of your business, Hannah.' He was enjoying himself. He'd only ever wanted to be equal with her, but Hannah had managed, sometimes quite ruthlessly, to gain the upper hand over him for a long time. It was good to be able to exploit her feelings for a change.

'How many times did you go with her?' she demanded.

'Really, Hannah, I can't see why you're interested. You didn't think I was a virgin at my age, did you?'

Hannah couldn't stand the thought of him being involved with another woman, even if it had been in the past. She'd assumed she had the sole rights to Matt's romancing, his lovemaking. She sprang to her feet, pushing back the chair.

'Who was she? Have there been others? Are you sleeping in anyone else's bed now?' Her voice rose the more she went on.

'Why are you shouting at me, Hannah? Are you jealous?'

It brought her up short. A few minutes ago she wouldn't have believed she could behave like this. 'Yes, yes I am!' She wanted to smash her hand across his face, pull his hair, hurt him. 'Damn you, Matt Penney, how dare you be so . . . so . . .'

'What, Hannah?'

'Attractive to me,' she said throatily, becoming suddenly still and sitting down on the bed close to him.

She gazed at him for some moments and he gazed steadily back. Then, all other thoughts pushed aside by the passion she felt rising for him, she put her arms round his neck and, careful not to hurt his hand, she pushed him down on the bed and crushed her mouth over his. Matt wrapped his arms round her and kissed her with equal ardour, making her realise how much she had missed this with him. She moved so she was lying on top of him. She devoured his lips for several moments then she kissed his eyes, his nose, bit his ears. Pulling open his shirt she ran her lips hungrily down over his chin, neck and chest. She went back to his lips again and again, feasting on him, exploring him in a way she had never done before.

Matt kept his hurt hand up out of the way but he returned her hungry caresses, undoing the buttons on the front of her dress and pulling it off her shoulders, exposing her perfect figure to his touch, to press against his bare flesh. His body was tingling deliciously. Hannah ran a row of kisses from his throat down to the pit of his stomach and he became intensely aroused. He lifted her face from his body.

'Stop it, Hannah, you're driving me crazy.' His voice was husky with desire.

She knew she should stop, common sense and respectability demanded it, but she reared over him and demanded his mouth again.

Matt couldn't bear it. He pushed her away from him, none too gently. 'I can't keep control if you go on like this,' he gasped, but he was desperate for her not to stop.

'Don't talk, Matt,' she breathed into his face.

Matt reversed their positions. He was so agitated that even if he'd had the use of both his hands she would have had to help him loosen the rest of their clothes.

Hannah didn't mind the moment of pain, pleasure ripped through her the next instant and with instinct born of her blossoming womanhood she moved in perfect timing with Matt. His need was so great his first release came quickly, then catching his breath he measured his pace, taking her with him to an exquisite simultaneous climax.

They lay on their sides, holding each other, allowing the wonderful moments of their fulfilment to wash over them. Hannah nestled into his hot, damp chest and marvelled that he could have driven her to such wild abandonment. She didn't regret it but it scared her a little and she had no idea what she wanted from him in the future. Perhaps her time in London would help her to decide.

Matt loved Hannah with all his being but he did not take their moments of lovemaking for granted. Hannah had changed a lot since she'd moved out of the village, she wasn't looking for a ring on her finger like most of the young women he knew. But if she never returned his love, if she refused for some reason to see him again, the beautiful moments of their passion and coupling, the knowledge that she had wanted him so much, and to be her first lover, would remain a triumph and a comfort to him for the rest of his life.

'I'm going away for a little while to London with Mrs Opie, Matt,' she said, keeping her face against his strong chest.

'Will you come and see me when you get back?'

'Yes.'

They didn't say anything else, content for now to leave it to fate to take them where it willed.

Chapter 25

Hannah lay in bed looking at the packed suitcases standing in front of the wardrobe. Inside them were the many new clothes and shoes Mrs Opie had bought for her; she had said she didn't want her to look like a servant on their trip away from Cornwall. There was also a new wool coat hanging in the wardrobe and a new hat and clutch bag sitting on one of the chairs by the window. One of the personal items Hannah was taking with her was Matt's jewellery box. Inside it was the locket Daniel had given her; she would wear it if there were any special occasions, but it didn't mean as much to her as Matt's gift.

Early tomorrow, Gregory Opie would take her and Mrs Opie to St Austell railway station and they would journey to London and stay for two weeks at the Dorchester Hotel. Hannah could barely contain her excitement. Few of the local women had stepped outside the village unless it was to go shopping in St Austell or occasionally to Truro, and here she was on the verge of travelling to the capital city. She intended to keep a diary and smiled at the thought that the first thing Leah would ask her when she got back was whether she had seen the King.

Mr Gregory hadn't been at all pleased when he learned Leah had been told her services wouldn't be required while they were away. 'It's a bit rough on Angie, isn't it, being left to do all the work?' he'd grumbled over the dining table that evening, glaring at Hannah who had been invited to eat with the family.

'There will be less work without Hannah and me here,' Mrs Opie said briskly. 'It's all arranged and that is the way it is going to be, Greg.'

Patrick Opie came out of his ruminations about the smaller meals he would cook for the next two weeks and listened to the end of the argument. 'We shall manage splendidly, won't we, Angie?' he said jovially to the maid who was in attendance. She coloured shyly. 'There's very little to do in the garden at this time of the year. Anyway, I thought you'd be up in London researching your new venture, Greg.'

'I can work just as easily down here,' Greg retorted irritably.

Hannah smiled smugly as she recalled how he had left the table and stormed off to his study.

She read a book for half an hour then turned off the bedside lamp and lay down and closed her eyes. As she had done for the last couple of days, she relived the wonderful moments in Matt's arms. Eventually she drifted off to sleep.

She was awakened some time later by a noise. She lay still and listened. It was the mysterious footsteps again. After a few moments she realised they were different tonight, they sounded a little heavier and they were definitely moving down the corridor – towards Mrs Opie's rooms.

Hannah got quietly out of bed and put on her dressing gown. She had to know who – or what – was walking about the house in the middle of the night. Picking up the poker in the hearth, her heart pounding, she silently opened her door and slipped into the dark corridor. Her heart nearly stopped in sheer terror and she put a hand to her mouth to forestall a scream. A large shadowy figure, clearly not either of the two Opie men, was passing through Mrs Opie's door. Hannah thought it had walked through the wood at first then she realised the door had been opened. Ghosts didn't walk through doors. Mrs Opie was in danger!

She made to dash after the intruder but then thought it best to wake up Mr Gregory who was just across the corridor from her. She rushed to his door, opened it quietly and went up to his sleeping figure which she could just make out in the darkness. She shook his shoulder.

'What the—'

'Shush!' Hannah hissed before his voice alerted the intruder.

Greg recognised her voice and immediately jumped to the wrong conclusion. 'Bloody hell, Hannah. If this is a ruse to sleep with me to prove to Leah—'

Hannah clamped a hand over his mouth. 'Shut up, Mr Greg,' she blurted out in a stage whisper. 'There's someone in the house. He's gone into Mrs Opie's rooms.'

Pushing her aside, Greg got out of bed. He was wearing only pyjama bottoms and didn't stop to cover his nakedness. 'Stay here,' he whispered. He took the poker from her hand and walked to the door.

As he stepped out into the corridor, Hannah heard him give a muffled cry and the poker rattle to the floor. She ran after him and screamed when she saw that he had been knocked down by another figure, shorter and wider than the first, who was standing over him. Hannah screamed again and the man's hand shot out and grasped her throat.

'Don't make another sound,' his rough voice threatened, 'or you'll follow him to the floor.'

There was a tall chest of drawers just inside the bedroom door with some of Greg's heavy volumes on it. Hannah reached out and clutching the heavy, bronze, bookend she thrust it into the attacker's chest. He howled in pain and fell backwards over Greg's still body. Hannah didn't waste a second, her every nerve and muscle pulsed with an energy born of the desire to protect Mrs Opie, and she clambered over the two men and ran to Mrs Opie's rooms.

Her screams had alerted Mrs Opie and the intruder. Mrs Opie had put on the bedside lamp and was sitting up in bed, trying to hold on to Pogo who was yapping and growling.

'Shut that blasted creature up or it'll be the worse for you,' the man snarled. He had a black stocking over his face and a cosh in his hand. He had been turning out her jewellery case and had a fistful of gems in his other hand. He stuffed them in his pocket and advanced menacingly on the bed.

'Leave my house this instant,' Mrs Opie shouted indignantly, seemingly unafraid.

Hannah flew at the man. 'Leave her alone!' she screamed, fighting and clawing like a wild cat.

'Hannah, don't fight him!' Mrs Opie cried fearfully. Letting Pogo go, she pushed back the covers and got out of bed to help.

The burglar tried to push Hannah off him but her flailing hands were scratching his face, her feet lashing out at his shins. He smacked her heavily across the face then thrust his head forward in a vicious head butt. Hannah cried as the skin above her eye split open. Her head was reeling and she was seeing stars but she still fought to bring the man down.

He raised his arm to smash the cosh down on her head, but Mrs Opie clutched at his coat and pulled on it with all her might. 'Leave her alone!' She was unsteady on her feet and lost her balance. As she fell, there was a horrible cracking sound and she howled with pain.

'Mrs Opie!' Hannah tried to reach her but the burglar grabbed her round the throat from behind and walked her from the rooms and out into the corridor.

Greg had come round and was grappling on the floor with the other burglar. Suddenly Patrick Opie was there in his dressing gown and slippers, and with a strength Hannah would not have believed he possessed, she watched amazed, dizzy and nauseous, as he picked up the burglar by the scruff of the neck and drove his head into the wall. The burglar sank down, unconscious.

Patrick moved away from him and facing the man holding Hannah, he put up his fists. 'Come on then, matey. Try and get past me, if you can.'

The burglar swore and produced a knife which he pressed against her throat. 'Get out of the way or I'll slit her from ear to ear.'

Hannah choked as she tried to breathe, her eyes wide with terror. Then Pogo ran up behind them and sank his sharp teeth into the man's ankle. He yelped and lowered the knife. Hannah brought her elbows back sharply into his guts and he doubled over. Patrick was upon them and, pushing Hannah to safety, he thumped the burglar cleanly on the chin and he joined his cohort on the floor. Pogo stood guard over him, growling low in his throat.

'Good heavens,' Patrick said looking about dumbfoundedly as he steadied Hannah on her feet. 'What on earth has been going on?'

Hannah rubbed her sore throat. 'Burglars, Mr Patrick,' she rasped. 'Mrs Opie is hurt. You must go for help.'

'Right. Mr Gregory isn't capable of driving. I'll borrow his car and fetch the doctor and the police. But first I'll tie up these vagabonds and lock them in a spare room.'

'Phone for an ambulance as well. I think her hip has been broken.'

Hannah hurried back to Mrs Opie, with Greg, shaking his head groggily, on her heels, shortly followed by Angie.

Mrs Opie was lying on her side, her face ashen, body twitching. The odd angle of her arthritic hip and the leg caught underneath her confirmed Hannah's suspicions.

'Is she all right, miss, sir?'

Hannah knelt beside her mistress and lifted her head on her lap. Mrs Opie was barely conscious. Greg pulled the covers off the bed and laid them over his grandmother. 'Go and make some tea and bring it up here, Angie,' he said, his voice telling of his shock at the sequence of events. 'Mrs Opie won't be able to have any but Hannah and I will be glad of some. Take the dog downstairs with you.'

'Yes, sir.' Angie gazed down disbelievingly at the huddled group for several moments then scampered away.

'Mr Patrick has gone to fetch an ambulance and the police, Mrs Opie,' Hannah said soothingly, having trouble keeping tears at bay.

'Are you . . . all right, Hannah . . . dear?' Mrs Opie got out between quivering lips.

'Never mind me. It's you I'm worried about.'

Mrs Opie held out a hand and Hannah took it in hers;

it was icy cold. Then the lady gave a long sigh and closed her eyes.

'Mrs Opie, Mrs Opie,' Hannah cried desperately, shaking her hand. She burst into tears and looked at Greg. 'Is she dead?'

Greg put his fingers on his grandmother's neck. 'She's got a strong pulse. It's better she's out of the terrible pain.' He crouched beside them with a pillow. 'Put this under her head. We can't do any more but make sure she's kept warm until the ambulance or doctor arrives.'

Hannah gently put Mrs Opie's head on the pillow then she felt Greg's hands on her.

'Come on, I'll put Grandmother's shawl round you. You're shivering.' When Hannah protested she wanted to stay close to Mrs Opie, he added, 'She'll expect me to look after you, Hannah.'

Hannah allowed him to help her to sit on the bed and wrap the shawl round her. He built up the embers of the fire to make a blaze then went to his room to get dressed. Hannah was crying softly, staring down at Mrs Opie, when he got back. He sat beside her and put an arm around her. Hannah rested against him, glad of the comfort. She remembered he had been struck on the head.

'Are you hurt badly, Mr Greg?'

He put a hand behind his head and grimaced. The fingers he looked at had blood on them. 'I think I'll need a couple of stitches. The doctor and a couple of aspirins will fix me up.' He gazed at her. 'You've got a cut on your forehead, but thankfully it looks as if it won't need stitching.'

'It's nothing compared to what has happened to Mrs Opie,' she sobbed, burying her face in his shoulder.

'Hush now,' he stroked her back. 'That was a brave thing you did for Grandma.'

'But if I hadn't gone for the burglar she might not have been hurt. She got out of bed to help me.'

Greg took her face in his hand. 'Listen, Hannah, Grandma is a light sleeper. If she had stirred, the swine might have bashed her in her bed. You may have saved her life.' He hugged her close. 'I adore Grandma. I can't thank you enough. And you might have lost your own life if it hadn't been for that silly little dog and Mr Patrick.'

Angie came back with the tea and she held a cup to Hannah's lips to encourage her to drink. Hannah took a few sips, then pushed it away and insisted she kneel beside Mrs Opie. It didn't seem right, leaving her lying on her own.

Angie left to get dressed. Greg watched Hannah as she tenderly stroked his grandmother's hand. With her hair falling about her pale face, her blue eyes looking twice their normal size, mouth turned down, she looked so very much like his late aunt.

'If only we had left a day earlier she wouldn't have been hurt,' Hannah said mournfully.

'There's no point in "if onlys", Hannah.'

'She'll be in hospital a long time, won't she?'

'A few weeks, then she'll have us to look after her when she comes out.'

Mrs Opie stirred. 'Stephanie . . . Hannah . . .'

'I'm here, Mrs Opie,' Hannah said softly, gripping her hand tighter. 'I won't leave you.'

Greg was sure her last statement was exactly what his grandmother wanted to hear. If she survived the trauma of the fall, he would demand to be told if Hannah Spargo really was Stephanie's daughter.

To arouse as little comment as possible, Greg walked to Porthellis rather than drive there the next morning. He didn't get past Miss Peters' eagle eyes. She appeared outside her little cottage, whip in tiny hand.

'Mornin' to 'ee. 'Tis a surprise to see you down here.' She recognised him from Hannah's description. 'Everything all right up at the big house, is it?'

'I'm looking for the Spargo cottage,' he said shortly, in no mood to be interrogated by the village gossip.

Miss Peters turned up her sharp chin. 'Which Spargo are 'ee looking for?' she asked tartly. 'There's Terence Spargo and Jeff Spargo, but if it's anything to do with Hannah then you'll be wanting her aunt, Janet Rouse.'

Greg wished he knew what Hannah's father was called. 'The Spargo who has a daughter called Leah,' he returned impatiently.

'Leah?' Miss Peters' voice rose suspiciously. 'What do 'ee want she for?'

'It's her father I'm looking for.' Greg gritted his teeth in exasperation. 'Are you going to tell me or do I have to ask someone else?'

The whip was brought up smartly and cracked over the cobbles. Greg jumped back, utterly startled. 'Carry on down the hill till you get to the waterfront,' the old woman cackled in glee. 'Then go 'cross the bridge to the dark side. 'Tis the first cottage you come to. Jeff Spargo lives there.'

Greg's feelings were as bruised as the back of his head and he felt insulted by the old woman's behaviour. He stalked off without saying thank you to her. He had set off from Roscarrock thinking he had a good excuse to see Leah, but recalling the brutal way, according to Leah, that Hannah had been thrown out of her home, he felt daunted now at meeting Jeff Spargo. Greg knew from Leah that the fisherman had delayed his return to sea until next week in the hope of keeping his son from leaving home rather than concern for his health. As he walked across the slab of granite, Greg hoped he would be out somewhere.

Leah answered the door to him. Her small face broke into a smile, then she exclaimed, 'Mr Greg, what are you doing here?'

'Hello, Leah.' He had the overwhelming desire to hold her to him for comfort. 'Is your father at home? I'd like to see him.'

Leah looked behind her, fearfully. 'I don't think he'd want to see you,' she whispered.

'I've come about Hannah. She hasn't gone to London. She's been hurt.'

'Oh, no!'

'Who is it?' a female voice said, and the door was opened wider. Prim had no doubt who the man on the doorstep was. 'What do you want?' she asked, not troubling to hide her loathing of an Opie even though she had never set eyes on the young man before.

'I've come about Hannah,' Greg repeated. 'She's been hurt.'

'Oh, my God,' Prim gasped. It must be serious for this man to be here. 'How bad is she?'

'Do you think I could come inside, Mrs Spargo? I'm sure you don't want all the neighbours listening.'

Her worry over Hannah banishing all thought of her husband's reaction, Prim beckoned him inside and closed the door. She showed him into the parlour where he positioned himself in front of the fireplace. 'Sit down please, Mrs Spargo,' he said melodramatically. He looked at Leah, careful not to give away he already knew her. 'Will you fetch your father please?'

Leah went to the kitchen. Jeff and Viv were waiting to be told who had been invited into the house. 'Dad, something terrible has happened to Hannah,' Leah blurted out, catching Greg's mood and hoping her father wouldn't throw him out. 'Mr Opie from the big house is here.'

Viv had been making pastry at the table. She wiped her hands on her apron and looked at Jeff doubtfully. 'Shall I go and fetch Aunty Janet?'

Jeff's face had darkened. He pulled his fading handsome features in tightly. 'Do what you damn well like. It makes no odds to me. I don't want to see the man.' Then he stared into the fire.

Leah was relieved. She hadn't expected her father to listen to Mr Greg but a few weeks ago he would have flown into a violent rage and declared he couldn't have cared less if Hannah had dropped dead, and Mr Greg would most certainly have been tossed out on his ear. As Viv took off her apron and put on her coat, Leah returned to the parlour.

'Father won't come in,' she said, sitting beside Prim on the lumpy couch. 'Viv's gone to fetch Aunty Janet.'

'Please, Mr Opie,' Prim pleaded, grasping Leah's hand, 'I don't want to wait until my sister gets here. Tell me what's happened to my daughter.'

'I thought you had the right to know before it gets about the village, Mrs Spargo,' Greg began. 'There was an attempted robbery last night at Roscarrock and Hannah was assaulted by one of the thieves.'

'Oh, dear God!' Prim shrieked. 'What did he do to her?'

'It's not very pleasant, I'm afraid. She was beaten and a knife was held against her throat. She was very brave as it was a particularly nasty incident. I was knocked out momentarily by one of the other burglars and my grandmother took a bad fall and broke her hip. I hate to think what might have happened if my cousin hadn't been there.'

'My poor girl. H-how is she now?' Prim asked, searching for her hanky. 'Hannah I mean?'

'The doctor has confined her to bed. This morning she was violently ill, because of the shock, he said. She is terribly upset. I know there is some sort of estrangement in the family but I thought, in the circumstances – well, to be blunt, she needs you, or at least one of you, to come and see her.' His eyes fell on Leah.

Prim shook her head and sniffed into her hanky. She could never bring herself to set foot inside that house again, even in these circumstances.

'Is your grandmother in hospital, Mr Opie?' Leah said.

He nodded. 'I'm afraid she'll have to stay in hospital for some weeks.'

In the other room Jeff had sat listening to the voices. He looked across at his mother's rocking chair, and for one heart-stopping moment pictured her there, emanating the hatred and spite that seemed to have become a living part of her. He shifted about uncomfortably, and it wasn't just physical discomfort. He couldn't get Mitch's words on the *Misty* about Hannah out of his head. There was no reason for him to hate Hannah, there had never been any reason to hate her. He wasn't proud to have the fact that he'd brought up all his children by bullying them thrown in his face. As far as he could tell, his mother hadn't repented of anything on her deathbed. Was she burning in Hell as Mitch had said she deserved? After a few moments he got up and put his ear to the parlour door.

'Would you like to come up to the house and see Hannah?' Greg asked Prim.

'I'll go,' Leah volunteered quickly.

'No!' Prim snapped. 'Perhaps Janet will go.'

Jeff pushed open the door. He hated Prim's attitude towards Hannah and Roscarrock as much as he had come to hate his mother's. 'She can go,' he said gruffly. 'Was one of the burglars a tall red-haired man?' he asked Greg in an unfriendly manner.

'Daniel wouldn't do anything like that,' Prim said, appalled.

'You never know with that swine,' Jeff hissed.

'No, Mr Spargo,' Greg said hastily, sensing the friction between husband and wife and realising to whom they were referring. 'Both men were known to the police. They come from the St Austell area.'

The next moment Janet burst through the front door, the first time she had stepped inside the cottage for ten years. She was amazed to see Jeff talking to the gentleman.

'I can't go today,' she said when she'd been told the story. 'I've got Roy's mother coming for the day. I could go tomorrow.'

'Leah can go today,' Jeff said, ignoring Prim's boiling pique. 'But she's not walking there with you,' he told Greg rudely. 'She can go this afternoon.'

Chapter 26

'How come you're going again today?' Janet asked Leah, who looked as if all her Christmases and birthdays had come at once. Janet had felt nervous at the thought of going to Roscarrock on her own and was surprised to find herself in Leah's company on the walk.

'Dad said I could.' Leah smiled secretively.

'Good heavens, he is turning over a new leaf. Be giving up the drink next.'

Leah playfully kicked at a pile of withered leaves heaped in the ditch. 'He's said I could work at Roscarrock.'

'Eh? Work there?' Janet had never been more astonished. 'How has all this come about?'

Leah told her aunt something of what had happened when she'd got back from the big house yesterday. Her father had asked her how her visit to Hannah had gone. Leah had been pleased with his interest, whatever his motive, and had been careful not to give away that she had been there before.

'Hannah was ever so relieved to see me,' she'd said dramatically. 'She has a terrible bruise on her face where the burglar hit her, a cut above her eye and marks on her arms where he dragged her along with his knife at her throat. She's been ever so sick, had to rush to the bathroom twice while I was there and she can't stop shaking.'

Jeff had not passed any remark and Leah couldn't tell what was really on his mind. Prim had listened in stiff-lipped silence, which puzzled Viv.

Prim's attitude stopped Leah mentioning that Hannah had been full of fear for Mrs Opie, even though Mr Greg had sat with them for some time and reassured her that his grandmother was receiving the very best of medical attention. On the way home, Leah had come to a decision that would probably send her father into a temper and might earn her a smack across the face, but in his present mood she thought it worth the risk.

Taking a deep breath she'd braced herself. 'Dad, Hannah said there's a job going at the house, as a house-maid for two afternoons a week.'

There was an angry intake of breath from Prim. She carried on darning a pair of socks, drawing the needle in and out in jerky movements. She wanted to smack Leah's insolent face but if she objected, Jeff would certainly allow her to take the job.

Viv had sensed the tension building up in the room and had excused herself to go upstairs. Since the violent row with her stepfather she avoided all confrontations if she could.

'What of it?' Jeff asked, his voice surly.

Leah clenched her hands to try to stop herself from trembling and there was a wobble in her voice as she answered. 'Well, I've been thinking about it. It's good money, six shillings a week. If I took it I could contribute to my keep and it will be needed if Mitch leaves.'

Jeff studied Leah's face then Prim's. It was a strange quirk that Leah should be eager to take a job in the same place he had forced Hannah into, whether she'd wanted to go or not. He had never showed his feelings for his children and although he'd been scathing about Leah on the *Misty* he was secretly pleased that she had emerged from her shell. A job away from the village would be good for her, and it would be one in the eye for his damned wife who had used Hannah's birth and presence in the house to get back at him for his womanising. Even better than that, giving his permission would be a shock to Feena Opie.

'How do you know they'd want you working there?' he asked Leah gruffly.

'Hannah has the authority to hire and fire the staff, Dad,' she said eagerly. 'She said she'd give me a chance to see how I got on if I was allowed to take the job.'

'You'll have to turn in half your money and buy all your own clothes and things and still keep your hand in round home.'

'I don't mind that. I'd just like the chance to make my mark in the world.'

Prim jumped up and threw her darning down in the chair. 'It'll be the end of the world for you, my girl,' she snapped, leaving the room.

Prim hadn't spoken a word to her since then, but Leah felt she had the right to strike out on her own and not always be tied to her mother's apron strings.

'I hope you're doing the right thing,' was all that Janet said. She felt sorry for Prim. Her world was falling in around her – but she was partly to blame for that.

When she entered Roscarrock Janet was as amazed and excited as Hannah and Leah had been.

'Good afternoon,' Greg said politely as he opened the door to them. 'You know the way to Hannah's room,

Miss Spargo. Why don't you show Mrs Rouse upstairs? I'll ring for Angie to bring you some tea.'

'That's very kind of you, I'm sure, Mr Opie,' Janet said in her most formal voice. 'He doesn't seem a bad sort,' she remarked to Leah as they climbed the stairs. 'He was good enough to let us know Hannah had been hurt.'

Leah nearly cooked her goose by exclaiming, 'Oh, Mr Greg is a very nice man.' Checking herself, she said, 'I agree with you, Aunty Janet.'

Leah tapped on Hannah's door and went in. Hannah was sitting in a chair by the fireside, covered by a blanket. Her face was a little swollen on the bruised side and around the cut and there were puffy dark circles under her eyes.

'Leah! You were able to come again. And Aunty Janet, come in, it's lovely to see you.'

'Good grief, my poor, dear girl,' Janet said, kissing Hannah's flushed face. 'Look what he did to you. You're lucky to be alive from what I've heard. Oh, Hannah, I've been so worried about you.' Janet ferreted about in her coat pocket and produced a hanky.

'I'm all right, Aunty Janet,' Hannah smiled. 'It looks worse than it actually is. Take off your coat and sit down. Tell me what you think of my room.'

Keeping her hat on, Janet unbuttoned her coat and laid it on the bed, looking around. 'I've never seen anything like it, it's like being inside a palace,' was her verdict. No wonder you like it here so much, she thought, worried at what other plans the mistress of the house might have for Hannah. She sat down in the chair Leah pulled forward for her. 'How's Mrs Opie?' It would have been too mean not to ask.

'Mr Greg has had a top orthopaedic specialist down

from London and he's operated on Mrs Opie and set her hip. She's in a lot of pain and is sedated much of the time. Mr Greg will take me to see her when she's a little better.'

'Don't overdo it too soon, Hannah,' Janet said, exercising her motherly rights.

Leah couldn't wait any longer to tell Hannah her news. She kept her face turned from her aunt's view. 'Hannah, you know that job you mentioned yesterday? About Roscarrock wanting a maid two afternoons a week? Well, you'll never guess. Dad has said I can take it.'

It took a few moments for Hannah fully to register Leah's ploy. 'Oh, that's good. Angie will be glad of the help while I'm laid up. Perhaps you can start tomorrow.'

Janet didn't want to be involved in this discussion, she felt that Hannah should not have mentioned the job to Leah. 'Are you still being sick, dear?'

'Just once this morning. I'm feeling a lot better than I was yesterday. I could probably resume my duties tomorrow but Mr Greg and Mr Patrick and Angie are all insisting I rest for a few more days.'

'I should think so too,' Janet said tartly. 'It wasn't they who had a knife to their throats.' She saw a wooden box on the table beside Hannah. 'That's pretty. Where did you get it?'

Hannah lifted up her jewellery box. 'Matt gave it to me for my birthday. Every time I feel like crying with the shock I listen to the music.'

'It means something to you then?'

'Yes, of course.'

'Does he?'

'I'm very fond of Matt,' Hannah replied to the blunt question, hoping she wasn't in for a lecture.

'Then why didn't you see him yesterday?'

Hannah frowned and it made her head ache. 'I didn't know he was here yesterday.'

'Came the moment he heard about the burglary after the boats came in, him and Daniel Kittow together. Mrs Penney told me in the bakehouse this morning. Your Mr Gregory wouldn't let them in. Apparently, Daniel was none too pleased about it and there was quite an argument.'

'I didn't hear any argument but I slept most of the evening from the sedatives the doctor gave me.' Hannah was glad Mr Greg hadn't let them in, she didn't want to see either of them until she was feeling and looking better. 'Perhaps Mr Greg thought it better not to disturb me.'

'I expect so,' Janet said briskly, keeping the slightly accusing tone in her voice. 'Do you have a message for Matt, if I happen to see him?'

'Tell him thank you for calling, and . . .' Hannah's head was beginning to spin and she couldn't think straight.

'And?' Janet prompted.

At that moment there was a knock on the door, and Leah, who had been wandering about the room, opened the door to Angie with the tea tray. Angie set it down shyly on the table beside Hannah.

'Are 'ee all right, miss?' she whispered to Hannah, nervous of her stern-faced aunt. 'Can I get 'ee anything else?'

'Um, no, thank you, Angie,' she said weakly.

Angie withdrew, but just before she closed the door, she said to Leah, 'I s'pose you can start work again now the mistress won't be going to London.'

'What?' Janet turned her head round sharply.

Angie could see she had said something wrong; blushing to the roots of her hair, she fled.

There was a dreadful silence in the room. 'I did hear right?' Janet asked in a harsh voice. 'Start work again?'

'Y-yes, Aunty Janet,' Leah admitted. 'You see, I—'

'I don't want to hear another word.' Janet shot up and headed for her coat. 'The pair of you have obviously been deceiving your mother for some time and I won't be a party to it.'

'You won't tell Mum, will you?' Leah wailed, seeing her dreams collapsing. 'She'll tell Dad and he'll be furious with us.'

'And justly so. What were you thinking of, Hannah? Your mother didn't want *you* to come here, let alone Leah as well. How could you go behind her back like that?'

Hannah's head was pounding, she was feeling hotter and hotter. 'Please, Aunty . . .'

'It's no good saying please. You can't expect me to keep quiet about your devious little scheme.'

'But Aunty, Dad's been a lot better about Hannah lately, he'll turn against her again,' Leah cried.

'I can't help that, you should have thought about that before you became deceitful, just like the people who live here – they must have been in on it too.' Janet fastened her top button and picked up her handbag. 'You were brought up good chapel girls . . .'

As her aunt prattled on indignantly and Leah begged and pleaded, the room seemed to fold in on Hannah. The sounds in her head were like the rushing of the wind, her sight blurred then everything became black. She slid to the floor, the jewellery box falling from her hands and spilling its contents with a clatter.

Leah screamed.

Greg had been hovering about the stairs in the hope that Leah would come out of Hannah's room on her own.

Perturbed by the raised voices, he had moved to the door and overheard some of Janet's outraged words. At Leah's scream he entered without knocking.

'What's going on here?' he demanded. Then he saw Hannah's crumpled body. 'Hannah!'

He rushed past Leah and bent and touched Hannah's brow. It was very hot. Gently, he gathered her up and laid her on the bed.

He didn't bother to hide the fact that he was familiar with Leah. 'Leah, run and fetch Mr Patrick. He's in the garden shed. Tell him to go and get the doctor. We must get a bloody phone put in the place,' he ended angrily.

Leah sped off at once and Greg turned to her ashen-faced aunt. 'I would never have asked you here if I thought you'd upset her. From what I can see, apart from Leah, Hannah comes from a nasty, small-minded family. She's better off here and I'll see to it that she stays.'

Wiping tears from her eyes, Janet looked down on Hannah's burning face. She was absolutely still, not a flicker of energy in her. Nodding meekly, she turned and left.

Chapter 27

Viv was upstairs in the bedroom she and Mitch were going to share on their wedding night. It had been Mitch and Josh's room but Josh was moving into his grandmother's room. The men's single beds had been taken out and replaced by one of the double beds from Leah's room. Viv wasn't happy about all this shifting about, even though the room overlooked the water and the quay and was larger, lighter and quite pleasant compared to her old attic room at Newlyn. If she could have had her way, she wouldn't have spent another night under the roof of what she had quickly come to see was a quarrelsome, unforgiving family. Josh in particular made her feel uncomfortable.

She had put clean sheets and blankets on the bed and was staring out of the window, her hands on her tummy. She hadn't realised Mitch had come into the room.

'What's the matter, Viv? You don't look very happy.'

'Oh, nothing. I was just thinking.' She didn't turn round to him, keeping her eyes on some men dragging a rowing boat up the slipway.

'If you've got something on your mind, I'd like to hear it,' he said kindly, coming to stand behind her. 'I've noticed you've become quieter.' Mitch hoped it wasn't

329

something he wouldn't like to hear but he wanted Viv to feel able to confide in him.

'I've been thinking about Hannah.'

'What about Hannah?'

With an embarrassed quiver in her voice, she said, 'Well, it's obvious why your father won't have anything to do with her, with her colouring being different to the rest of your family. Will you really be able to love my baby, Mitch? I hate to bring up Daniel's name but if we have children of our own will you prefer them to his?'

Mitch put his hands on her shoulders and said earnestly, 'I love you, Viv. I'll love the baby because it's part of you and because it was what made you turn to me. I'm not like my father, please believe that.'

Viv patted one of his hands. 'I believe you, Mitch. I just wanted to be sure you knew what you were doing by marrying me.' She turned round to him now. 'There's something else about Daniel. He told me he was engaged to a girl called Hannah. He could only have meant your sister but they don't behave as if they're going to get married.'

'They're not and he's a blooming liar,' Mitch said crossly. 'He went after Hannah the moment Matt Penney took an interest in her. I wish Hannah would see him for what he really is.'

Mitch didn't want to talk about Daniel. He was longing to get closer to Viv but since the night his grandmother had died she had shied away from all physical contact with him. He remembered her words that she had never liked the liberties Daniel had taken with her and he was keen for her to know he wanted her for more than just that side of life. She made to move away from him. He gently restrained her.

'Can I hold you in my arms, Viv? Just for a little while. I promise I won't try to kiss you or anything.'

She looked at him and smiled shyly. She wasn't sure if she was ready to submit to another man but she trusted him not to try anything before their wedding night. And Mitch was good to her and she owed it to him to make an effort. She placed her head on his chest and allowed him to hold her for a long time.

When Mitch left her, he borrowed Jowan's bike to ride to Portmellon to ask the fishermen of a lugger called the *Lady Sylvia* if they had finally made up their minds to take him on. Viv hoped he would bring back good news as she hung her few clothes up next to Mitch's in the wardrobe and put her brush, comb and hand mirror on the washstand. On top of the chest of drawers were the wedding presents they had been given, still wrapped and waiting for tomorrow, when she and Mitch would open them during the spread Jeff was laying on after the simple ceremony in the chapel.

In a short while she would go to Janet Rouse's house; it was there that she would spend the night and leave the next day in Janet's wedding dress. Prim and Leah were already there, the women going over the last-minute arrangements. Jeff and Josh were in the pub.

As Viv closed the wardrobe door, a prickle of fear shot through her. Someone had come into the room and she feared it was Constance Spargo's ghost. Peeping in the wardrobe mirror she saw it was Josh. He was standing in the doorway, his hands held casually on his hips. Viv sensed she was in a different kind of danger.

Turning round, she said edgily, 'I'm just on my way out.'

He was leering at her, his dark eyes travelling over her

body in the unwelcome way she'd come to dread since her arrival here. 'No hurry, is there?' he said throatily.

'Your Aunty Janet, your mother and Leah are expecting me. I'm already late.' She walked towards him, hoping he would let her leave. He stood his ground and Viv was afraid to move past him. 'Get out of my way, Josh.'

He grinned salaciously. 'I thought we could spend a little time together. I don't think you're the sort of girl who'd object to that.'

Viv's pulse was racing and a cold wave of terror swept down her back. 'P-please, Josh, I don't want any trouble.'

'But you're already in trouble, Viv. You've got Daniel Kittow's bastard growing in your belly. You didn't think we'd all fall for your little story, did you? Mitch is a fool to take you on, but that's his problem.'

'It's not Daniel's baby,' Viv cried, backing away. 'It's Mitch's.'

'Then that makes you a whore.' Josh advanced on her until her back was against the wall. 'You let both of them have you. I know Daniel did, he told me all about it. How he broke you in and how you cried, how you thought he was going to marry you. But after that you couldn't get enough of it.' Josh made a crude gesture. 'He said you were a nice little mover, Viv.'

'It's lies,' she hurled at him, tears of anger and humiliation streaming down her face. 'All lies! Get away from me.'

'Not until I've had what you gave the others.'

His hands flew out and grasped her arms. Viv fought against him but he was too strong. Twisting her arms behind her back, he held her wrists in one powerful grip and pulling her head back by her hair he forced his mouth over hers. Viv couldn't cry out or breathe. He pulled her cardigan off her shoulder then yanked her dress at the collar. The material wouldn't give and he tugged harder, ripping the dress and scratching her neck.

Viv struggled with all her being and managed to free one hand and rake her nails down his face. He yelped in pain and fury and struck her violently across the cheek. Viv screamed shrilly, then he forced his hand over her mouth and dragged her to the bed. They fell down on it and he was like a wild animal, tearing off her clothes, punching her when she struggled. Viv was in the deepest despair, in a few moments this man would violate her and she knew she couldn't live with the memory. She hoped he would kill her, because if he didn't, after what she'd been through already, she would take her own life.

Suddenly Josh was wrested off her and Viv watched, stunned, as Daniel, holding Josh by the back of his collar, drove his fist into his jaw and then his guts. As Josh doubled over, he brought both his fists down on the back of his neck, laying him out on the floor. Viv pulled on the bedspread to cover herself while Daniel dragged Josh's inert body from the room. She sat up, trembling uncontrollably and in terrible pain from the beating.

Daniel came back into the room and she whimpered, wide-eyed in fear, scrambling up the bed to get away from him.

'It's all right, Viv. I'm not going to hurt you and he'll be out for some time. I heard your scream and the struggle. Thank God I was about, the street is empty.' He moved closer to her but stopped when Viv made a strangled sound. 'I'm sorry this has happened to you. I've never trusted Josh Spargo.'

'H-he's no different to you,' Viv hissed between clenched teeth.

'I would never have gone as far as he did.' Daniel took his wallet out of his coat pocket. 'Look, I know things haven't gone well for you, not even since you came here to live. I believe Mitch is looking for a new boat to work from and is trying to find you your own home. You'll need something to get started.' He took ten crisp one pound notes out of the wallet and put them on the bottom of the bed. 'This should help. I hope you'll accept it with my good wishes. Mitch is a good bloke, he'll do right by you. I'd have never made you a good husband.'

Keeping the bedspread over her tattered clothes, Viv crept forward and picked up the money.

'That's right,' he smiled with the charm he had first used on her. 'I'm glad you understand I'm only trying to help.'

He watched as Viv's face contorted into an unrecognisable mask. 'What is this, Daniel Kittow? The ten pounds you got back because I didn't get rid of your brat?' Twisting it in her hand she threw it at him. 'Keep your conscience money. I don't want anything from you, not now or ever. You may have saved me from an attack by another man but it hasn't stopped me hating you. After that revolting gesture you just made, I hate you even more. I hate you so much it frightens me that I could end up like Constance Spargo. Get out! Get out of here before I scream the village down and say you both tried to rape me!'

Daniel didn't need to be told again, the expression on Viv's face told him she meant every word she said. Picking up the ball of money, he quickly left the house.

When she heard the door close, Viv got off the bed, her limbs shaking. She stripped off every item of her clothes and threw them on the mangled bedcovers. It would show the Spargos when they got back what had happened to her, proof of Josh's obscene assault on her, to add to the marks and scratches on his body. And they would know why she had packed her things and left their home for good.

Viv hurried up Porthkilt Hill with her head bent over and wrapped in a scarf. Miss Peters was on her doorstep, about to go inside out of the cold, blustery October weather after visiting old Mr Nunn. Despite the fact that dusk was drawing in fast, she saw the marks on the girl's face and knew there was terrible trouble here. The old lady walked over to Viv and took her arm.

'I can see you're leaving the village but there's nowhere to go at this time of the day and 'tis getting dark. Come in by my fire. I don't know what your problem is but I promise I won't interfere or send for anyone.'

Viv was numb with shock and at regular intervals an agonising pain gripped her lower body, but she understood what Miss Peters had said and allowed herself to be taken into the cosy little cottage. Miss Peters led her to the kitchen fire and Viv sat down in the armchair there, holding her bag of belongings on her lap and staring into space. Miss Peters said nothing as she took off her hat, coat and boots and busied herself with the kettle.

Viv didn't drink the tea or eat the plate of food put beside her. An hour passed and it was pitch dark outside and the wind was picking up. If it had been a working day tomorrow, the odds would have been against the boats going out. A spark exploding on a log in the fire brought Viv out of the trance she'd slipped into. Her knuckles were white from clutching her bag and her hands were aching. She loosened her grip.

'I can make a fresh pot of tea for 'ee,' Miss Peters

offered kindly. She was sitting on a three-legged stool on the opposite side of the hearth to Viv and looked like a wise elf.

'Thank you. My throat is awfully dry.'

A few minutes later Miss Peters pulled Viv's hands away from the bag and put it on the floor close by her. She spooned lots of sugar into a cup of tea and put it into her cold hands. 'Try to take a few sips, my dear.'

Viv put her quivering lips over the rim of the cup and drew in some of the hot liquid. Miss Peters tilted the cup until she had drunk half the contents and motioned she didn't want any more. 'Th-thanks for bringing me in here,' Viv said, hearing the chill in her voice.

'You can stay the night and decide what you want to do in the morning. You have my word I won't tell a soul you're here.' Miss Peters added defiantly, 'I ain't afeared of no man, even the one that hit you round the face.'

'It wasn't Mitch,' Viv said quickly, afraid Miss Peters had leapt to the wrong conclusion.

'I didn't think it was. You don't have to talk about it if you don't want to.'

Viv didn't know what she wanted to do and fell into another silence.

'I was going to have a baby once,' Miss Peters said suddenly.

'Were you?' Viv was totally surprised. Another pain hit her and she shifted about uncomfortably.

'Oh, I never got married, my dear, but I know what it's like to fall for the easy tongue of a handsome man. Few people knew about it and they're all dead now. It won't hurt to tell you. I don't think you're the sort who would spread it around, and anyway, you're not staying in Porthellis by the look of things. His name was Robert

Jago, the last descendant of a man who used to work at Roscarrock many, many years ago. If you care to look in Gorran churchyard one day you'll see his headstone. I was eighteen years old and he was nineteen, and he had the fairest face a maid had ever set eyes on and the disposition of a saint, or so I thought. He wooed me and one thing led to another and I ended up in the condition you're now in. I was naive back then, I told him I thought it was wrong what we were doing, but he convinced me a woman couldn't have a child unless she was married. "You pray for children in the marriage ceremony," he said.

'I was nearly four months gone before I realised I was pregnant. He said it wasn't nothing to do with him and he'd tell my father I'd gone with any amount of men. I saw then just what a weak man Robert was. He was more afraid of getting whipped by his father than getting married to me. There was hell to pay in my family. My father wasn't the sort to throw me out and it was arranged for me to stay with a relative and give the baby up. The night I was due to leave I lost the baby and that was that. Things carried on as if it had never happened but I could never bring myself to marry, although I had an offer or two.' Miss Peters told her sorry tale straight-faced and dry-eyed; too many years had passed for her to feel emotional about it now.

'What happened to Robert?' Viv asked, moved that the old lady should tell her this. 'You mentioned his grave as if he had died young.'

'Aye, he did. He went out on his father's boat and disappeared over the side. Was never known what happened to un. My father said he was took by God's hand, his reward for getting me into trouble, but I don't see

God that way. He's always prepared to give us a fresh start whatever we've done, and whatever fix you may be in, Viv, He'll help you make a fresh start too.'

'Josh Spargo tried to rape me,' Viv said in a rush, suddenly feeling the need to talk about her ordeal. 'He would have succeeded but for Daniel Kittow stopping him. Then Daniel tried to give me money, for my new home, he said, but I threw it back in his face. He's responsible for the trouble I'm in and he turned his back on me when I first told him. He paid the same ten pounds for me to get rid of the baby. I turned to Mitch after my stepfather threw me out. Mitch offered to marry me, he's been good to me. But I don't like most of the Spargos. They're always arguing, going behind one another's backs. After what happened tonight I had to get away.'

'I can understand that. Don't you want to marry Mitch now?'

'I don't know.' Tears filled Viv's eyes. 'I don't know what to do.' The next pain was unbearable and she cried out, clutching her stomach.

'What is it?' Miss Peters asked, going to her. 'Is it hurting where Josh Spargo hit you?'

Viv gave a groan. 'I'm all wet.' She put a hand down between her legs. 'The chair's all wet.'

Miss Peters saw the red stain appearing on Viv's dress. 'I'd better get you upstairs. You could be losing the baby.'

When Viv was lying down in Miss Peters' other bedroom, gritting her teeth against the pain, she gasped out, 'If I lose it, it would get rid of all my problems.'

'Never mind that now,' Miss Peters said, helping her out of her underclothes. 'I'm only concerned for your safety.'

Two hours later, with Viv's permission, Miss Peters

went up to the Manse and asked the minister if she could phone the local midwife. Before she rushed back to Viv, the Reverend Skewes and his wife offered to help the girl in any way they could. Miss Peters grimly said she might hold them to that.

The midwife arrived quietly just over an hour later and soon after that delivered the tiny scrap of humanity that was Viv's child.

'It never stood a chance, dear,' the midwife said briskly as she wrapped what she had delivered in a towel. 'Wasn't formed properly and far too small if you reckoned you were about twelve weeks along. It's the kindest thing, nature's way of clearing you out.'

Viv cried wretchedly. 'I really wanted my baby. What was it?'

The midwife was about to say it was too early to tell but received a hard stare from Miss Peters. 'A little girl, dear. It's better that you don't see her. I'll take her away and dis— see she's treated properly.'

Miss Peters stroked Viv's damp forehead. 'The midwife will clean you up then I want you to try and get some rest.'

Downstairs, the midwife quickly drank a cup of tea before putting on her coat. 'The girl's not from round here and not married. I suppose her father knocked her about and threw her out, that's what usually happens. It's what made her miscarry.'

'It was something like that,' Miss Peters said a trifle tartly. 'I'd rather you didn't mention your visit here. There's some in the village who would make trouble for her.'

'It's not my job to talk about my patients, Miss Peters,' the midwife answered in an offended tone. 'I feel sorry for girls like her. It's me who has to pick up the pieces. I trust you'll point her in the right direction in future.'

'You have my word on it,' Miss Peters said curtly as she showed the midwife out.

Chapter 28

Mitch was whistling cheerfully as he sped back home along the darkening lanes. The three share owners of the *Lady Sylvia* had said he could start work with them on Monday week, after he had given his father notice, and he would receive the same pay as he did now. One of the fishermen had taken him to an old man who had a small cottage to rent. Mitch had taken the three pounds, ten shillings he had managed to save since he had left school and he had parted with a month's rent in advance. The cottage had only one bedroom and very little furniture, it badly needed whitewashing outside and a lot of attention inside, but it was a start and he had a few shillings left to brighten it up. He would take Viv to their new home on Sunday and they could clean it up and make plans.

He left the bike outside the Rouses' back door and smiled as he heard female voices chattering in the kitchen, assuming Viv was in there. He was dying to let her know the good news but he'd wait until she came home and he could tell her privately.

When he got home he went to the food cupboard to get himself something to eat, but before he could put the jam sandwich to his mouth he heard a strange moan. It sounded as if it was coming from upstairs. A chill ran through him, he had thought there was no one else at home and like Leah and Viv he was a little afraid his grandmother's spirit hadn't left the house. When the moan came again he listened at the bottom of the stairs. There were other noises and they were coming from the room that was now Josh's.

Taking his courage in both hands, Mitch crept silently up the stairs. Gingerly, he pushed open the bedroom door then rushed into the room when he saw Josh struggling to get to his feet, clutching his stomach. 'Good heavens, Josh, what happened to you?' He saw the scratches on Josh's face and his bruised and swollen jaw. 'Who did this to you?'

Josh groaned and turned his head away from him. Mitch dragged him to the bed and laid him on it. 'I'll get you a wet cloth and fetch Mother,' Mitch said and he left the room.

As he passed the room now allocated to him and Viv, Mitch saw it was in disarray. His heart did a queer flip as he walked into it. It took only one terrible moment for him to realise what had happened here. Viv's ripped clothes were on the bed, her knickers completely torn apart at one side. Mitch bellowed like a raging bull. The wardrobe door was open and he could see only his clothes inside it. He was terrified for Viv's safety. He raced to the other two bedrooms and finding no sign of her or the rest of her belongings, he returned to his brother. Josh had crawled off the bed and was cowering in a corner, proof that the crime was his and he hadn't received his injuries trying to protect Viv.

'Where is she?' Mitch pounced on him, grabbing him by the throat and dragging him to his feet. 'What have you done with her, you bastard? Where's Viv?'

'I-I don't kn-know,' Josh gagged, trying to loosen his brother's stranglehold.

Mitch rammed his head against the wall. 'Why did you do it, you filthy bastard? Why did you have to hurt her? Viv was my girl. She was good and kind and honest.' The more the dreadful truth burned inside Mitch's mind, the angrier he became until finally he was totally out of control. He smashed Josh's head against the wall over and over again, leaving bloody smears to trickle down it. 'How dare you touch her! You're not fit to lick her shoes, you bastard! I hate you! I'll kill you!'

Mitch might well have killed him if Leah hadn't come home to find out why Viv was taking so long to come to her aunt's house. Alerted by the shouting, she couldn't believe her eyes when she ran upstairs to see Mitch unmercifully beating Josh. She knew it was no use pleading with Mitch or trying to wrench him away from Josh. Picking up the jug on the washstand, and letting out a fearsome scream to give herself added strength, she swung it at Mitch's head. It hit him on the temple and shattered. The sudden blow sent him staggering away from Josh who fell to the floor. Mitch sprang back immediately, his hands out like claws, but Leah threw herself over Josh's unconscious body.

'Stop it, Mitch!' she shouted. 'You'll kill him. What's the matter with you? Why are you fighting?'

Mitch stayed his fists just in time so as not to hurt Leah. On unsteady feet, he swayed and fell to his knees. 'He raped Viv,' he wailed breathlessly. 'She's gone, her things are gone, and I don't know where she is.' He appealed to Leah like a small frightened boy. 'Is she at Aunty Janet's?'

'No,' Leah replied, trying with difficulty to control her

own emotions at what he had said. 'She must have left the village, Mitch. You'll have to go and look for her.'

Mitch got shakily to his feet. 'Yes, you're right. She couldn't have gone far. I'll borrow Jowan's bike again.' He glared down at Josh. 'What about him?'

Leah looked at Josh. He was breathing heavily and making spluttering noises. 'He needs the doctor. I'll get Mum, she'll help me get him on the bed. You go, Mitch, and find Viv, she needs you.'

Mitch clattered down the stairs and was soon wheeling the bike up the village hill. He hadn't passed Viv on his way home and he rode along the lanes that led to St Michael's Caerhays. She couldn't possibly have gone any further, he thought when he reached the road outside the castle's boundary wall, so he turned round and cycled along the only other way she could have taken, to Roscarrock, in case she had gone to Hannah. When he got to the big house Mitch scrambled off the bike and threw it to the ground. Dashing up the stone steps he hammered on the door.

Several moments later, a woman nervously opened the door a little. 'Yes?' she squeaked.

'I'm Hannah Spargo's brother,' he blurted out, his breath coming out in ragged gasps. 'Please let me in, I need to see her at once.'

'I'm afraid Miss Spargo isn't here,' Angie Miller said in her small voice. 'She's gone to the hospital to visit Mrs Opie. She won't be back for ages.'

Mitch raked his hands through his hair. 'Has anyone called here this evening wanting to see her? A girl?'

'No, we haven't had a visitor for days. Can I give Miss Spargo a message when she comes back?'

Pacing about on the step, Mitch tried to think clearly.

There was no point in dragging Hannah down to the village, there was nothing she could do. 'No, no, don't say anything to her. I . . . I have to go.'

He took off again, leaving a very worried Angie to shut the door and lock it.

As he rode back to Porthellis, Mitch tried not to think about the other explanation that might account for Viv's disappearance, that in her grief and horror at being raped she had drowned herself in the sea or thrown herself off the cliff. He ran up and down the quay and searched the beach, looking for sign of her. Then he went into the village, methodically asking at every door if the occupants had seen Viv or taken her in, leaving behind him a wake of curiosity and speculation. It was late and he was getting frantic, when he saw the midwife coming out of Miss Peters' cottage. If Viv was hurt she might need the midwife to check her over; there could be no other reason for her to be leaving the old lady's cottage.

When the midwife had cleared the hill with her bicycle, Mitch battered his fists on the cottage door. Miss Peters opened it with her whip in her hand. 'Please, Miss Peters,' he implored her. 'Is Viv here? Something terrible has happened to her and she's left Cliffside Cottage taking all her things. I've been searching for her everywhere. I've even been up to Roscarrock. I'm out of my mind with worry.'

Miss Peters eyed the young man on her doorstep. If he had demanded entrance or had adopted a surly tone, she would have sent him on his way. But there were tears of anguish streaming down Mitch Spargo's face. She peered out either side of the door to see if they were being watched, then stood back from the doorway. 'Get inside quick and be very quiet.'

Mitch did as she said, then drying his eyes he waited hopefully for the old woman to speak.

'She's upstairs in my spare room,' she said in a low, grim voice. 'I saw her walking up the hill a few hours ago when it was getting dimsy and I asked her in. She was in shock, but after a while she told me your brother tried to rape her.'

'Tried?' Mitch breathed in relief. 'You mean he didn't actually do it?'

'She was saved by Daniel Kittow. Viv was took bad a little later and I sent for the midwife. Viv lost her child, and though it's a cruel thing to say, she's told me who fathered it and perhaps it's for the best.'

'Oh, my God.' Mitch wiped his hand despairingly over his face. 'Is she going to be all right?'

'It all came away without any trouble, thank goodness. It's her mental state I'm worried about. The poor girl has been to Hell and back.'

'I realised what Josh had done when I got home. I beat him senseless,' Mitch told the old lady. 'Can I see Viv, Miss Peters?'

'I'll go up and ask her but, Mitch Spargo,' she wagged a warning finger, 'if she don't want to see you, I won't go against her wishes. Do I make myself clear? I'm quite able to put you out of my house.'

Mitch nodded feebly.

Miss Peters left the room and Mitch fell down on a chair at the kitchen table, making an effort to pull himself together.

Her mind numb, her body battered and sore, Viv had been praying for sleep when she'd overheard Mitch talking to Miss Peters on the doorstep and in the kitchen, and she was gazing at the bedroom door waiting for the old lady to come in.

'You know who's here?' Miss Peters said gently.

Viv nodded.

'Do you want to see him?'

'I don't know. I can't think straight.'

'He's been searching like a madman for you. I don't think you have anything to fear from him or I wouldn't have let him in.'

'All right,' Viv said, her voice weak. 'Mitch has never done me any harm.'

Miss Peters tucked the covers in around Viv and stroked her brow. 'I'll send him up, but I'll be in my own room if you need me.'

Mitch tidied his hair as he climbed the stairs, holding his breath and praying that Viv wouldn't send him away now she had no reason to marry him. Miss Peters showed him into the room and closed the door. Mitch was shaken to see how pale Viv's face was, a stark contrast to the ugly red mark where Josh had struck her. She looked totally bewildered. He wanted to find something soothing and comforting to say, but instead burst into tears.

'I'm so sorry about this, Viv. I would've taken you away if I'd known anything like this was going to happen. I've been so scared, Viv. Don't leave me because of this. I love you so much.'

His tears pierced through her anguish and his love took away her despair. Viv held out her hand to him. He clutched it and sobbed over it.

'I shouldn't have let you worry, Mitch. I had to get away, it was all I could think about.'

'I understand. I know there isn't going to be a baby but I still want you to marry me. We could still have a future together.' He forced a smile through his tears. 'I got the job at Portmellon and a cottage for us to live in. It needs a lot of work on it but I've paid the first month's rent and we can move in straightaway. I've got enough money left to keep us going until I start work. Just give me a chance and I'll make you happy. We don't have to be a proper man and wife if you don't want that, I'll sleep downstairs.' Tears were flowing down his face again. 'I just want to look after you, Viv. Please say you'll marry me.'

Viv lifted her other arm and put it round his neck. 'I will, Mitch, and not just because I've got nowhere else to go.'

They cried in each other's arms, then Mitch called Miss Peters into the room. When they told her they still wanted to get married, a look of determination appeared on her tiny wrinkled face.

'Right then, you two stay here quietly while I go up to see the minister – he's offered to help. I'll see that everything works out for the pair of 'ee, never fear.'

That night Mitch slept in the Manse. Very early in the morning, while the streets were still dark, he carried Viv, wrapped up warm in his arms, to the chapel where the minister married them and Miss Peters and Mrs Skewes bore witness. A short time later, with gifts of food, clothes and money, and after the couple had thanked Miss Peters and promised to keep in touch, the Reverend Skewes drove Mitch and Viv to their new home, understanding completely why they vowed never to set foot in Porthellis again.

Chapter 29

Dressed in the hat and coat she was to have worn to London, Hannah gazed at her pale complexion in the cheval mirror. She'd have to put on a little rouge or Mr Greg, who seemed to have taken on the role of her protector since the break-in, would continue the fuss he had started last night over her intention to stand outside the chapel and watch Mitch and Viv emerge after their wedding. A feeling of queasiness came over her for a moment and she thought she would have to rush to the bathroom again. She had got over the shock of the burglary but was still being sick. Thankfully her stomach settled and she went to the dressing table.

After the twelve-thirty wedding she was going to see Matt. He had called at the house again, as had Daniel, but Mr Greg had refused to let either of them see her. Matt had written her a short, friendly, get-well letter and she'd replied saying she was looking forward to seeing him today. She had thought about him a lot since the time they had made love and she knew she cared deeply for him, which was just as well, because it looked as if the minister might soon be performing another rushed wedding. It had been a terrible shock to realise she must be pregnant, hard to believe she had conceived the first and only time she had made love. She did not regret making love with Matt and she couldn't blame him for it happening. It had been entirely at her instigation and she flushed every time she thought about how she'd practically seduced him. They should have been careful. She didn't know how it would affect her job; she hoped Mrs Opie would allow her to work here for a few more weeks.

Hannah sighed as she put on the make-up. She hated the thought of leaving here. She loved Roscarrock and her life here as much as she did Matt, perhaps more.

'Are you really sure you want to go, Hannah?' Greg asked her as she came down the stairs. He was standing at the bottom, wearing the expression of a stern parent.

'It's not just any wedding, Mr Greg. It's my brother's.'

'But except for Leah, your family are horrid to you.'

'Mitch isn't, he never has been,' she said determinedly.

'But you're not well enough,' Greg persisted stubbornly.

'I'm perfectly fine. I keep telling you.'

The telephone, which Greg had pulled strings to have urgently installed, rang on the side table and Hannah jerked in fright. 'There you are, anything startles you these days. Don't go away,' he ordered gruffly then picked up the receiver.

Worried it was the hospital with bad news about Mrs Opie, Hannah listened carefully to his responses.

'Good morning, sir, it's kind of you to ring . . . Grandmother is getting better slowly, thank you . . . Yes, the break was on her bad side but at least she won't have two bad hips, though of course she'll need help getting around for a very long time. She'll be home in about four weeks and she will be employing a nurse to care for her.' There was a long silence while the caller spoke. Greg's fair face broke out into a satisfied smile. 'You've rounded up Ken Blee and all his gang? I'm glad to hear it.'

Hannah realised Mr Greg was talking to the Chief Constable. Mr Greg glanced at her and she wondered if Daniel had really been involved with Blee's gang and was now in prison. It was an unpleasant thought and she repressed a shudder.

'Yes, sir. I hope they throw away the key,' Greg said. After some moments, 'I'll tell Grandmother you called. We'll have to have a meal together soon. Goodbye, sir.'

He didn't mention the telephone call but carried on with his earlier argument. 'Grandmother doesn't think you ought to go.'

'I know, but it's my decision to make, Mr Greg,' Hannah said stubbornly, picking up her umbrella and heading for the door. She would not be put off; apart from seeing the wedding and Matt she wanted to assure her aunt she bore her no grudge over the faint. Aunty Janet had written her a letter apologising for her behaviour and Hannah had replied that there was nothing to forgive and as far as she was concerned it was all best forgotten. But Leah had said their aunt was beside herself with worry and had muttered something about 'driving Hannah away for good'.

'Well, if I can't talk you out of it then I'll drive you to the top of the village hill.' Greg was on her heels and breathing down her neck. 'It'll save you being out in the cold for so long.' When Hannah seemed to be about to protest, he added hastily, 'It looks as if it's going to rain in a minute. Surely you don't want your brother to see you on his big day looking like a drowned rat? Go and sit down by the drawing room fire for fifteen minutes and then we'll leave.'

Knowing Mr Greg expected his orders to be obeyed just as Mrs Opie did, Hannah complied. He had sent her to the drawing room several times in this way since the burglary, saying that his grandmother had expressly ordered him to look after her. Hannah marvelled that she didn't feel out of place here in the magnificent room, sitting like one of the family on the plush sofas with Pogo on her lap, drinking tea from the best china that Angie brought in to her. Mr Patrick had fussed over her too, saying she was invaluable as his great-aunt's housekeeper and companion and she must regain her full strength to help nurse Mrs Opie when she got out of hospital. He'd added bashfully, 'None of us could do without you,' and had called her Hannah for the first time.

Mrs Opie was making a better recovery than the doctors had first thought. The time when she was due home couldn't go fast enough for Hannah. She went to the hospital with Mr Greg nearly every day, sitting close to the bed in Mrs Opie's nicely decorated private room, and chatting comfortably until the nurses told them visiting time was over. Hannah had felt a lurch in her heart on her first visit, to see her employer lying in the bed grey-faced and semi-conscious from pain and drugs. She couldn't explain it, not even to herself, but she felt that a bond of some sort had grown between them, and it hurt her to see Mrs Opie suffering. Although there would be a full-time nurse in the house – Hannah had already had a room prepared for her – with Mrs Opie at home things would soon return to normal. But of course, with a baby on the way, things would never be the same again.

At midday Jeff and Prim Spargo sheepishly knocked on the Manse door. Mrs Skewes kept them on the doorstep while she fetched her husband. The minister appeared some moments later with a grave expression.

'We've come about the wedding, Minister.' Jeff cleared his throat in embarrassment. 'We're, um, not sure if there's going to be one. You see . . . well, my son and the bride seem to have left the village.'

'I know,' the Reverend Skewes said coldly. 'I drove them myself to their new home early this morning, after I had married them. I know what happened to Miss Hickey at the hands of your other son. I don't hold with violence, but he deserved the beating Mitch gave him. I've never seen a young couple more distraught or starting out on their married life on such a bad note. Miss Hickey lost the child she was expecting.'

Prim gasped in horror. She had known there would be no possibility of Mitch ever coming home again after what Josh had done to Viv but it hurt that they'd not wanted her at their wedding or to bid her goodbye. Josh was seriously hurt with head injuries and needed nursing but hearing that his attack had been vicious enough for Viv to miscarry, she felt she couldn't go near her one remaining son again.

'There seems to have been nothing but trouble coming from your house over the years, Jeff Spargo,' the Reverend Skewes went on in a tone of reproach. 'I suggest you go home and put it in order, and leave the newly married couple to live their lives in peace, or at least as best they can in the circumstances. Good day to you.' The minister shut the door in their faces.

'You've done it again,' Prim said bitterly as they started off, embarrassed and humiliated, down the hill. 'You've got rid of another of your children.'

'Don't you bleddy well blame me,' Jeff snarled, not

caring that there were people about and they were making an exhibition of themselves. 'I didn't make Josh attack the flaming girl.'

'He did it because he's just like you!' Prim screeched. 'You can't keep your hands off women.'

'Damn and blast it, woman, I've never raped anyone. I've never needed to,' Jeff raged.

'Mitch would have left anyway.' Prim wasn't going to let the subject drop. 'You drove him away with your nasty tongue and bullying ways.'

They were nearing the waterfront and Daniel looked up from the *Sunrise* on which he was doing maintenance work. 'Did you hear that, Granfer?' he grinned as he scrubbed gull droppings off the top of the wheelhouse. 'The Spargos are going at it hammer and tongs again.'

Rufus rubbed at his dirty beard and chuckled. 'And they say we're the rough ones in the village. Folk should look next door to us instead.'

Jeff and Prim separated by the net lofts, Jeff to knock up Maggie in the pub to console him, Prim to tell Janet the wedding had already taken place.

Twenty minutes later, Matt, dressed in his good quality winter coat and best shoes, walked down from Cobble Street to the chapel. Unless Hannah was waylaid by an eager gossip, he doubted she would know anything about the latest violence in her family until she turned up at the chapel and found it empty. News of the Spargo wedding being performed several hours early was reverberating round the village, with neighbours popping in and out of each other's houses as the rumours multiplied. It was known that Mitch Spargo had beaten the daylights out of his brother and people thought there could be only one reason for that, even without Jeff and Prim's rantings to confirm it. The midwife had been seen in the village last night, and as none of the pregnant women had delivered, and no other woman had been reported requiring her services, it was assumed Viv Hickey had lost her baby. From a few indiscreet moments by the Reverend Skewes' cleaning woman in the bakehouse, people knew that Mitch and Viv had got married secretly and were now settled in their tiny cottage at Portmellon. Matt was hoping that the warm reply he'd received to his letter from Hannah, in which she'd mentioned she had something to tell him, meant she wanted their courtship to resume.

He opened the chapel door and closed it behind him, passed through the vestibule and went into the main body of the building. Much of the wooden interior was painted dark blue and brown, and the light was dim, but he quickly picked out Hannah. She was several feet away, gazing at the flowers in a wrought-iron pedestal, her tall graceful body striking in her elegant new clothes. He allowed himself a few seconds to enjoy looking at her.

'Hannah.'

She turned round with an uncertain smile. 'Matt, where is everybody? I thought the congregation would be here by now. When I saw no onlookers outside I came in here to investigate.'

As they walked towards each other, he said, 'It's believed the wedding has already happened.'

'What?' Her beautiful face fell and she instinctively reached out to him. 'They changed the time without telling me?'

Matt hugged her to him and kissed her cheek before telling her about the rumours flying round the village.

Clinging to him, she said, 'That's terrible. Poor Mitch, poor Viv. I only met her twice but she seemed a pleasant girl. I was looking forward to seeing their baby. I'll go over to Portmellon soon, I'm sure they won't mind me turning up. I might be able to help them in some way.'

'I'm sure they'd appreciate that,' he smiled into her eyes. 'Are you pleased to see me, Hannah?'

She lifted her face and placed a tender kiss on his chin. 'Yes, Matt. I'm sorry Mr Greg wouldn't let you see me at Roscarrock. I would have liked you to have tea with me.'

'Never mind, you're here now.'

They weren't in an appropriate place but their lips met and the kiss soon became passionate.

Matt squeezed her until she thought he'd cut off her breath. 'I've missed you so much, darling. Does this mean we can start again? What have you got to tell me?'

Hannah gently disentangled herself from his arms. 'Not here, Matt. Someone might come in.'

'Will you come home with me? We can talk in the parlour.'

'Yes, then I want to see Aunty Janet. I'm afraid I can't stay long in the village today. Mr Greg dropped me off and has insisted he comes back for me in two hours' time.'

'I'm glad he's looking after you,' Matt said, but he felt jealous that the other man saw so much more of Hannah than he did. 'I hope you'll tell him to let me in if I call at Roscarrock to see you again.'

They heard a patter of rain on the tall chapel windows. 'We'd better make a dash for it,' Hannah said, putting her arm inside his.

Daniel had had the same idea as Matt, to see Hannah outside the chapel and tell her the wedding was already over, but he hadn't been able to get away as quickly as he'd wanted from the *Sunrise*. When he saw Hannah and Matt emerging from the chapel, arm in arm and chatting happily, he felt betrayed and fell into a dark mood.

'Hannah!' He marched up and thrust himself between them. 'How long have you been here?'

'Hannah is with me,' Matt said angrily.

There was a bright flash of lightning followed quickly by a clap of thunder and the next moment the heavens opened.

'I want to talk to her,' Daniel insisted, taking Hannah's arm and pulling her away. Her umbrella clattered on to the chapel forecourt.

'Stop it, Danny.' Hannah crossly tried to struggle free. The rain was soaking them. 'I'll talk to you later, but right now—'

'No, you talk to him later.' Daniel dragged her out of the chapel grounds so forcefully Hannah could hardly keep her balance. She had seen him in ugly moods but never in such a vile temper. He spoke into her face. 'I've been your friend longer than him, and he's a bloody lame misery guts anyway. He's not for you, you have nothing in common. Remember all the adventures we used to talk about? Matt Penney will turn you into a downtrodden old woman before your time, you'll be bored to death in a few months. Stop wasting your bloody time with him and stop fooling about with my feelings.'

'Danny, let me go!' she shouted, horribly aware that even though the rain was teeming down, an audience was already forming in doorways and under porches to witness this latest spectacle.

Infuriated, Matt grabbed Daniel's jacket and wrenched him away from Hannah. Daniel had been expecting this and he spun round and brought his fist up into the softest part of Matt's belly. Matt yelled, but managed to keep upright and aimed a successful punch at Daniel's jaw. A full fist fight started and Hannah was obliged to get out of their way.

'Stop it, Danny,' she screamed. 'Matt's hand hasn't healed yet.'

'Don't let that stop you, Kittow,' Matt spat, his dark face on fire. He took off his coat and hung it on the chapel gate. 'I'll make you pay, you piece of scum, for manhandling my woman.'

'Matt, don't! Danny!' Hannah pleaded.

It fell on deaf ears. The men were pacing about like warring stags, eyes locked, sizing each other up.

'Hannah belongs to me, Penney,' Daniel seethed, throwing his jacket on the wet cobbles.

'You're hopelessly wrong, Kittow. You may have been closer to her in the past but you don't really know her. Tell him, Hannah. Tell him about us.'

Daniel glanced at her for confirmation, then kept his eyes rooted on Matt in case he tried something underhand.

'Tell him, for goodness sake,' said old Mr Dunn leaning on his two sticks at his door, 'or there'll be more blood spilt over a Spargo.'

'I'm sorry, Danny, but Matt means more to me than you,' Hannah said firmly. 'Now move away from each other, there's no need to fight.'

'You're not good enough for her, Penney,' Daniel snarled. 'You're a pompous bastard who thinks he's better than he is, but I could name a couple of whores who've had you in their beds.'

'Well, Hannah doesn't want a rotten, no-good criminal,

358

Kittow,' Matt sneered. 'Hannah's mine and it's her choice.'

'I'll kill you before I let you have her!'

Matt beckoned with his hands, one still bandaged. 'Come on then, try it, if you think you're man enough.'

'No, Matt!' Hannah cried desperately, running to him and gripping his jumper. 'Walk away, there's no need to—'

'He's not going anywhere until I've beaten his bleddy brains out!' Daniel ripped her away from Matt, sending her hurtling backwards until she was stopped and steadied by a pair of strong hands. She was pulled back gently into the shelter of a porch and screamed when Matt hit Daniel on the jaw before he could raise his fists. As they laid into each other again, Hannah could hear Mrs Penney imploring the watching men to stop them.

'They've gone mad. Nothing's going to stop them now,' a harsh male voice muttered. 'I'm not going to risk myself getting hurt.'

Daniel got a vicious blow in under Matt's nose and his lip split. Blood spurted down his face and he staggered back against the chapel railings. He gripped the wrought iron for a second then plunged forward, butting his head into Daniel's chest. Daniel rained blows on his head until Matt managed to haul himself away. He danced about on nimble feet, aiming punches into the air about Daniel's face. Daniel ducked and dodged, looking for an opening to inflict some damage on Matt's body. Finally, Matt lashed out and his fist struck Daniel's temple, making the skin there part in a two-inch gash. As the blood poured and Daniel fell to the cobbled ground, Hannah's legs felt so shaky she was grateful for whoever it was who was supporting her. She didn't look round, afraid to take her eyes off the fighting men for a second.

'Come on, Matt,' someone called grimly as Daniel reared up, ready to pitch in again. Something akin to hatred was on the two men's faces. ''Tis time that cocky sod was taken down a peg or two.'

'Watch his left, Danny,' Rufus guffawed, standing in his filthy jersey and ragged trousers in the rain, looking gleefully round the crowd. He wasn't concerned that two of his crew were fighting, as long as it was not on the boat. 'Danny'll soon finish un off. He's got no bleddy chance.'

As some people bawled out encouragement, the outraged Reverend Skewes added his voice to those who were shouting at Matt and Daniel to stop. There was another flash of lightning and a clap of thunder which seemed to shake the cove. Fred Jose was thoroughly enjoying himself, hoping Daniel would come off worse. PC Burt would be interested to learn about what was going on, fighting in public. There were so many witnesses no one would know who had made the phone call.

Several blows later, both men were weakening but gritting their bloodied teeth and wiping the rain water from their eyes. They were determined to go on fighting until one of them dropped unconscious to the ground or begged for mercy. They were grappling by the railings and as Daniel got a grip on the back of Matt's neck, Hannah was terrified he was going to smash Matt's face against the railings. She screamed and made to run forward but the hands on her shoulders held her tight.

'Stay here, 'tis too dangerous,' a familiar voice said. It had come from a man she wouldn't have believed would ever seek to protect her. She turned her head to find herself staring into her father's face.

Jeff gazed back at her for a moment, then he took his hands from her shoulders and walked away. Hannah was still looking after him when some men in the crowd suddenly rushed forward. Matt and Daniel were both in a desperate state, their clothes torn and stained with blood. It was now easier to restrain them and a spontaneous decision had been made to put an end to the fight before one of them was irretrievably hurt.

Hannah didn't see it happen and by the time she turned back, three men were holding Matt tightly in their grasp and three had Daniel.

'I haven't finished with you yet, Penney,' Daniel hissed, panting heavily and making blood and spittle drool down over his chin.

Mrs Penney was moving forward, holding out a handkerchief which was far too insubstantial for the job of mopping up her son's face.

'Any time, anywhere, Kittow,' Matt replied, spitting blood out over the cobbles.

The Reverend Skewes was trying to make himself heard above the voices of the excited crowd. 'The show is over. I suggest you all go home and let these two young men bow their heads over their shameful behaviour.'

It was some time before the first bystander moved off but when Mr Nunn went inside and closed his door, a steady trickle followed his example. Jowan touched Hannah's arm. 'Come home with me, Hannah. There's no use standing here. You won't be able to reason with either of them until they calm down.'

'In a minute, Jowan,' she said tightly. 'I have something to say first.' Only the minister, Mrs Penney and the men holding Matt and Daniel were left. Her heels clicked over the cobbles as she marched up to the two bruised and battered men with her head held high. 'How dare you fight over me as if I was a piece of property,' she accused them both.

'You're worth fighting over, Hannah,' Matt mouthed painfully with a feeble smile.

'Don't be ridiculous!' She turned on him, furious that except for his anger at Daniel he did not find the situation the least bit serious. 'You've behaved like a savage. You ought to know better with your education and beliefs, but you were more eager to fight than Danny and had less reason.'

'That's right, you tell him, Hannah,' Daniel jeered. Matt didn't seem to mean more to her than he did now.

'Shut up, Danny,' she hurled over her shoulder, then continued berating Matt, whose face had lost its look of triumph. 'There's a part of you I don't know and I don't like. I'd prefer it if you were more like the quiet, retiring person people suppose you to be. You've made a fool of yourself today, behaving like a common lout. I'm going to my aunty's and I don't know if I ever want to see you again.' Shaking her head haughtily, she marched into the courtyard, picked up her umbrella and set off down the hill with Jowan.

'Let me go,' Matt grimly told the men holding him. 'I promise I won't lay a hand on Kittow.' The men knew Matt never lied and let him go. Mrs Penney was holding his coat but he shrugged it away as she tried to put it over his shoulders. There was another clap of thunder, but Matt's face looked fiercer and darker, and deeply malevolent. His mother, Daniel, the minister and the six men watched, dumbstruck, as he took after Hannah.

He caught up with her as she and Jowan reached the next street and he roughly swung her round. His voice was loud enough for everyone to hear. 'Don't you ever speak to me like that again. Who do you think you are, Hannah Spargo? One of the blasted Opies? You may not approve of me fighting but I won't be insulted and pushed aside by a useless bastard who lives one step ahead of the law. Don't you realise he's almost certainly up to his neck in dealings with the same men who tried to rob Roscarrock? Doesn't it matter to you that he could be partly responsible for you and Mrs Opie being hurt and nearly killed? I don't know what you wanted to say to me but let me tell you this, I'm not going to run after you, Hannah, and beg you to tell me. I believe there's something too deep between us just to throw our relationship away. If you come to your senses, I'll be waiting, but it's you who will have to make the first move.' Shaking with fury, he stalked away.

Chapter 30

Mrs Opie was coming home the next day and Hannah was personally preparing her rooms. With Pogo asleep on his favourite chair in front of the cosy fire in the sitting room, she put clean linen sheets on the bed, affectionately plumping up the pillows and smoothing the deep, lace-edged hem of the top sheet over the soft wool blankets. Then she draped the silk bedspread over the top in just the way Mrs Opie liked. She cleaned the bathroom until the tiles and brass fittings sparkled. Next she polished the furniture and laid out the lace runners and doilies she had made during Mrs Opie's stay in hospital. She dusted the ornaments, then replaced the array of cosmetics, perfume and the silver hairbrush and trinket box on the dressing table. The day after the robbery Mr Greg had bought a safe and locked the jewellery inside it; in future Hannah would have to tell him when his grandmother required her jewellery.

When she had arranged the last cushion and attended to the clocks, Hannah stayed awhile, smiling as she pictured Mrs Opie back home in her rightful place. Since she had come here she'd shared nearly all her feelings with Mrs Opie and hoped the nurse would not encroach on their close relationship. From her hospital bed Mrs

Opie had noticed her sadness the day after the wedding and had found an excuse to send Greg out of the room before inquiring the reason.

'Is something wrong, dear? Were there problems at your brother's wedding?'

Without a second thought Hannah told her why the wedding had taken place secretly.

'That's absolutely appalling,' Mrs Opie said indignantly, delicately touching her hair which had been recently cut and styled; she looked every bit the elegant, confident, self-controlled lady Hannah had first seen. 'No wonder you look down in the dumps. I'm so glad your brother and his poor wife have got away from Porthellis. I must think of a way to help them, nothing patronising of course. It's a wonder to me why you want to go down to the village, Hannah.'

'I don't think I'll be able to face it for a long time,' she answered mournfully. The violence between Matt and Daniel had seen to that, and although she had pondered the unexpected kindness shown to her by her father and was cheered by it, the risk that her hopes might be misplaced and that she would face his usual hate-filled attitude towards her was too painful to bear right now. And while she wanted to ask Danny about Matt's allegations that he was mixed up in the burglary, she didn't really believe he could be involved in something so unlawful and violent.

When she and Greg had left, Mrs Opie had asked a nurse to pass her her writing things. Out of the gold initialled, tan leather case she took her journal and fountain pen and wrote, '*Nothing left for me to do now. Hannah is mine for good.*'

It was time for Hannah's morning break and she took

a tray up to her room, sat in front of the fire and ruminated over the future. Mrs Opie was coming home, the
burglars who had put her in hospital would be locked up
for a very long time, and if not for the fact that she was
pregnant things would have quickly returned to normal.
They might even have taken the London trip when Mrs
Opie's hip had mended properly. There could be no
doubt she was pregnant. The morning sickness had
stopped abruptly but she had missed two monthlies. She'd
leave it a little longer then go to see the doctor and look
for the right moment to tell Mrs Opie.

She would have married Matt, she didn't doubt he
would have asked her, if events hadn't taken another turn.
She had tried to shut out the memory of the dreadful
fight between Matt and Daniel and especially Matt's last
harsh words to her. She felt her anger with him was
justified, but he had been right, it wasn't so much what
she'd said to him but the way she'd said it. In unguarded
moments she would recall the way she had felt alive and
complete in his arms, his tender touch, the wonderful
sensations as they'd given themselves to each other completely. She would be filled with a terrible ache and tears
inevitably followed.

Apart from visiting Mrs Opie in hospital, she had left
the house only to call on Mitch and Viv at Portmellon.
Greg offered to drive her there and dropped her off just
outside the village. The road ran across the beach of the
village and he did not want to risk getting the car stuck
in the sand. Hannah asked at a cottage close to the
water's edge the way to Mitch and Viv Spargo's home.
She found it in a quiet, sheltered spot at the back of the
village. The view of the sea was blocked by other houses
but it had a scrap of garden at the back and front and a

backdrop of sloping fields which formed the side of a natural valley.

Mitch, bleary-eyed from a hard night's fishing, had been delighted to see her. 'Hannah! Come in,' he exclaimed, pulling her through the door. 'Viv, sweetheart, come down here,' he called up over his head. 'I'm putting the kettle on. Hannah's here.'

The door opened into the only downstairs room which doubled as a kitchen and parlour. It had oddments of old furniture, a patched, faded cloth on a small square table, and a fresh coat of paint, pale blue on the walls, white and sky-blue on the woodwork. There were two small, square-paned windows, one with blue and green floral curtains, the other pink with frilled edges, not new but in good condition. It was spotlessly clean, bright and appealing. There was a sense of promise here and Hannah was thrilled to see how happy Mitch was in his snug home.

'You have it lovely in here, Mitch,' she said, handing him a straw shopping bag and a parcel. 'I've brought you and Viv a few little things and a present for your new home.'

Mitch put them on the table and enfolded her in a bear hug. 'It's so good to see you, Hannah.'

'You too, Mitch,' she said, patting his back.

Viv came down the narrow flight of twisting stairs from the bedroom and opened the other door to the room. She had a bundle of laundry in her arms. 'Hello,' she said, a note of welcome in her shy voice.

Hannah gazed at her sister-in-law for a moment. Viv looked a picture of health. Her auburn hair, hanging in one long plait down her back, gleamed and her eyes shone with a healthy energy Hannah hadn't seen in them before. She couldn't help hugging her, it seemed the natural thing to do, and Viv responded in the same way. 'I didn't realise you were so pretty,' Hannah said.

'I've got the most beautiful bride in Portmellon,' Mitch said proudly. 'All the villagers here say so.'

'You forgot to put the kettle on, Mitch,' Viv chuckled, seeing to it herself.

'Sorry, sweetheart. Come and look what Hannah's brought us, a bag of goodies, I shouldn't wonder, and a present for the house.'

No one mentioned the wedding or the harrowing events surrounding it and if Mitch had heard about the fight that day, he didn't bring it up.

'Real sheets and pillowcases,' Viv exclaimed as she opened the parcel and held up the lengths of white cotton. 'We'll have the grandest bed in Portmellon, Mitch. Thank you, Hannah.'

'I'm glad you like them. I bought them in St Austell before Mrs Opie broke her hip and I thought I'd wait until you had your own home before giving them to you.'

The bag was filled with Mr Patrick's baking, items of lace Hannah had made and some odds and ends that Mrs Opie had said Hannah could take from the house. 'When she comes home she's going to send Mr Patrick up to the attic to turn out a few things for you. She said she hopes you won't be offended, but she'd rather think about someone other than herself just lying in bed all day with little to do.'

'It's very kind of her, we're grateful,' Viv said, nibbling on a piece of Patrick Opie's shortbread. 'Mitch is teaching me to read and write and when I've learned enough words I'll write and thank her. How's Leah? We became close friends when . . .'

'She's very happy now she's working openly at Roscarrock. She sends you both her love.'

'You must bring her next time,' Viv said.

Hannah promised she would.

'Did you walk here, Hannah?' Mitch asked, slipping his hand round Viv's small waist. Viv pressed her head against his shoulder for a moment.

'No, Mr Greg brought me.'

'We'll be the talk of the place,' Mitch puffed out his chest. 'Having a grand lady visit us who's driven up in a car.'

'I'm not a grand lady,' Hannah protested mildly.

'You look like one, doesn't she, Viv?'

'Yes, you do, Hannah,' Viv agreed. 'I haven't seen clothes on anyone like that since I passed the mayor's wife in the street at Newlyn.'

Hannah blushed. 'I'm only wearing what Mrs Opie bought for me to go to London in.' She changed the subject. 'How are things on the boat you work on, Mitch?'

'We're not doing too bad. Course, not as many boats go out from here. Like the other villages, we're pilchard driving up round Looe and Polperro. 'Twas a poor catch last night, but we're making ends meet, aren't we, Viv?'

Viv smiled shyly.

When Hannah left, Mitch walked her across the beach towards the car in which Greg Opie was sitting and making notes for his novel, quite oblivious of the interest he was stirring among the villagers. 'I'm glad to see you so happy, Mitch.'

'Viv was a bit depressed at first, but when she got better after the miscarriage and started doing things round the cottage she cheered up no end. Everything's fine between us, Hannah.' Mitch went quiet but Hannah knew he had something else to say. 'I'm going to hate telling you this, but I feel you ought to know. It wasn't my baby Viv was expecting, it was Daniel's.'

'Danny's!'

'Please be careful of him, Hannah. He seduced Viv, as good as forced her against her will, and when she told him she was pregnant he became angry and hit her. He arranged for her to get rid of the baby. Viv told me everything. It was painful and she cried a lot, but she wanted our marriage to be based on trust, with nothing hidden in the past. Daniel also told Viv he couldn't marry her because he was engaged to a girl called Hannah.' Mitch was deadly serious. 'For God's sake, you mustn't get involved with him. It would be better if you had nothing to do with him at all.'

Hannah found it hard to believe that Daniel could be so ruthless and heartless, but she couldn't keep setting aside what people were telling her about him. 'Don't worry, Mitch, I don't see Daniel at all now.'

Leah had been thrilled when Hannah told her she could go to Portmellon on the next visit. It was through Leah that Hannah knew what was happening in Porthellis. Josh wasn't expected to recover fully from Mitch's beating, his speech was slurred, his mind slow in taking in information. He couldn't go to sea and stayed home all day, following Prim wherever she went, like a young child frightened to let her out of his sight. Bitter over losing Mitch and Hannah's decision to keep away from Porthellis, Prim had accused Janet of not doing enough to stop Hannah from taking the job at Roscarrock and they were no longer speaking.

Three days after the fight, Constable Burt had arrived in Porthellis with a police vehicle, after an anonymous tip-off. He arrested Matt and Daniel and kept them locked up in separate cells for the night. The next day the magistrate fined them five pounds for breach of the peace and issued a stern warning about their unacceptable behaviour. People said Daniel was lucky that was all he was charged with. Since then there had been a series of thefts in the village – a fine pocket watch stolen from old Mr Nunn's house, some of Mrs Penney's best pieces of porcelain, a cameo brooch from Miss Peters, and cigarettes from the shop. People were pointing their finger in Daniel's direction; the thefts only happened when the boats were home, and they were wondering if they ought to begin locking their doors, which was almost unheard of in the village.

There had been a big change in the ownership of the *Sunrise* and the *Misty*. Matt had swapped shares with Terence Spargo, who'd declared he wanted nothing more to do with Jeff, and Terence was paying Matt the balance on the more modern, better equipped boat. He had taken Morley with him to work with the Kittows and Joses. Matt now fished off the *Misty* and two middle-aged unmarried brothers called Chellew had thrown in their lot with him and Jeff. All these events had left a sour atmosphere in the village and Leah said she wished that she, too, could move out for good.

Leah sat at the kitchen table slowly peeling vegetables for the evening meal. She was daydreaming, about Mr Greg. Hannah and Patrick were out visiting Mrs Opie. That afternoon Greg had said he'd come to a vital part in the plot of his book and so Patrick had driven himself and Hannah to the hospital. Angie went occasionally, but when asked if she wanted to join them she'd complained of a headache and Hannah had sent her to lie down in her room.

Hannah had made it clear to Leah that she didn't like the familiarity that existed between her and Mr Greg; did she think he might want to get her into bed? Leah smiled ironically to herself, she knew all about that sort of thing. Hannah seemed to think she was totally ignorant about what went on between a man and woman in bed, but Hannah hadn't lived at home in her adult years to hear their father having his way with their mother.

Leah's scar had been the main reason she had never shown any interest in young men, but her father and Josh's unhealthy attitude to sex had quashed all desire she might have had to look for a husband and have a family. She was sure Greg's kindness towards her was sincere, but even if there was more to it she still trusted and liked him.

Ten minutes after the car had gone he came down to the kitchen. 'Could you bring me some coffee, please, Leah?' He smiled at her warmly. 'I'm working on a tricky piece and the old brain cells need lubricating.'

'Right away, Mr Greg.' She got up from the table and washed her hands. 'You should take a walk round the gardens, that'll clear your head.'

'Not in this weather.' He lingered, leaning on the table and fiddling with some carrots. 'It's getting dark early. Looks like we're in for rain.'

Leah leaned over the sink to get a view of the sky over the top of the railings. 'And it looks like I'll have a wet walk home.'

'Mr Patrick will be back by then. I'll drive you.'

'Thank you, Mr Greg.' He had occasionally driven her home and they had chatted comfortably on the way.

He went back to his study and waited for the coffee, leaving the door open for Leah to carry it through. He shut it after her and watched her willowy form as she poured it out of the silver coffee pot. Her long black hair was tied back with a red ribbon and he had a strong desire to touch it. She smiled at him as she put two sugar lumps into the cup.

'Thank you, Leah,' he smiled back, slipping into the conversational mode he enjoyed with her. 'Pity you can't type. I've got a couple of boring letters to answer.'

'To people in London?' she asked with interest as she brushed up some fallen ashes in the hearth.

Greg noticed her attentiveness and responded to it. Often when he spoke to her she seemed to slip off into a little world of her own. 'Yes, I've been invited to a university reunion party, which I've no intention of going to,' he told her. 'I get asked every year and I never go, can't think why they keep asking me. The other's to a barmy old colonel who likes to find fault with my books. He says he was a spy in the Great War and knows what he's talking about. He probably does, and much better than I do, but judging from his bumptious way of writing he'd never succeed in getting it down on paper.'

'Do you mix with writers, actresses and people like that when you're in London?' Leah watched him sipping the coffee where he'd parked himself on the desk, and it struck her that he really was a handsome man – and tall and rich like the classic storybook hero.

'No, can't abide them.'

He'd said as much to her before. Becoming a little daring, she asked, 'Do you like many people, Mr Greg?'

He grinned. 'No, not many.'

'You'll turn into one of them recluses if you're not careful.'

'I suppose coming from a big family you like lots of people round you all the time.'

'Not really, I like to be on my own. My grandmother used to call me weird for it, but I'm not. When you've had to share a bedroom with three sisters it's nice to have some space. That's why I like working here, there's so much space and it's peaceful and quiet.'

'We have something in common, Leah.'

That remark made her smile shyly. 'Is there anything else, Mr Greg?'

'Not for now, Leah.' He was disappointed he could think of no reason to keep her here longer.

She raced back to the kitchen with her hands over her pounding heart. She stood on the flagstones and trembled like the last leaf hanging on a tree in the wind. For the first time she had noticed a man in the masculine, sexual sense. She had never felt so excited in her life; she was nervous, a little confused and light-headed, but one thing she knew clearly, she wasn't afraid to feel this way.

As the afternoon wore on, the sky became more overcast, the wind howled round the house and the expected rain came down in torrents. Leah turned on the kitchen lights and worked through Hannah's list of jobs as quickly as she could, so the last thing she had to do was collect Mr Greg's tray. Hopefully they would have time to chat before the others came back from the hospital. She was disappointed not to find him in the study. She washed the coffee things then tried to think of a reason to go back to the study and see if he'd come back. Then she remembered Angie and felt guilty about forgetting her. Perhaps Angie would like a cup of tea. She went upstairs to ask. As she started up the second flight of stairs she heard a noise, and thinking it was Mr Greg coming out of his room she pattered back down and made her way to the long corridor. She would say she was popping to Hannah's room for something; Hannah didn't mind that.

As she turned into the corridor she froze. Fear clamped her spine rigid. In the gathering gloom she could make out a figure floating along in a white gown, arms outstretched, coming towards her. Roscarrock's ghost! A real ghost this time, not someone who'd sat in old clothes for a portrait. It was obviously the ghost who owned the steps that Hannah had heard at regular intervals. And it was coming for her! Leah tried to back up and run away but her legs wouldn't move. The ghost had passed Hannah's room and was steadily gaining on her. Leah was terrified out of her wits.

Somewhere from deep in her chest she found her voice and let out a high-pitched scream. The ghost shrieked at her and she screamed again. The ghost stopped moving but still Leah screamed. And the ghost screamed every time she screamed, frightening her more and more until she was in a total frenzy.

Suddenly someone rushed past the ghost and grabbed her arms.

'Leah, Leah, stop screaming, it's me, Greg.' He tried to gather her to him but she clutched his sweater with feverish hands.

'M-Mr Greg, the g-ghost . . . coming to get me,' she jabbered like an imbecile.

'No, Leah, look closely,' he raised his voice in her ear. 'It's Angie. It's only Angie.'

It was several seconds before the cloud of fear controlling her brain cleared enough for her to understand his words. Her legs had turned to jelly and Greg had to hold her tightly to prevent her falling. She stared at Angie from huge saucer-like eyes, hardly daring to believe she wasn't in some terrible danger. 'A-Angie?'

Angie was standing shivering in her white underslip, her arms across her chest, hugging herself. Leah's screaming had terrified her as much as she had terrified Leah. 'I'm s-sorry, Leah. I-I dropped off to sleep and must have been sleepwalking. I'm sorry I frightened you.'

Leah felt more foolish than at any other time in her entire life. 'Oh, dear,' she cried, wishing the floor would open up and swallow her. 'I'm sorry too, Angie.'

'I must go,' Angie muttered, acutely embarrassed to be standing in front of Mr Greg in a state of undress.

'You have another lie-down to get over the shock, Angie,' Greg said kindly. When she'd gone he looked down at Leah's ashen face. She was trembling from head to foot and he gathered her up in his arms.

Leah realised she was nearly shredding his sweater and she let her hands drop. 'Where are you taking me?' she murmured, lapsing into the small whispery voice she'd once had.

'To Hannah's room. It'll be warm in there to help you get over the shock,' he said softly.

He put her down on Hannah's bed and sat beside her, holding her gently against him. He heard her sniff. 'It's all right to cry, Leah.'

Leah didn't want to cry because she'd had a shock but because she'd shown herself up as an utter fool in front of him. 'I . . . I feel so stupid,' she said, taking her hanky out of her apron pocket and dabbing at her eyes, her hand shaking uncontrollably.

'There's no need to feel like that. I would have been

just as afraid and screamed just as loud if I'd thought I'd seen a ghost. You weren't to know Angie was a sleep-walker.'

He's being nice to me again, as if I'm a silly child, Leah thought miserably. She said, 'Hannah's heard these footsteps sometimes at night. It must have been Angie all the time.'

'It's a pity none of us thought to tell her. Roscarrock isn't haunted, no matter what the locals say.'

'Mr Patrick told Hannah it was.'

Greg gave a small laugh. 'That was Mr Patrick being melodramatic. He's like that sometimes.' Leah was still shivering and he rubbed her arms tenderly. 'Feel better now?'

She nodded and allowed her head to sink against his chest. They sat quietly for some time, each enjoying the sensation of being close. Suddenly Leah had to know, 'Why are you so nice to me, Mr Greg? You didn't seem to like Hannah when she first came here and she says you have very little patience with most people, and now my foolishness has stopped you working on an important bit of your book.' She looked up into his face, her bottom lip quivering.

He gazed into her eyes, his own turning a warm smoky grey. Finally he said, 'I find you more important than my book.'

Leah swallowed. The pleasant friendship they'd shared had changed its footing in a few quiet moments. She had never dreamt that he cared for her and now she realised he was holding her in a way that had much more to it than simply giving comfort.

Greg hardly dared breathe. Leah had changed some-how this afternoon. His grandmother had warned him she was a mere child and would stay that way for a very long time and if he didn't keep his feelings in check he could hurt her unforgivably. He had resigned himself to wait until she grew up, until her emotions caught up with her age, but now it seemed they had. She was looking at him with her typical childlike innocence yet he recognised the new maturity in her, a woman's need even, but if he made one wrong move he'd end up regretting it for ever.

Leah sensed he was as nervous as she was; she knew this wasn't wise and was unlikely to lead anywhere that would benefit her, but she wished she could stay like this in his arms for ever. She took in every tiny part of his face, the strong nose and jaw, high cheekbones, proud brow, the slightly arched line of his fair eyebrows, and most of all the deepset eyes that had lost their sharpness and darting impatience and now looked velvety, open and honest. She put her face closer to his, not dropping her gaze.

Greg returned her gentle quest for knowledge of him by using his eyes to travel and linger over her, then feeling he was on safe ground at last, he lowered his head and fleetingly caressed her lips. Leah instinctively closed her eyes and put her arms round his neck when his tender touch came again.

Chapter 31

Hannah ran nimbly down the steps to meet the ambulance bringing Mrs Opie home and stood a little behind Greg and Patrick. Angie plodded down after her in a more ungainly manner and kept well back out of the way. Greg opened the back of the ambulance and a nurse, large-bodied, starchly uniformed and severely-shoed, got out first and shuffled him aside.

'Mrs Opie needs space, young man,' she said in a voice that boomed like the sea passing through a channel of rock.

'I'm her grandson,' Greg protested, pushing the wheelchair in front of her.

The nurse moved her thin lips disparagingly, then eyed him, Patrick, Hannah and Angie one at a time with an 'I'll soon sort you lot out' expression, but she changed her tone to the more gentle wash of a friendly wave caressing the summer sand. 'I do beg your pardon, Mr Opie. I didn't know who you were. Now, we must all be quick and get Mrs Opie in out of the cold and into her bed,' adding unnecessarily, 'mustn't we?'

Mrs Opie made a face at the nurse's back as she boomed instructions, again unnecessarily, to the two ambulance men on how to carry the patient up the steps and inside the house. 'She comes highly recommended,' Mrs Opie said rather mischievously, all smiles, as she was lifted past Hannah and the others.

'Lovely to have you home, Great-Aunt,' Patrick said as the ambulance men put her wheelchair down in the hall. 'I'm cooking you the most super lunch.'

'Thank you, Patrick. I've missed your cooking.'

'It's turbot dugléré . . .' but Mrs Opie had turned her attention to Hannah and Angie.

'It was good of you to meet me, my dears,' she said. 'Come upstairs with me, Hannah. You can unpack my things.'

'You may come up later, when I say you can,' the nurse broke in officiously, ignoring Hannah and taking no notice of her surroundings, as if she was used to living in such grandeur.

'Come up in ten minutes, Hannah,' Mrs Opie said, treating the nurse to an uncompromising stare. 'Nurse Collins, allow me to introduce you to my housekeeper and companion, Miss Spargo. The other gentleman is Mr Patrick Opie, my great-nephew, and the maid is Angie Miller.'

Myra Collins smiled at those she had been introduced to, a smile that was a little too wide to be genuine. Middle-aged and of medium height, she was a curious looking woman. The hair under her cap was iron-grey with fuzzy tight curls, her brow was smooth and formidable, but the whites of her pale brown eyes were yellow and her cheeks and the flesh under nose and eyes were fissured from a heavy smoking habit, the smell of which emanated from her clothes. Her head, hands and feet seemed much too small for the rest of her.

She folded her hands together and said briefly to one and all, 'Pleased to meet you.' Then she turned to Greg. 'Mr Opie, if you will be good enough to lead the way to Mrs Opie's room, we can dispense with the services of the ambulance crew.'

'Well, really,' he muttered under his breath, and Hannah exchanged a worried look with Angie as Mrs Opie was carried upstairs.

'I hope she don't come down to the kitchen,' Angie whispered nervously, heading that way to get on with her work.

'I don't think she will,' Hannah said tightly. 'I think Nurse Collins is the sort of woman who jealously guards her poor undeserving patients.'

'A battleaxe if ever I saw one,' Patrick observed. 'I wonder if she'll like my turbot in dugléré sauce. I'd better take the suitcases upstairs.'

Hannah showed the ambulance men out and didn't take a second longer than the ten minutes to knock on Mrs Opie's door and make her way into the bedroom. Nurse Collins was putting the wheelchair out of the way and Mrs Opie was sitting up in bed. Hannah felt a rush of emotion to see her, wearing a matching blue silk nightgown and bed jacket, regally occupying her home again. It seemed so long since she had fallen and broken her hip in this very room.

Nurse Collins scowled at Hannah. Hannah ignored her. Now the nurse had taken off her voluminous cloak, Hannah saw that her generously proportioned frame was not fully contained by her uniform; wedges of superfluous fat hung here, bulged there and wobbled everywhere. Definitely a candidate to appreciate Mr Patrick's cooking, she thought wryly.

'I'll start your unpacking, Mrs Opie,' Hannah said, smiling.

'Ring for some tea first, dear.'

From the haughty look on the nurse's face it was clear she didn't approve of her new employer using terms of endearment to a member of staff. But Nurse Collins had a more pressing need to attend to than to wonder why Mrs Opie appeared to be so fond of her rather too young housekeeper. She was desperate to light up a cigarette. 'I wonder, now that Miss Spargo is here, and you're quite comfortable for a few minutes, Mrs Opie, if I might go to my room,' she said loudly.

'Of course,' Mrs Opie replied graciously. 'Hannah, will you show Nurse to her room, please?'

'No need to bother, Miss Spargo,' Nurse Collins said briskly. 'Just tell me where it is, I'm sure I can find it.'

Hannah gave her directions to the previous housekeeper's quarters at the back of the house, and picking up her cloak and suitcase Nurse Collins left the room, leaving her stale tobacco smell behind. Hannah waved a hand in front of her face and opened a window on the mild November day.

'Don't worry,' Mrs Opie said humorously, marking Hannah's displeasure, 'she'll only be here for a few weeks.'

'All that matters is that you get well properly,' Hannah said, ringing for the tea.

'How sweet of you to say something like that.' Mrs Opie examined her closely as she opened a suitcase and starting unpacking.

Hannah paused in her work. 'I meant it.'

'Thank you, Hannah. I can't tell you how glad I am to be home. I'll have my writing things here beside me. Where's Pogo? I thought he'd be here to say hello to

384

me. I've missed him terribly too.'

'Here he is,' Greg said, carrying the little fluffy creature into the room. 'We thought it best to keep him out of the way until you were settled in. Just as well with that old harridan of a nurse. Where is she?'

'As the working men say, gone for a fag,' Mrs Opie laughed.

'If you ask me, she'll be a health hazard. I can't wait until we can get rid of her,' he said with feeling, sitting on the bed and kissing his grandmother affectionately.

'Is Leah coming this afternoon?' Mrs Opie asked.

Greg, blissfully happy and rather emotional since the wonderful events of yesterday with Leah, let Hannah answer that she was.

'Good, then we can all settle down to something of our old pattern.'

Five minutes later Nurse Collins was back. 'What's that?' she demanded in her mannish voice, pointing an accusing finger at Pogo. 'I won't have animals in the sickrooms I attend.'

As Mrs Opie's facial muscles tightened ready for an argument, Hannah and Greg exchanged looks. There were stormy times ahead.

As Leah walked along Turn-A-Penny Lane on her way to work, Daniel jumped over the hedge in front of her and made her squeal. 'What the heck do you think you're doing of, Daniel Kittow? I nearly died of fright.' She was angry at being rudely awakened from her thoughts of Greg. Neither of them had said much after they'd kissed or when he'd driven her home in a torrent of rain, but there was an unspoken agreement between them that they had a special relationship – and a secret one. Leah had been thinking up excuses to go to his study.

'Stop fussing,' Daniel said impatiently. The boats of Porthellis were laid up; although the weather was quiet and meek enough now, yesterday's fierce southerly wind had made the sea too dangerous to risk fishing today. Fed up with Hannah's non-appearance in Porthellis, Daniel had decided to do something about it. 'Who did you think I was? A highwayman?'

'It wouldn't surprise me,' Leah muttered, walking on, recalling the rumours about him stealing from people's houses. Her Aunty Janet had reported that her mantelpiece clock, a Rouse heirloom, had gone missing.

Daniel softened his mood. He had alarmed Leah and if he couldn't get round her she would refuse to do him the favour he was about to ask. 'Sorry I startled you, Leah,' he smiled with his old charm.

It was lost on Leah; she glared at him, she'd rather trust a snake.

'I want you to ask Hannah to meet me,' he said.

'She doesn't want to see you,' Leah said, hastening her steps.

'Tell her I'll be in the woods. She can meet me there when she takes that silly dog for a walk,' Daniel persisted.

'I'll do no such thing,' Leah retorted stubbornly.

Daniel was walking backwards in front of her. It irked him to have to plead. 'Please, Leah. I only want a few words with her.' He could see his words were falling on deaf ears so he stood still, making her stop, and said in a sterner tone, 'Well, I'll just have to go up to the front door and demand to see her then.'

'Don't do that. Hannah wouldn't like it, nor would the Opies.'

'You're not giving me any other choice. I'd ask to speak

to her over the telephone but it's too easy for her or Greg Opie to make excuses and I really need to see her. Hannah and I have been friends for years, I don't want that to end just because I was stupid enough to get involved in a fight. I rescued her from your old man once, remember? Not to mention it was me who saved you in the sea that day.'

Leah couldn't deny that and she could see he wouldn't give up unless she agreed to do as he asked, and it would be preferable for Hannah to meet him for a few minutes in the grounds than have him banging on the front door of Roscarrock. 'All right, I'll tell her. She usually takes Pogo for a walk about three o'clock, before it gets dark.'

'Thanks,' he moved out of her way, 'I won't forget I owe you a favour.'

Greg went back to his grandmother's room when Nurse Collins was eating her lunch. Mrs Opie was reading a magazine and pretended not to notice the serious look on his face. She had a shrewd idea what was coming. He took the magazine away from her and held her hand.

'You know what I'm going to ask, don't you?' he said softly. 'You can't hold the truth back from me any longer, Grandma. Is Hannah the daughter of Aunt Stephanie?'

'Is that what you think?' Feena Opie kept her face expressionless.

'You're more than fond of her and the resemblance to Aunt Stephanie at her age is too close for it to be a coincidence.'

She didn't answer and Greg took it as confirmation. 'Have you known all along, while she was growing up in the village, that she was your granddaughter?'

Several emotions now crossed Feena's features. She

gripped his hand tightly. 'Promise me you won't say anything, Greg.'

'You have my word, Grandma. Are you going to tell her?'

'Perhaps one day, if the time is right. I have Hannah's trust and loyalty and her affection and that's all that matters for now.' Feena smiled. 'I'm so glad you've grown fond of her too, Greg. I had lots of time to think while I was in hospital and you probably won't mind that I consulted my solicitor and have made provision for her future. Roscarrock will be yours of course one day and that will never change. In fact I may sign it over to you sooner rather than later, providing you always keep a place here for Patrick. When my wretched hip has mended I want to take Hannah away from here, far away from Porthellis and the other half of her family. We can start a new life together.'

'I think that would be the best solution, Grandma,' Greg replied, kissing her gently and leaving her to rest. He was truly pleased for Hannah that their grandmother would elevate her position in the world and hopefully make her happy, something he'd noticed she hadn't been of late. And Greg was happy for himself; the secret he had been asked to keep would ensure there would be no objections to what he planned for himself and Leah, if all went well between them.

Carrying Pogo so he wouldn't get his paws wet, Hannah met Daniel at the appointed time and place. He tried to hug her but she pushed him away. 'I don't like being summoned like this, Danny,' she said crossly.

'What else could I do?' he said taking Pogo, who was excited to see him, into his own arms and receiving a furious licking about the face. 'You won't come to me so I've come to you. Don't you think I'm missing you, that I don't care for you any more? Surely you don't believe I was involved in the burglary?'

'No, it's not that,' she said, walking further in among the trees, afraid they might be seen, blinking as moisture dripped off the branches of an elm tree and hit her forehead. She had noticed Nurse Collins glanced often out of Mrs Opie's windows. 'I've been to see Mitch and Viv. He told me it was your baby she was expecting.'

Daniel was thunderstruck, he hadn't expected Hannah to find out about his involvement with Viv. He thrust his hands into his jacket pocket and stayed quiet.

'Do you deny it?'

He knew he couldn't lie his way out of it. 'No. It was a mistake, it shouldn't have happened.'

'Too right it shouldn't have happened,' she hurled at him. 'Viv is little more than a child. How could you, Danny?'

'She's the only girl of her age I've gone with,' he tried to excuse himself. 'She was giving me the eye every time I was in Newlyn. She was so pretty I just lost my head for a while. But things have worked out for her all right now,' he pointed out.

It drove Hannah wild with anger. How dare he shift the blame to Viv. Rounding on him, she smacked his face with all her might. Daniel didn't see it coming and stumbled into a tree, banging his head. Pogo yelped and scrabbled up his chest as he felt himself falling. Daniel stared in disbelief, his hand to his red cheek, as Hannah let fly at him.

'You make me sick, Daniel Kittow! I don't believe for one minute that Viv led you on. You've always been too forward where women are concerned, you think you're God's gift to the female species. You're a liar and I hate that about you. And as for the fight with Matt, you deliberately provoked it and just as we were getting things worked out between us. The trouble with you is you like your own way and will do anything low, mean and underhanded to get it.' Out of breath, and wanting to get away from him, she ran through the woods and up to the edge of the cliff. She looked down on Porthellis with her heart breaking. Daniel's presence here had brought back every painful moment of the fight, how she had hurt Matt's feelings, and his harsh words.

Daniel walked slowly after her, giving her time to be alone. When she realised he was standing behind her she angrily wiped away her tears. 'Give Pogo to me,' she demanded.

'I'm sorry, Hannah,' he said, putting the dog down and letting him sniff about instead. 'I treated Viv badly and I'll always regret it, whether you believe me or not. I was jealous of you and Matt, but we've been close friends all these years and I know he isn't the man for you. You don't want a quiet, moody bloke who's inclined to sulk and get depressed. Remember the way he spoke to you? He can't love you and treat you like that.'

'You don't really know Matt, Danny. Yes, he's inclined to moods but only when he's upset. I've hurt him so much. He was right in what he said to me.'

'Will you go to him, like he said?'

'I don't know,' she shook her head, 'probably not. Right now I'm concerned with Mrs Opie and that's all I want to think about. I've got to go.' She called to Pogo and he obediently came to her, dragging his wet lead along behind him.

'You don't really hate me, do you, Hannah?' Daniel asked forlornly as they tramped back through the woods. 'We've been through a lot together.'

She didn't know what to say. Daniel turning up like this had made her all the more confused. Suddenly he stumbled and fell to the ground, clutching his shin.

'What's the matter?'

'I thought I was walking through a clump of grass but I hit my leg on something hard.'

He looked the exact opposite of his usual confident and proud self, the man who strutted on the quay at Porthellis, displayed his muscular torso for the local girls, breezed his way into the pub, demonstrated his prowess on the boat, that Hannah couldn't prevent a wry laugh. He hauled himself up and rubbed at his painful shin, grinning boyishly. Then he parted the grass he had walked into. 'There's something hidden here, looks like a blocked up rabbit burrow.'

Putting Pogo down, Hannah crouched beside him and pulled aside more grass. The top of the 'burrow' grew the more they uncovered it; it was much too big to have been made by rabbits. It was blocked off by concrete. 'I know what this is,' she said excitedly. 'It's the tunnel the Bodinnicks made to hide their gold from the Roundheads and then it was used by smugglers. I thought it would come out on the cliff top and not in the woods – no wonder I couldn't find it.'

'There you are, me girl,' he said as they stood and gazed down at the entrance to the ancient tunnel. 'We've stumbled on an adventure together, just like we used to dream about when we were children.'

Hannah was taken back to those years when her happiest moments had been spent in Daniel's company, when life had been uncomplicated, feelings given over only to fantasies and simple things like wondering what was for tea. 'Oh, Danny, why can't real life be like that?'

'I'd hate it if I lost your friendship, Hannah,' he said, a quiver in his voice. 'It's the thing I value most. I want to see you, regularly, like we've always done and I don't want it to be secretly like this, as if we've something to be ashamed of. Will you come down to the village again?'

'No, Danny.'

'Not even to go to chapel? You haven't lost your faith, have you? Not because of the fight? I promise I won't needle Matt again. Anyway, we hardly see each other now we're on different boats.'

'It isn't that.' Her faith was as strong as ever and she was sure she'd get a letter any day now from the Reverend Skewes inquiring why she wasn't attending chapel. She couldn't go again, soon her swelling middle would show she had erred and strayed – and Matt would know their union had conceived a child. 'I just can't.'

'Then I want you to ask Mrs Opie if I can come and visit you once a week. You've always said how kind she is to you, she'll understand why you need your friend.' He lifted her chin and made her look at him. 'And although I'm a bad man in a lot of ways, I'm the best friend you've ever had, aren't I?'

'Yes, Danny, but—'

'No buts. You ask her and send word to me by Leah. I'm not giving you up, Hannah. I love you and I'll come anyway.'

Chapter 32

'Waste of ruddy time, this is,' Graham Chellew, one half of the new shareholders of the *Misty*, remarked to Matt as they shared the watch one very cold night in the middle of December. For several nights in a row they had shot their herring nets round the Eddystone Rock lighthouse, off Plymouth Sound, and hauled in either small or no reward. And every night Graham put the fishing industry and the world in general to rights. They were now trying in Bigbury Bay further up off the Devon coast. ''Tis the fault of they buggers back in thirty-four, trawling the herring in the bay when they were about to spawn. Never seen a decent shoal since then, and all for the sake of one season's easy catch. Ruined it for all of us, they did.'

'I know,' Matt said grimly. 'I was around then.'

Graham looked at him thoughtfully as he cut off a chew of tobacco and pushed it into the side of his mouth. 'S'pose you were, but you look younger than 'ee really are with that sombre look you always have about 'ee.'

'What are you doing for Christmas?' Matt asked, to change the subject.

'Same as always. Me and me brother'll go to chapel, roast a chicken, treat ourselves to a bottle of brandy and curl up in front of the fire. Course, there won't be much joy around this year, not after night after night of all but empty nets for all the boats. Be a hard struggle for those with young'uns. Empty stockings all round, 'less someone's lucky enough to have a bit put by, but who in Porthellis has savings?'

I've got some, Matt thought bitterly, for all the good it does me. When Hannah had hugged and kissed him in the chapel he'd thought he might have been spending it on a honeymoon.

''Tis a crying shame,' Graham carried on with his woebegone theme. 'Boats coming down here all the way from Yarmouth and Lowestoft for sweet nothing.' He nudged Matt's arm, making him shiver and realise how cold he was. 'You're a more devout chapel man than me. Offer up a prayer or two.'

Hunching his shoulders and stamping his feet in a bid to feel warmer, Matt said sourly, 'I think God's stopped answering my prayers.'

Graham surveyed him in the starlight for some moments. 'When?'

'When what?' Matt replied, about to go off and get mugs of hot tea before he fell into a deeper depression.

'When do 'ee reckon He stopped answering your prayers?'

'I don't want to talk about it.' Matt moved away. 'I've said too much.'

Graham restrained him with a huge paw. 'You were friendly with Jeff's only fair-haired daughter. You'm talking 'bout the day that pretty little Hannah gave 'ee lip when you had a set-to with Daniel Kittow. I heard about that. That's it, isn't it? That's why you're going round with your mouth screwed up like a duck's fert. Well, don't just hang round moping about it, me handsome. Go tell her you're sorry. She's a nice maid. She'll come round.'

'Hannah's got a new life at Roscarrock,' Matt said, coming out with a statement that had revolved inside his head day and night since that fateful day, something he knew he had been right about when he'd reprimanded her after the fight with Daniel. 'She has to want me more than that or I could never make her happy.'

'I take your point,' Graham rambled on, not that he was a master of the affairs of the heart. Thick-set, snow-white hair sporting a spiky cut that should have seen the barber rightfully out of business, short bull neck, fat nose, small eyes, hands like hunks of meat and skin fissured like well-worn granite, not even the most ardent husband hunter had been tempted to give him, or his twin brother Malcolm, a second look. 'But have 'ee spoken to her since?'

'No.'

'Well, don't be so hard-minded. How could you possibly know what she's thinking now?'

Matt glanced across the sea at the navigational lights of an unknown lugger and wondered how its night was faring, then he gazed down at the water over *Misty*'s stern, looking for signs of silver fish in the first net. He saw nothing but total blackness, the same emptiness that filled him. He knew that Hannah was seeing Daniel regularly once a week at the big house – Daniel had gloatingly spread the news all over the village. Matt didn't believe that there was necessarily any special meaning attached to it as some of the other villagers did, but he had received no such invitation.

'I'll get some tea,' he muttered, walking slowly to the cabin, not finding the sea motion of the *Misty* as good as the *Sunrise*'s.

Jeff hadn't been able to sleep and had left his bunk over Malcolm's snoring hulk to make a fresh brew. He and Matt exchanged brief nods but not a word as Matt poured tea for himself and Graham and left the cabin. Matt had seen Jeff protecting Hannah that day and he wondered how he felt about his daughter now, but neither of them mentioned her. From the day that Matt had approached Jeff with the idea of him pulling out of the *Sunrise* and buying into *Misty*, their relationship had been strictly business. It worked well with Jeff who was gruff and occasionally fractious but quieter now that he had no family to push around on the boat. All that really mattered on the *Misty* was the size of the catches and condition of the weather.

At six o'clock in the morning the crew tested the first few nets, pulled in a few herring and shot the nets again. An hour later they tried again and eventually headed for Plymouth where they would berth at Coal Quay. The catch in the fish berth was small but slightly better than that of previous nights.

While the country was rocked with news of the King abdicating so he could marry the woman he loved, while disquieting news came daily about the Spanish civil war and Germany moving its troops into that country, and British men protested over the lack of jobs and their lack of hope for the future, Hannah shrugged it off, uninterested. When Nurse Collins loosened the suffocating hold she kept on Mrs Opie after the first few days, Hannah delighted in doing what she could for her mistress and being in her company. The household would breathe a hefty sigh of relief when the nurse could be sent on her way, and not just because of her heavy, offensive tobacco smell or her brusque manner. Myra Collins was very efficient about her work and surprisingly dextrous in performing the most intimate and embarrassing tasks so that her patient hardly noticed she was being attended to, but it had soon become apparent that she was unpleasantly inquisitive, prying into and asking blunt questions about matters that did not concern her.

A week before Christmas Hannah was angered to find her in her room. 'What do you think you're doing in here, Nurse Collins?' she demanded tersely.

'I heard you pacing about your room last night,' the nurse boomed, taking the further liberty of going to the window and peering at the wintry sky, the bare oak tree on the lawn. 'I've heard you on other nights too. I thought perhaps there might be something about your room that gave you restless nights. I've had patients sleep like a log after I've advised they changed their room.'

'I'm perfectly happy here,' Hannah answered acidly, fighting back further harsh words as the nurse ran a heavy finger over the jewellery box Matt had given her.

'This is a very nice room,' Nurse Collins observed, her long nose seeming to twitch hungrily as she looked in all the corners. 'Why were you given it?'

'That's Mrs Opie's business.'

'So it is,' Nurse Collins replied, finally heading for the door. 'You're well in with her. I wonder why.'

'Horrid old cow,' Hannah muttered venomously, wiping the woman's fingerprints off the jewellery box, feeling it had been violated somehow.

Later in the day, Hannah was upstairs with Mrs Opie, pleased that she had her to herself for a while, Patrick was out in his garden shed, and Angie was enjoying a quiet hour or two in her room. Leah had assumed Nurse

Collins was also taking a nap and slipped into the study, carrying a tray of coffee as an excuse.

Greg immediately encircled her in his arms and they kissed tenderly. 'Happy?' he whispered close to her ear, holding her waist from behind as she poured the coffee.

'Yes, very.' She shivered delightedly, revelling in the sensation of his warm breath on her neck.

He kissed the top of her head. 'It's about time I told my grandmother about us,' he said, turning her round to him.

'No, not yet.' She pressed the flats of her hands on his chest to prevent him kissing her more ardently.

'Why not?' He searched her lovely round dark face. 'You aren't having misgivings?'

She hugged him. 'No, but I'd rather wait until that horrible nurse has gone before we say anything. If Mrs Opie and Hannah raise objections I'm afraid she'll stick her oar in and make what we have seem sordid and wrong. She should be gone by the end of January, let's wait until then.' Leah didn't want anything to risk spoiling their romance and end up like Hannah who, despite her pleasure in having Mrs Opie home, was as desolate as a fish out of water.

'All right, if that's what you want,' he smiled to cover his disappointment. During the moments they could snatch together in the house and the longer hours they spent together covertly off the premises, they had talked at length about their steadily growing love. Nothing seemed more right in his life to Greg than to make Leah his wife, and if his grandmother did move out of Roscarrock with Hannah, he would install her here as its mistress and she would have servants of her own. Failing that, he'd take her away and set up home elsewhere. He pressed his lips once more to hers.

Nurse Collins was mooching about in the hall. Hearing voices coming from the study, she tiptoed on her ungainly small feet and put her ear to the door. It had gone quiet. What were Mr Greg and Leah, for she assumed it was them, up to exactly? Her hand strayed to the doorknob. She didn't know what she'd say when she burst in but she probably wouldn't have to give an explanation if she caught them up to no good.

Just then, Pogo, who had managed to slip out of Mrs Opie's rooms, saw the woman he disliked and ran yapping at her ankles. Nurse Collins shouted and ordered him off but Pogo made her back away from the study to the top of the kitchen stairs. Not sure what the disturbance meant, Greg hastily poured the coffee back in the pot and opened the door for Leah to carry the tray back to the kitchen.

'You're not afraid of Pogo, are you, Nurse?' Leah said cheekily as she caught sight of the woman cowering on the kitchen stairs.

'No, of course not,' Nurse Collins stated, rearranging her features into some semblance of calm. 'I was just about to see if the creature wanted to go for a walk when he got all excited.'

The herring season had put a stop to another of Nurse Collins's lines of inquiry. She wanted to know the exact nature of the friendship between Hannah Spargo and the tall, handsome, red-haired man who turned up once a week at the servants' hall. The nurse thought him a rough, sly individual and couldn't understand why Mrs Opie allowed such a caller. There were things going on in this house which were out of the ordinary and Nurse

Collins was burning to learn what they were all about.

Hannah played cards that evening with Mrs Opie. She didn't win a single hand, for her heart and mind were not on the game. As a flurry of snowflakes floated down and hit the windows, she looked wistfully outside into the white-flecked darkness.

'Close the curtains, will you, dear?' Mrs Opie said, expertly shuffling the cards in her smooth hands. She watched as Hannah rose from the opposite side of the card table and pulled the heavy velvet drapes, her pale, drawn reflection lingering on the glass before she covered it. 'I've had enough for tonight. Why don't we sit beside the fire?'

Mrs Opie wheeled herself to one side of the hearth and Hannah sat down in a plush armchair opposite her. As usual Hannah waited for Mrs Opie to raise the topic of discussion. 'What is it, Hannah? Don't tell me there's nothing wrong. I know you so well and it's obvious you're not at all happy.'

Hannah returned the shrewd gaze and felt that Mrs Opie could read her innermost thoughts. She would have to tell her soon that she was pregnant, she had been looking for the right moment and this was probably it, but she was afraid her wonderful life here would come to an abrupt end. Mrs Opie was extremely kind to her but even if she wasn't shocked or outraged by the revelation, what could she do with a pregnant housekeeper and then her infant? Hannah had no clear plans. She had saved a little money out of her wages and, despite his attitude to Viv's pregnancy, she would ask Daniel if he knew some-where in one of the fishing ports where she could rent a room and find a job, somewhere where somehow she

could look after her baby; she didn't have Matt but
she desperately wanted to keep his child.

She was confident Matt still loved her and many times
she thought over his words that she must go to him
if she wanted him, that he would not run after her. If she
turned up on his doorstep and told him about their baby,
she didn't doubt for a moment he would take her in his
arms and ask her to marry him, overjoyed that she had
come to her senses and that he was about to become a
father. But although she ached for him, being at Roscarrock for all these months had changed her, something he
had understood better than she had. She didn't think she
was one of the Opies as he had accused her, but had
she changed so much she'd be stifled by life as a fisherman's wife? And she felt she couldn't live again in the
village where so many bad things had happened to her,
where Viv had been brutalised and her aunt and mother
were estranged. Hannah felt guilty about not seeing them
and had written asking them to come to Roscarrock or
meet her elsewhere. Janet had replied politely that she
was very busy and Prim had not replied at all.

'You've taken a long time thinking about what you're
going to say,' Mrs Opie said eventually. 'I want nothing
less than the whole truth, Hannah. Is it something to do
with Daniel Kittow?'

It had taken a lot of deft persuasion to get Mrs Opie
to agree to Daniel visiting her. Mrs Opie had said she
felt she ought to cut herself off completely from the village, adding that what she had heard of Daniel Kittow
suggested he was a totally unsavoury character. Hannah
had pointed out that nothing had ever been proved
against Daniel, and in the end had pleaded that she
needed to see her childhood friend, that she would meet

him anyway up on the cliffs no matter how rough the weather was. Mrs Opie had reluctantly agreed, secretly telling Greg, who had objected strongly to the arrangement, that this was the best way to keep an eye on Hannah. Hannah had kept Daniel strictly to the two-hour weekly visit, and it had been warming to see him and talk to him in much the same way as they'd done before her romance with Matt.

'I do miss Daniel,' she said, uncomfortably aware of being under the spotlight of Mrs Opie's sharp eyes.

'How much do you miss him?' she asked softly. 'Are you in love with him?'

'No, not at all. Daniel would like something more to be between us but I'll only ever see him as a close friend. I think he's accepted that.'

'Good.' Mrs Opie leaned forward, only the slightest movement but it made Hannah pull herself back in her chair. 'Then I take it he wasn't the man who made you pregnant?'

Hannah sprang to her feet, hands to her burning face, tears spilling over her rigid fingers. 'H-how did you know? I-I'm sorry. I'll pack my things at once.'

'You'll do no such thing.' Mrs Opie wheeled herself over to her and took her arm. 'You'll sit down and tell me how you find yourself in this situation. And before you wonder if I'm angry or about to throw you out, I'll tell you I was young once and not always sensible. I've had children of my own and I've had my suspicions about your condition ever since the burglary, fuelled by a few mutterings from that wretched nurse. When you closed the curtains just now I saw how tight your dress is.'

Hannah sat down and sobbed into her hands. Mrs Opie stroked her hair. 'Come now, my dear,' she said kindly.

'It might be the end of the world for some girls but not for you. Did you think for a moment that I wouldn't help you?'

'I'm sorry,' Hannah repeated, searching in the sleeve of her cardigan for a hanky. 'I've let you down, after you've been so kind to me, giving me the job and a good future.'

'I don't see it that way,' Mrs Opie smiled. 'Now dry your eyes and we'll talk this over. First, will you tell me who the father is?'

'It's Matt,' she sniffed, dabbing at her eyelashes. 'Matt Penney, the man who carried my suitcase here for me when I arrived to stay.'

'He didn't force you?'

'Oh, no, Matt's a wonderful man. I was greatly attracted to him. It . . . it was more my idea to . . . to make love. It only happened once and now . . .'

'You're bearing the consequences,' Mrs Opie finished for her. 'Does he know about the baby?'

'No. If he did he'd want us to get married straightaway, but we quarrelled and—'

'And that was the end of that,' Mrs Opie cut in forcefully. 'Well, things have a way of working out for the best, Hannah. We missed the London trip but for some time I've been thinking of moving out of Cornwall and starting a new life, somewhere peaceful in the countryside and near the sea. I've allowed myself to stagnate here for far too many years. Greg loves Roscarrock and it will be his one day and he might as well have it now. We'll go away together, just you and I. We could say you're my widowed niece or something – I don't want you to go on being a servant, I value you far too much. The baby will have the best possible start to its life and we'll have nothing to do but enjoy each other's company and lavish all our love on it. Would you like that, Hannah?'

Hannah had never really thought Mrs Opie would treat her unkindly when she found out about the baby, but this was beyond her wildest dreams. All she could do was nod and burst into tears again.

Mrs Opie came closer and held her in her arms, caressing her hair and telling her that she would make sure everything would be all right.

'I'll start looking for property straightaway. We'll have a quiet Christmas, then I can let the nurse go and we'll move away before you start showing.' There were tears in her own eyes as she said huskily, 'Trust me, Hannah, we'll have the most wonderful life together when we get away from this place.'

Chapter 33

As part of her plans to move out of Roscarrock with Hannah, Mrs Opie had sent Patrick up to the attic to make an inventory of what was stored there, and to put aside some more things to be sent over to Portmellon for Mitch and Viv. He was wearing his coat and scarf because it was fearfully cold up in this part of the attic. Hanging a lantern from a nail on a sloping beam, and careful not to bang his head, he took a notebook and pencil out of his coat pocket.

'Where to start, where to start,' he ruminated, stroking his soft moustache. 'I wonder why Great-Aunt Feena wants to know what's up here now. It would have been an easier and a warmer task in the spring.' Feena Opie was keeping her plans a secret until she had secured a property.

Quickly becoming covered in cobwebs and looking around warily for spiders – the years he had spent in Africa among giants of the species had not reduced his fear of them – he began by writing down everything collected in the furthest corner, intending to work out towards the door, noting only the items he felt were of some importance. Soon he fell to wondering whom the various items had belonged to and when and why they had been relegated to these cold, dark corners. What had happened to the glass of a four-foot-square gilt mirror frame? Had it brought its owner seven years' bad luck? Who had used the rickety mahogany spinning wheel, a lady of the house or a servant girl? And what story lay behind the cutlass once owned by a seventeenth-century Bodinnick? Had it been wielded against Cromwell's troops intent on robbing the family gold? There was no proof a Roundhead had ever set foot on Roscarrock land but Patrick imagined a long, bloody battle, with soldiers and lace-adorned Bodinnicks scurrying over the house, the lawn, in and out of the wood and fighting to the last on the cliff top. 'I must tell Greg, he could write a book about it . . .'

There were several pieces of furniture including two ancient commodes, chests and chairs of various styles and sizes, a livery cupboard, a set of bedsteps, a wobbling gateleg table and a wardrobe so huge the mind boggled at how the unfortunate people responsible for carrying it up the narrow stairs had got it round the corners and through the door.

'Perhaps they cut it in half,' Patrick said to himself, opening the doors to look for a join and releasing a cascade of sundry items which had been carelessly stuffed into the wardrobe. 'Dear me, one could get oneself killed up here.' He threw the pile of mouldy smelling old clothes back in then spent ages going through boxes of twenty-year-old comics, cigarette cards, a scrapbook of matchbox fronts, one of newspaper cuttings of the Great War, the slides of a magic lantern depicting rural scenes. Patrick sat back in a dusty armchair, thoroughly enjoying himself, journeying through the four decades of his life.

Angie was cooking a nourishing old-fashioned stew

today and he was so absorbed he missed the lunch bell. Angie was too nervous to venture up into the attic and Hannah came looking for him. 'Mr Patrick, didn't you hear the bell or me calling you?' She was amused to see him scrunched up in the chair, an expression of boyish concentration on his curious, likeable face. 'Brr, it's cold up here. You were wise to put your coat on.'

'Ah, Hannah,' he grinned. He reminded her of an eccentric, bungling wizard called Rubblestubb in one of Jowan's boyhood storybooks. She could almost imagine him casting the muddled spell that had caused all this disorder. 'I've found a veritable chest of treasures up here. There's a lovely Victorian firescreen made of pretty cutout pictures over there. Would you like me to carry it down to your room? It's a shame to have all these fascinating things hidden from view.'

She didn't want the firescreen – she wouldn't be living here much longer – but to please Mr Patrick she said, 'Yes, please, that would be lovely. Are you coming now? You'll catch a chill if you stay here like this much longer.' She would miss Mr Patrick more than some of the members of her own family.

He got up with difficulty, his limbs had become stiff with cold and the ungainly position he had been sitting in. 'You are right, Hannah, I need a hot meal to warm me up but I can't wait to get back to it. Why don't you put on some old warm clothes and sort out a few things for your brother? You know better than I do what sort of thing he and his wife would like.'

'Yes, I will. Thank you, Mr Patrick.' She was looking at the back of a row of paintings he'd uncovered in a gloomy recess. 'I don't suppose Mrs Opie did any of these.'

'She might have. Great-Aunt Feena has sent anything not in use up here out of the way. We'll take a look later.'

After lunch, armed with a flask of tea and plate of biscuits, Patrick was soon busy again about his task. He looked at the row of paintings first. Most of them were ugly portraits of grave old men and women in Victorian and Georgian dress, goodness only knew of whom; none of them were signed so obviously they were of no importance. There were one or two weak attempts at sea and garden views by his great-aunt, signed 1916 and 1917 when she had first started to paint. 'Couldn't bear anyone to see them but hadn't the heart to paint over them,' he supposed out loud.

The last picture, wedged in tight against the wall, dreadfully out of proportion, the colours weak and watery, was of a young woman in 1920s dress standing in front of the walled garden. It was signed like the previous two, F. Opie. Patrick recognised the subject immediately, proud face, blonde hair, tall, graceful stance, striking blue eyes. He scratched his head in puzzlement. 'Hannah? How come?' Then he read the title of the picture. 'Stephanie. Stephanie!' What Greg had been hinting to him about Hannah when he'd first arrived from London hit him like a ton of bricks. 'Good heavens . . .'

A low shuffling noise behind him made him slam the painting back to the wall and pile the others against it. 'Ah, Hannah,' he began, turning round with a flushed smile on his shocked face. 'Oh, Nurse Collins, what on earth do you think you're doing up here?' he asked crossly.

'I thought I might be able to help, Mr Patrick,' she said, her loud voice bouncing off the rafters and echoing oddly in the corners. She peered and prodded and riffled through anything that was to hand. 'I heard Miss Spargo talking to Mrs Opie. It sounds like fun. I love secrets.'

'Secrets?' Patrick said heatedly. 'What do you mean secrets?'

'Well, there's always something mysterious to be found in the things abandoned in a cupboard or attic, isn't there, Mr Patrick?' Stepping over a cracked, floral-decorated chamberpot she made her way through the clutter to the huge wardrobe. 'I'll take a look in here. There might be some old clothes. I love old clothes, might be some going back several years.'

'Thank you, Nurse Collins,' he fumed, 'but Miss Spargo is coming to help me shortly and that is all the help I shall require.'

The nurse ignored him. 'Many hands make light work.'

Hannah climbed into the attic at that moment and let out a sigh of displeasure to see Nurse Collins ruthlessly handling the heap of clothes lying on the wardrobe floor.

'There you are, Hannah.' Patrick was mightily relieved to see her. 'Nurse Collins is just going.'

'I'm sorting—'

'Oh no you're not,' Patrick bellowed, making Hannah blink in astonishment at his unexpected forcefulness. 'If you please, Nurse.'

Nurse Collins tightened her robust features and threw down the clothes in her hand. She pushed past Hannah and muttered at her, 'It won't do for you to get cold, Miss Spargo.' Then she gave Patrick a decidedly smug look and left.

'That woman makes me feel most uncomfortable,' he said to Hannah, picking up his notebook and pencil. 'Perhaps you'd care to tidy up the wardrobe and shout out anything you find of interest.'

'Nurse Collins does have a knack of turning up at unwanted times and in places she has no right to be in,' Hannah said tightly, still smarting that the woman had trespassed in her room. She picked up the clothes, a port-coloured velvet evening dress, a fur stole and long silk scarf and put them in a neat pile, wrinkling her nose at their mouldy smell. 'What a pity there aren't enough coathangers. I was wondering, Mr Patrick, what usually happens at Roscarrock for Christmas?'

Patrick made a new heading on his list – toys. 'Well, we attend church and have a traditional Christmas lunch, we're having goose this year by the way, and actually I should be seeing to the festive fare rather than being up here but Great-Aunt Feena insisted. We exchange presents afterwards in the drawing room, that will include Angie and you, and I suppose that abominable nurse, this year. We have tea with Christmas cake and mince pies. Then we might play cards, listen to the wireless, swop stories and sometimes Mr Greg plays the piano. I'll be decorating the tree in the drawing room soon. Perhaps you'd like to help me. Actually, we might as well set aside the decorations while we're up here.'

'I'd love to help you decorate the tree. What sort of tree will it be?'

'A fir tree and it will be a tall one, six or seven feet at least.'

'At my Aunty Janet's we always had a holly tree or branch, depending on what me, my cousin and uncle could find on the hedges,' Hannah said, pausing in putting the clothes on the wardrobe floor and becoming painfully nostalgic. 'Sometimes we had to walk miles to find one a good size and shape.' As she said this she felt a sudden pang of homesickness and was full of guilt for staying away from her family; she knew that before Christmas she would have to go down to the village and see them, especially the woman who had been a kind and loving mother to her. There was a tremble in her voice as she went on, 'When I lived at home with my parents my grandmother wouldn't let us celebrate much over Christmas. My grandfather, who I never knew, died on Christmas Eve and she said it would mock his memory.'

'Well, I don't agree with that.' Patrick saw her wistfulness and wanted to reach out and comfort her, but that was not his way. He'd felt a rapport with Hannah from the moment he'd met her on Hidden Beach and now he understood why after the discovery of the painting. She was his cousin and he was pleased about that. How long his great-aunt had known about Hannah's real identity and what her true motive was for arranging for the girl to work here he didn't really want to know and he'd never ask about it. 'You miss your family, don't you? All of them, your mother and father too?'

'Yes,' she admitted gloomily, wishing also that she hadn't cut herself off from those living at Cliffside Cottage just when her father seemed to be at long last coming round. He probably saw it as a snub and hated her as he had always done.

'Then go and see them,' Patrick said, standing close to her and smiling sagely. 'It's never right not to keep in touch with flesh and blood, no matter what they've done. I'm taking Mr Greg's car to St Austell tomorrow afternoon to buy Christmas presents. Why don't you join me and buy them all a little something then take it down to the village?'

'Yes, I'd like to,' she replied, brightening. She was leaving here soon so she had nothing to lose.

They got on with the work, Hannah putting aside some things for Mitch and Viv, a pitcher and bowl, candle holders, a small bookcase and three small pictures – a duck on a pond, a galleon on high seas, and a view of the coastline around the Dodman. She'd fully expected to find a stuffed bear, stag's head or suit of armour in the attic and was slightly disappointed that there were only more mundane household things.

'Why don't you take some of these toys in case they have children?' Patrick said. 'Shouldn't think they'll be wanted again here. Oh, I say.'

'What is it?' she asked, watching him put a small box on the seat of a chair.

'It's a jack-in-the-box, in its original packing too. Looks like it's never been played with. I saw one just like it out in Africa about twenty years ago when the uncle of a family I knew brought one out for their baby.' He frowned. 'It was new on the market then, I remember him saying so. It must have been bought and not wanted.'

Hannah took the toy from him and opened the packing then the wooden lid. A colourful smiling clown popped out. Her eyes lit up. 'It's lovely. I'll ask Mrs Opie if I can take it with the other things to my brother and his wife.'

'I'm sure they'll be delighted with it.'

Hannah didn't intend giving any toys to Mitch and Viv. It wouldn't be kind in the circumstances; it was her own baby she wanted the jack-in-the-box for.

When she left the attic, something made her slip along to the nursery. She went straight to the cradle and pushed it gently, making it swing and creak on its old hinges. She pictured what her baby would look like lying in the cradle and saw a strong, determined, tiny face topped with earth-brown hair and bearing the darkest of eyes – the image of its father. Suddenly it seemed as if the baby was no longer inside her, clinging to its first vestiges of life, but was actually in the cradle and Matt was in the room with them. He was so proud, so happy they were all together. He took his beautiful eyes off their child and gazed deeply and lovingly at her.

'Hannah? Hannah?'

It was several moments before she realised someone was nudging her arm. Hastily she wiped her tears away.

'What are you doing here?' Leah asked, peering at her. Hannah turned her face away. 'I've been looking for you everywhere. Angie made tea for you ages ago. You should be getting cleaned up. Mrs Opie will be ringing for you soon. Are you all right? Have you been crying?'

'I'm fine, Leah.' Hannah gave her a watery smile. 'I was just thinking and came over all silly, that's all.'

Leah put her arm round her waist. 'What were you thinking about?'

'Oh, Christmas, old times.'

'I thought perhaps you were thinking about Matt.'

Giving one last glance down into the cradle, Hannah turned and quickly left the room.

Mrs Opie forbade Nurse Collins to be in the room while she was resting, but eager to discover more about the young housekeeper who resembled the woman in the painting she'd glimpsed in the attic, the nurse slipped back into her employer's rooms to root about when she reckoned Mrs Opie had dropped off to sleep. She opened several drawers and cupboards in the sitting room but found nothing of interest, then, remembering the journal Mrs Opie often wrote in, she crept into the bedroom.

Holding her nicotine-laden breath, she carefully opened the top drawer of the bedside chest and pulled out the journal.

She flicked through the pages, seeing nothing of interest until a certain day last year when Stephanie Opie had suddenly died. After that, all the insertions made very absorbing reading indeed. A touch of malice played at the corners of her mouth as she looked down at the lady reposing elegantly in her sleep. Mrs Opie was one of her difficult patients, insisting on this, arguing about that. She had even threatened to dismiss her this morning when she caught her having a crafty puff on a cigarette in the en suite bathroom.

I wouldn't upset me, if I were you, the nurse thought triumphantly. Or I'll make sure your precious Miss Spargo knows what's written in this book.

The door to the rooms opened and Nurse Collins hastily put the journal back in its place. She met Hannah in the bedroom doorway. 'Mrs Opie isn't awake yet,' she whispered officiously. 'I'll get her to ring for you when she's ready.'

Hannah peered round her to check.

'You may go, Nurse,' Mrs Opie said firmly, woken by the voices. 'I'll ring for you if I need you.'

'Very well, Mrs Opie.' Nurse Collins walked out, reaching for the packet of cigarettes hidden in her uniform pocket.

'I don't really need her at all,' Mrs Opie said, sitting herself up against the pillows. 'I can do just about anything for myself now. Did you find anything suitable for your brother in the attic, Hannah?'

Hannah told her what she had set aside for Mitch and Viv. 'And there was a jack-in-the-box. It's never been played with by the look of it.' She lowered her eyes shyly. 'I was wondering if I could have it for my baby.'

Mrs Opie's eyes narrowed. 'I'd forgotten about that toy. Yes, you may have it. Make arrangements with Mr Greg to drive you to Portmellon. I daresay Leah will want to go too.'

'Mrs Opie, I want to talk to you about Leah and Mr Greg.' Even though they had been very careful, Hannah had noticed the new closeness between them. Certain that Nurse Collins was spying on them and would cause trouble if she could, Hannah wanted to air the subject before there was a major row and Leah was hurt.

Mrs Opie sighed resignedly. 'I know what you're going to say. You suspect they're having a romance. I'm sure they are, my dear. I've given it a lot of thought. If I confront them they will either deny it or Greg will become angry. I don't want them eloping and ending up regretting it. It's better to let whatever is between them run its course. You needn't worry about Greg being irresponsible, he has taken Leah's youth and simplicity into account, I'm sure. We're about to start a new life, so perhaps, if they do have a future together, we should allow it to happen. And talking of that, I had a telephone call from the estate agent while you were in the attic. He's found what sounds like a delightful property in Torquay on the seafront. It's ready to live in, with servants standing by, and it has all we need. The estate agent's a friend of my late husband's and I trust him. So, my dear,' she took Hannah's hand, 'as soon as Christmas is over, we'll pack up and move. I'm delighted.' She saw the mixed emotions on Hannah's face. 'How about you?'

'It's wonderful news, Mrs Opie, but it will be strange moving away, perhaps not seeing my family . . . or Matt again. I want to go down to the village before Christmas. I must see them all at least one last time.'

'Do you think that's wise?' Mrs Opie said rather sharply.

'Well, it wouldn't be right just to go off and not tell them.'

'I suppose not but I don't think you ought to say anything until we're packed and ready to go. I don't want to risk your father causing trouble.'

'I don't think he will. Matt and Daniel had a fight over me and I was nearly knocked over. My father pulled me to safety and held me.'

'What? You've never mentioned this before.' Feena tried hard not to sound as alarmed as she felt.

'I started to tell you about the quarrel Matt and I had,' Hannah pointed out. 'When we first talked about the baby.'

Mrs Opie remembered cutting her off. She changed tack. 'If I'd known Daniel Kittow was involved in a fight I doubt if I'd have allowed him here in the house.'

Hannah turned down her bottom lip and didn't reply. Telling Daniel she was moving out of Cornwall would be worse than telling anyone else but she fully intended seeing him again, to say goodbye properly, no matter what Mrs Opie said.

'Well, never mind that now.' Mrs Opie recognised that stubborn look. Stephanie had made similar expressions. 'But I still don't think you should see your father.'

'I won't,' Hannah said. 'The boats are away at Plymouth. The men won't be home until Christmas Eve.'

Including Matt Penney, Mrs Opie thought with much relief. She feared him the most. If anybody could snatch Hannah away from her, he could. She prayed that

Hannah wouldn't realise just how much she loved the young fisherman. 'You had better go down to the village as soon as possible, Hannah,' she said. 'I only hope they appreciate your good will.'

Chapter 34

Hannah walked into 7 Quayside Street with an armful of parcels. Janet looked up from her sewing machine at the kitchen table. They stared at each other. Hannah put the parcels down on the table, nervous of the welcome she would receive.

'Hello, Aunty Janet.'

'Hannah.' Janet pushed back her chair and her eyes filled with tears. 'I knew you'd come to see me.'

Hannah ran to her and they hugged each other tightly. 'I'm sorry I haven't been for so long.' She kissed her aunt's cheek. 'How are you and Uncle Roy, Jowan and Ned?'

'Oh, we're all right.' Janet went to the teapot. 'They haven't had hardly any luck with the herring, a very poor season for everyone so far. Be lovely to have them home again on Christmas Eve. You'll come back and see them soon? Jowan in particular has been missing you.'

Hannah wondered if Janet was trying to make her feel guilty, but her aunt was smiling tearfully as she put cups and saucers on the table. 'I've brought you all a Christmas present,' Hannah said. 'Jowan's is a book about the stars. The man in the shop said it was a comprehensive one so he should be able to learn all he wants from it.'

'That's kind of you. The boy's always looking up at the sky with that telescope Leah brought from Roscarrock for him. We've got a present for you. I was going to ask Leah to pass it on to you. I'm so glad you're here so I can give it to you myself.' Janet took a flat box in holly wrapping paper out of the dresser cupboard. Hannah thanked her and kissed her again. 'How are you then, Hannah?' Janet viewed her with a mother's critical eye. 'You look a bit pale. Are you eating properly? Not that you're in the least skinny. Are you sleeping well?' Janet looked embarrassed. 'What I mean is, have you got over all that robbery business? And me upsetting you?'

With her emotions all mixed up about leaving Cornwall, wondering exactly what her new life with Mrs Opie and the baby would be like, perhaps never seeing her family or Daniel again, and her raw feelings for Matt, Hannah hadn't in fact been sleeping or eating properly lately. Of course she hadn't lost any weight, in fact she was finding her clothes were getting too tight round the middle. She couldn't mention the baby although she would have liked to talk to Janet about it, but she was sure her aunt would only go running to Matt the moment the *Misty* moored and that would just complicate things.

'There's nothing to worry about, Aunty Janet,' she said cheerfully as she took Ginger the cat on to her lap and stroked him. She didn't want Janet to feel guilty about the day her nagging had brought on the faint. That wouldn't be fair. 'I've just been very concerned about Mrs Opie, that's all.'

'You're very fond of Mrs Opie, aren't you?'

Hannah detected a hurt note in her aunt's voice. 'Yes, she's been very good to me.'

'You won't stay away from us for so long again, will

you?' Janet pleaded. It had broken her heart that Hannah had kept out of the village. Prim had blamed Feena Opie, but Janet had argued that it had been her own family who had driven Hannah away.

'I'll come again soon after Christmas,' Hannah promised. How long it would be before she came again after that she couldn't say but she made her mind up there and then that somehow she would come back to Porthellis regularly, at least to see Janet, and bring her child with her. 'I've brought a present with me for Mum and Josh . . . and Father. I'll see Sarah, Naomi and Lizzie before I go today and ask one of them to pass them on.'

'There's no need,' Janet said, looking out of the kitchen window at the sound of approaching steps. 'Your mother and Josh are coming now.'

'I'm glad you and Mother have made it up,' Hannah said, putting Ginger back in his basket and feeling even more nervous at facing her mother.

'We have,' Janet said sadly, 'but things aren't the same between us.'

Prim let out a gasp of shock at seeing Hannah and Hannah did likewise to see Josh trailing into the room behind her. Her eldest brother, big and tall and as dark as ever, was like a frightened child, holding on to their mother's coat, his Spargo good looks gone and replaced by an imbecilic stare and drool and a persistent twitch under his left eye.

'Hannah's come with Christmas presents,' Janet said quickly, to break the icy atmosphere Prim had brought with her.

Prim glared at Hannah. 'If you've brought anything for me then you can take it back to Roscarrock with you. I've finished with you, Hannah Spargo.'

'Mum!' Hannah protested, reaching out beseeching hands to her.

'I think you stopped thinking of me as your mother a long time ago,' Prim said tartly, then added bitterly, 'You can speak to your brother if you like, or rather what your other brother left of him.'

It was hard for Hannah to sort out her feelings for Josh. He'd deserved the beating Mitch had given him but to see him like this, his mind damaged beyond repair, his life as good as over at the age of twenty-eight, was heart-rending. He sat in the chair Prim had led him to, gazing uncomprehendingly into space, making strange muttering noises. She said, 'Hello, Josh,' but he didn't respond and she couldn't tell if he heard her. He certainly didn't recognise her.

'In case you're thinking otherwise,' Prim said harshly, 'I don't feel bitter towards Mitch. Josh should never have done what he did to that maid, but it's not only him who's suffering the consequences, I am too. I'll have an idiot child tied to me for the rest of my life. He follows me everywhere I go, afraid to let me out of his sight. I don't get a minute's peace from him. I've moved out of the bedroom I shared with your father and have to sleep in the room with him.' Prim looked at Josh, his head lolling to the side, saliva trickling down his chin from the corner of his twisted mouth, as if she loathed him. It made Hannah's blood run cold. Prim went on, 'I would have left your rotten, evil father after Mitch went if it hadn't been for him. With Mitch gone, the girls married and leading their own lives and you having deserted me, I had no more ties. Leah can look after herself – she could go and live in at Roscarrock too for all I care. All my adult life I've worked and suffered because of the

Spargos and now I can't get away from the man I hate with all my heart because of his equally rotten son.'

Hannah was shaken to the soul by the pure venom in her mother's words and the extent of her self-pity. She sat down, gazing sightlessly at the floor, tears of hopelessness searing her eyes. She wished she had not seen her mother today but it reinforced her desire to go away with Mrs Opie.

It was some moments before she felt Janet's hand on her shoulder. 'She's gone, Hannah. I'm sorry it happened but it's just as well you know how she feels.'

Hannah stayed another hour with Janet, both trying hard to talk and behave normally, but Hannah was glad to put her hat and coat back on and leave. She left the presents for her father, Josh and her mother with Janet in case Prim changed her mind and decided to accept them, and called on Sarah, Naomi and Lizzie in turn. The few minutes she spent with each of them were a little easier; she was interested to learn how their pregnancies were progressing, each of them at a different stage, Lizzie's baby due first in March. Envying them their settled lives, she wondered how they would react when they knew she would provide their offspring with a new little cousin.

As she walked up Porthkilt Hill she hoped she wouldn't meet Miss Peters. The tiny old woman's sharp eye and tongue were the last things she wanted to face, but the person she met made her feel far worse. Mrs Penney was on her way down to the bakehouse.

'It's good to see you again, Hannah,' she said as graciously as Mrs Opie would have done.

'Hello, Mrs Penney. Happy Christmas to you.' Hannah fell into an embarrassed silence, unable to think of anything else to say.

Mrs Penney had something to say. 'Will you be coming to chapel on Christmas Day?'

'Um, no, I don't think so.'

'Will you be seeing Matt at all?'

It would tear her in two to see Matt. Part of her wanted to throw her arms round his neck and implore him to take her back, to tell him about their baby, to be with him for ever, but she didn't know if it was the right thing to do, and another future beckoned her. Gulping back the painful lump in her throat, she murmured, 'No. Wish him a happy Christmas for me please.' Then she hastened on her way.

Mrs Opie had arranged for Greg to take her to and collect her from the top of the village hill, saying she shouldn't exert herself unduly in the cold in her condition. She had also exhorted her grandson to keep a close eye on Hannah and go down into the village and fetch her if she was a minute late. When Hannah saw the car she broke into a run.

Greg got out of the car and met her. 'Take it easy, Hannah, you'll fall over and do yourself an injury running so fast.' He saw at once she was distressed and put her gently in the front passenger seat.

'They haven't upset you again, have they?' he asked sourly, getting in beside her. 'And at Christmas of all times.'

'It's not that.' She could no longer hold back the tears.

'What then?' He put his arm round her. 'What is it?'

She couldn't speak and he pulled her into his arms. Hannah sobbed her heart out wretchedly, soaking his coat and clinging to him as if she would drown if he let her go. When the worst of her terrible loneliness had been purged and the whirling storm in her mind had calmed down to a gentler sea of emotion, she pulled away from him.

'Can you tell me what's the matter?' he said softly.

'H-have you . . . ever been in a position . . . when you didn't know . . . what to do, Mr Greg?'

'A few times.' He stroked her arm. 'What you need is a good stiff drink. I've got a drop of brandy in here.' He reached across her to the glove compartment. 'Here, take a few sips of this.'

He held the miniature bottle of brandy to her trembling lips and Hannah allowed a few drops to burn into her mouth. She swallowed it with difficulty but welcomed the warming it gave her churning stomach. She pushed the bottle away. 'Thanks . . . I'm all right now.'

'I don't suppose you can tell me what upset you but I think you should talk to Grandma. Can't be anything she can't fix up.'

'She knows all about it,' Hannah said, gazing out of the windscreen at the familiar lane and hedges that led past Porthellis, wondering if she could ever steel herself to take the route down into the village again despite her earlier determination to visit Janet regularly. Mrs Opie was 'fixing up' part of her problem but Hannah couldn't tell her grandson that. 'Can we go home now, Mr Greg?'

When they were carefully taking the narrow bends of Turn-A-Penny Lane, she said, 'Please don't tell Mrs Opie I was crying. I don't want her to worry or spoil Christmas.'

'Okay, if that's what you want.' He glanced at her, his grey eyes warm and soft and full of concern. 'I suppose Christmas is the time for feeling extra emotional over our troubles. I know we didn't hit it off at first, Hannah, but I want you to know you can always talk to me.'

'Thank you.' In any other circumstances she wouldn't have asked the question that had been on her mind for some time but her inner pain gave her boldness and he had been so kind to her. 'I know I shouldn't bring it up but I'd like to know if you are in love with Leah.'

'As you've asked, yes, I am,' he replied and a broad smile spread across his fair features. 'I know you're concerned about her and that's only right and fair, she is your younger sister and as you have pointed out to me, Leah's not at all worldly. I was attracted to her naivety and innocence at first but my feelings for her have grown. I adore her and can't imagine living without her. We're going to tell Grandma in the New Year, after Nurse Collins has gone. I hope one of your parents will sign the consent form so we can get married and I hope you'll give us your blessing, Hannah.'

'I will, if you're sure Leah loves you.'

'There's no doubt about that or I wouldn't have made my feelings plain to her.'

'Then I wish you all the happiness in the world. You're lucky to know exactly what you want.'

Chapter 35

The fishing fleets headed for home throughout the morning of Christmas Eve. The *Misty* left Plymouth Sound some two hours later than the rest of Porthellis's luggers and behind the last of the boats going downcoast for Christmas because they had to wait for Jeff to come ashore from visiting a woman he knew. He climbed aboard the boat to three mute, grim faces; even Graham Chellew was disinclined to be chatty. They had made two hundred and fifty-five pounds for the season, an amount well down on other years. They were tired and dispirited and the satisfaction on Jeff's face grated on their nerves.

They got under way in a freshening south-easterly wind and on a sea that was gradually growing in strength and power. Huddled out of the bitter cold in the wheelhouse, Malcolm Chellew at the wheel, they stood close together watching the sails flapping wildly, the bows of the boat rising and dipping over the iron-grey white-flecked water, willing the four and a half hour journey to be over soon.

'Be lucky if there'll be any herring at all next year,' Graham said, true to his grumbling form.

'Aye,' Malcolm replied, the only one who was listening as he expertly read the mood and pitch of the waves. 'Couldn't get much worse.'

Jeff was looking at Matt, as he had done often over the last few weeks, noticing his growing despondency; today he appeared to be in a pit of deep despair. He said suddenly and unexpectedly, 'You got anything for Hannah for Christmas?'

Through his gloom Matt barely heard the question. Knowing something personal was going to be said, and not insensitive to Matt's mood, the Chellew brothers started a quiet conversation between themselves.

'Why do you ask?' Matt frowned, deepening the furrows of his brow.

'I know you think a lot of her. I heard what you said to each other after the fight. You're not going to let her pride get in the way of your love for each other, are you?'

Matt was dumbfounded to hear these words from the man who had treated Hannah more cruelly than any other. 'Why are you interested in what goes on between me and Hannah?' he asked suspiciously, hoping there wasn't trouble brewing. 'I thought you hated her. You ordered her out of the village. Have you changed the way you think about her or are you up to some other bloody cruel game?'

'I'm a man who's faced death and who's lost a bitter-tongued mother who never had a good word for any of his children,' Jeff said seriously, grabbing the roof of the wheelhouse as the lugger lurched wildly. 'I should never have listened to my mother though there were other reasons why I turned against Hannah. But I see things in a new light now. I don't want to spend eternity suffering in Hell for turning against one of my own.'

'Maybe you don't,' Matt said warily. 'But that doesn't explain why you're concerned about what goes on between Hannah and me.'

'I don't know what your differences are about but I can see there never was a couple more suited to each other than you and her.'

'She doesn't see it that way.'

'She would if she was thinking straight. Hannah's got a bit above herself working in the big house, but she would never have spoken to you the way she did if she didn't care about you. She felt let down by you fighting with Daniel Kittow and that bastard's not worth spitting on. He's after her himself but even if he wasn't I reckon he'd try to come between you. He's got a hardness about him she can't see. Surely you aren't going to let him win?'

'Is that the way you see it?' Matt said thoughtfully.

'How do you see it?'

'That she could never be truly happy with me unless she loves me more than Roscarrock.'

'She may have had her head turned, what young woman wouldn't given the circumstances? But she kept on with you, didn't she? Kept coming back to you no matter how you fell out. That must mean something. I'll tell you one thing, Matt, I know it was mostly because of me she went to Roscarrock but it won't do her any good if she stays there for ever. You're a proud bugger too, you know. Jump down off your high horse and go to her. She's worth one more try, isn't she?'

Matt gazed out of the sea-lashed window at the waves being whipped up by the increasing wind. He had gone through every emotion since he'd given her his ultimatum, at times seriously thinking of throwing himself into the depths and letting himself drown rather than face the rest of his life without her. But was there a safe port of calm still to be had with her? He didn't know, but Jeff was right, he had been letting his pride rule his heart.

'Hannah's worth anything and everything. Perhaps it wouldn't hurt to talk to her again.'

Jeff slapped him hard on the shoulder. 'That's the spirit. Take that bleddy miserable look off your face and when you get ashore clean yourself up and go straight up to Roscarrock. I'll stake my life on it that she'll be glad to see you.'

The men ate their crib and chatted more amiably as they got nearer Porthellis. As they caught up with other boats going home they waved to the crews, shouting Christmas greetings to Mevagissey men and those from Mount's Bay and wishing each other good luck for the New Year.

As the *Misty* sailed the stretch of coast between Polperro and Fowey, a fierce gust of wind rocked the boat and a stay holding the mizzen mast to the gunwale at the stern snapped and ran through the pulley. The mast swung about like a twig and was in danger of being damaged. Matt and Graham volunteered to make the repairs.

'Watch your footing,' Jeff cautioned them. 'The sea's riding like a good man on a whore.'

Matt frowned at Jeff's vulgar expression and put on his oilskins and followed Graham outside. The wind was now gale force. The sea was pounding against the boat, hurling freezing cold water up over the top of the cabin and wheelhouse, hitting the men angrily in the face and stinging their flesh. It was dangerous to the unwary but the two men had weathered these conditions, and worse, many times before.

Inching cautiously along the deck as the boat rolled, ducked and dived, holding tightly to the sides, Graham

grabbed the end of the rope while Matt gripped the swaying mast. In a few minutes they had the rope back
through the pulley and the mizzen mast firmly lashed in
its place. Graham gave Matt the thumbs up and they
started to make their way back to the wheelhouse and
welcome shelter.

They didn't see the freak wave until it was washing
over them with the force of an avenging angel. Matt was
thrown to the deck like a piece of flotsam, banging his
head on the hatch of the fish berth as he was sent sprawl-
ing. He clawed at the hatch to stop himself from being
flung against the side of the boat and probably having
his ribs broken, raising his head in time to see Graham
disappearing over the side.

'No!' He waited until the terrible rush of water had
cascaded back over the side of the boat and scrambled to
his feet, lurching forward until he was clinging to the
gunwhale. Graham was holding on to the side of the boat
but was in danger of being swept away at any moment.
Throwing his body over the side, Matt got hold of his
wrists.

'Pull yourself up,' he shouted above the roar of the
elements. Like Graham, he had lost his hat and salt water
dripped off his chin and stung his eyes.

Graham used all his strength in one huge effort to get
a grip on Matt's oilskins. Matt felt as if his arms were
being torn from their sockets as he started to haul him in.

'I've got him too!' a voice shouted at Matt's side and
he knew Jeff was there. 'Pull! Pull!'

They nearly had Graham chest high over the gunwale
when the boat dipped and Graham was slung back down
into the surging water.

The two rescuers gritted their teeth and strained every

muscle to pull on the stricken fisherman. Matt got a glimpse of Graham's face; he was terrified, it was a perilous sea to be lost in. Their lungs at bursting point, they pulled and strained and slowly, a bit at a time, Graham was hauled towards safety. Graham cried out in pain as they got him stretched over the gunwale. Then his hand slipped off Matt's slippery oilskins. Afraid they'd lose ground again, Matt took one foot off the deck and leaning further overboard tried to clutch a handful of Graham's oilskin jacket. The boat gave a tremendous stagger downwards on that side and losing his footing, Matt spilled out of the boat, over Graham's body and into the sea.

Malcolm, fighting to steer the lugger to the best advantage to get his brother safely back on board, cried out in disbelief as he saw Matt's body being hurled into the boiling spume. There was nothing he could do for him; he couldn't even get to the flares for he daren't take his hands off the wheel. He watched, hardly daring to breathe, as Jeff brought Graham to safety and laid him out on the deck. Then he bent over the side to look for Matt. His dark eyes darted over wave after wave, he peered in all directions but there was no sign of him. Jeff put his fist in the air and howled in anguish. 'Almighty God, why must this happen now?'

When he'd got Graham back to the wheelhouse, he set off the distress flares and then the *Misty*, staying close to the spot as they waited for the lifeboat, searched the area again and again.

It was dark when they stopped for a few moments to eat and drink to keep their strength up. Just after midnight, Christmas Day, they hailed the lifeboat, but there was no sign of Matt. The men bowed their heads and prayed but they knew it was hopeless. Matt was lost for ever in the murky black waters.

Chapter 36

Greg was taking Leah home, the headlights of the car spotlighting a steady fall of rain but they were warm and happy to be alone together again.

'Looks like we're in for a wet Christmas,' she observed, not the least bit concerned with the weather. On the back seat of the car were the presents she had been given by Hannah, Mrs Opie, Angie and Mr Patrick. This was going to be the best Christmas she had ever had.

'Pity we can't spend Christmas Day together,' he said wistfully. 'But hopefully it will be the last one we have apart.'

They were pulling out of Roscarrock grounds and into the lane when Leah gave a squeal as a man suddenly appeared in front of the car. Greg slammed on the brakes and the man leapt out of the way, narrowly missing being knocked down. Without even a glance into the car, he passed through the gateway.

'Damn it,' Greg thumped the steering wheel. 'That was Daniel Kittow. Obviously on his way to see Hannah. I hope he doesn't stay long. Are you all right, darling?'

'Yes,' she said shakily. 'It gave me such a fright. I think Hannah will be glad to see him.'

'Why?' Greg asked as he continued on their way.

'Well, she's a bit moody despite it being Christmas, isn't she? Daniel has always been able to cheer her up.'

Greg wanted to talk only about himself and Leah. 'I don't suppose there'll be much of a festive atmosphere at your house. If it gets too bad and you can slip away, come up to the house tomorrow.'

'I'd love to, especially to sing carols under the beautiful Christmas tree.' Leah had been fascinated by the six-foot fir Patrick and Hannah had decorated in the drawing room. 'But what would Mrs Opie say if I suddenly turned up?'

Greg pulled the car into a gateway near Hemmick Farm and turned off the engine. He took Leah into his arms. 'I don't think she'd mind, in fact she'd probably welcome you. I'm sure she knows about us.' He kissed her cheek very tenderly. 'Hannah does. She asked me about us yesterday and said she gives us her blessing as we're in love.'

In love. The words bounced around inside Leah's head. They had talked a lot about their relationship, even marriage, but love had never been mentioned. When she thought about Greg at night in her bed, she told his image she loved him. She had imagined them in all sorts of romantic situations, but they had been dreams rather than something she thought could actually happen.

Greg didn't notice her quietness and carried on talking. 'I can't wait until that horrid nurse leaves the house. The moment Christmas is over, I'm going to tell Grandma about us, that we want to get married. Goodness,' he grinned, 'I haven't actually asked if you will marry me yet. Will you, Leah? Say yes and make me the happiest man on earth.'

Leah had fallen into something of a stupor. It was one

thing to fantasise about marrying Greg, of living as his wife at Roscarrock and not as a servant; it was entirely different to be actually faced with his proposal of marriage. 'How can I become your wife?' she asked, feeling panicky. 'You're a gentleman, your family and friends will never accept me. They wouldn't want you marrying a girl so much below you and who's disfigured.'

'We've been all through this, darling, and your scar doesn't matter at all. I forget you've even got one. But whatever you looked like, I'd still love you. Don't worry, I don't want to plunge you into a life you wouldn't be suited to. I thought we'd either live quietly at Roscarrock or go somewhere else. It's all I'll ever want. It'll just be the two of us, and perhaps Patrick and Angie.'

'But what about Mrs Opie and Hannah?'

'I'm going to tell you something, darling, and you must promise to keep it a secret or it might cause all sorts of trouble. My grandmother and Hannah will be moving away soon. They're going to live in Torquay. Grandma thinks it will be good for Hannah – you've seen for yourself how events have upset her recently.'

'Hannah's going away? I can't imagine living without her around.'

'She'll be much happier starting again somewhere else.' He held her face in his hand. 'Could you live without me, Leah?'

Suddenly Leah understood what falling in love was all about. It was wanting that person with you every moment of your life. The thought of no longer seeing Greg, of not having his arms around her, his devotion and his love, was the most frightening thing she'd ever experienced. 'No, I couldn't,' she said, moving in closer against him.

'So if we can get either of your parents to consent, you'll marry me as soon as possible?'

'Yes, Greg,' she breathed.

Thinking of her youth and moment of panic, he made himself ask, 'Are you sure, Leah?'

'Yes, because I know I love you.'

'Oh, darling, then here's your present from me.' He took a tiny box out of the inside breast pocket of his coat and opened it. It contained a sparkling solitaire engagement ring and he proudly put it on her finger.

He usually kissed her first but this time she offered him her lips, and for the first time he kissed her with some of the passion he felt for her.

When they reached the top of the village hill, Leah reluctantly gave the ring back to Greg for safekeeping until their engagement was announced. He handed her another parcel to open the next morning. They stayed a long time in the darkness of the car before she got out and skipped home, her presents held safely out of the wet under her coat.

Prim attacked her with a sharp tongue the instant she got inside Cliffside Cottage. 'Where on earth have you been? Your father's boat hasn't come in yet and Mrs Penney has been here worrying about Matt. Why do I always have to face everything like this alone?'

'Are all the boats home?' Leah asked, unperturbed. It was only about seven o'clock, too soon to start worrying.

'The last boat came in over three hours ago but apparently the *Misty* didn't put to sea with the rest of them.'

'There you are then. It shouldn't be too much longer. Do you want a hand with those mince pies?'

'You can finish them off,' Prim snapped, plonking the glass she was using to cut out the pastry on the flour-laden table then flopping down wearily in a chair. 'I've been on my feet all day getting ready for tomorrow, though I don't see any point, I haven't got much family left at home. It's all right for you, gadding about with those blasted Opies. I don't know why you don't go up there to live.'

Leah ignored her mother's spite. She might be doing just that soon, but not as a servant. She put the rounds of pastry into the patty tins, filled them with mincemeat and put on the lids. 'Has Josh been playing up?' she asked her mother kindly. 'You know I'd look after him more if he'd let me.'

Prim didn't answer. She was thinking about the late return of the *Misty*. Maybe the boat had engine trouble, or it might have hit a stormy patch of water and was taking the passage home very slowly. It might have sunk for some reason. Jeff floating dead in the water was very appealing to her, as long as it was only him. If it turned out that that was what had happened, she'd put Josh in an institution and go off somewhere. Leah could do what she liked. She had plenty of relatives living in the village. Janet could take her in like she had her other daughter. Hannah, my daughter – that's a bloody laugh, Prim mused bitterly. If only I'd never seen her, wanted her; it was my undoing.

Leah put the mince pies into the small oven of the range. 'Hannah said she visited Aunty Janet and the others the other day.'

'She did. I saw her,' Prim said, suddenly bone weary and not caring about anything any more. Rather than getting out of this house for good, an easier way out of her misery had occurred to her.

'She didn't say she'd seen you.'

'She wouldn't. I was nasty to her.'

''Tis the season of good will, Mum.'

'Oh, shut up, Leah, and make me a mug of cocoa. Then go up and see if Josh is asleep. I managed to get him off early tonight.'

At eight thirty, with still no sound of the familiar tramp of her father's sea boots heading for the door, Leah went down to the quay, lit up by lantern light, and found herself among a group of people, including Sarah, Naomi, Jowan and John Jacobs, Lizzie's husband, and two cousins of the Chellew brothers, all concerned that the *Misty* was overdue. Mrs Penney was among them. 'Is your mother coming?' she asked Leah, her face pinched with cold and worry.

'No, she's very tired. I told her I'd keep vigil.' Leah's insides were cramped with fear for her father and the rest of the crew. She wondered if Hannah would want to know about Matt and considered telephoning the big house, but decided it would be better to wait for some definite news.

'The Coastguard's been informed,' Jowan told her gravely. 'They said they saw some flares late in the afternoon off Fowey and sent out the lifeboat but couldn't give us any more details.'

'Oh, God,' Leah groaned, wishing Greg was with her.

One man who wasn't interested in the fate of the *Misty* was Fred Jose. Seizing the opportunity, he entered the Penneys' cottage by the back door, took off his shoes and crept along to the parlour. He knew his way about from a previous excursion here. Wearing gloves, he took a piece of porcelain out of the glass cabinet. Putting his shoes back on, he closed the door and made his way to the dark side of Porthellis.

He went home and up to his bedroom and added the figurine to the bag of goods he had been stealing over the last few weeks. Then he slipped out of the house again and went next door to the Kittows' cottage. He knew Daniel had left the village and Rufus was in the pub; he had plenty of time. He stole through the mess and clutter that made up the Kittow home and went upstairs and looked inside the two bedrooms. He couldn't see very much but was careful to identify Daniel's room by his clothes and belongings. There was a built-in cupboard next to the top of the bed, and making sure its light didn't shine through the window, he switched on his torch. The door was half open so it didn't matter about keeping it tidy. Pulling some of the things out, Fred put the bag of stolen goods in a corner at the back of the cupboard and piled clothes back over, to make it look as if the bag had been hidden.

He turned off the torch and stood back in the room. 'Get out of this, you bastard,' he chuckled to himself.

In Cliffside Cottage, Prim stood over her sleeping son and by the light of the oil lamp she was holding watched his slightly twisted face as he breathed heavily and twitched every so often. 'Just like your rotten father,' she hissed at him. She had loved Josh, her firstborn, but as he'd grown up and turned out more and more like Jeff she'd come to dislike his surly ways and finally the young man himself. Now she loathed him.

Another hour had slipped by and she was getting hopeful her husband would never come home. She knew the authorities wouldn't easily take Josh into an institution; he might have lost his mind but he wasn't physically disabled and he had a fit and able mother to look after him. Prim couldn't face caring for him for the rest of her life, even if Jeff was lost at sea and she was free of him; and if she simply left Porthellis, Josh would be foisted on Sarah or Naomi and she didn't want that. There was only one thing she could do.

Putting the lamp down, she held up the pillow she had in her other hand. Slowly, she lowered the pillow until it covered Josh's face. She pressed as hard as she could and after a few moments he struggled, thrashing his arms about in the air and making dreadful guttural noises in his throat.

'Die, you miserable creature,' she uttered, her mouth ugly and distorted.

'M-umm.' Josh had said few intelligible words since his brain had been damaged but there was no mistaking this. He had cried out, 'Mum.'

Her heart rising to her mouth, Prim snatched the pillow away and threw it on the floor. Josh's face was red and crumpled and full of fear. She sat on the bed and lifting him up hugged him in her arms. 'Oh, dear God, forgive me,' she cried, sobs racking her body. 'What was I thinking of? I must have gone mad.' She had never once smacked her children and here she had just been trying to take Josh's life. It wasn't his fault his father was rotten, that he'd turned out the way he had because of him. It was Jeff's fault too that Hannah and Leah had gone to Roscarrock and she had turned against them because she couldn't bear the thought of losing them. 'Forgive me, Josh, forgive me. I promise I'll make it up to you and the girls.'

She held Josh until his fear and shaking stopped and he fell asleep. She kissed his face, laid him down and covered him as tenderly as she had done when he'd been a baby. 'It's all right, son,' she whispered through the long and lonely night, her voice thick with emotion. 'I'll look after you and if it ends up just being the two of us at least we'll have each other.'

Daniel held a sprig of mistletoe over Hannah's head and kissed her cheek then he slid his mouth along her face to kiss her lips. In need of comfort after her harrowing time in the village, Hannah leaned against his strength and enjoyed the closeness as he encircled her in his arms.

'It's good to see you, Danny,' she said against his broad chest.

'I hate these long weeks away from you, Hannah,' he said huskily. Lifting her face he gazed down at her warmly. 'You look as beautiful as ever but not too well. Everything's all right, isn't it?'

No, it's not, she wanted to cry, but she couldn't tell him her troubles. 'I think I'm getting another cold.' She smiled to fool him; Daniel knew her so well, he wouldn't easily be fobbed off with a lie. 'Did you have good catches?'

'Nothing to speak of, nor the other boats. It was only thinking of you that kept me going through the long cold nights.'

'Are all the boats home safely?'

'Yes.' He knew the *Misty* wasn't but he didn't want her thinking about Matt. He lowered his head and placed his lips over hers. He knew she would pull back if he became passionate and he held himself in check. She didn't respond at first then she put her arms round his neck and kissed him back.

Immediately regretting her action, she pulled away from him. But Daniel was satisfied for now. 'Why don't we exchange presents now,' he suggested in a tender voice. 'I bought you something special in Plymouth. I scoured the shops until I saw just the right thing.'

Hannah had been sure Daniel would call on her this evening and she had his present ready. Sitting close on the bench at the long table in the servants' hall, she unwrapped her present first. 'Oh, Danny, it's beautiful.' In her hands was a figurine about three inches tall of a fair-haired girl in a long blue dress, the dress and her long hair swirled as if by the wind.

'Of course it's beautiful. It's just like you. If it had a name it would be called Hannah.'

'I'll treasure it all my life.' She kissed his cheek and gazed wonderingly at her gift again.

'Will you treasure it, Hannah?' he said, the catch of emotion in his voice drawing her attention. 'I've never seen you wearing the locket I gave you.'

She tried not to blush guiltily. 'I wear it on special occasions. It means too much to me to risk losing it if I wore it all the time. Open your present. I hope you like it. It's hard to know what to get for a man that isn't boring like socks or a scarf.'

He unwrapped the long narrow box she'd placed in his hand. He took out an ebony, silver-tipped fountain pen. He turned it over in his big rough hand, looking at it from all angles. 'It's lovely. Thanks. But I don't know when I'll use it.'

'You're bound to want to write to me.'

Her sentence had been worded wrongly and he was on to her in an instant. 'What do you mean? Where are you going?'

She put the figurine down on the table and moved away to the fireside. 'Well, I thought you could write to me on the boat and post a letter from Plymouth, as we miss—'

'That wasn't what you meant.' He got up and gripped her arm. 'Is that bloody London trip on again?'

'No, it's . . .' She'd backed herself into a corner and knew she'd have to come clean. When Daniel got the bit between his teeth he never gave up until the outcome was satisfactory to him. Raising her chin to meet his deep blue, narrowed eyes, she said, 'Mrs Opie and I are going away to live, at Torquay.'

'When?' he snapped, a dark shadow passing over his handsome features, a cruel downwards twist at the corners of his mouth.

'In a few days' time.'

'For good?'

She couldn't hold his accusing stare and looked away. 'Yes.'

He moved in closer and took her other arm, jerking her slightly so she was forced to look at him again. 'And why has this all come about?'

'Mrs Opie has been thinking of getting away for some time, she's had enough of being cooped up here. She wants me to go with her and as things haven't worked out for me—'

'They haven't worked out between you and Matt but it's not the same situation with us.' He was angry and gave her a little shake. 'When were you going to tell me, for goodness sake? After you'd packed up and gone? Is that all our friendship means to you?'

'I wouldn't have left without telling you, Danny, please believe me.' He was hurting her and she tried to free herself. 'Our friendship means everything to me.'

'Then there's no problem, is there? You don't have to

go away with that old woman.' His expression softened and he looked pleased with himself. 'We'll get married straightaway. I've got a large amount of money stashed away. I'll buy a big cottage on the waterfront. You can be your own mistress and you won't have to work your guts out like some of the other women to make ends meet. We'll have a good life together. I never thought I'd fall in love but I have with you. I love you so much, Hannah.' He thought that it was arranged, that Hannah couldn't possibly disagree with him. He took her possessively in his arms and brought his mouth, open and full of passion, down over hers.

All that had gone through Hannah's mind as he'd proudly given his speech was the memory of how Matt had offered her marriage in similar circumstances, so she wouldn't have to go away to start a new life. She hadn't loved Matt then and didn't love Daniel now. He had acted so quickly and his grasp was so tight she couldn't move a muscle and she stayed passive, her head forced uncomfortably backwards, feeling she would suffocate, until he brought the kiss to an end. His smile lit up his handsome features but she couldn't be swayed like all the other women who had put themselves so readily in his arms.

'I can't marry you, Danny,' she said, breathless from his embrace.

'Don't be silly, Hannah, there's nothing to stop us. We'll see the minister tomorrow. I'll even go to chapel and we can see him then.'

She had to get through to him. 'I don't love you, Danny.'

'Of course you do,' he said, letting her go, not wanting to believe what she was saying. He went to his coat and pulled out a bottle of wine. 'I bought this to toast Christmas but now we can drink to our future.'

'Danny, you're not listening to me,' she said desperately. 'I'm going away with Mrs Opie. My mind's made up and nothing will change it.'

He slammed the wine down on the table, making the figurine jump dangerously near the edge. 'I don't believe you!'

Trembling at his sudden outburst, she said firmly, 'You'll have to.'

'You can't do this to me.' For the first time she saw the hint of tears in his eyes. 'I won't let you. I love you, Hannah. For God's sake, doesn't that mean anything to you?'

'We're friends, Danny, we can only ever be friends.'

'No.' He raked his hands through his hair. 'We're more than that, we always have been, but I haven't seen it until this year. You'll marry me if I have to drag you to the bloody altar.'

Angie, ordered by Mrs Opie to stay at hand in the kitchen when Daniel arrived, wished Mr Greg was back from taking Leah home. Disturbed by the shouting, she was trying to pluck up the courage to go into the servants' hall. Nurse Collins suddenly swept past her like a tank at war and swung open the door.

She strode straight up to Daniel. 'You're disturbing the peace of the house, young man. I suggest you leave at once,' she boomed.

'Go to hell, you interfering bitch,' Daniel hurled at her. 'This is between Hannah and me.'

'Danny,' Hannah pleaded.

'Oh no it's not,' the nurse bellowed, advancing further until she was just a few inches away from him, completely unafraid of the furious red-headed young man. 'When things get out of hand and threaten to alarm one of my patients, it concerns me. Leave at once or I'll get the maid to phone for the police.'

Daniel looked at Hannah with cold eyes. 'Do you want me to go?'

'You'd better, Danny,' she said, watching the rage increasing in him.

He grabbed his coat. 'I'm not leaving this here. I'll be back.' He stormed out, slamming the door behind him.

Angie crept into the room and seeing Hannah shaking violently and looking as if she was about to faint, she led her to an armchair. 'Shall I get 'ee a cup of tea, miss?'

'It's not tea she needs,' Nurse Collins mocked. 'It's a ring on her finger. You should have accepted his offer. It's the only decent thing to do.'

'Mind your own business,' Hannah snarled viciously at her. The nurse might have saved her from further argument with Daniel but she had no right to get personal.

'Of course, I've known for some time,' Nurse Collins went on regardless, enjoying herself. 'You get a sixth sense about women in your condition in my profession. You'll regret sending your lover away.'

'He is not my lover,' Hannah seethed, appalled that her news was out. Angie would know what the nurse meant.

'Good Lord, how many men have you got dangling on a string? You've got loose morals to go with your pretty face.'

Hannah couldn't take any more. 'Get out! Get out!' she screamed at the top of her voice, frightening Angie into believing she was about to have a seizure.

'Don't worry, I'm going.' The nurse made to leave with

a smirk on her ugly face but before she could add a further insult, she was faced with Patrick Opie's outraged indignation.

'Oh, go you will, Nurse Collins. Right out of the door first thing in the morning, Christmas Day or not. My great-aunt will agree with me.'

Daniel had not left but was leaning against the wall of the steps, smoking a cigarette. He heard the row going on inside but couldn't make out the words. He didn't care what it was about. He drew in deeply on the cigarette and blew out a long plume of smoke. The unthinkable had happened to him. He had been rejected by a woman. Hannah had resisted his attempts to get closer to her before but he hadn't taken her seriously. Why had she refused his offer of marriage, rejected his love? There must be more to this than her wanting simply to move out of Roscarrock with her employer. She had often told him over the years that she could never bear to leave Cornwall. What had changed her mind?

She had looked different tonight, he couldn't put his finger on why. She had felt different in his arms, a little fuller in the figure. The truth hit him like a slap in the face. So that was why she had to get away. He threw the cigarette down in disgust, his face a distortion of hurt, hate and revenge. Matt Penney was a dead man. And he hadn't finished with Hannah yet.

All Hannah wanted to do was go to bed, but Mrs Opie had to be told about Daniel's outburst – she had heard the altercation from the other side of the house – and the nurse's impertinence. Mrs Opie was appalled. She told Patrick to telephone round the hotels and find a room for Nurse Collins for the next week. He was to drive her there after breakfast. Then Hannah had to convince Mrs

Opie she was all right, that she didn't want to sit with her and talk things through any more. Mrs Opie gave her a sleeping pill and at last she was able to slip away to her room for an early night. It was nine o'clock and she prayed she'd quickly drift off to sleep and not wake until long after dawn the next morning.

The moment she stepped inside her room, the door was pushed shut behind her. She knew a moment of terror. She saw at once who it was but shrank from the malevolence emanating from him. 'My God, Danny, what are you doing here? I don't want any more trouble.'

'Then don't raise your voice or I swear I'll tear this bloody house apart.'

'Wh-why haven't you gone?'

'Let's say I have some unfinished business,' he mouthed sarcastically. 'You can't send me packing like that mealy-mouthed Matt Penney.'

She saw him then as Viv had, and no doubt other women who had tried to resist him, a part of him she had foolishly ignored. What Daniel wanted he took and nothing stopped him, she had seen that in all other aspects of his life but it had never occurred to her that he could ever hurt her. 'Pl-please go.'

'Not on your life.' His top lip curled. 'How could you lie down for Matt Penney? Now he's got you stuffed up you're going to run away.'

'How do you know? Did you hear the nurse?'

He shook his head disdainfully, still keeping her a prisoner against the door. 'Is that what that bitch was saying to you after I left?' Spreading the fingers of his other hand he ran them down over her face to clutch her throat. Hannah's heart leapt in fear. She knew he could break her neck as if it was a flower stem. 'Poor sweet little

Hannah. Her father didn't want her, her grandmother hated her, she was wronged and rejected. But she kept her innocence, waiting for the right man to marry her and make all her dreams come true.' He swore at her viciously.

'Please, Danny, stop. You're frightening me.'

He ran his thumb over her trembling bottom lip. 'Am I now? Were you frightened when Matt got inside you?'

'No,' she spat at him, outraged that he should think Matt had forced her. 'Matt isn't like you. He's a good, honest man, loving and gentle and it was me who wanted him.'

For one terrible moment she thought Daniel was going to hit her. He hissed into her face, 'You obviously haven't told him about his brat. Why don't you want him any more?'

'I do,' she threw in his face. 'You've just made me realise it. And I'm going to tell him the first moment I get the chance.' She prayed that after the way she had treated Matt he would still want her.

Moving his hand to cover her mouth, Daniel balled his fist and looked with menace at her stomach. 'If I beat his brat out of your guts, you won't have no reason to go to him.' He grinned, a wide evil smirk, and straightening out his hand he placed it on her breast and squeezed, making her eyes widen at this new terror. 'Matt Penney's a righteous man. He won't want a whore. I'll tell him you came to me willingly, that we've been carrying on where he left off.'

Keeping his hand over her mouth, he lifted Hannah off her feet and carried her struggling to the bed. He pushed her down and threw himself on top of her. She beat at him with her fists. He gathered her wrists together and held them above her head. As she opened her mouth to scream, he smothered it with his, his teeth cutting into her lips. The room was growing dark and started to spin. She fought hard to keep conscious, knowing if he succeeded in raping her she'd be sucked into the terrifying empty darkness it would bring and she'd be lost in a limbo world of hate and self-loathing for ever. Her only hope lay in not struggling, in making him believe she wanted him too. She lay still and as she'd hoped he took his hands from her wrists so he could more easily remove her clothing. She put her arms around his neck and stroked his hair. He stopped kissing her and looked questioningly into her eyes. She could feel his body, ready to invade and destroy her.

'Please, Danny,' she whispered. 'We're friends, remember? Friends don't hurt each other.'

With a low, anguished moan he rolled off her and lay on his back on the bed beside her. She covered herself but didn't dare move away from him in case it sent him into another rage. He was breathing heavily, harsh ragged sounds, and it seemed an eternity before he calmed down. He sat up and looked down at her. 'It should have been me, not some other man,' he said, his voice rasping.

Going to the door, he picked up the sleeping pill she had dropped there. He flung it on the bed beside her. 'You'd better take that tonight and one every night from now on, because I hope I haunt you in your dreams for the rest of your life.'

She said nothing, afraid of reawakening his lust and the need for revenge at what he saw as her betrayal of him; she prayed fervently that he would go. His eyes rooted on her, he straightened his clothes, tidied his hair, then without another word left the room.

Hannah couldn't be sure that he would never try to

harm her again and she prayed to God that one day he would get his just desserts.

When she found the strength, she got off the bed, undressed, put on her nightdress and washed her face. She took the sleeping pill and got into bed. She didn't feel the need to run to Mrs Opie for comfort like she had at other times. She had something to tell her tomorrow, that she might not be going away with her, because first thing she was going down to the village in the hope of finally putting things right between herself and Matt. She had his jewellery box in her hands and she played the music over and over again until she fell asleep.

Chapter 37

Leah and Mrs Penney watched the sea from Janet's house for sign of the *Misty* coming in. Finally, at midnight, Leah walked home through the icy-cold damp air. The smell of salt was heavier than usual and the wind threatened to rip the scarf from her head. She found her mother snoring softly in her chair in the kitchen, and rather than wake her to inform her there was no news, she left a note and went back to her aunt's. An hour later her Uncle Roy and Jowan went up to the Manse to telephone the Coast-guard for news.

When the two men came in, the women looked at them with a mixture of hope and fear. 'Well?' Mrs Penney asked bravely.

'They've given us some news at last,' Roy said gravely. 'The flares they saw came from the *Misty* and the reason they were fired was,' he paused, 'because they lost a man overboard.'

Mrs Penney grabbed Leah's hand. 'Do they know who it was?'

'They said they didn't have any names.'

'Why don't they know any more than that?' Janet said heatedly, looking helplessly at her niece and Mrs Penney.

'They're doing their best, dear,' Roy said softly, helping

himself to tea from the teapot that had been on the go all night. 'Anyway, names wouldn't help at this point – could be the wrong one.' Roy stuffed a sandwich into his mouth and took a big bite. 'I'm going out with the men on the quay.'

Jowan was about to follow his example. Leah took him aside. 'If it is Matt I think we ought to let Hannah know. She thinks more of him than she realises and would be devastated to hear it second-hand.'

'If that's how it turns out we'll go up to see her together,' Jowan said, his young weathered face creased with worry. 'Sounds like someone's lost his life, whoever it is.'

The night wore on and at intervals all the fishermen in the village, except Daniel, trooped into Janet's kitchen for hot drinks and food.

'I'm so grateful to you, Mrs Rouse,' Mrs Penney said from her position at the front room window. 'I'll reimburse you for everything that's come out of your cupboard as soon as I get home.'

'No need for that,' Janet said, peering at the whites of the waves filling up the basin of the cove. There was activity on the quay as men prepared to put to sea at dawn to help in the search. 'They brought plenty of bread and splits down from the bakehouse and people have been bringing things in all night. I'm only too glad to be able to help. Could be one of mine out there.'

Mrs Penney's kindly face was ashen and drawn. 'Poor Matt, he's had such a terrible second half of the year, losing his finger . . .'

'Losing Hannah?' Janet ventured, voicing what she knew the other woman was thinking.

'I hope he was being careful on the boat.'

'Matt's one of the finest fishermen in the village.'

'Yes, but he's been so unhappy, depressed . . .'

Janet was appalled at what was going through Mrs Penney's mind. 'Matt wouldn't do nothing like that,' she said stoutly. 'He's got a strong faith and even if he's given up on Hannah he'll realise there's other girls about.'

Mrs Penney took a deep breath to forestall a flood of tears. 'Matt's only ever been interested in Hannah. It's as if she's the only one he could ever want. I don't think he'd ever consider someone else. It might not be him who's gone overboard but he's got a lifetime of heartbreak to face.'

As she couldn't think of anything to say, Janet rubbed Mrs Penney's arm in a comforting gesture and went back to Leah, who was dozing in the kitchen. The back door was opened and Prim came in. She had seen for herself that the *Misty* was not moored at the quay but wanted to know if there was any news.

Leah woke at the sound of her mother and aunt's voices. She stretched her aching limbs and was pleasantly surprised when Prim smiled at her. Janet looked puzzled too as she said sweetly to Leah, 'Why don't you go home and have a couple of hours in bed, my handsome?'

'I'd rather stay here, Mum, if you don't mind.' Leah wanted to be ready to go to Roscarrock with Jowan if need be.

'I suppose I'd better be there when Josh wakes,' Prim said; she knew Josh wouldn't remember the pillow being pressed over his face but the terror he had felt would linger and he would be very nervous all day. 'Is there tea in that pot?' Janet nodded. 'How's Mrs Penney? She must be worried sick.'

'She's in the parlour, looking out the window,' Janet

replied, pouring tea for Prim and putting ginger biscuits on a plate.

'I'll drink this then go in and have a word with her. We're in the same boat, so to speak.'

When Prim left the kitchen, Leah and Janet exchanged looks, wondering what had happened to bring Prim back to her old self.

A few minutes later, as the first shaft of light showed itself in the eastern sky, a shout went up on the quay. The women pulled on their coats and scarves and ran to join the men on vigil.

Jowan met Leah as she put her foot on the first paving stone of the quay. 'It's the *Misty*. She's coming in.'

Leah's stomach twisted into a painful knot. Now they would find out who had been lost and whether or not he had been found. She stood on the front of the quay with Mrs Penney, Janet and Prim, clutching one another's hands, watching the *Misty* coming closer and closer.

One of the Chellew brothers was on the prow ready with the mooring rope. When the boat nudged the quay wall, he jumped woodenly ashore and Roy Rouse took the rope from him. It was Malcolm. Hands reached out to help Graham ashore and see to the boat.

Graham and Malcolm Chellew stood on shaky legs, almost too weary and cold to stand up. Blankets were thrown round them and all eyes were on the only other man aboard, coming out of the wheelhouse. Prim gasped in disappointment that it was Jeff. It meant that Matt was the man who was lost. She squeezed Mrs Penney's hand and found it rigid.

Leah was glad to see her father but grimly caught Jowan's eye. They had an awful task in front of them.

There was silence as Graham Chellew walked stiffly to

Mrs Penney. He was soaked through, chilled to the marrow from looking down into the sea without a break for several hours for Matt. 'I'm very sorry, Mrs Penney. I was tossed overboard by a freak wave but managed to cling to the side. Matt was hauling me back in when the boat lurched and he went over. The lifeboat and other boats who were in the area are still looking for him. We had to come in because we're nearly out of fuel.'

'Thank you for telling me, Graham.' Mrs Penney's voice was small and dignified, only a slight quake in it betraying her effort to stay in control. 'Thank you for staying out to search for Matt. I'll carry on waiting.'

'Come back to my house, Mrs Penney,' Janet said, and when the grieving woman could make her legs work, she led her away.

There was a flurry of activity as men went aboard their boats to join in the search. The survivors of the *Misty* would be taken home and looked after. All three would have preferred to refuel and continue the search for Matt, but they were too cold, too weary and would have been a hindrance rather than a help.

Leah ran up to Jeff and hugged him. 'Thank God you're all right, Dad.'

He put his face on the top of her head. He said nothing, there was nothing he could say.

'Dad,' she said, shivering in his arms. 'I hope you won't object but Jowan and I think we ought to go up to the big house and tell Hannah about Matt.'

Prim had moved towards them and waited for her husband's reply. It made all who heard it stare at him curiously.

'I'll go with you, Leah. Jowan can stay on watch on

the quay. Just give me a chance to change my clothes and have something hot to eat.'

Angie Miller was the only one up and about when the knock came at the door just before seven o'clock. She showed Leah and her father anxiously into the drawing room where she had just lit the fire. Then, thinking it best, she woke Mr Greg and told him who was downstairs wanting to see Hannah at this ungodly hour on Christmas morning.

'You did the right thing, Angie,' Greg said, deeply worried that Jeff Spargo of all people should be here. 'Leave them there and go about your work. I'll see to this.' When Angie left the room, he dressed hastily and went to his grandmother.

'What on earth do you think he wants?' Feena Opie said, as worried as Greg.

'He wouldn't tell Angie but obviously it's bad news. Perhaps Hannah's mother has died. Leah's with him but it doesn't look as if he's come to cause trouble about us.' With that, Greg brought his relationship with Leah out in the open but Mrs Opie wasn't in the least bit interested in that right now. 'Don't let him see Hannah until I'm downstairs. Give me fifteen minutes to get dressed. Don't disturb Patrick or the nurse.'

Leah was sitting on a sofa near the fire, Jeff was standing, despite his weariness and the walk here, with his hands clasped behind his back, as Mrs Opie wheeled herself into the room with Greg at her side. Leah got to her feet. She was pale and pinched, cheeks red and raw from the cold, and Greg had to fight with himself not to go to her.

'Whatever your reason for coming here like this, let me

460

tell you I won't have any trouble, Jeff Spargo,' Mrs Opie said in a voice to rival the unfriendliest sea. She took in every detail of Jeff Spargo. Even with the ordeal of the many hours just spent at sea, the need of a shave, the toll of natural ageing, he was still a handsome man.

Jeff was thinking that time had been less kind to her, but Feena Opie was still a striking looking woman. 'I haven't come to cause trouble. Leah can vouch for that. I want to see Hannah,' he said in a similar tone.

'What about?'

'I'll only tell Hannah that.'

Without taking her eyes off Jeff, Mrs Opie gave her orders. 'Greg, ask Angie to get Hannah up. Tell her she must not say why, only that I require her in the drawing room.'

As Greg did this, Jeff and Mrs Opie glared at each other across the room, and across twenty long years of hatred.

When Greg came back he stood at his grandmother's side again but gazed warmly across the room at Leah who returned his look. Jeff noticed and a low rumbling noise of displeasure came from his throat.

Hannah had washed and dressed and was running a brush through her hair, standing at the window and looking out at the grey churning sea, when Angie knocked and entered. She had been awake for some time, and when she'd heard Mrs Opie and Greg going downstairs at such an early hour she'd thought it was part of their Christmas morning tradition. She had been rehearsing the words she would say to Mrs Opie about her intention of seeing Matt the moment breakfast was over and she hoped she wouldn't meet too much opposition.

She pattered down the stairs after Angie and went into

the drawing room with 'Happy Christmas' on her lips. When she saw Leah and her father, the last person she'd expected to step over the threshold of Roscarrock, she froze.

Before Jeff could speak, Mrs Opie said, 'Hannah, your father has come with some news for you.'

Hannah glanced at Leah, who looked down at the carpet, her pale lips quivering. She moved past Mrs Opie and Greg, her heart thumping wildly, bracing herself for what was obviously some terrible news. 'Dad, what is it? Is it Mother?'

Jeff licked his cracked, sore lips and gulped. Hannah looked young and vulnerable and very frightened, as she had done on the day he had beaten her and thrown her out of his house, when she had been just a child, bewildered and hurt by his incomprehensible hatred and rejection of her. And in spite of all that he had done to her, she still called him Dad. What he had to say now would be harder than he'd thought. There was no haughty pride in him now, no desire to be master over his flesh and blood.

'It's not her, Hannah. I wanted you to hear this from me.' Her blue eyes grew bigger and he saw there was a lot of pain behind them, pain she should never have had to bear. If he hadn't insisted she come here to live and work she probably would have been married to Matt by now, there would have been no fight over her with Daniel Kittow, Matt wouldn't have pulled out of the *Sunrise* to come to the *Misty* and his body wouldn't be out there now being tossed about and smashed in the sea. He swallowed the lump in his throat. 'There's been . . . an accident on the boat.'

She took an involuntary step backwards, knowing in

the depths of her soul what he would say next but not wanting to hear it.

'Matt fell—'

'No, no,' she put her hands instinctively over the slight swell of her middle. 'Not Matt, d-don't tell me he's dead.'

'I'm sorry, Hannah. He's been missing for over fifteen hours. The *Misty*'s not long come in but the lifeboat and other vessels are still searching for him.'

Tears ran down her face, her heart felt as if it had been wrenched in two. 'No, not Matt. He can't be in the sea. I love him. I was going to tell him today.' She rounded her fists in pure anguish and raised them in the air and screamed, 'No! Oh, God, not Matt!'

Both Leah and Mrs Opie made to go to her but Jeff beat them to it. He enclosed Hannah in his arms and she sobbed wretchedly on his shoulder. 'Don't give up hope,' he whispered tenderly. 'There might still be hope.'

Hannah lifted her head from him. 'Yes,' she wiped at her tears with agitated hands. 'I-I must go down to the village and wait.'

'I'll take you to your Aunt Janet's. Mrs Penney is watching the sea from there.'

'Hannah,' Mrs Opie said from directly behind her.

Hannah turned round to her. 'Please don't try to stop me. I have to go.'

Mrs Opie wasn't going to try and change her mind. It was painfully obvious how much Hannah loved Matt Penney. He was almost certainly dead and she would need comfort, and Mrs Opie wanted it to be her comfort. 'I was going to say that I'll come with you. Greg, will you get the car ready please? We'll all go together.'

Patrick Opie came into the room and was told the bad news. 'Nurse Collins is outside in the hall,' he said uncomfortably. 'She is wondering about her wages.'

'There's an envelope on my dressing table, Patrick. Give it to her then telephone for a taxi. I'm sure you'll be able to find someone willing to earn a double fare, even on Christmas Day. I don't want her in the house when we get back.'

Hannah ran upstairs, ignoring the nurse as she passed her at the drawing room door – still snooping – to fetch her and Mrs Opie's coats.

Leah could contain herself no longer and rushed to Greg's open arms. Jeff made to snatch her away from him, but Mrs Opie put her wheelchair in his path.

'Leave them alone. She is one child's life I won't allow you to ruin,' she muttered acidly.

'You've got no room to talk,' he snarled back. 'You can't tell me the reason you wanted Hannah here isn't purely selfish. You didn't want her when she was born.'

'You didn't want her when she was expected,' Mrs Opie retorted.

'What are they talking about, Greg?' Leah asked, wide-eyed.

'If you two want a quarrel then do it at a later date,' Greg said sternly although he was curious to know more himself. 'Think of Hannah's feelings now.'

Greg brought the car round to the front of the house and carried his grandmother down the steps and into the front passenger seat. Hannah, Leah and Jeff got into the back and Greg made the car roar down the drive, leaving Patrick and Angie to see the nurse off the premises and cook a Christmas dinner and wonder when it would be eaten.

An hour later Nurse Collins handed her suitcase to a taxi driver from St Austell and passed him the money

Patrick Opie had given her for the fare. She smiled sardonically as the taxi pulled away. She had overheard the tragic news being given in the drawing room and guessed that the fisherman lost in the sea was the father of Miss Hannah Spargo's baby. The nurse had no pity for her. When she got back, the girl would find out who her real mother was. Nurse Collins had left Mrs Opie's journal, marked at appropriate pages, on her bed.

Chapter 38

Greg drove his car all the way down Porthkilt Hill and as close to the quay as he could. Under the watchful eyes of the villagers he opened the door for Hannah, Leah and Jeff to get out then took his grandmother's wheelchair out of the boot. Someone had run to tell Janet and she met the group as they walked away from the car, Greg pushing Mrs Opie over the bumpy cobbles. It was raining lightly and Mrs Opie held a black umbrella over her head.

Janet had never met Mrs Opie before and was shocked that she should arrive here now. Her expression made clear that she wasn't the least bit in awe of the elegant lady who lived in the big house up on the cliff.

Hannah rushed to Janet and fiercely grabbed her arms. 'Has there been any more news?'

Janet hugged her. 'Nothing, I'm afraid.'

'Is Mrs Penney with you?'

'Yes. Are you coming to wait with her? She's bearing up well but is very tired, she hasn't slept a wink all night.'

'I should have been told sooner,' Hannah said crossly.

'There would have been no point, Hannah, we didn't know who it was that was missing until the *Misty* came in.' Janet studied her waxen face. 'How do you feel about Matt? I think Mrs Penney will want to know.'

467

'It's very simple, Aunty Janet,' and the tears fell hotly down Hannah's cheeks. 'Last night I realised just how much I love him and I'll probably never have the chance to tell him.' Her worry that her rejection of Matt might have made him lose his love for her, or that if he still loved her he might not trust her enough to want to marry her had turned into real anguish.

'I'm sorry, Hannah.' Janet hugged her again. People were closing in on them to catch what they could of their conversation. 'Come along inside. The last thing you need now is to catch a chill in the wet and cold.'

'No, Aunty Janet, I'm going to wait on the quay. Can Mrs Opie go inside?'

'She can wait in her grandson's car,' Janet said sourly; she considered it a ruddy cheek that Feena Opie had come at all.

'Please, Aunty Janet,' Hannah pleaded, 'for my sake? She's been so good to me.'

Moved by Hannah's stricken face, Janet reluctantly agreed and Hannah led the way. Greg pushed his grandmother to the house and carried her inside because the passage was too narrow for the wheelchair. Hannah showed them into the parlour and the others followed them in. Hannah took one look at Mrs Penney at the window and a sob caught in her throat. Mrs Penney held out her arms tentatively and Hannah went to her. They embraced and cried together, alone in their grief, although the room was filled with people.

When they were more composed, Janet took it upon herself to introduce Mrs Opie and Greg to Mrs Penney.

'It's kind of you to come,' Mrs Penney said, keeping the emotion out of her voice. She wasn't at all pleased to see the woman who she considered had taken Hannah away from Matt.

'I'm very sorry about your son,' Mrs Opie said smoothly. 'Anything that concerns Hannah concerns me.'

Mrs Penney turned back to the window. There was an unpleasant atmosphere in the room. Greg knew that even if there weren't undercurrents of mutual antipathy here, he and his grandmother would not be welcome and indeed were intruding. 'Shall we wait somewhere else?' he suggested to Leah. 'I think your aunt's house is bursting at the seams.'

Leah looked uncertainly at her father for permission. He nodded curtly. 'Go on, but I'll be wanting to talk to the pair of you later.' She left on Greg's arm, making Janet's eyes widen with amazement. So the Opies had wheedled themselves into the lives of both her nieces.

Janet felt she must be a good hostess despite having an unwelcome visitor in her home. She offered tea and Mrs Opie accepted.

Hannah refused tea. 'I'm going outside now,' she said, her thoughts only for the man she loved and feared was lost for ever.

'Wouldn't it be better if you waited in here, dear?' Mrs Opie said, holding out a hand to her.

'No, I want to be there if the lifeboat comes in.' She went before there could be further argument and Mrs Penney went with her.

Left alone, Mrs Opie and Jeff ignored each other for some time but eventually their eyes settled on one another.

'You haven't changed much in appearance,' she said coolly.

'Can't say the same for you,' he replied, reaching for a

cigarette in his coat pocket but not lighting it as he remembered Janet wouldn't allow smoking in the house. 'But you have kept a certain something about you. I heard somewhere that Stephanie is dead. Is it true?'

'Yes,' Mrs Opie said tightly, 'not that it's any concern of yours.'

'I thought it had to be something like that to make you suddenly show an interest in Hannah.'

'I would never have let you take her if I'd known then how you would treat her.'

'Don't come all self-righteous with me. You never stooped to do anything about it.'

Mrs Opie raised her chin in the superior manner he had seen before, over twenty years ago. 'That is something I shall regret until the day I die. Why have you changed towards her?'

'That's between me and God.'

'God?' she scoffed. 'Since when have you cared about your rotten soul?'

Moving to the wheelchair, he lowered his dark head and hissed in her ear, 'It's no more rotten than yours.'

Before he said something he'd regret, Jeff joined the villagers on the quay, leaving Janet to serve Mrs Opie tea on her best teak tray. The women sipped demurely, avoiding each other's eyes, not speaking since they had nothing pleasant to say to each other. After a while, bad manners or not, Janet excused herself to prepare the next meal. Her menfolk wouldn't feel like a Christmas dinner unless there was good news but they had to eat sometime today.

Jeff stayed close to Hannah, wishing he could think of a way to comfort her as she paced up and down the quay or peered out to sea with a pair of borrowed binoculars. Vision was poor with the low grey sky and the rain gusted into the harbour. She could see no further than Slate Rock and sighed in sheer frustration. Her face was drawn and often she wiped tears from her eyes.

'Do you think he could be alive, Dad?' she said the next time he hovered at her side on the edge of the quay.

In Jeff's experience, there was no possibility Matt had survived but he didn't have the heart to crush the tiny bit of hope she was clinging to. 'There was that fisherman from St Ives last year, he was found after two days in worse seas than this.'

Hannah was comforted but only for a moment. She knew very well that most people lost at sea perished. 'Can't someone phone the Coastguard again?' she wailed suddenly. 'They might know something by now.'

'I'll go up to the Manse, my handsome,' Roy Rouse said. 'The minister said we can use his phone as often as we want.'

Hannah thanked him, mopped the rainwater dripping off her chin then went under the tarpaulin cover the men had rigged up for shelter out of the biting wind to tell Mrs Penney. They gripped icy hands, and listening to the hushed tones of those keeping vigil with them waited ten long miserable minutes for Roy to come back.

Roy swept the despair from his face before he reported, 'The Coastguard says they're still searching for un and also for another boat reported t'be in trouble.'

Hannah gulped to forbid fresh tears; she must keep calm, for Mrs Penney's sake as much as her own, and Matt's, if he was found alive. There was a mutter of concern for the missing boat and the watchers sank into deeper despair. The lifeboat was more likely to concentrate on a missing boat than a single fisherman who stood little chance of surviving. Hannah put her face in her hands for a few moments and mouthed a desperate prayer. She didn't realise she was shivering violently. She shook off the blanket someone tried to put round her shoulders and went out into the wet again.

About an hour later Prim went to her sister's house for an update on the news and was shocked to learn that Mrs Opie was there. She had not dreamt the car parked close to the quay belonged to an Opie. Ignoring Janet's plea to be civil, she marched to the parlour and didn't mince her words. 'You have no right to be here. Hannah's nothing to you. She's my child.'

'I have more right to her than you,' Mrs Opie returned, unrattled by the other woman's venom.

'Flesh and blood's not the same as the one who fed her, clothed her and comforted her for ten years. I bonded with Hannah the first time I held her. She's mine, I tell you.'

Mrs Opie smiled smugly. 'Your sister thinks that too. We'll see who she goes to when this is over, shall we?'

Prim felt like ripping the other woman apart. Instead she dashed outside to be with Hannah.

Hannah saw her coming and clung to her for the first time since Jeff had thrown her out of his house. 'Oh, Mum,' she cried. 'I can't bear this waiting.'

'He'll be all right.' Prim had to fight to control herself over Hannah's distress. All she could say was to repeat the encouragement Hannah had heard over the last three hours. 'You mustn't give up hope.'

There was a sudden shout and Hannah pushed her way through to the edge of the quay as people rushed forward. From his vantage point on top the quay wall, Jowan cried, 'The lifeboat's coming in!'

Mrs Penney was now beside Hannah. Holding their

breath they linked arms and watched the churning waters anxiously for the first sign of the lifeboat. Hannah's mind was a turmoil of hope and fear. She clenched her fists until her nails dug into her flesh as the prow of the clinker-built boat lurched round the end of the quay on a surge of surf. The seven-man crew of the Fowey lifeboat, holding on as the boat rolled, were visible in the wheel-house and on the deck in their familiar oilskins, sou'wes-ters and lifejackets. There was no sign of anyone else. The coxswain threw the mooring rope to Jeff.

Hannah's heart was like a hard lump in her chest. It seemed they hadn't come with good news. She moved closer to the edge of the quay, trying to get a better look. Then as the boat was pulled along parallel to the quay, she saw a figure huddled under a blanket, sitting against the wheelhouse.

Without a thought for her own safety she jumped down into the boat, making it rock and scattering two lifeboat men who had been about to climb ashore. One tried to restrain her but she beat him off. Nothing would stop her seeing if the person under the blanket was Matt.

She ripped the blanket off the head of the figure. Her heart stopped then speeded up violently. Even with his head down nearly over his knees, she knew it was him. 'Matt!'

He raised his face, looking up at her numbly out of large dark-shadowed eyes.

'Oh, Matt.' She threw herself on her knees and pulled him into her arms. Her tears wetted his chilled rough skin as she kissed his face again and again. 'Oh, darling, I thought I'd lost you,' she laughed and cried together. 'Thank God you survived. I'm sorry I've been so beastly to you, Matt. I love you, I really do. Please forgive me. Say you still want me.'

He was almost too weak to speak but a rasp came from his throat. 'You mean it, Hannah?'

'Yes, Matt. I love you with all my heart.' She kissed his lips and looking lovingly into his eyes.

'Me too,' he smiled weakly and put his lips on hers. She held his head against her breast, crying with relief that he was alive and still loved her.

Hannah was pulled away from him by two of the lifeboat men. 'That's enough for now, m'dear,' the coxswain said firmly. 'At least we know for sure he's the man we were searching for from the *Misty*. All we've been able to get out of un was the name Porthellis. We came across a Mount's Bay lugger drifting out to sea with engine trouble. They picked him up last night. Another lifeboat's looking after they. He's been out of it for most of the time. What he needs now is a doctor and his bed.'

Hannah was aware of the cheers going up on the quayside. She stood aside and let the lifeboat men lift Matt to his feet and with help from the men ashore he was pulled safely on to land. Mrs Penney went to him as he was supported by two pairs of brawny arms. After she'd hugged and kissed her son she turned to thank the lifeboat men who took Matt's details from her.

Matt sagged and it was suggested he be carried home without further delay. Hannah was beside him, holding his frozen hand, when there was a scuffle in the crowd and Daniel shoved his way through to stand in front of them.

He threw back his red head. 'You should have stayed in the sea, Penney,' he cried like a madman, 'because I'm going to put you straight back in it!'

People screamed as Daniel rushed at Matt with outstretched arms, but he was stopped by PC Burt and a plainclothes policeman who made a grab at his body. He howled and fought them off, scattering the shocked crowd and smashing his fist on the constable's jaw, knocking him to the ground. He was brought under control by Jeff and the detective, who together twisted his arms behind his back and brought him down to the ground. Rufus tried to intervene but other men dragged him away. PC Burt scrambled to his knees and slapped a pair of handcuffs on Daniel's wrists. The crowd listened in stunned silence as the detective, with his knee in the small of Daniel's back, formally arrested him.

'Daniel Kittow, I am arresting you for the theft of several items stolen from property in Porthellis, of resisting arrest and striking a police officer in the course of his duty.'

Daniel struggled against his captors. 'I didn't steal anything, you bastards. I don't know what you're talking about.'

The policeman hauled him to his feet. Daniel glared at Matt with pure hatred. 'I haven't finished with you yet, Penney,' he spat.

Hannah let go of Matt's hand and marched up to Daniel. 'Oh yes you have.'

Daniel eyed her stonily. 'I really loved you, Hannah.'

'You don't love anyone but yourself, Daniel Kittow.' She sent her hand across his face in a hard stinging slap. He lunged his head at her but PC Burt yanked on his hair. Her voice was as cold as the grave. 'Now we're taking Matt home. We've got better things to do than watch you being brought at long last to justice.'

As Daniel was hauled away to a waiting police vehicle,

Fred Jose talked excitedly about him getting at least a year in prison and how he'd watched the policemen search the Kittow cottage and come out with a bag of stolen items.

Matt was carried home by two fishermen. Hannah called in at her aunt's house before going up to Seaview Cottage. Mrs Opie held out her hands to her as she came into the parlour. 'Greg has told me the good news. I'm so pleased Matt is safe. We'll go home now, dear, and leave your aunt in peace.'

'I won't leave Matt, Mrs Opie,' she said in a no-non-sense tone that the lady herself often used. 'Mrs Penney's said I can sleep at her house tonight.'

Worried that Hannah might not come back to Roscar-rock, Mrs Opie decided to risk playing her trump card. 'You will come back tomorrow? I've got something very important to tell you.'

Impressed by Mrs Opie's quiet seriousness, Hannah asked, 'What's it about?'

Mrs Opie gave a dramatic sigh. 'I think I'll tell you now. It's something you should have been told years ago. It's about who your real mother is.'

'My real mother?' Hannah sat down on a chair, all her energy draining out of her and making her feel light-headed. After all that had happened, she had no strength to spare for any more shocks. 'Don't you mean who my real father is? I've assumed for years my mother had an affair and that was why Jeff Spargo resented me. It accounts for my different colouring.'

'No, Hannah, Jeff Spargo is your real father. Your colouring comes from your mother.' Mrs Opie dropped her voice theatrically. 'She was my late daughter, Stephanie.'

Hannah's hands flew to her face. 'Y-you mean you're my grandmother?'

'Yes, I am, Hannah. I've known it all your life and I'm ashamed to say I didn't want anything to do with you when you were born. I had no dealings with the village after that. I didn't want to risk seeing your father, who for obvious reasons I detested. Time went on and I forgot all about you but last year Stephanie died and I was curious to see how her child had turned out.' Mrs Opie's voice faltered. 'The moment I saw you, Hannah, I felt a strong affection for you and wanted to make up for all those lost years. Now I have grown to love you.'

Hannah was dumbfounded. 'So that's why you gave me one of the best rooms at Roscarrock and have been so kind to me? Why my other grandmother said I belonged there?'

Mrs Opie smiled indulgently. 'You have turned out to be a lovely young woman, it's been easy to be kind to you. It's been a pleasure having you in the house. Patrick has found it so and it's why Greg – he knows about you, my dear – has grown so fond of you. After all, you are his cousin.'

Hannah could hardly take this in. She got up and paced the room. 'But my mother, Prim, why did she take me in if what you say is true?'

'Stephanie wrote Jeff a letter saying his child had been born, that she didn't want to bring you up because she wanted to continue her travels round the world. The boats were away and Prim opened and read the letter. She came up to Roscarrock for a confrontation. You were only two days old but Stephanie had already left. I was going to give you up for adoption but Prim asked to see you. She had just given birth to a stillborn daughter and as soon as she saw you she wanted you to fill her baby's place. As Jeff was your father, I let her take you. It seemed the ideal solution at the time.'

'But why if he's my real father did he turn against me? Why did my grandmother hate me?'

'I think you'd better ask your father that.'

'I will, but not now.' Hannah felt there was more to this than what Mrs Opie – her grandmother – was telling her but right now she wanted only to be with the man she loved. 'I must go to Matt, he needs me and I need him. Of course, I won't be going away to Torquay with you now.'

Mrs Opie reached out to her. 'Don't make a hasty decision, Hannah, I beg you. You're full of emotion now and you might regret it for the rest of your life. I can offer you and the baby so much more than Matt can. Think about it.'

Hannah resented her last words. 'Life with Matt could never be a mistake. You've given me a lot to think about, Mrs Opie. I'll come up to Roscarrock only when I'm sure Matt is all right. Now I'll find Mr Greg and tell him you're ready to go home.'

One by one the Porthellis boats that had put to sea to search for Matt came safely home. The families made the most of what was left of Christmas Day, thanking the Lord that one of their own had cheated the cruel sea. Hannah stayed by Matt's bedside as he slept, happy that at last she knew where her future lay. But what of her past? She really did have the right to the name Hannah Spargo, but she did not look forward to learning all the circumstances that had made it something of a curse to her all her life.

Chapter 39

Matt slept round the clock until the afternoon of the day after Boxing Day. It was some moments before the stinging and heaviness left his eyes and he could see properly. He was lying on his back and moved gingerly to ease his stiff limbs under a mountain of bedclothes, pushing them away because the crackling fire had made the room stuffily hot and a jumper had been put on over his pyjamas. He groaned in pain, feeling battered and bruised all over his body, which indeed he was.

He remembered the fall off the *Misty* into the sea, the battle to tread water in its icy, monstrous grip. Then as he'd pessimistically thought that Hannah wouldn't want him if he went to her, the desire had come like a welcome balm to let the water drag him down into its depth and end the misery of facing all those long lonely years on his own. He couldn't recall being dragged on to the Mount's Bay lugger, of being stripped of his clothes and put into dry clothes. The fishermen must have looked after him well otherwise he would probably have died from the effects of his prolonged drenching in the sea even if he hadn't drowned.

His body and bones had stayed remorselessly frozen and there had been voices and an unwelcome disturbance as he'd been lifted out of the strange, hazy succour of numbness back into the harsh, cold weather and then into the lifeboat. The lifeboat men had rubbed his arms and legs and kept talking to him to keep him awake. Then there had been a woman's voice. Hannah's? Yes, she'd told him she loved him. Matt was still hopelessly weary and drifted off to sleep again in a state of bliss. Then he came to in a terrible panic. What if the part about Hannah had been a dream, an hallucination brought on by his ordeal?

'Hannah!' His voice wouldn't come but he kept shouting.'Hannah! Hannah! Hannah!' He wanted to die if the beautiful words she had spoken to him were just a cruel trick of his imagination. 'Hannah!' Sheer desperation forced sounds from his throat.

Hannah and Mrs Penney came running up the stairs together and found him in a state of near hysteria. Mrs Penney clutched one flailing arm while Hannah dashed round the other side of the bed and took the other.

'Speak to him, Hannah,' Mrs Penney cried. 'He's calling your name.'

He was too weak to fight against them and allowed his arms to be pressed down at his sides. Hannah sat on the bed and took his shoulders. 'Matt, it's Hannah, I'm here. Calm down, darling.'

The glazing over his eyes cleared and finally he saw her. 'Hannah? I was so afraid your coming to me was only a dream,' he whimpered and her heart went out to him. She kissed his forehead and placed the covers back over him.

'I came to you on the lifeboat, Matt,' she smiled down on him and stroked soothing fingers over his damp brow, 'and I've been with you ever since. Your mum and I were just downstairs having our tea.'

'Wh-what did you say to me, in the lifeboat?'

'I told you I loved you. I do love you, Matt, and I'm never going to leave you.'

'Stay with me. Don't go downstairs.'

Mrs Penney, content Matt was alive and well and had secured Hannah's love, made a tactful withdrawal.

Matt couldn't tear his eyes away from Hannah, still afraid she'd disappear like a puff of smoke. He pushed the covers off but she piled them back on.

'You have to keep warm, Matt. You'll soon start shivering again.'

'I want to feel you against me.'

Certain that Mrs Penney wouldn't come back, Hannah slipped off her shoes and got into bed with him. She took him in her arms, her face on the pillow looking into his. He smelled slightly sweaty and salty and wonderfully of himself. She kissed his cheek, and brushed her lips over his. 'Better now?' she murmured tenderly.

He lifted his arm, it felt as limp as a dried-out vegetable leaf, and placed it over her firm feminine body. He had longed to touch her again for so long. 'Thanks, darling. I feel as weak as a baby.'

'The doctor says it will take a few days to recover your strength. He's kept a close eye on you. You're lucky not to have gone down with pneumonia.'

He closed his eyes, smiling faintly, immediately slipping into a warm comfortable sleep. When he woke about fifteen minutes later, Hannah's beautiful blue eyes were gazing adoringly into his. He felt a little stronger and took advantage of it by kissing her with some passion.

'What made you realise you loved me, Hannah?' he

481

asked, his voice low and husky. 'The thought I might be dead?'

'No,' she ran a row of gentle kisses along the line of his eyebrow, 'it was before that. I knew it deep down but with Mrs Opie offering me a new life – we were about to leave Cornwall and live in Torquay – I didn't see it clearly. I was dreadfully unhappy and confused. Then on Christmas Eve, Daniel came to Roscarrock. He was as friendly as usual at first but when he found out I was going away he got agitated and demanded that I marry him. The nurse looking after Mrs Opie heard us shouting and she ordered him out of the house and I thought he'd gone.'

Matt listened, serious and quiet, but Hannah could feel him getting tense, she could hear his heart thundering and she wondered if she should go on. 'What happened next?' he said, moving his face closer to hers.

'He came to my room. You see, he realised something about me and he went berserk. He pushed me down on the bed and nearly raped me.'

'I'll break his bloody neck when I get out of this bed,' Matt exploded, making himself cough and gasp for breath.

Hannah held him tighter. 'No, you won't. Don't talk like that, darling. He can't come between us any more. It was a frightening experience but I managed to talk him out of going any further. I want you to forget about him now. I don't want him to spoil what I'm going to tell you, the reason behind me and Mrs Opie going away.' She smiled into his concerned eyes. 'Matt, I'm going to have a baby.'

His splendid velvety dark eyes widened then shone with wonder. His handsome face broke into a wide smile. 'A baby? My God, that's wonderful!' He kissed her as long and as hard as he could. 'Is that what you were going to tell me that day?'

'Yes.' She clung to him.

'I would have asked you to marry me. What would you have said?'

'I would have said yes, with mixed feelings. But now I know I want nothing but you. So, Matt Penney, will you marry me?'

'I'd better,' he laughed, placing a gentle hand on her tummy and glorying in the slight swell he felt there. 'You need to be made an honest woman, Hannah Spargo, and pretty darn quick.' Matt knew a moment of doubt. 'Will you be happy living here after life in a grand house?'

'It wasn't really the house that had a hold over me, Matt, but Mrs Opie and now I know why. She told me something, just after you were brought ashore. You see, she will be our baby's great-grandmother.' She gave Matt a brief account of what Feena Opie had told her in Janet's parlour. 'In a couple of days, when you're better, I'll go up to Roscarrock and see if there's any more to the story.'

'Don't you believe she was telling you everything? How do you feel about what she said?'

'I've no idea,' she snuggled into him. 'I've only been thinking about you and that's all I really care about.'

Hannah spent some time at Janet's, called on Sarah, Naomi and Lizzie and on the very welcome invitation from her father, left before he'd gone back to the herring grounds on Boxing Day, she finally crossed over the granite bridge and went home to Cliffside Cottage. In ten years nothing had changed in the small dark kitchen, except her grandmother wasn't sitting in her rocking chair to put a blight on the occasion.

Prim fussed over her as if she was royalty and plied her with her favourite treat, pilchards roasted on the grid iron. Hannah spent a happy afternoon with her mother and Josh. She kept what Mrs Opie had told her about Prim not being her real mother to herself, she wanted to talk to her father first, but she shyly told Prim she was expecting Matt's baby. She thought her mother would at least express disappointment in her but her chubby face broke into a sunny smile.

'That'll be three new grandchildren next year after all. I take it you and Matt are getting married?'

'Yes, we asked the minister to call on us and have set the date.'

'A proper wedding is just what we need after the miserable time we've had lately.' This was the best news possible for Prim; it meant Hannah would be staying in the village and Feena Opie had lost her tight grip on her. 'Though we might be having two weddings in the family,' she went on, trying not to sound bitter because she might be losing a daughter to Roscarrock after all. 'I can't get used to Leah being so familiar with that Greg Opie.'

'I have misgivings too, Mum, but if it's what Leah wants, I don't think we should stop her. You'll find Mr Greg is a good man when you get to know him.'

'Well, if anything comes of it we'll just have to get used to it, I suppose. Your father has warned him to behave like a gentleman and in view of her age he won't give consent for a year. If Greg Opie really loves Leah, he'll be happy to wait.' Prim looked down in her lap. 'Will you be going back to live at Roscarrock until you get married?'

'I haven't really thought about what I'll do,' Hannah

said carefully, going to her mother. 'I have to give her two weeks' notice whatever happens.' If she moved out of Roscarrock, and Hannah was sure Mrs Opie wouldn't want that, Janet would probably hope she'd live with her. She kissed Prim, whose kindness and forbearance had been large enough to adopt her, and they hugged emotionally. 'It's so good to be able to come home at last, Mum.'

Chapter 40

On New Year's Day Hannah went up to Roscarrock. Greg saw her coming along the drive and met her in the hall, surprising her by taking her into his arms in a friendly bear hug.

'It's good to see you again, Hannah,' he said, guiding her towards the stairs in the warm house. 'Now we can enjoy a belated Christmas – we've held over our celebrations until you came back. Leah's been keeping us informed about things in the village. I'm glad Matt is making a good recovery.' Another surprise came when he grinned perkily, looking nothing like the stony young man in the portrait. 'Look, we might as well bring everything out into the open. I know you're expecting a baby and I'm thrilled you'll be giving me a little cousin.'

Hannah stared dumbfounded at him for a moment. 'Thank you, Mr Greg. Does Mr Patrick know too?'

'We had a family discussion on Christmas Day when Grandmother and I came home. No more of this Mr this and Mr that, you're family now. Grandmother is in her rooms. Go up and see her straightaway, she's been missing you terribly and has been very troubled.'

Having heard her voice, Angie appeared hesitantly in the hall and Hannah couldn't resist giving her a little peck on one ruddy cheek. Blushing to the roots of her hair, the maid said bashfully, ''Tis some good to see 'ee back, miss.'

'I won't be coming back to work, Angie,' she said, including Greg in the conversation so he knew exactly how things stood. 'I'm getting married in less than two weeks. I hope you'll both come to my wedding.'

'Aw,' Angie uttered in disappointment. 'We'll miss 'ee here, but congratulations. I'd like to see 'ee married, miss.' Then she lost her nerve and scuttled away.

Greg went back to his study and Hannah climbed the elegant staircase. She walked along the corridor, feeling strange now that her time here had come to an end; she had been happy here but she would be even happier as Matt's wife in Seaview Cottage. She tapped on Mrs Opie's door and went straight in.

She was sitting at the fireside, half-heartedly reading a book. 'Hannah!' She put the book down and held out her hands. 'Come over here, my dear. I wish I'd been at the window and seen you arrive.'

They were both feeling awkward. Hannah went over to her grandmother but didn't take off her coat or sit down.

'So, my dear,' Mrs Opie said with a brightness she did not feel. She was worried about Hannah taking five whole days to come back to her, she hadn't even telephoned, and she felt rather slighted. 'How is Matt? And what have you decided to do?'

'Matt is well enough to sit in the parlour now.' Hannah smiled fondly to herself at the memories of all she had done for him, bringing his meals, taking up newspapers to keep him occupied, the more personal things like helping him wash and shave. There had been many times she'd slipped into bed with him when Mrs Penney was out. She had been totally absorbed in Matt and, partly because she didn't want to, had given Roscarrock and those who lived here little thought. Now she must face the implications of what Mrs Opie had told her and try to find out what else there might be to learn. 'We're getting married, it's all arranged.'

Mrs Opie's heart dropped like a brick but she wasn't very surprised. 'Then I shall see to it you have a truly splendid wedding. I'll arrange for my dressmaker to come here with materials and patterns and you can choose the dress of your dreams.' She would have thrown open Roscarrock for the reception but she knew the Spargo family wouldn't come and Hannah would refuse the offer.

Hannah frowned. She hadn't made any arrangements. Janet would be sure to want to make her wedding dress and would be very hurt if she was refused. Prim would want a say in what happened too. Hannah wished she and Matt could slip away and get married secretly. 'I'll have to talk things over with Matt first,' she said, hoping to forestall any more suggestions.

'Very well, but I want to be involved in some way with your wedding and future life.' Mrs Opie got down to more immediate things. She knew Hannah would never give up Matt Penney, but once she was settled back in the house, there would be opportunity enough to influence her again before her wedding took place. 'Angie has lit a fire in your room every day in case you came back so you'll find it lovely and warm. You may do as much or as little work as you please. All I ask is that for the next few days you spend plenty of time with me.'

Matt hadn't been pleased that she would be spending any more nights under Roscarrock's roof but she had promised she would come down to the village and see him as often as possible before he travelled to Plymouth to rejoin the *Misty* for the last week or two of the herring season. He'd wanted her to collect her belongings today and move out but she'd explained her close relationship with Mrs Opie. Although it was on a different footing now, it forbade such a discourteous course of action and he'd reluctantly understood.

'Where are you and Matt going to live?' Mrs Opie asked.

'In his cottage in the village. It's quite big, has four bedrooms, an indoor lavatory and proper bathroom,' Hannah answered proudly.

'I'm glad you won't be living in poor cramped conditions but doesn't his mother live there? Will you be happy sharing another woman's home?'

'It's gone on in the village for generations. Mrs Penney is very kind, I'm sure we'll get on very well.' Hannah would not let Mrs Opie interfere in her new life.

'And will Matt continue as a fisherman after his recent ordeal?'

'Yes. It's a hard life but he loves it.'

Hannah was no less respectful to her but Mrs Opie sensed she was wary of her. She would have to step carefully. She hated the thought of Hannah being married to an ordinary fisherman: she had hoped to give her and the baby a better life, but at least Matt Penney's occupation would allow her lots of leeway.

She gave her most gracious smile. 'Perhaps when he's away at sea you and the baby will spend a few nights here. It will only take a very short time to modernise the nursery. After all, you'll have family here. Greg has told me he intends to live here with Leah when they are married.'

As she'd intended, mention of Leah living at Roscarrock swayed Hannah greatly to her side. 'Well, I suppose that would be nice for all of us. You are reconciled to Leah marrying Greg then?'

'Yes, my dear. Like you, I didn't like it at first but we mustn't fly in the face of true love.' Mrs Opie laughed and it was sincere. 'Who knows, we could have babies running about all over the house. The only thing now is for me to advertise for more staff.'

Hannah felt that when she knew all about her birth, when she had spoken to her father, things might work out very well for all of them. 'I'll go and take off my coat and settle in.'

'Come back in a little while and we'll have tea together.' Mrs Opie's hopes were similar to Hannah's but she was burdened by a terrible worry.

The first thing Hannah did in her room was wind up the jewellery box Matt had given her and listen to its music. She missed him already. She smiled at the jack-in-the-box. Maybe it had been bought for her, perhaps Mrs Opie had hoped Stephanie would keep her baby; now her own baby would play with it.

As she made to take off her coat, she saw a book on the bed. Thinking Mrs Opie had ordered it placed there for a specific reason, she sat on the bed and opened it at the first page marked with a thin piece of card sticking out. Reading the underlined sentences she quickly found it wasn't a housekeeper's order book, it was writing very personal to Mrs Opie.

17th May 1935. *Stephanie is dead. I've seen very little of her in the last ten years but I can hardly bring myself to believe it.*

How very sad, Hannah thought, rising to take the book to Mrs Opie, not understanding how it had come to be in her room. But her eyes roamed over the next few sentences and she sat down rigidly on the bed. Her fingers trembling, she turned to the next marked page and the next and the next. The more she read, the more horrified she became. She felt chilled to the core and her breathing became shallow as if the air was trapped in her lungs. When she had read all the pages, a curious pain was twisting inside her, a pain nearly as dreadful as when she had thought she'd lost Matt.

There was a taste of sour plums in her mouth. Her arms and legs felt too weak to get up. She wanted to cry but the tears were locked in her throat. She had never felt such revulsion. The room was spinning and she had to wait for her head to clear and her sight to focus. A scream of rage and disbelief built up inside her, as if her soul was being ripped out of her. She had been betrayed. For the first time in her life, she felt hate and wanted revenge.

Holding the journal out in front of her as if it was some accursed thing, she walked on legs that felt they could barely hold her up to Mrs Opie's rooms.

'You were qui—' Mrs Opie saw the journal in Hannah's hands and the utter contempt disfiguring her lovely face. She paled and Hannah saw something she'd not witnessed even on the night of the burglary. Feena Opie was frightened.

'Have you been looking for this, by any chance?' Hannah said, her voice seeming to flow across the room on dark waves of disgust.

'Hannah, dear, please let me explain.' Mrs Opie tried to get out of her chair but fell back clumsily.

'You lied to me!' Hannah hurled the journal across the room. It hit the side of the mantelpiece and Mrs Opie winced. 'You're not my grandmother. God help me, you're my mother! It wasn't Stephanie who had an affair with my father and didn't want me, it was you! And you only wanted me because Stephanie died. If it hadn't been for that I would have lived and died in the village and you wouldn't have cared a damn. Then when you decided you wanted me in your life, you planned to take me away from here and I would never have known who I really was. You only told me half the truth after Matt was rescued to try to break us up, didn't you? You even used Leah in a scheme to get back at my father.'

'Hannah, I . . .' Mrs Opie clutched her chest as panic threatened to prevent her breathing. 'Please, if you'd just—'

'I'll do nothing for you ever again!' Hannah was screaming at the top of her voice and she was aware of heavy footsteps running towards the room. 'You're an evil calculating bitch and I never want to see you again!'

Ignoring Mrs Opie's pitiful cries, she ran from the room. Greg and Patrick were coming down the corridor and she would have marched straight past them if they hadn't barred her way. Both men were alarmed by her look of pure hatred. It was as if she had taken leave of her senses.

'What's going on, Hannah?' Greg asked. 'For goodness sake, we could hear you shouting all over the house.'

'Ask your grandmother,' Hannah hissed venomously. 'If you can get her to tell you the truth. That's something she's not very good at. Now get out of my way.'

Greg took her arm but she wrenched his hand away and pushed between him and Patrick. 'Hannah,' Patrick began, but he could see it was no use. Whatever the trouble was, she couldn't be reasoned with now. The men exchanged puzzled looks and hurried to the woman whose wretched sobbing was clearly audible in the corridor.

Hannah stopped only long enough to take Matt's jewellery box out of her room then she ran down the stairs and out of the front door, not seeing Angie hovering fearfully about the servants' stairs. She ran along the drive, through the gateway and into the lane, not stopping until her lungs were bursting for air. She leaned against the hedge and opening the jewellery box took out the locket Daniel had given to her. She tossed it as far away as she could over the hedge. She wanted nothing to remind her of the other totally selfish and manipulating swine who'd tried to make her life his own. She walked on as fast as she could, halting only to accommodate a painful stitch, carried along by a vortex of emotion.

When she got to Seaview Cottage she burst through the back door and ran to the parlour, glad Mrs Penney wasn't in the house.

'Hello, who's there?' came Matt's voice from the parlour, thinking he had a visitor come to keep him company.

He saw at once something was terribly wrong and got to his feet. 'Darling, what is it?'

Hannah rushed into his arms. Her strength finally left her, she crumpled and he carried her to the sofa. She clung to him as if she would die if he let her go, his closeness enabling her to unleash the flood of weeping she had been holding back.

'Oh, Matt, hold me,' she whimpered when at last she could speak, her face seamed with pain, 'and never let me go.'

Chapter 41

Hannah was alone on Hidden Beach. She was standing on the shore, as still as a statue, the keen wind plastering her coat against her legs, whipping her scarf away from her neck and stinging her face. She didn't feel it or the cold water seeping into her shoes.

It was over a week since she'd made her distressed flight from Roscarrock and the first time she had left the Penneys' cottage. For some reason she had ended up here, the place where she had met Patrick Opie and her dealings with Roscarrock and Feena Opie had begun. Greg had come down to the village and then Patrick, but she had refused to see them. Rumours as to what had gone wrong at the big house were rife. She had made Matt promise not to tell anyone what she'd learned, and Janet and Prim had gone away from Seaview Cottage shaking their heads at her inability to talk to them about it. She was still numb inside over the things she had read in the journal. The doctor had been sent for but only Matt's love had warmed her out of the shock and torment she'd suffered. Worried about her and the baby, he had refused to rejoin the *Misty* and stayed close, until now, when she had suddenly wanted to be alone, to be outside near her beloved sea, to try to come to terms with who she was, and what those who were her flesh and blood meant to her.

She had been here for nearly an hour but not one lucid thought had formed in her mind. Something touched her shoulder gently from behind; she didn't feel it at first, then there was a light tap and she turned round. Her body went stiff and as straight as a ramrod. It was her father.

Jeff met her hostile blue eyes squarely, acknowledging he deserved her contempt. She was pale and drawn and looked forlorn, as she had done so many times as a child when he'd spurned her affection and withheld his own.

'Matt wrote to me at the Seaman's Mission. He told me what's happened. He's desperately worried about you. I came back at once. We need to talk, Hannah, and not just you and me. Will you listen?'

She nodded.

'I don't think it's fair that you just hear my side of the story. Will you come to Roscarrock with me now and talk to Feena Opie?'

She hesitated. Part of her abhorred the thought of seeing Mrs Opie but how else could there be even a chance of everything being straightened out once and for all? 'All right, but only if Matt comes with us.'

The three of them walked to Roscarrock without speaking, Jeff slightly ahead, Matt keeping his arm round Hannah's waist. Jeff knocked on the front door and Angie Miller, her flat features working in agitation as she looked worriedly from one grim face to the other, showed them into the drawing room.

Mrs Opie was escorted downstairs and into the room by Greg and Patrick on either side of her wheelchair. Her eyes fastened on Hannah's face. She looked haggard, as if she had aged ten years since Hannah had seen her last. Hannah kept her feelings in check, reminding herself that all her past kindness had been tainted with an ulterior motive; it would be all too easy to give way to a rush of pity.

'We're pleased that you've come,' Greg said, speaking for all of the Opies. 'My grandmother has told Patrick and me the true facts behind Hannah's birth and if you have no objection, we'd like to stay. Perhaps we could all sit down.'

Hannah wanted to remain standing but Matt, eager for this meeting to be as unconfrontational as possible, eased her down on the sofa beside him, keeping his arm round her. Greg and Patrick sat down on the opposite sofa. Jeff sat on a chair. Mrs Opie's wheelchair completed what was roughly a circle, all of them able to see each other's faces.

There was an uncomfortable silence, then Jeff, red-faced, cleared his throat. 'Hannah's agreed to come here so she can learn how she . . . um, came into being.' He looked at Feena Opie. 'Perhaps if I start?'

She nodded, quite unable to talk for the moment but glancing often at Hannah, her expression a mixture of hope, pleading and shame. It had been difficult and embarrassing admitting to Greg and Patrick that she was Hannah's mother, but the pain of coming to terms with what she had done to Hannah through her selfishness had been far worse. She had spent hours sitting in Hannah's room, more bereft than when she'd heard Stephanie had died, the daughter whose memory she had sullied. It was this that Greg and Patrick had liked the least in her confession.

'There is a tunnel leading down from Roscarrock to

the cliff,' Jeff began, his colour deepening as all eyes in the room turned to him. He spoke directly to Hannah. 'It was dangerous and had been blocked up at the cliff end many years ago to stop the children climbing up inside it. I went there one day to get Josh. He'd stayed out longer playing on Hidden Beach than he was supposed to and your mother – Prim – she was worried. I found Josh and some other boys up the cliff trying to unblock the tunnel. They'd been doing it for weeks, they said, and had nearly succeeded. I boxed your brother's ears and sent him and the others home.

'I intended to get some men to help me secure the tunnel once and for all, but something, a sense of boyhood adventure I suppose, made me pull out the last bits of driftwood and other stuff and I climbed inside. I struck matches and came across an old lantern. I lit it and I kept going. It was tricky and downright dangerous in some places. I could have been trapped or killed and my body might never have been found. I didn't think about that, I was too excited.

'I came out inside Roscarrock's woods and frightened the wits out of a lady walking a dog.' He glanced at Feena Opie who dropped her eyes. 'That of course was Mrs Opie. She was furious and threatened to inform the police.' Jeff's voice took on an apologetic tone. 'I won't go into details. I found Mrs Opie to be an attractive widow, she was lonely and I soon charmed her. I never came here by the tunnel again. Mrs Opie and I made sure it was blocked off properly. We started an affair which went on for two years, then Mrs Opie told me she was pregnant. She wanted us to go away together but I didn't want to be a kept man and told her so. We quarrelled and I thought we'd gone our separate ways. I admit

I wasn't curious about the baby. I thought that with all her money she'd have it well taken care of.'

As Jeff paused to take a breath, Mrs Opie continued the tale. It took every ounce of control for her to look Hannah in the face and speak without emotion. 'I think for your sake, Hannah, your father is trying to spare you some of the details, but you've come here for the truth and you shall hear all of it. When I found out I was having his child I had this cosy picture of us going away together and being a family. But he was tiring of me by then, partly because I was besotted with him and behaved very possessively. Yes, we quarrelled, violently, and our passion turned to hatred. I felt rejected and I bided my time, waiting to get revenge. I gave birth to you and wrote to your mother saying her husband was the father of my child. I didn't know he'd had other affairs and Prim was used to them, that it wouldn't break up their marriage. Prim came here and laughed in my face and there were bitter feelings between us, but then we both saw a way of getting revenge on Jeff.'

Hannah glared at her disbelievingly. 'I read in your journal that you were glad at the time my mother had asked to take me, but she did it out of love and kindness. How could she have used me for revenge?'

'It's true, Hannah,' Jeff said. 'Prim's behaviour wasn't much better than ours where you were concerned. I was shocked at first when she brought you home, but you were my child and if she was willing to take you on I wasn't going to worry about it. Your mother always took it badly when one of her babies died, she genuinely loved you in place of the little maid we'd just lost. But I didn't realise the other reason behind it. You weren't dark like the rest of my children and Prim paraded you in front of me as a reminder of my sins. She never tired of throwing it in my face. It turned me against you until I couldn't stand you near me. Then my mother started. She'd always despised Prim because she'd wanted me to marry another girl and she objected to the way she was treating me. She kept urging me to throw you out of the house. It took me a long time to realise what a spiteful twisted woman she was. As you know only too well, things got worse over the years until I thought I hated you, and it all came to a head when Edwin drowned in the boat accident. I knew it wasn't your fault, Hannah, but I needed someone to blame.' Jeff noisily cleared his throat to hide the fact that he was close to tears. 'I'm really sorry for the way I've treated you. I hope one day you'll forgive me.'

During her parents' tale, Hannah had leaned closer and closer into Matt. Her expression had not changed and Jeff became earnest. 'Despite the terrible way you've been treated, Hannah, don't let it ruin your future with Matt. It all started with the birth of a baby – you. Try to let it end with your own baby coming into the world.'

'Yes, Hannah,' Mrs Opie implored her. 'Don't let your suffering turn you into the way Prim and I became.'

Matt gazed into Hannah's eyes to see if this full explanation had eased some of her pain. 'Has anything they've said brought you comfort, darling?'

She gave him a small smile, his love and closeness giving her strength. The others were waiting for her to speak. She gave the deepest sigh. 'It's all about sad love affairs really on Mother's and Mrs Opie's part. They fell in love with a vain and selfish man.' She was able now to look with a little sympathy and understanding at the woman who was her real mother, then her eyes turned to her father. 'There's a lot of men like you in the world,

Jeff Spargo, and I've had the misfortune to know one even worse. I can only thank God that He didn't allow Daniel Kittow to hurt me and that I love a good and honest man in Matt.'

Jeff looked down guiltily. 'What will you do now? About me, your mother and Mrs Opie?'

'I shall take your advice. I won't let myself sink into self-pity and spoil the future I have with Matt. I love him too much for that. I'm used to your ways, Father, and you've already shown me that you've changed. Mother's still my mother and I'm grateful she took me in and loved me, whatever her motives.' Hannah turned to Mrs Opie. 'It's you I find the hardest to forgive. You are my real mother and yet you gave me up purely for revenge, deserting me for the first twenty years of my life and then only wanting me for your own selfish reasons.' She flung her hands out in a gesture of hopelessness. 'I loved living here at Roscarrock and I grew to love you.'

Mrs Opie broke down in tears and Greg put his arm round her. He said to Hannah, 'Please try to forgive her, you'll only end up hurting yourself even more.'

'If I may say, Hannah,' Patrick said, quietly adding his opinion, 'my great-aunt might be the most calculating figure in all this but she's also the most pathetic. She has the most to lose.'

'She was a quiet respectable woman until she met me,' Jeff put in, feeling he owed his old love that much. 'I started off the whole sequence of events.'

Matt whispered in Hannah's ear, 'If you can't forgive her then Leah probably won't want to live here when she and Greg Opie are married and Mrs Opie will lose her grandson too. She'd end up with nothing while you have a large family, our new life together and plenty of love to go around. And, darling, I believe Mrs Opie really does love you.'

Hannah remained thoughtful. Mrs Opie stopped crying and dried her tears. She looked across the room at Hannah and Hannah saw the same loving, protective expression she'd seen when Mrs Opie had tried to stop the burglar hurting her, her actions costing her dearly. A huge chunk of ice fell off her heart. She got up and kneeling at her side, put her arms round her. Mrs Opie clutched her and they both cried.

'Forgive me, Hannah,' she sobbed. 'I do love you.'

'I love you too,' Hannah whispered back.

When she stood up, Jeff was shyly holding out his arms to her. A few days ago she'd never have believed that what she had wanted for over twenty years would actually happen. She fell into his arms and the last of her unforgiveness melted as she cried more healing tears against him.

'Does this mean all will be well from now on, Hannah?' Matt asked.

She smiled through her tears. 'Yes, I think we can look forward to the future now.'

'I think we could all do with a good stiff drink,' Greg said in a relieved voice.

'I agree but before we do that there's something else I want to say,' Jeff said. 'I'd like it to be known I've given up bullying my children. I've written to Mitch asking him to forgive me and I'm hoping he'll come round.' He flushed with embarrassment. 'If you'll let me, Hannah, I'd like to give you away at your wedding. And I'm hoping you'll agree to come home until your wedding day and leave on my arm, like a father and daughter should.'

Hannah left her father for the man she loved with all

her heart. 'Yes, I'd like that,' she smiled happily, 'living at home for the next few days until I become Mrs Matt Penney.'

Kilgarthen

A charming saga of Cornish village life from the
author of the PENGARRON trilogy

Gloria Cook

Laura has one last duty to carry out as the wife of
Bill Jennings – to take his body back to the Cornish
village where he grew up. But she can't share in the
villagers' grief. Kilgarthen's 'local boy made good'
was actually a devious trickster who had only married
the impressionable eighteen-year-old Laura to secure
a position on the board of her father's construction
business. By the end of the Second World War,
Laura's father having died, Bill was chairman of one
of the biggest companies in London.

Laura is determined to leave Kilgarthen as soon as
the funeral is over, but a shattering phone call from
her lawyer forces her to reconsider. She is given the
devastating news that Bill had squandered her
father's company funds. The only money Laura has
left is tied up in the cottage Bill owned in the village
from which she is preparing to make her escape.

Laura's enforced stay in Kilgarthen turns into a
journey of self-discovery. She is soon drawn into the
lives of the villagers and one person in particular
captures her heart – five-year-old Vicki Jeffries. But
any lasting relationship with the little girl is cruelly
interrupted by Vicki's father, Spencer. He wants
nothing to do with Bill Jennings' widow and Laura is
determined to find out why . . .

FICTION / SAGA 0 7472 4903 2

Sheila Jansen

DELLA
DOLAN

In the great tradition of Catherine Cookson

Della Dolan's girlish dreams of romance quickly evaporate when her parents forbid her to see her cousin Jonathan: there is bad blood between the families and he must take the blame for his father's sins.

Thanks to her friend Rose – who some say is no better than she should be – Della is not short of other suitors and in Jerry she finds a loving husband who has the full approval of her parents. But their marriage is doomed by his past and, in the uncertain days of 'the phony war', Della is alone once more.

Although World War II brings hardship to Newcastle, Della and her friends find new freedom and excitement, too, as social barriers are broken down. But for Della, love remains elusive until a chance meeting reawakens feelings long buried . . .

FICTION / SAGA 0 7472 4241 0

A selection of bestsellers from Headline

LAND OF YOUR POSSESSION	Wendy Robertson	£5.99 ☐
DANGEROUS LADY	Martina Cole	£5.99 ☐
SEASONS OF HER LIFE	Fern Michaels	£5.99 ☐
GINGERBREAD AND GUILT	Peta Tayler	£5.99 ☐
HER HUNGRY HEART	Roberta Latow	£5.99 ☐
GOING TOO FAR	Catherine Alliott	£5.99 ☐
HANNAH OF HOPE STREET	Dee Williams	£4.99 ☐
THE WILLOW GIRLS	Pamela Evans	£5.99 ☐
A LITTLE BADNESS	Josephine Cox	£5.99 ☐
FOR MY DAUGHTERS	Barbara Delinsky	£4.99 ☐
SPLASH	Val Corbett, Joyce Hopkirk, Eve Pollard	£5.99 ☐
THEA'S PARROT	Marcia Willett	£5.99 ☐
QUEENIE	Harry Cole	£5.99 ☐
FARRANS OF FELLMONGER STREET	Harry Bowling	£5.99 ☐

All Headline books are available at your local bookshop or newsagent, or can be ordered direct from the publisher. Just tick the titles you want and fill in the form below. Prices and availability subject to change without notice.

Headline Book Publishing, Cash Sales Department, Bookpoint, 39 Milton Park, Abingdon, OXON, OX14 4TD, UK. If you have a credit card you may order by telephone – 01235 400400.

Please enclose a cheque or postal order made payable to Bookpoint Ltd to the value of the cover price and allow the following for postage and packing:

UK & BFPO: £1.00 for the first book, 50p for the second book and 30p for each additional book ordered up to a maximum charge of £3.00.
OVERSEAS & EIRE: £2.00 for the first book, £1.00 for the second book and 50p for each additional book.

Name ....

Address ....

....

....

If you would prefer to pay by credit card, please complete:
Please debit my Visa/Access/Diner's Card/American Express (delete as applicable) card no:

Signature .... Expiry Date ....